Praise for these other novels of spectacular
medical suspense by Michael Palmer

TRAUMA

"Start reading *Trauma*; you won't stop. A chilling medical thriller." —*New York Times* bestselling
author Tess Gerritsen

"Fast-moving, nicely detailed." —*Booklist*

"A riveting medical thriller that will grab you by the throat and won't let you go until long after you have read the intense climax . . . A must-read for all!"
—*Suspense* magazine

RESISTANT

"Palmer, the master of medical suspense, captivates readers with [this] stunning thriller."
—*Library Journal* (starred review)

"Of all [Palmer's] novels, this one has the most ambitious plot and a fascinating array of characters . . . [including] one of the best action scenes to ever appear in a medical thriller." —Associated Press

"Palmer's growing audience will find much to enjoy here, as will medical-thriller fans of all stripes."
—*Booklist*

POLITICAL SUICIDE

"Action/mystery reading at its best. Palmer just keeps delivering good stories, one right after the other."

—*Huffington Post*

"This book goes from great to outstanding . . . a definite keeper!"   —*Suspense* magazine

"Palmer writes terrific medical suspense, and he has thrown political intrigue into the mix . . . fans won't be disappointed."   —Associated Press

OATH OF OFFICE

"One of the most exciting thrillers of the year."

—*Huffington Post*

"A shocker."   —Associated Press

"Suspenseful . . . Palmer's easy mix of science and individual courage should please his many fans."

—*Publishers Weekly*

A HEARTBEAT AWAY

"When it comes to inventive plots for medical thrillers, nobody does it better than Michael Palmer . . . This premise is explosive and compelling and grabs the readers from the very first page."   —*Huffington Post*

"Michael Palmer anchors his thrillers in high concept and steeps them in medicine. *A Heartbeat Away* opens with a prologue, and from the opening line, the reader knows things are not going to go well . . . This is the book for readers who wholeheartedly believe politicians are capable of anything." —*Boston Globe*

THE LAST SURGEON

"Prepare to burn some serious midnight oil."

—*Boston Herald*

"Highly suspenseful and compelling." —*Booklist*

"Palmer has always been a good writer but he has never crafted a story as suspenseful as this one . . . This is the kind of book you read with a bright light on and all the doors locked . . . Franz Koller is one of the most deadly villains to grace the pages of a novel since the introduction of Hannibal Lecter." —*Huffington Post*

THE SECOND OPINION

"A heart-pounding medical thriller . . . satisfying, expertly paced [with] enough suspense to keep readers happily turning the pages." —*Boston Globe*

"The novel is not merely a thriller but also an exploration of its central character's unique gifts and her determination to communicate with her comatose father despite overwhelming odds. Another winner from a consistently fine writer." —*Booklist*

MICHAEL PALMER
AND DANIEL PALMER

MERCY

St. Martin's Paperbacks

This is a work of fiction. All of the characters, organizations, and events portrayed in this novel are either products of the author's imagination or are used fictitiously.

MERCY

Copyright © 2016 by Daniel Palmer.
Excerpt from *The First Family* copyright © 2017 by Daniel Palmer.

For information address St. Martin's Press, 175 Fifth Avenue, New York, NY 10010.

ISBN: 978-1-250-03085-6

Our books may be purchased in bulk for promotional, educational, or business use. Please contact your local bookseller or the Macmillan Corporate and Premium Sales Department at 1-800-221-7945, ext. 5442, or by e-mail at MacmillanSpecialMarkets@macmillan.com.

Printed in the United States of America

St. Martin's Press hardcover edition / May 2016
St. Martin's Paperbacks edition / March 2017

St. Martin's Paperbacks are published by St. Martin's Press, 175 Fifth Avenue, New York, NY 10010.

10 9 8 7 6 5 4 3 2 1

To Donna Prince,
my caring aunt, my dad's beloved sister,
and a dear friend to us both

Love and compassion are necessities, not luxuries.
Without them humanity cannot survive.

—DALAI LAMA

CHAPTER 1

You really don't know what you've got till it's gone.

On nights like this, when Walter McKenna could barely get air into his lungs, and each breath came ragged and raw, the lyrics from the Joni Mitchell tune popped into his head and he'd grimace, thinking she was right. Damn right. In Walter's case, it was heart disease that had paved over the paradise of his good health. It zapped most of Walter's remaining strength and left him perpetually exhausted.

With great effort, Walter managed to sit up in his hospital bed. He had to do something to take the pressure off his bedsores—decubitus ulcers, his doctors called them—that had again formed on his buttocks and back.

Even in this new position, Walter felt them rubbing on the bedsheets. The pain brought him to tears. To keep new ulcers from forming, Walter endured daily chemical debridement. But that was better than the hives that had broken out a few weeks ago. Those were brutal little suckers. The pale red bumps came on like a speeding train, coating his entire body, and causing horrible itching that antihistamines could barely subdue.

If he were back home, Walter could at least enjoy some familiar comforts, but he was long past that possibility. Walter cursed softly. The hospital was his home now, and had been for months. Tomorrow's debridement was just another bit of suffering to add to his growing list of miseries.

He shifted position again, but it was impossible to get comfortable. His legs and arms were weighted with so much fluid he felt like a human water balloon. He also felt intense pressure on his bladder, and relieved himself into his catheter. Peeing into a tube, shitting into a bedpan: this was life with end-stage heart disease.

In the morning, Melinda, Walter's wife of twenty-five years, would show up and they would watch television together and talk pleasantly during the commercials. She would bring him updates from the high school track team where he ran as a boy and coached as a man, and this would make him feel both happy and sad. She would try to hold his hand, but his fingers were stiff and achy, grotesquely engorged, and it hurt to be touched.

Now, just the thought of Melinda tightened Walter's chest, squeezing his heart. He made a loud sucking sound through his oxygen cannula, like the last gasp of a dying breath. But it was not his last gasp. Even though Walter's arteries were clogged with plaque, the surrounding muscles starved for oxygen, and his ventricular function had downshifted from a sprint to a limp, he was still very much alive. A permanent resident in what he morbidly referred to as God's waiting room.

When the figure appeared in the doorway, Walter wondered for a second if he were dreaming. But the pain was present as always, and thank goodness his dreams were not that cruel. Still, doctors rarely stopped in at night unless they had good reason. Walter listened to the beeps, hums, and buzzes—the white noise of all the monitors attached to him—without a sense that anything was abnormal.

But the doctor was here, so Walter figured he had to have a good reason. This doc wore a waist-length white lab coat, a crisply pressed shirt, and a bold red tie. He was Walter's hospitalist, a specialist in administering general medical care to hospitalized patients. Lots of different hospitalists looked after Walter—so many, in fact, that he had taken to calling all of them Doc.

"What's up, Doc?" Walter croaked. He needed a sip of water, but was too weak to reach the glass himself. Doc noticed and gave Walter a drink.

"Just making rounds," Doc said.

"This late?"

Doc said nothing. From a black leather medical bag, Doc removed a bag of medicine, some clear liquid, and hooked it up to Walter's IV.

"Hey, I've got more bags hanging on that IV tree than a luggage carousel at Logan. What's with the new meds?"

Doc returned a half smile. "Just a refresh of your ACE inhibitor," he said.

Walter, who'd taught high school physics for more than two decades, had little trouble absorbing all the medical jargon tossed his way. The angiotensin-converting-enzyme inhibitor would lower his blood pressure by decreasing oxygen demand from the heart. It was all duct tape and glue to keep a leaky vessel afloat another day longer, but Walter preferred that to the alternative.

Doc titrated the new IV medication and did a quick check of Walter's vitals.

"How you feeling, Walt?" Doc asked.

"Like I'm dying," Walt said.

"Everyone is dying, Walt. We're just moving at different rates of speed, is all."

Walter could not argue there.

"Any unusual discomfort?" Doc asked.

Walter paused, as if he could have a new pain to which he was not yet attuned, but, no, nothing was out of the ordinary. He said as much.

"So, any big plans for tomorrow?" Doc's tone was a bit too sardonic, but Walter appreciated any hint of levity, even if it was gallows humor.

Several loud beeps rang out, and Walter's EKG burst into an erratic series of peaks and valleys.

"Just the meds kicking in," Doc said as he adjusted something on Walter's EKG monitor. "I gave you a big dose, so it will take effect right away." Walter's heartbeat revved up several notches. His lungs, already thick with fluid, felt as if they'd been put in a vise.

The evening nurse popped her head in. "Oh—hi, Doctor. I was just checking on him because his monitor is alarming."

"Thank you, Judy. We're all set here. With his paperwork, I mean."

The nurse returned a look of grim acknowledgment that set Walter on edge. Paperwork. Walter thought he understood the reference. Alarms were a constant on this floor, and he had a signed DNR that meant caregivers were not to perform CPR if his breathing should stop or his heart stop beating.

I'm having a reaction to the meds, Walter thought in a panic. *Got to relax. Take it easy. I'm not ready.*

"What'd you give me, Doc?" Walter asked. A stab of chest pain took his breath away.

"Just a little something to take care of people who have no business living," Doc said.

Walter waited for a hint of a smile, some indication this was Doc's tasteless humor on display once more, but his expression was cold as stone. Walter glanced toward the doorway, hopeful the nurse would reappear, but she had already left, probably headed back to the nurses station. No rush. No urgency. *Damn that DNR.*

Walter found himself gasping for breath. His body grew hot, and sweat blanketed his forehead. Gripping the bedsheets like a horse's reins, Walter tried to slow the canter of his heart.

"I feel kind of funny, Doc," Walter wheezed.

Stinging drops of perspiration rolled into Walter's eyes. The pressure on his chest intensified. Walter took in several sharp, short breaths, but could not seem to fill his lungs.

A sharp, crushing pain took away what little breath remained. Unable to speak, Walter pawed the air, trying to get Doc's attention. A wave of nausea overtook him, and a strange pressure built up at the base of his neck. Walter's fingers turned a horrifying shade of dark violet. The gurgling in his lungs bubbled up to his throat. His heart skittered with irregular beats. A spasm of coughing shook Walter's ribs so violently he thought they would break. His arms began to ache, and Walter felt an overwhelming sense of dread, of impending doom. Something was terribly wrong with him.

"Doc . . . Doc," Walter coughed in breathless sputters. "I think . . . I'm . . . having . . . heart attack."

Doc titrated the IV once more. "You are, Walt. A big one. *The* big one, in fact."

Walter's eyes rolled into the back of his head. His heart seemed to bounce freely around his chest. From somewhere in the whiteness and the blackness of this strange place where Walter now found himself, he heard a familiar sound. A melody. Some song. A tune he once loved. Yes, there it was, echoing softly in his mind. The words came to him, as did the angelic glow of Melinda's face.

You don't know what you've got till it's gone . . .

CHAPTER 2

There was no "normal" to Dr. Julie Devereux's work-day. Life as a critical care doc at White Memorial, a five-hundred-bed hospital in the heart of Boston, was suited to people who could roll with it when the emergency department interrupted morning rounds for an immediate consultation, or when a patient who had been stable moments ago was suddenly and inexplicably teetering on the edge of death.

Having Trevor, her twelve-year-old son, tag along for the day was not on Julie's schedule. But go with the flow, right? In no way did that mean Julie was pleased. If this were some official take-your-kid-to-work day, she would have had a different attitude. But this was a take-your-kid-to-work-because-he-got-suspended-from-school-for-fighting day. Not endearing. Not by a long shot.

Trevor, a lanky, sweet-faced boy with thick, shoulder-length brown hair just like his father's, brooded behind Julie as she headed for her office down the hall.

"Wish I didn't have to be here," Trevor grumbled.

Julie stopped walking, turned around, and gave her son a hard-edged stare. "Well, I'm sorry, Trevor, but people do have to work for a living."

Two nurses strode past and said a warm hello to Julie. She was beloved here—a lot more than at home, it seemed.

Julie reminded herself to be patient with her son. Change was not easy, and Trevor, her only child, had to adjust to the fact that his mother would soon be remarried. She wondered if this acting out was Trevor's way of processing a slew of conflicted emotions. He liked Sam, or maybe tolerated was the better word, but resented the idea of a man other than his father living with them. He had said as much to Julie. Maybe the kid held out hope that Julie and Paul would reconcile one day. That was not going to happen.

Perhaps once she and Sam were married and living together, Trevor's recent string of bad behavior would come to an end.

"I still don't see why you couldn't have left me at home like I wanted. I would have been fine on my own. Better than being stuck in your office all day."

Julie shook her head in frustration. "Getting suspended two days for fighting isn't exactly how to earn trust," she said in a matter-of-fact tone.

"Well, he started it," Trevor shot back.

Julie sighed. Trevor always had an answer for everything.

"How come I can't just stay with Dad?"

"Because your father isn't home. Believe me. I called."

"Where is he?"

"In New Hampshire, collecting scrap metal for his next sculpture."

Trevor seemed to think this was cool. His dad was cool. Of course he would think that. His dad thought homework was a waste of time and sugared cereal was a four-course meal.

"Dad let me weld the last time I was there." Trevor made this seem like an off-the-cuff remark when he knew he had tossed a barb that would sting.

"He did what?" Julie arched one of her delicate eyebrows and tried to block all sorts of horrible images from her mind. She had seen enough third-degree burns in her career to have some stern words with her ex-husband before this day was over. Paul had good intentions, but when it came to good judgment, he could be worse than Trevor.

"If it sells, I'm going to get a cut," Trevor announced with pride.

"Well, before you pick out a new iPad with your earnings, ask your father how many sculptures he's sold in the last few years."

Trevor looked away because he knew the answer was zero. Paul was quite talented, and his art fairly inventive, but he was not particularly ambitious or motivated. He did not make much money from his sculptures. Julie accepted that, as long as he paid the court-ordered child support. Paul could do this because of a substantial inheritance from a grandmother, one that allowed him to lead an artist's life. Paul paid his share of the child support on time and with no grumblings, but still Julie wished he'd be a stronger role model for his son.

Sam Talbot would never replace Paul as a father—nor

would he ever try—but with his kindness, maturity, and stability, Sam was sure to be important in Trevor's life. As a high school history teacher, Sam was not exactly rolling in the dough, but the way he loved her and the way she loved him made Julie feel like the richest woman in the world.

Julie set a hand on Trevor's delicate shoulder. Her son might have been obstinate, disrespectful at times, a little mouthy, but he was still her pride and joy.

"Look, kiddo, you're here for the day," Julie said, "so do your homework and try to make the best of it. And I hope you brought a good book, because you're not going to be glued to your electronics all day."

Julie tugged on her white lab coat so it fit better over her beige blouse. Everything fit better since she'd lost the weight gained during the divorce. She told people it was diet and exercise, but really the weight came off after she jettisoned the stress. For that, Julie had motorcycles to thank—a Honda Rebel 250, to be precise, which Sam, an avid rider, had bought for her as an engagement gift. Julie was looking forward to their upcoming ride to the Berkshires, and showing Sam the new hip-hugging leather pants she'd bought online from Cycle Gear. But the weekend was several days away, which meant plenty of time for Julie to work, look after Trevor, and feel like she was shortchanging both.

Since her separation from Paul, Julie had come to know a lot of single, career-oriented mothers who tried to be all and do all. Her advice to them, whenever asked: go ride a motorcycle. The moms might not lose the worry and doubt, she explained, but they'd have a blast forgetting some of their troubles for a while.

Julie's first patient of the day was Shirley Mitchell,

a seventy-seven-year-old woman with a nasty case of pneumonia to go along with the initial stages of peripheral artery disease. Despite her illness, Shirley had a fairly decent quality of life. This could not be said for many of Julie's critically ill patients in the thirty-three-bed unit, who sometimes endured debilitating and costly treatments in order to squeeze out only a few more months of life.

Julie was an advocate for death with dignity. She wrote papers and frequently spoke at conferences with the goal of bringing about policy change. Self-determination was a fundamental right, and the courts were beginning to agree. It was coming to health care whether the providers liked it or not. High-profile cases like that of Brittany Maynard, the twenty-nine-year-old woman dying of brain cancer who ended her suffering on her own terms, would continue to be a force for change. Death with dignity laws did not, as some critics said, kill people who did not wish to die. Julie could produce thirty years of data as proof.

She, and others who thought like her, wanted to take government out of the equation and let the patient and the patient's doctor come to a decision on what was best. The option to have an option was what Julie fought for, not some death mandate, as her opponents feared.

Her activism, of course, was controversial among her colleagues who viewed her stance as anathema to their profession. *It violates the Hippocratic oath to do no harm. It demeans the value of human life. It will lead to abuse or reduce palliative care options.* All valid arguments, but Julie believed that even those most vocal in their opposition had at some point wrestled with doubt while helping to keep alive a supremely sick patient who wished only to die.

Sometimes dead is better.

Shirley's nurse was Amber, a petite twenty-six-year-old blonde who one day—not quite yet—might turn Trevor's head. For now, Trevor seemed oblivious to Amber's beauty and was content to wave hello from the doorway after Julie made introductions.

"Trevor, you know where my office is. Why don't you go there now and wait. I'll come get you for lunch."

Trevor gave a nearly imperceptible head nod, and away he went.

Somehow Amber had managed to turn Shirley onto her side, not a simple feat given this particular patient's size, and was applying moisturizer to the backside of her body. ICU nurses were some of the most compassionate Julie had ever worked with. They did an incredible amount of work, almost always with a smile regardless of the unpleasantness of the task.

Shirley was not aware of Amber. She was sleeping soundly, thanks to the propofol, and breathing normally through the endotracheal tube inserted down her throat.

"How was her night?" Julie asked. Since this was the morning shift, Julie would get Amber's take on what the night nurse had relayed.

"I heard it went pretty well," Amber said in a cheery voice. "Fever is down to a hundred and one. WBC is fifteen thousand."

"Fifteen thousand for the white blood count," Julie repeated, sounding pleased. "That's approaching normal."

"And there's less secretion in her endotracheal tube," Amber added.

"Less secretion, eh?"

Another bit of good news. When Shirley arrived at the ICU, her chest x-ray showed substantial infiltrate clogging her lungs.

Amber said, "The respiratory therapist titrated down her oxygen and now she's only on forty-five percent. When I left yesterday she was on sixty."

Julie went to the Medi-Vac unit mounted on the wall and inserted a catheter down the tube. She engaged the suction, producing a whirring sound, and up came a soupy, yellowish, highly viscous, putrid-smelling liquid. It was less than Julie had expected.

"Looks like Shirley really is getting better," Julie said. "Maybe today you can give her a wake-up and lighten the propofol."

Amber acted disappointed. "Shirley can be a handful. I'm really going to miss the milk of amnesia," she said.

Julie smiled at the long running ICU joke; the milky white drug had the same color and consistency as the popular over-the-counter laxative. A sleeping patient makes no trouble, said the adage on the floor. But staying on the ventilator long term increased the likelihood of going from sleeping to dead. The breathing tube keeping Shirley alive was also a gateway for getting bacteria into the lungs. Ventilator-associated pneumonia was a real risk. For people already seriously ill, it could be a death sentence.

"Let me know how Shirley is doing when she's awake. Maybe we can reduce the ventilator further, and if that goes well, we'll move on with a spontaneous breathing trial."

If Shirley were able to breathe for two hours under

her own power, Julie would consider taking her off the ventilator.

"I'll get her awake right away," Amber said.

"Good," Julie answered.

So far the day was off to a banner start.

A raven-haired nurse named Lisa, dressed in floral scrubs, poked her head into Shirley's cubicle.

"Dr. Devereux, I need some help. It's the quarterback. I'm worried. We're cranking vasopressors, but his BP is unstable and trending down."

Julie darted out of the room and Lisa fell into step behind her. ICU nurses were not only compassionate, but were some of the best trained in the field. They seldom worried over nothing.

CHAPTER 3

The quarterback in question was Max Hartsock, a six-foot-five, two-hundred-twenty-pound star of the Boston College Eagles football team. Max was in the ICU with kidney failure and on dialysis following an exceptionally nasty MRSA infection. Instead of running plays, he lay on his back, spread-eagled, with a damp sheet covering his barrel chest.

Max's dark skin was an ashy shade. A thin layer of sweat glistened over muscles bloated with fluid. His numerous tattoos were stretched out and badly misshapen.

Tubes were inserted in all parts of his body. Most of the tubes put medicine into him, but a red one carried Max's blood to the dialysis machine, which was on and turning in a circular motion, removing waste products and essentially doing the work his kidneys could not. A different red tube put the cleaned blood back in.

A native of Dorchester, Max Hartsock was something of a legend, a local boy from a tough neighborhood who overcame adversity to become a Division I football standout.

Trevor's dad, who like Julie was a BC alumni, was still slightly obsessed with BC football, and Julie had fond memories of going to the games as a family. Paul's devotion to the team had rubbed off on Trevor. Her son, a soccer player and self-proclaimed ESPN addict, had plastered his bedroom walls with various Boston sports paraphernalia. In deference to his parents' alma mater, Trevor designated a special section of wall exclusively for BC football's annual team poster, which this year featured Max Hartsock front and center.

Julie came to Max's bedside. "How are you feeling?"

"Like I just got sacked by the entire Florida Gators football team." Max's voice came out thick and raspy.

"That good, huh?"

"What's wrong with me, Doc?"

"Well, a lot. The MRSA infection caused your body to go into shock, which then shut down your kidneys. And now, for some reason, your blood pressure isn't stable."

She checked the carotid pulses on either side of Max's muscled neck. They were regular, but a little thready. Lisa's concern had been valid. Julie sensed a crisis might be looming and, paradoxically, she relaxed. Maintaining a level head was essential for making smart decisions.

Max had an arterial line in for continuous blood pressure monitoring. Julie glanced at the digital read-out: ninety-five systolic, lower than it should have been with all the vasopressors in his bloodstream. He was also running a fever, 102 according to the readout on the monitoring system. He had almost every hookup the ICU had to offer, but nothing could explain why his BP was not stable.

"He's had a heparin infusion?" Julie asked Lisa.

"A few hours ago," Lisa said.

Julie gave a nod. This was standard practice for preventing thrombosis during intermittent dialysis.

"I'm already at the max dose of Levophed, thirty micrograms," Lisa said, as if reading Julie's thoughts.

"Well, his BP should be higher. Give him fluids while we're sorting this out."

"Is that your son?" Max asked Julie in a raspy voice.

Julie spun her head toward the door.

"Trevor, what are you doing here?" she said in a sharp tone. "You're supposed to wait for me in my office."

"I needed a charger."

"Read a book," she said with a scowl.

Trevor gave Max an awkward wave.

"Yes, that's my son, Trevor," Julie said. "He's actually a very big fan of yours. But he shouldn't be here." To Trevor, Julie said, "Should you?"

"That's okay, Doc, I don't mind." It took effort, but Max waved Trevor into the room.

At the same time, Lisa went to the door and yelled into the hall, "Hey, can someone help me?"

A second nurse soon arrived. "What do you need?"

"A liter of saline," Lisa said. "No, make it two."

"You're a BC football fan, eh?" Max said to Trevor.

"Yeah. Big time."

"Ever go to the games?" Max's voice came out just above a whisper and Trevor had to lean in close to hear.

"Yeah," Trevor said. "Saw you play against Syracuse with my dad. Three hundred twenty-five yards passing, three TDs, and no picks. Awesome game."

Max managed a half smile. "Kid, you know my stats better than me."

Trevor blushed. "I doubt it."

"Your mom's taking good care of me. You being cool with her?"

"Yeah, pretty cool."

Julie set a damp cloth against Max's forehead to soak up some of the perspiration. The saline arrived and a nurse went to work getting the bag hooked up. After scanning his body head to toe, Julie double-checked Max's lines and glanced at the screen of the dialysis machine. She kept an even keel as she ran through her list, conducting a rapid-fire differential diagnosis in her mind.

Two-port line for the dialysis catheter seems okay . . . no signs of bleeding there . . . dialysis machine says the blood flow is appropriate . . . no blockages . . . lines don't appear to be stuck against a blood vessel wall . . .

In the middle of her exam, Max's BP crashed.

"BP is down to seventy-five!" the monitoring tech called, talking only about the systolic reading, a common practice during an emergency.

A loud beeping startled Trevor. For a few seconds nobody moved, no sound other than the incessant churning from the dialysis machine as it cleaned Max's blood. Trevor moved back a few steps as Max let out a soft moan.

Julie felt her pulse quicken.

"Trevor, please wait in my office." There was no room for negotiation. Trevor departed with haste.

We're giving him fluid, max vasopressors, lowered dialysis, and he's still shitting the bed . . .

A monitoring nurse out in the hall yelled, "Hey, is anybody seeing this? The BP in room fifteen is dropping like crazy."

Lisa yelled back, "Yeah, we're seeing it!"

"When was he last fine?" Julie asked Lisa. "Was he okay after the line went in?"

"Yeah, he was fine then," Lisa said. "Then the nurse turned on the dialysis and he got worse, so she turned down the flow, thinking that would help."

Max took several short, sharp breaths that barely moved air, and let out another moan. Julie eyeballed the monitor, taking in the oxygen saturation reading, and saw it was within the normal range. She reviewed Max's heart rhythm as measured by the telemetry and noted an increased heart rate that often accompanied episodes of low blood pressure. The rhythm in his pulse gave no indication of any cardiac trouble. The usual culprits appeared not to be at play here.

What the hell is going on?

Julie slipped her stethoscope into her ears. She listened carefully for the telltale rubbing sound that signals when renal failure causes fluid to build up in the sac around the heart, essentially squeezing the life out. She heard the fast lub-dub of Max's heart racing to send blood to his vital organs.

"Did you get a chest X-ray?" she asked Lisa.

"Yeah, we did the X-ray," Lisa said. "But it hasn't been read yet."

"Dammit," Julie said. "Well, get someone to read it, will you?"

Setting the diaphragm of the stethoscope on Max's back, Julie gave a careful listen to the chest posteriorly. Next, she put it near the armpit, and then to the front of the chest, hearing bilaterally symmetrical breath sounds. Even with those normal sounds, Julie could not rule out the possibility that the insertion of his central venous catheter might have caused a pneumothorax. If air were leaking into the space between the lungs and the chest, it would explain Max's hypotension. She needed those X-rays pronto.

Lisa soon returned, while Julie continued to listen with her stethoscope. A second nurse and a monitoring tech also entered the cramped quarters.

"We got a rush on the read," Lisa said. "I'm trying to pull it up on the computers, but the system is down for maintenance."

"Damn computers," Julie muttered.

"They said it won't be long before the system is back online," Lisa said. "We can try to get it from the backup."

"No, by then the main system will be back. Did he ever spike a fever?" Julie asked.

"It's been gradual," Lisa said.

A series of alarms sounded louder than any previous alerts. The BP monitor rang loudest and grew in volume as Max's blood pressure sank lower, to sixty-two.

"Should I call a code?" Lisa asked.

Julie had been thinking the same herself.

She needed that damn radiological read.

Julie's composure began to fracture. The code blue seemed a likely course of action. She shot Lisa a fierce look.

"Get someone to call down to radiology and tell them we need that reading now! Fix whatever they have to fix, but get me that read! Lisa, tell me again, what dose of Levo is he on?"

"Thirty micrograms," Lisa answered.

"Are you *sure* that's the right stuff?" Julie asked.

Lisa looked at the bag and nodded.

"We've already given fluid," Julie said as the calm

returned to her voice. "Let's get a second vasopressor going. This time use vasopressin."

You are not going to die, young man. No way!

Max was groaning incoherently and sweating profusely. Lisa got the new medicine hooked up while the second nurse left the room to call radiology. She returned a few moments later.

"The system is back online. Radiology said no pneumothorax," the nurse said, glancing at her note. " 'New dialysis catheter in place adjacent to previously seen subclavian line.' "

This struck Julie as odd. Typically the catheter for the vasopressors and the one for the dialysis would have been positioned opposite each other. There was a computer in Max's room, and this time Julie was able to pull up his X-rays and read them for herself. The frontal X-ray showed that the lines were in fact overlapped, easy for her to see.

"BP is fifty-nine!" the tech reported. The alarms were really going.

Julie looked at Lisa. "Why did the radiologist put the dialysis line on the same side as the subclavian line for the vasopressors?" she asked.

Lisa thought before answering. "Max had a broken collarbone that ripped the subclavian vein, so that's why they switched to the right. They capped the port and he was fine."

A thought tingled. "Fine until when?" Julie asked, an edge to her voice.

"Um, for a while after we started the dialysis. I don't know exactly how long."

Julie studied those lines on the X-ray once more. It was uncommon but not unprecedented for the two catheters to be on the same side of the body. In optimal placement the catheter tips would be right next to each other, but on Max's X-ray Julie observed a noticeable gap between them.

The image called up a memory of a time she ran out of gasoline while on a long ride with Sam. To get her bike started, Sam had to siphon the gas from his tank into hers using a tube he carried in a satchel for just such emergencies. The siphon did not function at all until Sam got the tube positioned properly, but once he did, the suction it generated was impressive.

Max was fine for a while after we started the dialysis . . . after . . .

Julie felt a surge of excitement. She had never encountered something like this, but those cath lines might be positioned in such a way to create a siphon inside Max's body. If that were the case, the blood filled with the vasopressors needed to keep Max's blood pressure up during dialysis was being siphoned into the very machine that was purifying his blood, removing all traces of the medication he needed.

"Shut off the dialysis!" Julie barked. "Shut it off right now! This is not the time to be dialyzing our patient. That can wait!"

"BP is fifty-five!" the tech called out.

Max's eyes rolled back into his head and his mouth fell open as he became unconscious. All sorts of alarms continued to sound, and several more nurses and two residents rushed into the room.

With the push of a few buttons, Lisa shut down the machine. Almost immediately, Max's blood pressure spiked to seventy. Then seventy-five.

Julie realized she had been holding her breath. She

let out a long exhale. Max's eyes fluttered open, but he was groggy, completely out of it.

"BP is up to ninety," the tech said.

Julie let herself relax a little only when Max began to move his extremities spontaneously and became somewhat responsive. Lisa set her hands on her hips and struck a pose as if to say that she'd filled her quota of excitement for the day.

"How did you know, Dr. Devereux?" Lisa asked. "Even the radiologist didn't think of that when he put in those lines."

"Well, maybe he doesn't ride motorcycles," Julie said.

When it was obvious that Max had stabilized, Julie went out into the hallway. To her surprise she found Trevor lurking nearby, with a clear view of the action. He looked at his mother with awe, a look Julie had not seen since her son was six years old. It erased all of her anger over his disobedience.

"That was pretty amazing, Mom. You saved his life, didn't you?"

Julie just smiled.

CHAPTER 4

Roman Janowski—Romey, to everyone who knew him—sat at his expansive desk fingering the embossed invitation. The black-tie celebration would honor Charles Whitmore as the "Hospital Administrator of the Year."

Anger and resentment rose in Romey's throat. Whitmore was a fraud, the exact sort of asshole John Fogerty sang about in "Fortunate Son," one of Romey's favorite Creedence Clearwater Revival tracks. Whitmore got the job at Boston General because his family had been at the center of Boston's illustrious medical history since the 1850s.

Big deal, Charlie, thought Romey as he gazed out his massive office windows at the green emerald square of the hospital quad five stories below. *Daddy got you a job running an internationally renowned medical center with arguably the best medical staff anywhere and a patient service area that includes every millionaire in the world, and so you succeeded. Bully for you!*

Romey knew *he* was the real deal. White Memorial

had been a second-rate hospital before he took over. By instituting some unique and unusual methods, he had managed to make the hospital one of the best-run medical facilities in the state.

"Anybody can do a Whipple procedure on a sheik with pancreatic cancer who will die in a year anyway," Romey had said during a board meeting. "The real trick, the reason you pay me so well, is because I can take the bread and butter of medicine—arthroscopy, gallbladder removal, and pneumonia—and create a margin of fifteen percent. Let the other hospitals battle to attract top doctors who want their egos affiliated with a worldwide organization. I'd rather have enough funds to give bonuses to my physicians so they will do what it takes to improve our bottom line."

Heads nodded, and no one objected to Romey's raise—a raise that pushed his salary into seven-figure territory and gave him another seven in bonuses. With that kind of income, Romey could be short and bald, with a noticeable belly and ears like radar dishes, and still attract plenty of leggy blondes, including the two who were his current mistresses. Nancy, his wife of thirty-five years, was willing to accept her husband's indiscretions in exchange for her cushy lifestyle as long as he had the courtesy not to flaunt the girls in her face. Romey obliged happily. He would do anything to keep Nancy from making good on her long-standing threat to divorce him in the most costly way possible.

Romey folded the invitation in half, then tore it in two. The difference between Romey and Charles Whitmore, Romey knew, was flash and renown. The time had come for Romey to step out of the shadows and build his empire.

He looked at the pile of folders on his coffee table and knew where to begin. Romey slipped on his headset and dialed the direct line for the president of Suburban West Medical Center.

"Allyson Brock's office," said the friendly voice on the other end.

"Is Allyson in? It's Roman Janowski from White Memorial."

"Just a minute, Mr. Janowski, she's just ending a meeting, but I know she will want to take your call."

Of course she will. She's drowning.

A brief interlude of insufferable elevator music followed before Allyson picked up the line.

"Romey, to what do I owe the honor of this call? You city boys rarely give us folks toiling in the hinterlands the time of day," said Allyson, her voice almost dripping with honey.

"Not true, my dear. I always think that those who run small suburban hospitals have a lot to teach us all."

"Well, what can I do for you, Romey?"

"Word on the street is that one has never played golf until they have played with you. A history with the LPGA, I understand." In fact, Romey knew everything about Allyson's brief time on the tour—just as he knew everything about her divorce; her two kids in college; her over-mortgaged houses in Wellesley, Martha's Vineyard, and Loon Mountain; and her addiction to Nordstrom and Saks.

"I didn't know you played."

"Well, I am just learning, but I figure I might as well learn from the best, so I am hoping you might be able to find some time next Wednesday for a round with an old duffer." Romey was sixty-five, hardly old, but Allyson was fifteen years his junior.

"Sounds like fun. I generally play at Beechwood."

"Actually, Allyson, I want to show you my home course in Duxbury. Shall we say two o'clock?"

Allyson's voice grew a bit tense as she agreed to Romey's offer. She was shrewd enough to know Romey had something else planned. Why else would he want her at a club where she had never played before, and would know no one?

Romey moved to his couch, where a stack of files sat in front of him. He had a lot of homework to do before the round of golf, and none of it involved a ball, club, or tee. He opened the files to review the audited financial statements of Suburban West Medical Center, its Medicare cost report, IRS 990 forms, and notes from physicians who'd once worked at SWMC. Plenty of ammunition to guarantee the only one who would score an eagle on Wednesday would be Roman Janowski.

CHAPTER 5

Back again, for the second time in a week.

Tommy Grasso had become a regular at White Memorial. Bad luck combined with bad choices had turned the hospital into his version of *Cheers,* a place where everybody knew his name. Nobody wanted to boomerang in and out of the hospital, occasionally multiple times in the same month. Nobody wanted COPD either, but everybody wanted to breathe, so the hospital was where he had to go.

This was Tommy's tenth trip to White Memorial since he rang in the New Year. Ten times Tommy had been processed through hospital admissions and wheeled into a bland and standard room where he would spend a few days, or maybe longer. Sometimes he was brought to the ICU and placed on BiPAP, a breathing apparatus that helped get air into the lungs. He was even placed on a ventilator a couple times. But they always sent him to rehab, then home for a short stint, only for the cycle to repeat.

What Tommy really needed was a new pair of lungs. What Tommy got was a spot on a waiting list that would probably never call his name because of his O-negative blood type. Even if they did find him a match—and that was a 7 percent possibility on the outside—he was saddled with an equally uncommon tissue type.

If smoking were not the single cause of Tommy's health issues, it was certainly the star of the show. At one time Tommy could catch the eye of most any girl, including his beloved Gladys. He had been tall and fit, with a stomach flat as an ironing board, and blessed with a thick head of dark hair. A three-sport athlete in high school, Tommy could swim like a fish and still smoke like a chimney.

Over the years, Tommy's dark hair turned gray and eventually fell out. His gut expanded as his lung capacity shrank, and a flabby chin overtook a jawline that once turned many heads. The two-pack-a-day habit that took away Tommy's good looks had started back when Brownsville Station made smokin' in the boys' room sound like a cool thing to do. The habit continued until his college-bound son extracted a promise to quit that came too late.

He had gone almost a decade without a cigarette before the first signs of COPD appeared. The seeds of the disease, however, had been planted long ago, and could not have cared less when Tommy last had a puff.

These days, Tommy's son was married, and there were grandchildren in the picture who lived a few hours away. They might as well have nested on top of Mount Everest. Tommy was too sick to travel even short distances. Being out of breath was a terrifying sensation,

and one Tommy did everything in his power to avoid—
well, everything but follow his doctors' orders to the
letter.

When he was not at the hospital, Tommy was either
in rehab waiting for too few nurses to help him from
his bed to his chair or the bathroom, or he was home-
bound and tied to a ratty recliner positioned strategically in front of the TV.

Tommy, who had hypertension to go along with
COPD, had been watching TV (as usual) when he experienced the familiar sensation of shortness of breath.
One second he was enjoying a Sox game and the next
he felt like someone had dumped a pile of bricks on top
of his chest. He fought to get sips of air into his battered lungs. He coughed and wheezed and managed to
squeak out a single panicky sentence directed at Gladys:
"I can't breathe."

Gladys, accustomed to the drill by now, encouraged
Tommy. "Pursed-lip breaths now, in and out. Remember, blow out the candle. I'll grab your hospital bag and
get the car ready."

Gladys drove Tommy to the ER, following a route
seared into her memory. In the car he coughed up a
thick, viscous ball of mucus. Trouble. His breathing
grew shallower, and Tommy knew that carbon dioxide
was building up in his blood, making it hard for him to
stay awake.

Once in the ER, it was an all-too-familiar scene. A
respiratory therapist and an ER nurse (Tommy knew
them both by name) stood at his bedside, talking to
themselves and to the doctor, dressed in a white lab coat
(Tommy knew him by name as well).

"Mr. Grasso, I'm sorry you're back so soon," the respiratory therapist said. Her name was Lynn and her sympathy came across as genuine. "We'll do what we can to make you feel better. Jill, can you listen to his breath sounds? Dr. Chan, Mr. Grasso is currently eighty-two percent on a four liters nasal cannula. I'd like to get him on the BiPAP."

"I agree," Dr. Chan said.

"How are those breath sounds?" Lynn asked.

The other nurse, Jill, was pretty and always sweet to Tommy, but he wished he did not have to see her again so soon, if ever. "Prolonged expiratory time and lots of wheezing," Jill answered.

"Respiratory rate is forty. He's barely moving air," Lynn said.

"Start a continuous nebulized albuterol," Dr. Chan said. "Go with fifteen milligrams, please."

To Tommy, the exchanges between the doctor and nurses were lines of a play he could recite before they were even spoken.

She's going to tell me about the mask, he thought.

"Mr. Grasso, I'm going to put a mask on, it will let you breathe a little easier. It will feel tight at first, but it will help assist your breaths."

Tommy wanted to laugh, but beneath the oxygen mask, he felt his own respirations diminish.

"Mr. Grasso, how are you feeling, sir?"

"Hard . . . to . . . breathe . . ."

And stay awake, he wanted to add, but lacked strength in his mind and lungs. The only thing Tommy could focus on was his need for more air.

Tommy's acute exacerbation of COPD could have been caused by an infection, some sort of bacteria, but most likely it was mismanagement of his medication again. He had so many pills and inhalers to keep track of, and a slew of complex instructions to follow.

"If these stats don't come up, we're going to have to tube him. Call the ICU and give them a heads-up."

If Tommy had seen that his oxygen saturation was down to eighty-one percent, he would have known that ventilation was inevitable.

"Did we get an ABG measurement yet?"

The arterial blood gas test measured acidity and levels of oxygen and carbon dioxide in the blood. Tommy guessed his number was 7.2, maybe as low as 7.16. Either way, he was most likely experiencing respiratory acidosis, a condition resulting from lungs that were incapable of removing all the carbon dioxide the body produced.

"Seven point one two," Jill said.

Her voice sounded far away . . . so far from here. Tommy's eyes began to shut. He was tired, tired of everything. What he would not give for a good set of lungs, for a decent breath of air again.

Dr. Chan said, "Draw up the succs."

Succinylcholine, Tommy knew the drug well. It was used for intubation.

WHEN TOMMY'S eyes fluttered open, he had a tube shoved down his throat and a machine to do all the breathing for him. It took a moment to get oriented to the fact that he was back in the ICU. Tommy had no idea if it were day or night. His cubicle had no windows; no other patients either.

There was, however, a visitor in his room. The room lights were off, and Tommy could not make out a face, and he couldn't ask for a name because of the tube shoved down his throat. His vision was badly blurred both from sleep and the sedatives he'd been given. His mouth felt like he had swallowed sand, it was so dry and gritty, and he had no way to alleviate that sensation.

"Hi there, Tommy."

The voice sounded soft and gentle, but somewhat distorted, with a bit of a delay, as though it had bubbled up from a deep well. It was like the voice in a dream. Tommy wondered if the sedatives also distorted his hearing. Or maybe it was just hard to hear over those awful mechanized breathing sounds.

"You're up again, I see."

I've been up before? When? Tommy could think those thoughts, but could not voice them.

He liked having company, any company, but what Tommy really wanted was Gladys. He figured it was at least the afternoon, because Gladys always spent her mornings with him in the ICU.

"You keep coming back here, Tommy. It must be awful. You really *should* learn how to manage your meds. Maybe try to eat a little better, or, God forbid, take a walk. It certainly would help keep you out of the hospital."

Tommy picked up something unsettling, as if he were being taunted, or maybe scolded. Either way, he wished he could speak, have a conversation. Then he would know for sure.

A phone rang. The visitor answered. "Hello. Yes, I did call . . . it's Mr. Tommy Grasso. He's back . . . yes, again, in the ICU of all places . . . what do you think? COPD, of course . . . yes, he has tested positive. . . . I think we did it the last time he was here . . . Oh, I

absolutely think we should give him the treatment . . .
I can do it so that there'll be a little delay before it
takes effect. Just enough so I'll be long gone . . . well,
if anybody deserves the treatment, it's Tommy . . . it's
best for him and that's my role here, that's what I care
most about . . . Good, I'm glad we're in agreement."

The visitor put the phone away and came to Tommy's bedside.

"I've got great news." The visitor sounded calm, the
way his doctors spoke, but somehow Tommy felt uneasy for reasons he could not comprehend. "You're going to get the treatment. Do you know what that means?"

I don't think I want to know, Tommy wished he could
say.

"It's the ultimate cure, Tommy," the visitor continued. "Once you get it, you'll never have to come back
here again. Think about it. No more hospital visits. Not
ever. You'll be cured for good."

Tommy's skin prickled. He did not know what this
treatment was, but it was something he did not want to
have. Helpless on his back, eyes wide with terror, unable to speak, Tommy could barely make out a bag of
clear fluid in the visitor's hand.

"The treatment won't take long, but I can't promise
it won't hurt. If you could talk, you'd thank me. Nobody
wants to live in a hospital, Tommy. It just isn't right.
Someone needs to show you a little mercy."

The visitor undid one of Tommy's IVs and hooked
the catheter line into the bag of fluid, then titrated the
flow.

The last words Tommy heard were, "I am merciful."

CHAPTER 6

Sam Talbot lived on the kind of wide, tree-lined street where Julie had once imagined she would raise her family. The houses here were spacious, but not too grand. Her ex-husband, Paul, had railed against the trappings of suburban life, so they'd ended up buying a condo in Cambridge. And Julie, to her surprise, fell in love with urban living. The conveniences were hard to beat. Once the excitement of her engagement to Sam had worn off, Julie made clear her concerns regarding living arrangements. She was a full-fledged city mouse, and Sam was of the country variety.

"We'll work it out," Sam had assured her.

That was almost a year ago. They had yet to reach any decision. Now the wedding was fast approaching—six months and counting down—and some sort of resolution was in order.

"He'll be fine here," Sam said, speaking of Trevor.

"Well, I know he'll adjust," Julie replied. "But how long will it take? How well can he manage?"

They were working side by side in Sam's two-car

garage. Julie had an underground parking space, but no storage, and a real garage was one of many amenities suburban living had to offer. Julie attended to her motorcycle and Sam to his in preparation for the day's long ride.

"He'll make new friends," Sam said. "How many middle school chums are you still close with?"

"Plenty," Julie answered. Julie did not make eye contact with Sam. She was too busy going through her pre-ride checklist, which she approached with the same fastidiousness she brought to a bedside exam.

Sam was less diligent, in part because he was far more experienced. He rode a BMW K1600, which had an engine roughly seven times the cubic capacity of Julie's bike. Julie's ride was plenty powerful and she had confidence in her ability to control her bike, thanks to fifteen hours of instruction from Training Wheels, a premier motorcycle riding school. It was the other motorists she worried about.

"Who are you still close with from middle school?" Sam asked.

Her focus still on her bike, Julie answered, "Sandy, Claire, and Eileen." She rattled those names off the top of her head, but she could have mentioned others as well.

"You talk to them only on Facebook," Sam said with a grin.

"They're still my friends, and isn't Facebook how *we* reconnected?" Julie strode over to Sam, giving her hips an extra playful swagger. She wrapped her arms around his neck. He was taller than Julie by five inches, but she did not mind stretching to meet his lips. His close-cropped beard, sandy-colored like his thick, wavy hair, tickled her face and she enjoyed the sensation. She threw herself into the kiss, making it clear that wherever she and Trevor lived, Sam would be in her life forever.

"Maybe I'll keep my condo for a while, you keep your house, and we'll see each other when Trevor is with Paul."

Sam frowned. "We sound like we're already divorced."

"I just don't know if I can move him now, sweetheart. He's acting out at school and at home. The whole notion is daunting."

Sam fell silent, not brooding, but thinking. "What if I sold my house and we bought a new place together in Cambridge?"

Julie was stunned. "You would do that for us?"

"That way Trevor could go to the same school, and we could be together as a family."

"Why not just move into my place, then? There's more than enough room for the three of us."

"That's your place with Paul," Sam said. "I want something that's just about us. A place where we can make memories from scratch."

"And you can make new cabinets," Julie said, smiling.

Mostly self-taught, Sam had painstakingly stripped his house down to the studs and rebuilt it using second-hand tools and limitless ingenuity. It was a true labor of love. From decorative moldings with intricate carvings to the kitchen cabinetry and furniture, Sam was an artist with wood.

"But you hate the city," Julie said. "And now you'll have a commute."

"I'd hate living apart from you even more. Trevor's not the only one who can adjust."

Julie purred and pressed her body against him, running her hands along his backside in a playful, teasing way. Sam's hazel eyes flickered with excitement.

"How about after this ride I help lube your throttle cable?" Julie whispered in his ear.

Sam laughed and kissed Julie with passion. "I love it when you talk motorcycle to me."

Julie pulled away and her expression became more serious. "We'll figure it out, okay? I love you and I'm excited to spend the rest of my life showing you how much."

Their lips met again.

"Thank goodness for Facebook," Sam breathed in Julie's ear.

Back in high school, Sam Talbot had hovered near Julie's close circle of friends, but they remained acquaintances and nothing more. Occasionally they would bump into each other at a party or some school happening, but Sam was a band and drama club kid. Julie was more of a jock, and for the most part, those groups didn't interact.

But then came life, and later Facebook, and suddenly Julie's friend list was replete with people from her past whose names she could barely recall, including Sam Talbot's.

When Sam posted about his divorce, a year after Julie's had been finalized, she worked up the nerve to send him a message. It was the tone of his post that had her so intrigued. She could still recall some of that text verbatim.

Life can be a magical journey and the only anchors

we have are the ones we tie to ourselves. So anchors away and bon voyage, my friends. I'm sailing off on a new adventure!

Julie loved the visual, and wanted to believe she embraced her own upheaval with the same degree of optimism. She wrote a friendly note to Sam, to whom she had not spoken since graduation. They made a date to meet for drinks, which led to more drinks, and now, almost two years later, plans to marry.

"I have a lot of papers to grade tonight," Sam said. "Can you stay over and keep me company?"

"I have to be home for Trevor," Julie said.

"That's it, I'm calling the real estate agent as soon as we get back."

Julie laughed warmly as Sam fired up his engine.

"Don't laugh, I'm serious," he said.

Julie climbed on her bike and blew him a kiss. "And I'm glad."

They backed their bikes out of the garage. Skill with a motorcycle had more to do with correct technique than brute strength, and Julie was all about doing things the right way. She led by example at work and at home. She hoped Trevor would adopt her ways, but it seemed Paul's influence was winning out.

Still, Trevor could recite on command Julie's list of three things in life not to waste—time, money, and potential—and this gave her hope that Trevor would one day mature into better life habits.

Soon they were on the road, headed west to the Berkshires. Julie felt peaceful and exhilarated all at once. Thin clouds scudded in front of the morning sun, darkening a splendid blue sky. It was the first Sunday of September, the long Labor Day weekend, and an unseasonable chill in the air hinted at summer's final good-bye. Julie's leather jacket provided warmth against the biting wind.

They took the highway so they could make good time getting to the day's main event, a thirty-five-mile stretch of Route 20 called Jacob's Ladder Trail Scenic Byway. The road wound through Russell, Huntington, Chester, and Becket before ending in downtown Lee.

Just beyond the Russell town line, the rambling Westfield River came into view. It was a spectacular sight, and Julie followed Sam into a scenic pullout. She dismounted and removed her helmet, shaking her head to let her long, chestnut hair tumble to her shoulders.

"I find it so insanely hot every time you do that," Sam said after removing his own helmet.

"And this is so insanely beautiful."

Julie took an invigorating breath. Already some flashes of color were brushed upon the leaves of the vast forest, just beyond the riverbank. The fall was always Julie's favorite season—a time for renewal and optimism, and of course pumpkin everything. This would be the first year Trevor had no plans to go trick-or-treating. Julie was surprised that this made her feel a little sad.

Her thoughts were interrupted by a phone call from Paul. "Hi, what's going on?"

Paul said, "Trevor has to do a book report and wants to know if you can pick up the book for him at the library."

Julie kept her annoyance in check. "Paul, I'm in the Berkshires. I believe you have the same access to a library as do I. And why wouldn't he want to go to a library? There's no place better."

"I'm working on a sculpture and Trevor's enjoying helping."

Her jaw tightened. "You better not be giving my son a blowtorch," Julie said.

"No. You made your feelings about that quite clear."

"Well then, let me make this clear to you, as well. Don't be lazy. Go take your son to the library. Give him a hug from me. I'll see you both tonight."

"But—"

"Good-bye, Paul." Julie ended the call.

Sam gave Julie a wry smile. "You really are a great ex, you know that?"

"My mother taught me how to do it right. She had plenty of practice."

"Third time's the charm."

"Paul means well. He's just a little, I don't know— immature, I suppose."

For all of Paul's deficiencies, he loved his son. Julie was happy that she and Paul kept a cordial relationship. She could wish all she wanted for Paul to be more mature, more reliable, more dependable. Then again, they were divorced for good reason. Paul might not have had full-blown Peter Pan syndrome, but indications of the condition were certainly there.

In college, Paul's carefree attitude, his spontaneity, his joie de vivre, had captured Julie's heart. Years later, and especially after Trevor was born, what had been endearing turned frustrating. Julie was all for carefree moments, but on a daily basis, what she wanted most was a partner.

Many of Julie's friends admired her ability to keep the acrimony to a minimum. She simply felt that it served no purpose. Trevor benefited from having two parents actively involved in his life.

"You know I rarely speak to Karen since our split," Sam said, "but when I do it's a lot less friendly."

"You don't have kids with her, so there's less of a reason to keep up friendly relations," Julie replied.

Sam gazed out at the rambling water, looking a bit wistful. "When we got married, I thought kids were in the plan."

"She thought you were going to go work for your father's company and become obscenely rich. I've said it before. It's not a coincidence that as soon as you decided to become a teacher, Karen decided she didn't want kids. It was emotional blackmail, nothing more."

Sam got that faraway look in his eyes again.

"I love what I do, but I regret not becoming a father."

"You're great with kids and with Trevor," Julie said.

"Speaking of Trevor, I bought the wood for the table we're going to make. I can't say he seems super excited to help me, but he didn't say no, either."

"He'll come around eventually," Julie said. "This is hard for him. It's a big adjustment for us all."

"I know I'm not Trevor's father, and I would never try to replace Paul," Sam said, "but I'm going to treat him like a son. That's a pledge and a promise."

A lump wormed into Julie's throat. "Just another reason why you're the man for me," she said.

They rode the rest of the byway and got lunch at a cute restaurant Sam had found on Yelp. The journey home was easy and wonderful. Julie rode alongside Sam whenever possible, and otherwise kept a safe distance behind him. For those few hours, all her worries about Trevor, the pressures of her job, nagging concerns about selling her home and moving in with Sam receded to the back of her mind. The road liberated her from anxiety. She loved the feel of her bike, and admittedly took pleasure in the looks she got from other motorists. Her engine hummed like a finely tuned instrument. The vibration against her hands relaxed her muscles.

Everything about that moment was perfect.

CHAPTER 7

They left 95 to merge onto 109, a busy two-lane road that wound through a number of quiet suburbs. Sam's home was ten minutes away. Julie planned to park her bike in Sam's garage and drive her Prius into Cambridge, arriving in plenty of time to greet Trevor—with his library book, she hoped. Her electric car did not turn heads like her motorcycle, but she got occasional questions from people considering a purchase, and a few scowls from some who typecast her as a tree-hugging liberal.

A white Honda Civic, driving erratically in front of Sam, triggered Julie's concern. The first sign of trouble came when the Civic swerved onto the shoulder where the road curved sharply. The car wheels chopped up dirt and gravel, kicking loose stone onto the road before the driver corrected the error. The sky had darkened enough so Julie could see light from a cell phone illuminate the driver in a bluish haze.

Damn menace, she thought.

Sam motored along behind the Civic while Julie

slowed to put some distance between her bike and the distracted driver. She wanted Sam to do the same; sometimes he trusted that his riding skills would trump other people's stupidity.

The road turned. Julie could not see around the bend, but she did note that the double yellow dividing line was a solid one.

Do not pass. Blind curve.

Maybe they need a line for "don't look at your phone while driving," she thought.

The Civic veered again to the right. Julie's breaths came in short bursts. She suddenly felt unsteady on her bike as her anxiety spiked.

She glanced at the speedometer.

Forty.

She had no wiggle room if that Civic did something really foolish. Before Julie could honk out a warning to Sam, the Civic swerved yet again, this time steering into the left lane just at the point when the blind curve straightened.

Immediately, Julie saw what was coming down the road. A red pickup truck (Ford, Dodge, impossible to say) was headed right for the Civic. The world down-shifted into slow motion.

Julie, who had sensed the danger, knew for certain that the Civic had drifted too far left to avoid a collision.

These cars are going to hit . . . slow down . . . pull off to the side of the road.

She braked, preparing to pull over. The driver of the pickup blared his horn and slammed on his brakes. The truck went into a skid and the Civic turned hard right. Long black skid marks marred the road where the

Civic's tires failed to gain traction. Sam braked maybe a second after Julie, but he was in front of her, closest to the coming crash.

The next moments happened fast, too fast to take it all in, and yet each brutal detail came at her like single frames of an advancing filmstrip. The pickup swerved to avoid a head-on collision, but the Civic smacked into the truck's rear. There was a ferocious crunch of metal on metal. Glass shattered. The impact changed the trajectory of the pickup and sent it at an angle into the oncoming traffic. It crossed the highway dividing line and came shooting toward Sam like a half-ton missile.

Sam was pulling to the side of the road, leaning his body and bike as far right as he could without tipping over. As this happened, the Civic spun in a complete circle before it skirted across the left lane, then shot off the road entirely and crashed into the trees. Branches snapped fiercely and more glass exploded as if a bomb had gone off inside the car, followed by a whoosh when the Civic's air bag deployed.

Julie applied her brakes hard. Her bike teetered without going over. Sam accelerated, trying to avoid a direct hit with the pickup as it veered into their lane. Julie was overcome with a terrible knowing. The pickup was traveling too fast and Sam was not going fast enough. The front left fender of the pickup collided hard with the rear tire of Sam's motorcycle. The pickup slipped into a harder skid as the rear wheel of Sam's bike lifted off the road.

The bike's front wheel spun across the pavement like a runaway gyroscope before it lost traction entirely. The bike went airborne, with Sam riding it the whole way.

How high was he when he finally let go—five feet? Maybe more. His body was still moving forward. It looked like both he and the bike were flying.

Sam flipped over in the air and landed hard on his back as the bike's rear wheel struck him in the chest. The bike bounced off him, then the pavement, with a loud metallic crunch. It flipped again, and again, until momentum carried the crumpled heap of metal off into the trees where it came to a stop, front wheel still spinning.

Julie threw her body weight hard right and skidded to a full stop, letting her bike fall away as she tumbled to the ground. She had slowed down enough for a soft landing.

Sam had not slowed at all. He skidded helplessly down the road on his back. Ten feet . . . fifteen . . . twenty . . .

Julie thought she heard him screaming, only to realize it was her own terrified voice. She pushed to her feet and ran toward Sam. Her body lurched awkwardly from side to side as she fought to regain her balance. Blood roared in her ears. A blaring horn was stuck on one long wailing note. From the corner of her eye, she could see the metal carcass of Sam's motorcycle caught in a tangle of weeds.

Sam lay spread-eagled on his back in the middle of the road, his head and shoulders extended over the yellow dividing line. An approaching car shuddered to a stop just before it would have crushed Sam beneath its wheels. A trail of blood followed Sam's path down the road, ending at his body.

Julie registered that Sam's leg was bent at an awkward angle. His right wrist looked misshapen, obviously fractured. But she saw Sam's head loll from side to side, and her heart leapt.

Thank God, he's alive. He's alive!

She ran toward him, screaming at full volume, "Somebody call nine-one-one!"

CHAPTER 8

Julie had done what she could. All that remained was to wait for help to arrive and keep up the ABCCs—airway, breathing, circulation, cervical spine immobilization. Sam lay motionless in the middle of the road, his hazel eyes open wide in a vacant stare focused on the sky and nothing else. Julie observed the rapid rise and fall of his chest and heard the distressed wheezing sounds of his breathing.

She had checked his pulses, both carotid and radial. Those were present, fast and weak. Naturally she worried about shock. The jugular venous pressure was elevated, and just by looking at Sam's neck, she could see the vein on the right side was engorged. She checked the left and it looked the same. If Sam were in hemorrhagic shock, which was her assumption, those veins should be flat as a pancake. Low blood pressure caused the body to shunt blood to the heart and brain to preserve life.

Why would the jugular veins be distended? she wondered.

"Sweetheart, it's going to be all right," she said in a shaky voice. "You were in an accident. Don't try to move. Help is on the way."

And it was.

The man driving the pickup had called 911 and retrieved the first-aid kit Julie kept in the satchel on her motorcycle. He let Julie know the driver of the Civic escaped serious injury, but they were sending two ambulances as a precaution. To Julie, it seemed a common occurrence for reckless drivers to escape the mayhem they caused unscathed. Julie pushed the thought from her mind. What mattered now was comforting Sam the best she could. She wanted to hold Sam's hand, but his riding gloves had shredded from the long skid down the asphalt. The skin of his palms was nearly sheared off. His fingers had yet to move.

Instead, Julie knelt beside the man she could hardly wait to marry, the man who made her heart swell with his kindness, and tried to comfort him as best she could. The helmet had safeguarded his head and face, but blood escaped from a grisly four-inch gash that had opened on Sam's chin. His beard, flecked with debris, looked red.

The panic that had gripped Julie in those first terrifying moments gave way to a gut-wrenching awareness. This was happening. This was real. This *had* happened.

A circle of bystanders had formed around Julie and Sam, watching the gruesome scene with grave expressions. The spectators were visibly shaken. Some were crying. Some looked away as Sam emerged from the initial shock enough to feel the first pangs of real pain. He groaned and his mouth contorted into an agonized grimace.

"Sam, can you hear me? Can you say anything? Baby, please, say something if you can."

Sam's lips trembled. "It hurts," he wheezed. "Oh God, this hurts. This hurts so much."

Tears streamed down Julie's face. "I'm sorry. Help is on the way. Wiggle your fingers if you can. Just a little wiggle."

Nothing.

Off in the distance, Julie heard the first wail of sirens on fast approach. She saw the flashing lights, and soon the first responders were on the scene. She counted three police cars, two fire trucks, and two ambulances.

Julie stood, waving frantically. She got the attention of the lead ambulance driver, who made a hard stop not more than ten feet away. Two paramedics, dressed in blue uniforms with EMT badges sewn into the pockets of their shirts, latex gloves already donned, burst from the vehicle and raced to Sam's side.

"I'm Dr. Julie Devereux," Julie said in a breathless voice. "I work in critical care at White Memorial Hospital." Julie got the names of the two EMTs. Bill was a thin man in his midtwenties with shaggy brown hair and deep-set eyes. Ashley, in her late thirties, was athletically built, with broad shoulders, strong legs, and muscular arms.

"Did you see the accident?" Bill asked.

Julie nodded. "Yes, we were riding together. The victim is my fiancé, Sam Talbot." Julie had to look away until she steadied herself.

"His airway is clear," she said, trying to find some authority in her voice. Julie did not hear any crackling, grating sounds of crepitus, indicating air had not penetrated the soft tissue. "No crepitus, but I'm fairly certain he has a flail chest on the left ribs seven, eight, and nine. Both carotid and radial pulses are present, but weak. I don't think there's bleeding in the abdomen, but I'm worried about hemorrhagic shock. I'm also concerned his jugular veins are distended. I checked for a pneumothorax, but he has good breath sounds."

Bill and Ashley crouched next to Sam.

"Is his airway still clear?" Bill asked.

Ashley checked. "Yeah, he's got a good airway. He's breathing on his own."

A firefighter wearing a brown turnout coat and pants with sewn-in yellow bands approached.

"Need any help?"

"Yeah, we need the backboard and a cot, please," Ashley said. "Bill, can you take a look at his lower extremities? I need to get his helmet off to make sure he has a really good airway. Dr. Devereux, are you in a position to assist?"

Julie did not respond. Her focus had been entirely on Sam, who moaned and made a low gurgling sound.

"Dr. Devereux, can you assist?" Ashley asked again.

This time the question hit Julie like a slap. *Get with it!*

"Yes, of course I can," Julie said.

Ashley gave a nod and took her position in front of Sam's head. Once there, she undid the strap to Sam's helmet. Bill brought out strong scissors, capable of cutting through the leather of Sam's motorcycle pants.

"Okay, straps off," Ashley said. "I got c-spine."

Ashley was stabilizing Sam's cervical spine with a hand behind the head supporting the base of the skull, while her other hand held Sam's chin firmly.

Julie got directly behind Sam and slowly, methodically, began to pull the helmet off Sam's head. To do so, she maneuvered the helmet up and down, pulling with gentle force, careful not to catch the sides on his ears or snag his nose with the chinstrap. Ashley kept tension in her arms so that Sam's head would not drop.

The moment the helmet came off, Sam let go with a deep, guttural noise that tore at Julie's heart. She looked down and got her first good look at her fiancé's face. It was the only part of him not horribly injured, though his grayish coloring was most unsettling. Julie's chest grew tight. Ashley moved her hands up higher on Sam's head to continue to support the c-spine.

"We got an open fracture in the left lower leg," Bill announced.

Julie cringed.

"Bill, I need a blanket under Sam's head right away. Please, quickly."

Bill stopped cutting and did as he was instructed.

"Dr. Devereux, can you continue to take c-spine?" Ashley asked.

Ashley sounded so calm, so composed, the way Julie was accustomed to being.

"Of course," Julie said, keeping her hands to the sides of Sam's head.

With careful, practiced movements, Ashley unzipped Sam's jacket and took scissors from a belt pouch to cut open his shirt.

"Trachea is midline, and those neck veins do look slightly engorged," Ashley said.

"Slightly? Check again," Julie said. "It's more than that."

Those veins were a symptom of something, but of what?

"Yeah, I agree," said Ashley. "How's your breathing, Sam?"

Sam groaned and made another noise that sounded barely human.

"Let's get oxygen on him," Ashley ordered. "I'm going to get two IV Lactated Ringer's going."

Sam needed a lot more than the fluid and electrolyte replenishment. Looking down at the pant leg Bill had cut away, Julie saw where the bone had sheared through the skin. It was a hideous, jagged cut, crisscrossed with strands of frayed muscle and ringed by clumps of fatty tissue. The bone poked out from the middle of a five-inch gash in the leg. It was barely a speck of white adrift in a sea of blood. The Lactated Ringer's infusion would replenish electrolytes, but contained no antimicrobial agents. With such an open wound, Sam's risk of infection had markedly increased.

Ashley set her hands on Sam's bare chest, an area of his body spared major cuts and abrasions thanks to his protective gear. Along with providing oxygen flow and bleeding control, stabilizing any chest wall defect was a first priority.

Julie thought back to the accident. Had Sam hit the pickup's side mirror? Did the motorcycle land on top of him? A crushing impact of either type could be devastating. Ashley listened with her stethoscope, and Julie resisted the urge to rip the instrument from her ears to give a listen for herself.

Time was of the essence. It had been five minutes or so since Ashley and crew had arrived on the scene. In five more minutes, they should be in transit. If Ashley or Bill detected any major issue in Sam's ABCCs, it would be a load-and-go situation for certain.

"Can you tell me where you are hurting?" Ashley asked.

No response.

"Sam, can you wiggle your toes at all?"

Sam groaned incoherently.

Bill dressed the leg wound while Ashley got the portable oxygen unit running and the mask secured in place. All of the essential equipment was bagged and at the ready, saving valuable time that might have been wasted running back and forth to the ambulance.

Once the IVs were hooked up, Ashley undid the snaps of Sam's pants and palpated his abdomen.

"Abdomen is soft. We need to get a c-collar on him, then we need to log roll."

"What about those jugular veins?" Julie asked. "I'm really concerned."

"Then the sooner we get him to the hospital, the better," Ashley said.

Not just any hospital, Julie thought.

Ashley got the plastic, bivalved shell secured in place around Sam's neck while Julie continued to hold his head still. The entire process took less than a minute.

"Okay, are we ready to log roll?" Ashley asked.

Bill, having dressed the leg wound as best he could, nodded and took up position by Sam's lower extremities. Ashley reached across Sam's body so that she could get enough leverage to roll him onto his side.

"On my call, on three," Ashley said. "One . . . two . . . three."

Ashley and Bill pulled Sam onto his side, while Julie twisted her body to continue to support his head. As he rolled, Sam let out another loud groan. A firefighter tilted the cot and Ashley quickly inspected Sam's posterior from head to toe before the backboard was brought up flush against his body.

"Lower on my count," Ashley said. "One . . . two . . . three. Now we slide on three."

Together they slid Sam onto the board. Ashley conducted another examination of the pelvis and lower extremities before the anti-shock garments, padded liners that could be inflated to protect the body during transport, were secured in place. Ashley removed Sam's socks and shoes while Bill thoroughly assessed Sam's body using inspection and palpation techniques. They checked his distal pulses once more as two firefighters secured the backboard straps around Sam at three points.

Everyone stayed in constant motion, and every action had a purpose, like a choreographed dance rehearsed thousands of times. Julie's only job was to hold Sam's head perfectly still until the blocks were put into place. It was the best job for her: her hands on him, touching him, comforting him.

"Sam, can you wiggle your toes or fingers for me?" Ashley asked.

He made no movement at all. Panic set in as Julie contemplated the extent of Sam's injuries.

"Sam, we're going to lift you now." Whether he heard her or not, Ashley was going to give Sam the play-by-play. "You won't fall, because you're strapped in," she said. "Okay, on my count of three we lift him onto the cot. Everyone got a good grip?"

Bill, Julie, and two firefighters nodded in unison. On three they lifted Sam onto a rolling stretcher. Additional straps were quickly secured around him.

As soon as Sam was loaded into the back of the ambulance, Julie pulled Ashley aside.

"I want to ride in the back with you," she announced. "You're going to need two people looking out for him during transport, anyway. And please—let's bring him to White Memorial."

Ashley did not look pleased with either request. "I have a third EMT who will ride with us. I'm sorry, but that's our policy. And White Memorial is simply too far away."

Julie's eyes welled. White was smaller than some other Boston hospitals, but the trauma team was unsurpassed.

"Ashley, I'm begging you. It's where he needs to be. We don't have time to debate it. Please, just do it. You know it's the right thing to do, and you know I can help."

Bill had climbed into the back of the ambulance so he could assess and reassess Sam's condition. He was looking for deformities, contusions, abrasions, and penetrating punctures, and constantly monitoring Sam's vital signs.

"Hey, Ashley," Bill called out. "I'm really worried about these distended jugular veins. This isn't right. Yeah, it's, uh . . . it's not good at all."

Ashley shot Julie a nervous glance.

"Climb in, Dr. Devereux," Ashley said. "White Memorial, here we come."

CHAPTER 9

The dead can speak. It just takes time and patience to learn their language. Dr. Lucy Abruzzo had spent her career studying this language, and as White Memorial's chief of pathology, she spoke it better than anyone on staff. These days, bureaucracy and administrative duties took precedence over the lab work that had fed her passion for years. Lucy's personality was better suited to working with tissue samples and cadavers than to managing budgets, personalities, and cost structures. But hospital CEO Roman Janowski was not somebody you turned down twice.

As a manager, she remained somewhat of an enigma. A detached personality, someone a bit aloof, she was well suited to the autopsy table, but around a conference room table that personality could be off-putting. Lucy was an infrequent contributor to any pre-meeting banter. Most jokes and pop culture references were lost on her, as someone who did not own a television. Away from the lab, Lucy read nonfiction compulsively, ran for distance, loved chess, and enjoyed cooking, but only when following a recipe. Improvisation was for wilderness medicine.

It was common for Lucy to be so overscheduled with meetings that she never had time for any actual pathology. Weekends were different, though. Lucy used Sundays to catch up on paperwork and assist in the lab. Someone was always here doing something.

The moment Lucy set foot in the lab, a powerful scent hit her nostrils. Someone was testing stool samples, probably looking for a toxin. The pathology lab was always full of unusual smells, and Lucy found them all oddly pleasing. Dr. Becca Stinson, a fresh-faced second-year pathology resident, waved Lucy over to her workstation.

Some cases Lucy's team managed were difficult to crack, while others were more straightforward. The pathology of the human body could be like the mystery novels Lucy once favored. Bodies had unreliable narrators, red herrings, good guys and villains, and answers that could be proved beyond a reasonable doubt using the right tools and investigative logic. The case Becca was working was evidently a tough one to solve.

Lucy pushed her shoulder-length brown hair away from her narrow face and put on her tortoiseshell glasses so she could read the case file Dr. Stinson handed her. It looked straightforward.

Becca, who trained at a CrossFit gym and discussed it incessantly, had about four inches and twenty pounds (all muscle) on Lucy, whose arms and neck were thin from years of running. Though she was petite, Lucy probably could have held her own in the CrossFit arena. Years of cutting ribs and sawing bones had built up a lot of strength in those delicate arms.

Lucy studied the file intently for several quiet moments, her focus unwavering, the noxious odor no longer even registering.

The doctor's report was succinct, just the way Lucy liked it.

> *The patient, Cliff Anderson, seventy-seven, has experienced progressive cognitive decline and increased incidents of lethargy, depression, and memory troubles. The patient has presented with decreased motor function, as exhibited by multiple recent falls at home. Physical and neurological examinations were both unremarkable. CT and MRI scans of the head did not reveal significant acute pathology and the EEG was negative for seizure-like activity. Cerebral angiography also negative for abnormalities. Temporal artery biopsy ordered to rule out temporal arteritis.*

That last line was Mr. Anderson's last best hope. If the vessels that supplied blood to the man's head were inflamed or damaged, it could cause his symptoms. The condition was also completely treatable. However, Lucy believed the real culprit behind Mr. Anderson's troubles was something no department at White Memorial could cure. The biopsy did in fact show inflammation, some possible blockage there. But sometimes lab results offered rays of false hope. The symptoms outlined in the report were standard for another ailment, one that would be heartbreaking for both Mr. Anderson and his family.

"Well?" Becca asked after Lucy had finished her review.

"Seems cut and dried to me. Mr. Anderson has Alzheimer's."

Alzheimer's disease had no official test that could be done on the living. Neuropathological signs of the disease, amyloid plaques and neurofibrillary tangles of tau, a protein involved in maintaining the internal structure of the nerve cell, could be confirmed only during autopsy. Diagnoses of Alzheimer's relied largely on documenting mental decline. The medical report indicated symptoms consistent with that diagnosis, and given the patient's advanced age, Lucy figured it would have been Becca's first best guess as well.

"You don't seem convinced," Lucy said.

Becca buried her hands inside the pockets of her lab coat. "He's not presenting in a typical fashion."

"How so?"

"The tissue sample from the temporal artery biopsy showed severe inflammation, more than I expected, and some evidence of tissue death. Also, the patient complained of headaches and anxiety."

"And you think it could be—what? His MRI was normal. No evidence of stroke, tumor, head injury, nothing structural like hydrocephalus."

"Even without excess fluid in the brain, at minimum we should order an erythrocyte sedimentation rate, and I'd like to do a toxicology screen as well."

"Which the insurance company is going to deny."

"Which is why I want your help," Becca said.

"Charm them with my infectious personality, is that it?"

Becca cleared her throat. "Well, something like that, I suppose." Clearly, Becca felt she was on to something, but pathologists were not supposed to treat patients like internists.

Lucy appreciated this doctor's doggedness, respected it. She also understood her frustration. The pathology lab, hidden in the bowels of White Memorial, was stocked with cutting-edge pathology equipment including cryostat machines, tissue processors, imaging systems, and a digital incubator. It was a large and well-lit space, complete with several workstations, each equipped with a powerful microscope. The lab could run almost any test or diagnostic requested by hospital doctors, but not without somebody to foot the bill. Like many hospitals its size, White Memorial operated on razor-thin margins, scrutinizing every penny.

Lucy considered her options. She knew one test would lead to another, and then another. Cliff Anderson's doctor would come storming back here, pissed at having to do battle with the insurance company for tests he did not order.

"It's Alzheimer's, dammit. What don't you get?"

The thought put a rare smile on Lucy's face. Becca was right to question the dearth of testing, and the tissue death, while not indicative of temporal arteritis, was still unusual. *Why not do some more tests?* Lucy asked herself. After all, didn't Mr. Anderson deserve the best that White Memorial had to offer?

"Let's do whatever tests you think are necessary," Lucy said. "We'll sort it all out later."

Becca's broad smile was the big win of the day. Lucy loved her team, and it felt good to see them feel successful. Pathology was hardly a lonely profession, though many held that belief. A good path lab required smart docs like Becca to operate at a high level. What it did not require was direct involvement with patient care, and this suited Lucy just fine.

From down the hall, Lucy heard the familiar sound of gurney wheels on approach. It was a bellwether of sorts—the dead were coming. They showed up here even on Sundays.

Sure enough, Jordan Cobb, the six-foot-two hospital diener and longtime White Memorial employee, poked his head into the lab.

"Hey there, Docs," Jordan said.

The diener always had a happy expression on his face despite the grim nature of his job. It was Jordan's responsibility to collect the dead, move them to the morgue down the hall from the pathology lab, and clean each body prior to autopsy. It was a necessary job, but one many found unsettling. Not Jordan, though. He was unemotional about the work, the way Lucy would have been.

"Death is coming for us all," Jordan once said to Lucy during his performance review. "I just hope whoever gets my body treats it with respect. That's what I'd want, so I guess that's what I do."

He got a raise.

Jordan had the broad shoulders and thick neck of a football player, though he had never played any organized sport.

"Living in Dorchester is sport enough," Jordan once said.

Lucy sometimes let Jordan watch her perform autopsies. He found it endlessly fascinating.

"Who's our new houseguest?" Lucy asked.

Jordan lifted back the bedsheet and squinted his big brown eyes to read the toe tag. "Tommy Grasso. He'd been on life support, but they just pulled the plug. Funeral home will receive him tomorrow, so he's going to storage, no autopsy needed, at least according to the paperwork here."

Lucy glanced at the documents Jordan handed her and gave a nod. "Okay, wheel him and seal him," she said.

"What's happening in here?" Jordan asked. "It's not my business, I know, but I usually don't see you in the lab these days, Dr. Abruzzo."

It was true. Lucy's Sunday shifts had lately been less about the lab and more about that catch-up paperwork.

"Oh, Dr. Stinson and I are talking about doing some tests that aren't officially sanctioned."

"Hospital stuff, huh?" Jordan said with a shrug. He had an innocent, boyish-looking face, though quite handsome, and kept his dark hair cut short. The patch of hair on his chin helped him look closer to his true age, twenty-six.

"Yeah, Jordan, hospital stuff."

Jordan wheeled Tommy away, and Lucy's attention returned to Mr. Anderson's case.

"I feel bad that you're going to take some heat on this," Becca said, "but I really think it's the right thing to do."

"I'm fine with it. Honest."

At that moment, Jordan returned to the lab, no longer wheeling Tommy Grasso, but holding a slip of paper in his hand. "Hey, I found this in the hallway. I think it dropped out of one of your file folders, or something."

Jordan handed the paper to Lucy. It was a test result for Cliff Anderson. Odd, because the only lab work

Becca had done was that temporal artery biopsy. At first Lucy thought it might be a result from one of the tests Becca wanted to run. Maybe she'd already ordered them, and was doing the "ask forgiveness before permission" thing. But this was a heavy metal test, specific for cobalt, and the result was quite puzzling.

"Becca, who ran this test?" Lucy handed the sheet to Becca.

Becca stammered, "I—I don't know."

"Something wrong?" Jordan asked. He sounded genuinely concerned.

"No, nothing you did. It's just this paper—this test result you found."

"What is it?" Jordan asked.

"Well, according to these findings, Cliff Anderson has a cobalt level of twenty-four micrograms per liter of blood. It's not enough to kill him, but it could certainly make him very ill," Lucy said.

"Loss of motor coordination, memory troubles, tissue death, headaches, anxiety," Becca added, sounding excited. "Sound familiar?"

"Has he had a hip replacement?" Lucy asked.

"I'd have to look up his full medical record. Give me a second."

Becca left and Lucy reviewed the lab result again. The line that would normally indicate the doctor who requested the test was blank, as was the field for the technician who ran it.

"Guess it's a good thing I found that paper," Jordan said.

"Yes, it could be a very good thing," Lucy said.

Becca returned soon after, with a surprised look on her face.

Lucy's eyes went wide with anticipation. "And?" she asked.

"And seven years ago, it appears Mr. Anderson got a hip replacement from Aberdeen Hip Replacement Systems."

"You know it?" Lucy asked.

"No," Becca said. "But does the company matter?"

"Some hip replacements have been known to cause cobalt poisoning," Lucy said.

"Is there a part number or something?" Jordan asked.

Becca showed him the tablet.

Jordan used his smartphone to run a search query for the part number displayed on Anderson's medical record.

"It says here that the product was discontinued, but never recalled."

"Why was it discontinued?" Lucy asked.

Jordan squinted to focus. "Says overuse. Metal-on-metal construction was supposed to help with failure rates, but instead caused an increase in met . . . metall . . . metallosis, if that's the right word."

Lucy's expression was one of stunned disbelief. "Well, well, well. Cliff Anderson doesn't have Alzheimer's, he has cobalt poisoning."

"Guess we're not going to have to battle with the insurance companies after all," Becca said.

"Glad I found that piece of paper," Jordan said, with the proud smile of someone who had just done something important.

"Yeah, but the question remains," Lucy said. "Who knew enough about Cliff Anderson to request we run this test?"

"And who the heck ran it?" Becca added.

CHAPTER 10

The siren's persistent wail rattled Julie's nerves and made it impossible to concentrate. Ashley, more accustomed to the noise, appeared unfazed by the racket as she conducted a thorough secondary trauma survey on Sam.

Julie had ridden in the back of ambulances before, but only as part of her training. She did not remember them being so claustrophobic. She found the constant jostling unnerving.

To put an exclamation mark on that thought, the ambulance lurched forward. Julie, occupied with Sam's heart rate and pulse oximeter readouts, tumbled to the floor.

"Are you all right?" Ashley asked.

Julie quickly got back to her feet. Her gaze went to the heart rate monitor, which showed a jump from 97 to 125 in less than a minute.

"What's going on with that?" Ashley said, and began to reassess Sam anew.

Sam's heart rate continued to tick upward: 125, 130, 145 . . .

Julie had a gut feeling it had everything to do with those distended jugular veins. Through one of the windows between the hard plastic struts that made up the cervical collar, Julie could see those veins were even more grotesquely engorged than before. Blood filled them from Sam's sternum to his jawline. It was a clear sign of impaired blood return to the heart.

His breath sounds were still solid, though, and the pulse oximeter read 96 percent, which was in line with the ten liters of oxygen flowing into Sam's face mask.

Julie recalled all of the anatomy she knew about the heart. It was an ingenious circulatory system that regulated blood flow from areas of high pressure, with less space for the blood to flow, to areas of low pressure, which included the body's veins. In a healthy person those jugular veins should be flat, with no noticeable bulge.

The bulge on Sam's neck was a clear indication that the whole system was in disarray. If pressure built up in the heart's right atrium, the first chamber to receive blood returning from the body, blood could begin to back up into the veins leading to it. That included those jugular veins, which drained the head and arms.

Julie centered her thoughts.

"His heart rate is still climbing," Ashley announced. "One fifty-five. His pulse is thready. I'm really worried he's going to arrest." Her calm exterior seemed to be fraying.

"It's those veins," Julie said, softly, almost to herself. "Something is causing the pressure to increase in his circulatory system. It's not building from inside the heart, but from outside of it."

The ambulance shimmied and shook. Its siren screamed. All of it combined to make it difficult for Julie to focus on a differential diagnosis. She fought the distractions, churning through the limited possibilities. Topping the list was a tension pneumothorax, common in chest trauma. A collapsed lung, pushing against the heart, could squeeze the vessels and the heart itself toward the opposite side of the chest. If enough air pressure built, blood could not enter the heart and it would back up into Sam's veins. But those breath sounds simply did not support the theory. *What then?*

"Dr. Devereux, heart rate is at one hundred sixty-five. BP down from one hundred to eighty-five."

Blood pressure dropping, heart rate going up. *What's the damn cause, here?*

"He's going to arrest any second!" Ashley's voice betrayed her fear.

Julie looked down at Sam and saw that his lips, ears, and nose had begun to turn an alarming shade of blue. She tried to get a carotid pulse, but checking was near impossible with the collar around Sam's neck.

"Can you get a pulse here?" Julie spat out the words.

Even Ashley, more experienced working around the c-collar, was hampered. It did not help matters that the ambulance swung violently from left to right as it zoomed around slower-moving traffic.

"Careful, Bill!" Ashley barked. "We're in crisis here."

Sam's readouts continued to go wild. His heart rate was nearing 200 and his blood pressure was down to eighty over sixty.

"I can't get a pulse," Ashley yelled. "We've got to start CPR now! He's in PEA." Pulseless electrical activity. Sam's heart was not pumping blood, but it still had a rhythm observable on the electrocardiogram. Julie knew she had only a minute or so before asystole ensued—what most people would call flatline.

Something held Julie back. A feeling, same as the one she'd had with the BC quarterback, Max Hartsock. Something simply was not right, and CPR was going to be a potentially tragic waste of time.

"Heart rate at two oh one and no pulse!" Ashley called out. "Forty milligrams vasopressin, ready to go."

Sweat dotted Julie's forehead. Heat rose through her body. The ambulance was cramped, cacophonous, and the constant movement kept her off-kilter.

Think . . . get your head around this . . . what could it be?

"Dr. Devereux! We need to code him. NOW!"

The accelerated beeping and increased volume of Sam's many monitors had reached a fevered pitch. Julie did not react impulsively. Her brain worked lightning-fast to weigh the probability of one condition over another.

What about a sternal fracture? Julie thought. It was an uncommon injury, but one linked to trauma. The breastbone sat in front of the heart and great vessels. A hard enough blow to the chest could push the bone into the thoracic cavity, blocking blood flow to the heart from the head and arms. If that were the case, there was nothing Julie could do from the back of an ambulance.

A voice whispered in the back of Julie's mind, telling her to focus on CPR and get Sam to the hospital.

But something—instinct, experience, fear—told her to wait.

Two paths. Did he need CPR or something else? Choose wrong, and he could die.

"Heart rate two oh five. He still has no pulse. We're going to lose him, Dr. Devereux, if we don't start CPR now!"

Julie looked down at Sam's lifeless face. The serenity of his expression unsettled her to the core. He looked so at peace, almost unbroken, except for those veins. Those damn veins.

And that's when Julie knew the answer.

"I need a needle, stat!"

"A needle? What for?"

"Just get it, dammit!" Julie barked out the words.

"What size?" Ashley asked.

Julie's brown eyes flared like embers from a fire. "The biggest one you got."

There was some fumbling before Ashley procured a forty-five-millimeter long, fifteen-gauge needle capable of piercing bone. She handed it to Julie. The IO needle, used in intraosseous infusions, was typically inserted into the shinbone. The needle's large bore allowed for huge volumes of intravenous fluids to be pumped into a patient through the rich network of vessels in the marrow space. But this was not about getting fluid in. It was about getting it out.

"Heart rate is still two oh five," Ashley announced.

Julie tightened her jaw and nodded that she understood.

If Julie did not do what had to be done, right here, right now, Sam would die before they reached the hospital.

She set the needle against the skin below Sam's ribs, just to the right of the little key-shaped bone that hung off the bottom of the sternum. Julie did not waste time cleaning the area with Betadine or isopropyl alcohol. If Sam got an infection, at least he would be alive to endure it.

Ashley looked deeply troubled. "Dr. Devereux, what exactly are you doing?"

The constant motion of the ambulance made it difficult to hold the needle in the proper place. The screech of the siren pounded at Julie's eardrums.

"He's bleeding into the pericardial sac surrounding the heart," Julie said. "It's compressing his atrium and backing the blood up into his veins."

Being an experienced paramedic, Ashley understood right away what Julie planned to do.

"You're going to perform a pericardial tap? Here? Now?"

"He's got cardiac tamponade. If I don't do it, he'll die."

There was no real test for cardiac tamponade, though echocardiography had improved the diagnosis considerably. A process of elimination and a gut feeling had brought Julie to this moment.

The needle trembled ever so slightly in Julie's typically steady hand. Fear was foreign to her when it came to performing lifesaving medical procedures, but Ashley was right to be concerned. In terms of risky maneuvers, this one, under these conditions, ranked near to the top. Sam should be in the ICU. He should be given more oxygen, plasma volume expansion with an infusion of blood or dextran. To do this properly, Julie should take between twenty minutes and an hour. Now, she had but seconds.

Most of the color had drained from Ashley's face. "We're not authorized to perform this procedure," she said.

"Yeah, well, I am."

The needle was attached to a plastic grip that fit comfortably in Julie's hand. Julie's fingertips rested at the tip of the needle, increasing her dexterity and control. She inhaled deeply and exhaled through her nose.

You can do this . . . for Sam . . . you can do this . . .

Julie twisted the needle back and forth and pushed hard enough to puncture the skin. A trickle of blood oozed out from tiny gaps around the circumference of the needle. Julie took in another readying breath and visualized the anatomy. If she didn't get this right, the needle could puncture the heart or liver, or collapse a lung.

"Bill, pull to the side of the road!" Ashley called out.

"No! Keep driving! I've got this."

"What do you want me to do?" asked Bill, who took his orders from Ashley.

Ashley locked eyes with Julie. "Keep going," Ashley said.

In one quick thrust, Julie drove the needle up toward Sam's left shoulder. But that was only step one.

"I need a syringe. Again, the biggest you've got."

The syringe Ashley handed her—twenty milliliters, not quite the size Julie wanted—screwed onto the plastic grip. Julie released a flange, and built-up pressure in Sam's pericardium pushed blood into the syringe at a rate much higher than Julie anticipated.

"I need another syringe, stat!" Julie yelled.

Blood quickly filled the syringe, but more was coming. Pressure steadily built up inside the syringe, and Ashley reached for a replacement. Too slow. With a popping noise, the plunger damming the blood shot from the syringe barrel like a bullet from a gun. A jet of dark blood exploded in a horizontal geyser that covered Julie's face in red. Blood splattered on her clothes, her neck, face, and hair.

Ashley gasped in horror as Julie reached for the flange to shut off the blood flow. With the back of her hand, Julie smeared more of Sam's blood across her face as she wiped her eyes clear. The coppery, metallic taste soiled her mouth and turned her stomach.

"Blood pressure is rising and I have a good pulse," Ashley said, her voice calm in spite of all the blood. "Heart rate is coming down, too."

"I need another syringe," Julie said, breathless. A trickle of blood dripped off her chin and left dots on the floor by her feet.

"Heart rate is one oh six, one hundred . . . goodness, it's down to ninety."

Julie got the second syringe in place. This time, as she opened the flange to allow blood flow again, she kept her hand on the plunger to control the pressure. Blood filled the second syringe as well, but at a normal rate.

Julie used a towel to wipe some blood off her face. The ambulance smelled like a slaughterhouse as it rocketed through the darkening night.

Soon they reached White Memorial. The ambulance came to a hard stop and Ashley pushed the back doors open. The team waiting to receive Sam gasped at the ghoulish sight within. Sam's blood had splattered the walls, floor, and equipment, and it covered Julie like a gory second skin.

"I did a pericardiocentesis en route," Julie said to one of the doctors on the scene.

The doctor grimaced and returned a sympathetic look.

"The OR is prepped," the doctor said. "We're moving him to trauma first. We'll take good care of him."

Sam was wheeled through the emergency doors and whisked down a hallway, out of sight. Julie, alone, stood for a moment at the back of the ambulance. Then she sank to her knees and began to sob.

CHAPTER 11

Julie was a spectacle, a true sight to behold, on her march through the hospital waiting area to the ER trauma room. A boy in his basketball jersey, his wrist encased in a bag of ice, huddled close to his mother as Julie passed. A woman with a hacking cough stopped long enough to fix Julie with an openmouthed stare. Another woman, baby clutched to her chest, turned away, but not before Julie caught her eye. How she must have appeared to them! Blood splatter across her face, in her hair, soiling her clothes. *What had happened to this poor woman?* Whatever scenarios they conjured, surely they were thankful for their own conditions over Julie's.

Inside the ER, Julie drew more shocked looks from nurses and doctors who knew one of their own had been involved in a terrible accident. A nurse dressed in blue surgical scrubs, her long blond hair locked in a tight ponytail, came rushing over.

"Dr. Devereux, I heard. I'm so very sorry. Can I get you anything? I'll grab you some scrubs to wear. You need something to drink. Some water?"

Julie nodded numbly. She did not know this nurse by name, but recognized her face.

"Where is he?" Julie asked. Her voice came out as a rasp, barely audible. Physically her body was inside the ER, but her thoughts were still on that bloodstained road, still in the ambulance.

"He's in trauma room two over there," the nurse said, pointing.

Julie handed the young woman her phone. "Please call my ex-husband, Paul Devereux. Tell him what happened. His number is in my contacts. Tell him where I am."

The nurse took the phone and nodded. "Yes, of course. I'll be right back with some clothes."

Julie approached the trauma room with trepidation, heart pounding, arms dangling limp at her sides. The space, twice the size of a typical ER suite, was crowded with people from the rapidly assembled trauma team. She noted, with a huge sigh of relief, that Dr. Wendy Benton was among them. Dr. Benton, a highly skilled trauma surgeon, conducted her primary survey while the phlebotomist scoured Sam's body for areas undamaged by impact so she could draw blood for labs. Had Sam not worn his helmet, the only people attending to him would be down in the hospital morgue.

At the foot of Sam's bed stood Dr. James Gerber, a slender ER doc with silver hair whom many nurses considered to be among the very best of the staff. His voice was calm but commanding, bringing order to the chaos. The triage team worked independently yet functioned essentially as a single organism, with Dr. Gerber taking in all the information while he performed his own exam.

Sam had been transferred to a hospital bed, where he remained lashed to that board. The cervical collar and cushioned blocks were both still in place. From the head of the bed, a nurse, her identity concealed beneath a surgical mask and head covering, spoke in a loud, clear voice.

"Sam, can you hear me? Give my hand a squeeze. Can you wiggle your toes?"

The nurses had already dressed Sam's palms in light gauze and were busy applying topical hemostatic agents using oxidized cellulose sponges to clean and sterilize some of the lesser cuts. Nearby, an intubation tray was prepped and ready with a complete set of endotracheal tubes, laryngoscope, and Magill forceps. Sam would be intubated before they moved him either to radiology for a CAT scan or to the OR for surgery. Two liters of normal saline hung from an IV tree and provided Sam with vital electrolytes as well as a source of water for hydration. EKG leads connected to the cardiac and hemodynamic monitors showed real-time vitals for his blood pressure, heart rate, rhythm, and oxygen saturation levels.

"02 SAT's ninety-four percent on a non-rebreather," a nurse called out to the medical scribe, who entered that information into a portable computer. "HR is one ten. Occasional PVC. BP measures ninety palp."

The numbers were not horrible, and certainly a lot better since Julie had drained Sam's blood from the pericardial sac. A respiratory therapist pulled aside Sam's oxygen mask to check his airway for soft-tissue laxity, tongue blockage, or potential hematoma from a swollen blood vessel. Julie knew the process, as she'd done it countless times herself.

"02 SAT's maintaining on a non-rebreather mask," the same nurse called out.

"Thank you," Dr. Gerber replied. "Dr. Benton, have you seen this? Both jugular veins are slightly distended."

Julie's effort had fixed the problem only temporarily. Those veins were still symptomatic.

"Dr. Julie Devereux performed a pericardial tap in the back of the ambulance on the way here. That's what I heard, anyway."

Drs. Gerber and Benton stopped their exam to lock gazes with the nurse who supplied that information.

"Is that true?" Dr. Gerber asked. He sounded incredulous.

Julie took this as her cue, and she stepped into view. "Yes, I did. James, can I be of help? Please. I'm here."

Dr. Gerber took one look at the blood caked onto Julie's face and clothes and his expression conveyed his deep compassion.

"Not yet, Julie," he said. "We'll get you some scrubs, though."

"They're coming," said Julie.

"Just hang back a moment. Nurse, let's get an IV of seven milligrams lidocaine in him with epinephrine, please. Buffer that with a milliliter of sodium bicarbonate." Dr. Gerber's voice held no edge.

Julie exchanged glances with an X-ray tech waiting outside the curtain with a portable unit. He would be called to the stage soon enough.

"BP measures eighty-five palp," a nurse called out.

"I'm okay with that," Dr. Gerber answered quickly.

Normally, this would be more concerning, but Julie understood Dr. Gerber's logic. Low blood pressure helped to lessen the bleeding, and the more blood they could keep in Sam's body, the better.

Dr. Gerber continued his primary survey, concentrating several seconds on Sam's abdominal area. Dr. Benton leaned over Sam to listen for any speech. The surgical resident, a spitfire Indian woman named Dr. Riya Kapoor, diminutive in stature only, listened intently with her stethoscope and announced in a clear voice, "Equal breath sounds."

"We have some slight bruising surrounding the umbilicus," Dr. Gerber noted. "Let's get two units of plasma from the blood bank, O-neg of course. And tell them to keep it coming. And grab some splints, please. Need them for both arms and the left leg."

The ER tech took off at a sprinter's pace to fetch the blood and splints.

"Oh two SAT's ninety-three percent on a non-rebreather."

"Fine. Fine."

The phlebotomist got Dr. Gerber's attention. "Trauma panel is set and ready . . . CBC, CHEM-7, coagulation profile, and tox screen. We'll also type and screen for blood transfusion and liver function. Any other special orders?"

"No, that's good," Dr. Gerber said. "We're going to finish this survey quick and get him to the OR."

"Agreed," Dr. Benton said. "With the blunt chest trauma and blood in the pericardium, I'm concerned about aortic injury."

Dr. Gerber's focus shifted from the abdominal area to a soft-tissue assessment. Dr. Kapoor conducted a neurovascular exam of Sam's open leg fracture, which would eventually require surgery.

"Left leg bleeding has slowed," Dr. Kapoor announced. "Maybe minimal arterial damage."

"Even so, I'd like to start him on cefazolin, two grams IV, right away. We've got infection risk with that open fracture, after all," Dr. Gerber said. "Can we get pulses?"

"I'll do it," Dr. Kapoor said. The head nurse left the trauma room in a hurry to get the medicine Dr. Gerber had ordered. The ER tech returned with the splints. The scene was similar to the kinetic choreography at the accident site, only with a larger ensemble.

"Let's get the FAST exam done," Dr. Benton said. "Arthur, can you please set up the ultrasound?"

The ER tech ran to the corner of the room and wheeled the ultrasound machine over to the exam table. He got the machine powered on while a nurse set to the task of splinting Sam's many fractures.

"Radial pulse is ninety-eight, weak and thready, equal on both sides," Dr. Kapoor announced. "Carotid and femoral same. Nineties. Weak and thready. Equal on both sides."

The scribe recorded all this information into the computer as it was presented.

"Finish the neuro check, please," Dr. Benton said to Dr. Kapoor.

Standing at the curtain opening, Julie watched Dr. Kapoor peer over Sam's mangled limbs in search of some body part she could use for the evaluation. She settled on Sam's big toe and gave it a hard squeeze. Julie bit the knuckle on her thumb. Anxiety seized her and would not let go. It was ironic that with all the advanced machinery hooked up to Sam, all the medicine he received, it was the outcome of this one simple test that would determine so much.

Squeeze the big toe and . . .

Julie closed her eyes tight and listened.

Please . . . please . . .

She prayed for Sam, she prayed to God as so many families of her patients did. She prayed harder than she ever had done before. It was not God who would save Sam; Julie understood this all too well. It was the amazing doctors and nurses who were treating him. Yet in Julie's heart, she knew that what she really prayed for was a miracle.

Dr. Kapoor spoke up. "No response in any extremity."

A sob burst from Julie's lips as the first wave of grief hit like a tsunami. *It's still early,* she told herself. *It can change.*

"Okay, FAST exam now, Riya," Dr. Benton said.

With the equipment prepped and ready, Dr. Kapoor had the first view up in less than a minute. She kept the probe marker pointed toward Sam's head to get the clearest picture, and started in the upper quadrant between the seventh and eleventh rib interspace.

Dr. Benton peered at the monitor and put her finger on something that bothered her. "Looks like some free blood in the intraperitoneal space."

Julie could visualize the black line on the monitor between the liver and kidney that signified the pooling blood.

"And there's free fluid at the lower tip of the liver," Dr. Gerber observed.

Dr. Kapoor moved the probe to show the right diaphragm and right pleural space.

"Pericardial sac still has fluid." She moved the probe

quickly onto Sam's abdomen. "Liver is clear, spleen is fine . . . seeing some fluid in the pelvis."

This was the only bit of good news Julie had heard.

"What's our list of injuries?" Dr. Benton asked.

"Broken radius and ulna each side," Dr. Gerber said. "Possible fracture of the left olecranon, open fracture left leg."

Sam had not moved; he had yet to speak.

A nurse leaned over him. "Sam, can you open your eyes?"

Please, open your eyes, Julie begged.

Nothing. No movement at all.

Julie felt the floor give way.

"Glasgow is a six," a nurse announced.

Dr. Gerber shined a penlight into both of Sam's eyes. "Pupils equal and reactive," he said.

The scribe was recording this when the nurse with the long ponytail and Julie's phone bounded over with a clean pair of scrubs.

"Paul and Trevor are on their way," she said, handing Julie back her phone. "That was the message."

"Thank you," Julie said. She clutched the scrubs in her hands and squeezed hard.

A six, Julie thought. The Glasgow Coma Scale was a simple but effective test of consciousness and nervous system status. Sam needed to be at a thirteen, and he was at a six.

Dr. Gerber put his penlight away and unsheathed a sharp needle from a sterile package. He moved the needle against the heel of Sam's foot up to the soft part of the pad. Though he was unconscious, Sam's large toe extended upward, as did the other toes, to a lesser extent.

It was Babinski's sign. The reflex was normal in children up to two years old, but went away with neurological maturity. In an older child or an adult, it was an indication of a spinal injury or brain damage.

Something was very wrong with Sam.

The second survey began as Dr. Gerber called for the portable X-ray unit. Dr. Kapoor and Dr. Benton reviewed the images from the FAST exam while two nurses rechecked Sam's vitals.

The X-ray technician inserted a plate underneath Sam's body and set about placing the films. Silence descended as Julie heard the familiar revving sound of the X-ray machine. The technician worked quickly, moving from several shots of the spine to the pelvis.

Dr. Benton and Dr. Gerber stepped over to view the display. They pulled up the images and studied them intently. Dr. Kapoor looked at the films as well.

"C4 burst fracture!" Dr. Benton called out.

Dr. Gerber's composure cracked, revealing alarm in his eyes and voice for the first time. He turned to the nurse closest to him. "Two point seven grams IV Solu-Medrol, stat!"

Julie's heart sank. All she wanted to do was collapse, but she was too numb to move.

Dr. Gerber, grim-faced, eyes downcast, emerged from the trauma room and took a single step toward Julie. She could see that he was forming the exact words to say. He didn't have to say anything: Julie knew the significance of a C4 burst fracture.

CHAPTER 12

The furniture in the modest waiting room on the first floor of the Saunders Building was upholstered in fabric but not very comfortable to sit on. The tissue boxes were equal in number to the dog-eared magazines. Off to the side were small consultation rooms where distraught family members could speak privately with a patient's surgeon. Sam had been in surgery for six hours. In that time, Julie had seen a number of people go into those rooms and emerge looking utterly destroyed.

What sort of expression will I have? Julie asked herself. No big smiles, certainly; Sam was too badly injured for that. She still hoped for good news, though the odds were not in their favor.

C4 burst fracture! Julie could not stop hearing Dr. Benton's voice.

The wait was unbearable. No matter how much water she drank, Julie's throat was persistently dry, her chest drum-tight. The guilt came and went in waves.

If only she had honked in time. If only she had

agreed to be home for Trevor an hour later, like Sam had wanted. If only they had taken a different route. If only she had made any number of other choices, they would have been someplace other than behind that Civic. Of course, Sam would tell Julie it was not her fault. He'd tell her that, if only he could.

Julie had showered and changed into scrubs, but felt no better for the effort. She could still smell Sam's blood in her hair, on her skin, even though all traces had been washed down the drain. The knots in her stomach made it impossible to sip from the second cup of coffee a thoughtful nurse had brought her.

Paul and Trevor were with Julie in the waiting area, and had been there for the past several hours. When they first arrived, Trevor's baffled expression had made it clear he did not understand why his parents embraced with such emotion. It was understandably strange for him to see his mom and dad being at all affectionate. It would come up later in conversation, and Julie would explain that while she no longer loved Paul as a husband, she regarded him as a friend and appreciated his support at a time of great need.

"Is Sam going to be okay, Mom?" Trevor had asked. His dark eyes were a little watery.

Julie was touched by his emotion. "We'll see. I don't know. I'm being honest."

"Don't ride motorcycles anymore. Please."

"I have no plans to," Julie said.

For the most part, Trevor was quiet now, reading the book he'd gotten from the library before any of this had happened.

"Tell me what I can do for you," Paul said to Julie. His eyes, brown and clear, brimmed with compassion.

He liked Sam, and had encouraged Trevor to embrace him as a stepfather. Sam's last birthday had fallen on a day when Trevor was with Paul, but Trevor phoned anyway and sang "Happy Birthday." That had been entirely Paul's doing.

Julie saw so much of Paul in Trevor. One day, her sweet-faced son would be the spitting image of his father. Paul was a tall, handsome man, with lustrous brown hair that could be unruly but today was pulled into a tight ponytail. He wore a faded brown leather jacket with a black T-shirt underneath, and a worn pair of blue jeans flecked with metallic paint from whatever sculpture he and Trevor had been working on. His craggy face was dappled with the trademark scruff that somehow managed to keep from blossoming into a beard.

"Let me get you something to eat," Paul said. They sat on adjacent chairs. Her hands were trembling, and Paul had noticed. "You look a little pale."

"I can't, Paul. I couldn't get down a bite."

"Jell-O, then. It's not even real food."

Julie almost managed a laugh. "Okay, Jell-O. Cherry. And maybe an apple."

Paul stood and put his hand on Julie's shoulder. "It's going to be all right," he said.

Julie swallowed hard, and her face twisted. "I don't think so."

"Are they going to arrest whoever caused it?" Trevor asked.

"I honestly don't know. Why don't you go with your father and get something from the cafeteria."

Trevor stood his ground. His sweet nature shone through like a beacon. He wanted to stay by his mother's side and help guide her through these treacherous waters.

"Go, honey. Go with Dad. Get something to eat. I'll be fine on my own for a bit."

Trevor followed his father out of the waiting room just as Dr. Lucy Abruzzo came walking in. Lucy, in her white lab coat, was visibly upset. She moved quickly toward Julie, and the two women embraced long enough for those pent-up tears to fall.

"I'm so sorry. I was down in the lab and didn't see your text until just now. Julie, what happened?"

The two friends talked together in hushed tones. No particular event had brought Lucy into Julie's life. They were colleagues at the same hospital who had struck up a conversation one day, and found in each other a dislike for bureaucracy, a love of science, and a passion for medicine. They would eat lunch together whenever possible and sometimes Julie would join Lucy, a seasoned marathoner, for a jog, which always turned out to be a humbling experience.

A prolonged silence followed Julie's account of the day's tragic events.

"I'm at a loss for words. I'm so sorry, Julie."

"What am I going to do?" Julie said, biting at her lip, trying to redirect the pain in her heart to someplace else.

"We won't know the extent of his injuries until after the surgery."

"Burst fracture, C4," Julie reminded her.

Lucy was not going to take the bait. "It's not a death sentence."

"A lot of my patients are on the verge of becoming your patients. I know the odds."

Lucy was too professional to offer false hope, but still did not seem as convinced as Julie.

"We've both been around this business long enough to see remarkable recoveries. Sometimes it takes months, years of rehab, but we've seen it happen."

Julie mulled this over. "We don't see it very often."

Lucy took Julie's hand and gave a squeeze. "Just have faith," she said.

"I know what I would want," Julie said.

"Don't get on your soapbox about death with dignity just yet. Sam is still in surgery, and you're projecting the worst."

"I'm not projecting, I'm protecting myself," Julie said.

"I understand completely," said Lucy. "And if I had any feelings—which according to the other department heads around here, I don't—I'd be doing the same damn thing."

The automatic doors opened with a whoosh. Dr. Benton appeared, dressed in a fresh pair of scrubs, her surgical cap still in place. Dr. Riya Kapoor, the surgical resident, was at her heels.

Julie jumped up, closing the distance between them in seconds.

Dr. Benton's cheerless eyes, glazed from hours of surgery, fixed Julie with a look of compassion.

"Hi, Julie. Let's go to one of the conference rooms."

The conference room was for long conversations. Julie had been hoping for something that could be said while standing—something like, "He pulled through surgery like a champ."

"Is he dead?" Julie spat out the words, her voice shaky. The world was turning black.

"No," Dr. Kapoor said.

Julie motioned for Lucy. They followed the two surgeons into the windowless conference room, which held a small table, a few chairs, and nothing more.

"Sam has stabilized and he's being taken to the ICU now," Dr. Benton began.

Julie tried to recall the shift schedule, wanting to know who was on the floor and would be looking after her Sam.

"You know that his injuries are severe. We found the hemopericardium. The cause was a small tear in his aorta. He was placed on bypass, and we repaired it easily in under fifteen minutes."

So Sam had died, if only for a few minutes. They had placed him on a cardiopulmonary bypass, stopped his heart, and rerouted his blood so they could repair that tear in the aorta.

Julie held her stony expression, knowing the bad news was yet to come.

"He sustained numerous injuries due to the high-speed impact of the crash," Dr. Benton continued. "Ortho cleaned up the wound from the open fracture. They plan to set it in a day or two, when he is more stable. His wrist and elbow are splinted, and will also need pinning. We'll try to have two ortho teams in the OR to minimize time spent in surgery."

That's not it . . . there's something else. I can see it in her eyes.

"He also suffered a pelvic fracture, and is in traction now." Dr. Benton reached across the table for Julie's hand.

Oh, no . . . here it comes . . . A pit opened in Julie's stomach.

"The major concern now is that the burst fracture of C4 splintered into the spinal column."

Julie visualized fragments of bone moving with enough velocity to shear the delicate strands of nerves embedded in the spinal column, the way shrapnel can shred flesh.

"Dr. Weinstein has been involved, and Sam is on the spinal cord trauma protocol."

High-dose steroids to try to help the swelling, Julie knew. It was like using aspirin to try and cure a cancer.

"Now we want to give him some time to stabilize and give you time to see him before we take him for an MRI."

"What's the prognosis?" Julie asked.

"We don't know yet."

"Give her your personal opinion, Wendy," Lucy said in a stern voice.

"I'm sorry, Julie," Dr. Benton said. "The injury was bad, as bad as I've ever seen. There's no easy way to break this news gently. My personal opinion is the accident is going to leave Sam permanently quadriplegic."

CHAPTER 13

Romey arrived at Duxbury Country Club at about one o'clock and changed into his golf outfit, khaki pants and a navy polo shirt. He had paid the pro for all the starting times between one and three, ensuring that he and Allyson would not run into anyone, especially not anyone he knew. A meeting between two rival hospital executives—on a golf course, of all places—could start rumors that might make others aware of the business potential. Like Warren Buffet, Romey saw opportunities others missed.

He was sitting on the veranda when Allyson Brock pulled up in her brand-new Lexus. The car was such an obvious choice for an executive. Romey drove a late-model, but not brand-new, Honda Accord. It was a sensible choice, and told his employees he was just one of them. While he was not about to surrender his spacious corner office, Romey thought his car made him appear more approachable. He knew how to play it smart.

As a boy, Romey had been blessed with a gift for

numbers, but it did not take a math genius to know his chances of fitting in would have improved greatly were he more athlete than mathlete. A lonely only child growing up in a nice New Jersey suburb, Romey had been small and skinny back then. He was pragmatic about such matters. He did not wallow in self-pity and focused instead on his strengths rather than his weakness. He studied hard, honed his analytic skills, and after graduation went to Rutgers on an academic scholarship, where he excelled at accounting.

He trusted numbers more than people. Board members did as well, which explained why many hospital CEOs and administrators were numbers people and not trained physicians.

Allyson walked toward Romey, pulling her clubs behind her. She was wearing beige capris that accentuated her athletic body. Her white knit shirt clung to her torso and was open just enough to show cleavage. With what he was about to reveal, Romey had no doubts he could get Mrs. Brock into bed. He thought he could juggle it even with his two current mistresses.

Allyson waved and flashed Romey a smile, but he sensed a slight air of superiority in her gesture and the way she carried herself.

Romey was shorter than Allyson by three or so inches. His belly was a bit soft, his ears too big for his head, his hair thinning. She was the sort of woman who equated appearance with power, and for that reason alone was blind to the threat he posed. A man who loved power and money as unconditionally as Romey did not need Kevin Costner's jawline—or a good handicap, for that matter—to have the upper hand.

Romey took Allyson's clubs and put them in the back of a golf cart. "I figured we'd drive, no need for a caddy. Is that all right with you, Allyson?"

"Sure. This is just a friendly game. If I can give you any pointers, I will."

Allyson placed her tee in the grass and with a driver hit an amazing shot that flew about two hundred yards, landing smack in the middle of the fairway.

Romey stepped up to the tee and with way too much effort, sliced the shot into the rough, about a hundred yards from the tee. His short torso and thick waist made it difficult to get the club around the ball. He gave Allyson a sheepish grin. "I told you I was just learning."

Allyson came up behind him and explained how he had to hold his hips steady, spin from the waist, and remember to follow through.

"The ball goes where you tell it to."

"Wish it were that easy with physicians," said Romey.

"Don't we know it," she said. "Some days I feel like I go into work just to do battle with my medical staff. They all want to become employees of the hospital, and they give me and the board such a song and dance about their productivity. We both know that they don't want to work the way the old guard did. They don't want the hassle and expense of owning their practice. They'd rather work four days a week, take no on-call, and sign their inpatients over to hospitalists. And for this they want a quarter of a million, and threaten to leave on an almost daily basis."

Romey had heard all this before. It was the administrator's lament, the theme song of those running hospitals in the early part of the twenty-first century. Physicians and hospitals used to have a more symbiotic relationship: the hospitals provided physicians a place to admit and serve their patients, and physicians, in turn, provided the hospitals with paying customers. In that model, many of the docs ran private practices and billed patients separately for their time and expertise, while the hospitals charged for inpatient stays, including room, board, and ancillary services: lab work, radiology, use of the operating rooms, physical therapy.

It worked fine until the government and other insurers changed the way they paid hospitals and physicians. After the change, it made financial sense for physicians to become hospital employees. The docs would no longer have to fight with the insurers, and the hospital would take over most of their expenses. With the physicians under the control of the hospital, administrators could force doctors to deliver competing services like lab, radiology, or even surgery centers through the hospital and generate larger profits for their institutions. It should have worked well for both parties, but an employee's mind set is different from that of an independent owner of a medical practice. The doctors wanted more and more perks for less and less work. At least, that was how the administrators saw it.

By the third hole, it was obvious that Allyson was feeling her most powerful. Romey knew she loved playing golf with male colleagues, especially since she was so much better than most of them.

She came up behind Romey and placed her hands on his hips. "Do you mind?" she asked.

"Not at all," said Romey.

Allyson moved his hips through the correct range of motion. The tutorial paid off. Romey's next swing was a straight, albeit relatively short, drive.

"That's right," she said. "If you keep your hips in line, it will give you the straight line you want."

"Who taught you this insidious game in the first place?" Romey asked.

"My father was a fanatic," Allyson said. "I was on the course with him when I was six, and by twelve I was playing eighteen holes. Good golfers wanted me to caddy for them because I was something of a natural and I gave great advice."

Romey might not have known how old Allyson was when she began to play, but he did know she got a golf scholarship to the University of Southern California, where she studied occupational therapy. Upon graduation she was able to join the LPGA tour. He knew other things about her, too. Things she would not want anyone to know.

They played through the hole and climbed in the cart to head for the fourth tee.

"So tell me, Allyson, how are things at Suburban West?"

Allyson gave him the party line. "Pretty good," she said. "We had a tough time last year, but we put in place some cost-savings measures that should turn things around. We're also in the process of recruiting two new orthopedists and a podiatrist that will really help us establish our sports medicine department."

She hopped out of the cart and sent her first drive right down the center.

"You are good," said Romey as he put his tee in the grass and addressed the ball. His shot was picture perfect and hit the fairway dead center, about fifty yards ahead of Allyson's ball.

Allyson watched Romey's shot, mouth agape.

"Never believe what you see," said Romey. "Just like I don't have to believe you and your 'everything's just perfect' routine."

A shadow crossed Allyson's face. "What's that supposed to mean?"

"It means, I know you're facing a seven percent loss for the past year. Not the kind of financial position that can be corrected with a sports medicine program, especially since I can assure you those two orthopedists are not coming near your hospital."

If Allyson was stunned by Romey's drive, she appeared in absolute shock at his knowledge of Suburban West's financial position.

"I also know that HealthSense Insurance is giving you a four percent haircut and Unified is considering dropping you from their network. That could hurt. They make up—what? Twenty-one percent of your patients?"

Allyson was too stunned to speak. Insurance negotiations and rates were highly confidential.

"So, Allyson, you're in a very weakened position, and my hospital is flush with cash. Unless you work magic, your days at Suburban West are definitely numbered."

Her body deflated. "How do you know all that?"

"You know that's a question I can't answer. But I am here to help you."

"How?"

"Tomorrow you will find a proposal on your desk for a management contract between White Memorial and Suburban West. You can read it if you like, but suffice it to say the terms are financially favorable for individual board members. In the end, however, White Memorial will have total control. You don't have the balance sheet to make it and we both know it. You can string the board along for a while, sure, but they'll see a better way forward in my proposal. So, you're going to include me in an executive-level meeting and together we're going to make sure you sell my proposal to your board exactly as it is written."

"What about me?"

"There will be a transition period where you'll share CEO duties with someone I select. When the merger's complete, I'll have a position open as director of support services at White that just may be right for you."

"Are you kidding me? I run the hospital. You expect me to take a director's position?"

"Let's face it. You haven't exactly done a very good job, have you? It's probably less than six months before your board cans you, so I think you're not in much of a position to negotiate."

"I'm a damn fine CEO. I climbed my way to the top and worked for everything I got."

Roman knew this was true. After Allyson's golf career came to an abrupt and unexpected conclusion, she went to Tufts and got her MS in occupational therapy. Upon graduation she landed a job in a private rehabilitation hospital run by the owner, a neurologist. In a few years she became the director of occupational medicine, and in that capacity implemented a winning strategy for attracting patients. Allyson was so successful she was promoted to COO, where she came to the attention of an executive recruiter looking for someone with panache and cachet to help turn Suburban West from a bleeder into a success story.

"I'm not saying you didn't work for what you got, Allyson. I'm just saying you were the right person for a time, and times have changed."

"And what makes you so great, Romey? How is it you're keeping so high afloat?"

Romey made a *tsk-tsk* noise. "Those are trade secrets, my dear. Let's just say my board is extremely pleased with my performance because I always hit my numbers.

"Now, here's how it is going to work, Allyson," he continued. "You will take whatever job I tell you, and you will do whatever I tell you."

"Please, Romey. Spare me the alpha male bravado. I can't be played like that."

"No? I disagree. Have a look at this." Romey pulled a folded piece of paper out of his pocket and handed it to Allyson.

Her body shook with anger as she looked at the confidential agreement between her and the LPGA.

"If you don't support me fully on this, Allyson, I will wait until you are fired by Suburban West—and then I'll make sure you won't be able to get a job selling Big Gulps at the 7-Eleven."

Romey's face was calm, but his interior glowed. The smell of dirty laundry always intoxicated him.

While Allyson told people she had left the tour because she wanted to pursue a career and family, the truth was far different. She had thrown several matches for a Vegas bookie who had blackmailed her with evidence of her scandalous affair with a tour director. The agreement was that if she left the tour of her own volition, the LPGA would not press charges, because they did not want the bad publicity that would result. If however, this information was ever made public, the tour would come after her personally and press criminal charges. The damages from litigation would be ruinous.

"I assume we have an agreement."

Allyson stared at the paper.

"I would like to hear it, Allyson."

"Yes, you prick. We have an agreement."

"Such language. Not a good way to start off our new relationship," said Romey, as he swung his clubs over his shoulder and sauntered back to the clubhouse.

CHAPTER 14

Jordan Cobb sat at the kitchen table in the two-bedroom apartment of his next-door neighbor, Ms. Mae Walker, with an algebra book open and a sharpened number two pencil in his hand.

Seated across from Jordan, with a scowl on his boyish face and his thin arms folded tight across his chest, was Emmett Walker, Mae's middle son. Jordan came to the Walkers' every Tuesday to tutor Emmett in math. Jordan wore his professional attire, a polo shirt and jeans, and looked about as hip-hop as Mr. Rogers. Emmett, who kept his dark hair trimmed short, was dressed in his full street regalia, including sneakers so white they looked like two giant teeth, baggy jeans, and a Rocawear hoodie.

"Come on, Emmett," Jordan said. "You know how to do this problem in your sleep."

Emmett leaned back in his chair, a playful hint in his big brown eyes. "Yeah? Keep talking about it and you'll put me under. Then I guess I'll figure it out."

Mae Walker, a full-figured woman whose kind face

could turn threatening in a blink, stopped stirring whatever delicious concoction she was cooking and glowered at her son.

"You mind your manners, Mister Walker," she said. "Jordan is here to help and you're here to listen and learn. Is that understood?"

"Yes, Ma. Sorry, Ma."

Mae held her stern expression until she felt her directive had taken, then turned up the volume on the small television on the kitchen counter and went back to stirring the pot.

Like a lot of the mothers Jordan knew (he tutored many of their kids), Mae Walker was both a stern disciplinarian and a loving parent. For kids like Emmett, it was an essential combination. Mr. Walker had not been a part of the family at any point that Jordan could remember, and Jordan had lived in the apartment next door since he was in diapers. In a neighborhood like this one—urban, tough, more sirens than birdsong—it was easy for a kid like Emmett to detour onto a crooked path.

Dorchester could be a bit like a checkerboard of good and bad neighborhoods, five blocks trouble free and then five blocks a whole lot sketchier. The better the neighborhood, the higher the rent, which was why Ms. Walker and Jordan's mom lived where a lot of the single mothers lived, in the not-so-nice part of town. Keeping kids in school meant keeping them off the street. That was good for the mothers and for Jordan's tutoring business.

"Come on, Emmett. We got this one. X minus three equals negative five. Now solve for X."

Emmett gazed out the window behind Jordan with a sullen look on his face. "Shit, man, I dunno."

"Emmett! Your language," Mae called out.

"Let's go, buddy. Pick up the pencil, put it on the paper, and solve it. I know you can do it because you've done it before."

"And let me tell you, those Beats by Dre headphones of yours are gonna be resting on the head of another child who learns his math, if you don't get this right," Mae said.

Emmett picked up the pencil and started to scratch. "Um . . . so it's plus three both sides—right?"

"That's right," Jordan said.

"So, I get . . . um . . . X equals negative two."

Jordan held up his hand. Emmett gave it a half-hearted high five, but behind the boy's tough exterior, he did look pleased with himself.

"You got it. Now just thirty more of these, and you'll be an expert."

Emmett leaned back in his chair and eyed Jordan with a crooked smile. "How you so smart at this stuff, anyway? They teach you that in prison?"

Mae Walker gasped. "Emmett! My goodness."

Jordan was unfazed by the question. "It's all right, Ms. Walker," he said. "I don't mind talking about it."

"How much time you do, anyway?" Emmett asked.

Jordan put down his pencil and gave some thought to how best to respond, how much to share. He decided to give Emmett the same thing he'd sworn to in court: the truth, the whole truth, and nothing but the truth, so help him God.

"I did five years at Cedar Junction. Hard time, too. Not a minimum-security stint."

"You shot a guy. That's what I heard, anyway."

Mae was half listening to the story and half watching

the news. She'd heard it all before and knew Jordan regretted his choices, had paid for his mistakes, and had done the hard work to make something out of his life.

"Yeah, that's just street talk," Jordan said. "I never shot anyone in my life. I got caught up in stuff, though. Thought I needed to fit in instead of doing the right thing."

"And what's that?"

"Learning. I loved school. Studying. Math. Science especially. I got straight As, but it wasn't cool, you know? It wasn't *hip* to be smart. I got teased a lot. I ignored it for a while, but there was only so much I could tune it out. I started believing the talk, and that's when I got focused on the wrong things. I wanted to prove them wrong, because I wasn't strong in here." Jordan tapped his finger against his chest, anatomically hitting a bull's-eye on his heart. "Or here." This time he pointed to his head. "I started running with the wrong crew, you feel me?"

Emmett shrugged, his way of showing that he felt something, but was not about to say it out loud.

"I was dealing. Pot mostly, but some other stuff, too. My grades, they stayed up, but I can't tell you how bad I felt inside. It was wrong, what I was doing, and I knew it, too."

Emmett arched his eyebrows. "Yeah, but at least you got mad respect, I bet."

Jordan was unsure how much to share with Emmett. It was five years of hell, no way to sugarcoat it. He'd been locked up with pissed-off lifers who had no qualms about sticking some rusty shank in your back just because they thought you looked at them funny. The best way to survive inside was to join a gang, something Jordan had sworn off doing right after his arrest, so he'd lived prison life as an outcast.

Eventually, the other black inmates offered protection after Jordan earned enough good behavior credits to teach GED prep classes. Prison life, Jordan came to learn, was a microcosm of the streets, but in a modified form. For five dollars you could get everything from a toothbrush to heroin, and there was constant pressure to buy product or help some merchant sneak it in. Failure to comply could easily net you a month's stay in the infirmary if they beat you bad enough. Constant vigilance was what kept Jordan safe and out of trouble, but it was an exhausting way to live.

He told Emmett, who sat transfixed, listening a lot more intently than he ever did in an algebra lesson.

"I did all right in there because I chose to use my time wisely. I read, I studied, I learned about a lot of things so I could get out and get a job."

"You push around dead people all day," Emmett remarked.

"Maybe so, but it's honest work, and I ain't going back to prison for doing it."

"Yeah, but now you broke."

"I'm not broke."

"Look how you dress."

"I like how I dress."

"Then why do this?" Emmett pointed to the algebra book with a scowl on his face.

"Because I like to teach, I like to learn, and if there's one lesson I want you to learn, it's to study hard and keep your nose clean. Don't make the same mistake as me."

"Yeah, yeah."

"No, I mean it."

Emmett looked serious, like he got it. "It's cool."

Something caught Jordan's attention, a snippet from the news broadcast Mae was half watching. Jordan rose from his seat.

"Ms. Walker, would you mind turning that up a bit?" he asked.

"Of course, sweetheart," Mae said.

The small television showed a Fox News report from outside the prison where Jordan had spent five years of his life. The broadcast reporter was a sharply dressed man in his late twenties. Behind him was the chain-link fence topped by razor wire, which Jordan still saw in his nightmares.

The television camera captured a group of nearby protesters who held handmade signs. FREE BRANDON STAHL, two or three of them said. MERCY NOT MURDER, said another. One sign in particular drew Jordan's attention: a picture of a dog being injected by a syringe, above the words STOP TREATING PETS BETTER THAN PEOPLE.

"Brandon Stahl, the former nurse from White Memorial Hospital, remains behind bars this evening following the State Supreme Court's denial of his appeal for a new trial," the reporter said. "Stahl is serving a life sentence for what some have called the 'mercy killing' of his patient, Donald Colchester, who suffered from advanced-stage ALS, or Lou Gehrig's disease. Protesters have gathered at the prison to object to the ruling and express support for Stahl, who maintains his innocence and claims that Donald Colchester had a heart attack and died of natural causes.

"The prosecution relied heavily on a last-minute witness after the court refused to admit a recording of

Mr. Stahl agreeing to help Mr. Colchester commit suicide. The defense had asked for a new trial, citing procedural violations with the witness's testimony, but the presiding judge disagreed."

"They're getting it all wrong," Jordan said, mostly to himself.

"Did you work with that man?" Mae asked.

Focused on the report, Jordan took a moment to respond. When he did, he sounded distracted. "Um, yeah. Yeah, I knew him."

The reporter corralled one of the protesters for an on-camera interview. Jordan watched with rapt attention.

"What's your opinion on today's ruling?"

The protester, a middle-aged woman wearing a bulky overcoat, flashed the camera her sign that read GIVE PATIENTS THE RIGHT TO CHOOSE.

"It's a tragedy," she said. "Donald Colchester was suffering, and Brandon Stahl was the only person who did something about it. The hospitals just want to keep people alive so they can squeeze out every last dime for profit, or try out their new drugs and treatments. We're nothing but lab rats to them."

The reporter knew when to end an interview on a dramatic high note.

"Reporting live from MCI Cedar Junction, I'm Stephen Wright, Fox News. Back to you, Jim and Carla."

Jordan turned away from the television, disappointment on his face.

Mae placed a comforting hand on his shoulder. "I'm sorry, honey," she said. "If he was a friend of yours and all, I'm sure it must be hard."

Jordan was visibly shaken, his lips tight across his

mouth. "It's not about the recording or the witness," he said. "Why don't they get that? Why doesn't anybody get that?"

"What, honey? I don't think I follow," Mae said.

Jordan went back to the table, where Emmett doodled on the paper instead of solving the next equation.

"It's nothing," Jordan said. "Come on, Emmett, let's get this work done. Time's wasting, and one thing I learned from prison is that you don't waste time."

CHAPTER 15

Numb.

That was the word Julie used to describe her feelings to anyone who asked. She was simply numb. With her mother and Lucy, Julie could be more candid, admitting to an unshakable malaise, loss of appetite, physical aches and pains, tears at unexpected moments. It had been a week since Sam's accident and Julie wondered if she was still in a state of shock. Some nights she would wake up confused, forgetting for a few blissful seconds how one person's careless actions had altered the life she and Sam had together so dramatically. She would close her eyes and wish it were a dream, but images of the horrific crash would come at her as fast as an out-of-control pickup truck.

For now, Julie could do nothing but battle through each day and try her very best to stay positive. It was not easy. Sam had shown minimal signs of neurologic recovery, but no miracles. His eyes came open only for brief periods and he had yet to be weaned from the ventilator, but that could happen any day now. Fortunately, he had been in excellent shape prior to the accident. This would help him in his recovery.

As chaotic as the past week had been, Julie had fallen into a rhythm of sorts. Work. Sam. Home. Repeat. She would have been at the hospital right now, at Sam's bedside, but Paul had gone out of town to visit with a gallery owner who had expressed interest in his work and Julie needed to be home for Trevor. She was happy to have the time with her son and grateful Paul had stepped up to spend most evenings with Trevor, doing everything he could to be helpful. This was a critical time, and everyone was on edge while also trying to be supportive and useful. Sam's parents had flown in from Michigan. They were staying at a hotel near the hospital. Julie would have let them stay with her had they asked, but was glad she did not have to play hostess.

The clock on the cable box let her know that soccer practice had ended twenty minutes ago. Trevor would be showing up any moment. Slumped on her sofa, Julie nursed a white wine, while on the television three strangers were marrying three other strangers at first sight. Julie preferred programs like *Downton Abbey* to reality fare like *Married at First Sight,* but these days her choices drifted toward the mindless. In that regard she thought nothing could surpass this program.

The viewing served no other purpose than as reprieve from Julie's endless worry, her regular bedside vigils. The police were still investigating the accident, and the insurance companies were on the case. Also on the case were a number of attorneys who wished to represent Sam in litigation. That would have to wait. Much would have to wait, including Julie's marriage to the man she loved.

Julie took another sip of wine and returned to the show. Susie cringed at the sight of Andre. Maybe it was his ghastly teeth that did her in. Julie thought about her own wedding plans and wondered if she and Sam would ever marry.

She knew Sam well enough to know he would not want her to commit to him should he be dependent for life. He had talked in the abstract about this very thing, because he knew another rider who had suffered a debilitating head trauma. Sam had seen the life-changing impact of the injury on the rider's wife and family. When it came to accidents, motorcyclists could do the Kevin Bacon six degrees of separation game. They all knew someone who knew someone who had been in one.

Sam would want a wife, not a caretaker. That was what Julie imagined he would say. But his broken body in no way severed her feelings for him. He was still the man she loved, in body, mind, and spirit. The Internet was full of stories of people who had married quadriplegics and made it work: blogs, message boards, Reddit. Julie knew this, because she had read them all.

A few minutes after her last time check, Julie heard the front door open. In shuffled Trevor. She listened to the familiar sounds of her son reentering his home. First came the thud when he dropped his backpack on the floor. Then the closet door swung open with a creak, followed by a clatter of hangers as Trevor hung his coat. Then she heard the bathroom faucet running while he washed his hands.

"Hi, sweetheart, I'm in the living room. Dinner is in the oven."

The apartment—fifteen hundred square feet of living space consolidated on one floor, with three bedrooms and two baths—smelled of chicken curry, a recipe Julie had stumbled on while browsing Pinterest. It was the first real meal she had cooked since the accident.

"I'm going to put Winston in his ball," Trevor said. "And I don't have any homework."

Winston was the family guinea pig, a woeful substitute for the dog Trevor had begged for since his eighth birthday. Julie was sorry she could not accommodate her son's wishes, but a dog simply did not fit their lifestyle.

"Come in here and talk to me. I want to look at your folder."

"It's fine." Trevor had perfected the "leave me alone" tone and gave it just enough edge not to be totally rude.

"It's not fine. We have an agreement."

No response. Bad sign.

The agreement was for Julie to review Trevor's schoolwork and check over his grades until he pulled them from Cs to Bs. She'd stop when it looked to her as if he was performing at or near his potential.

"Trevor?"

"I'll be there in a minute."

A rolling rattle alerted Julie to Winston's imminent arrival. Sure enough, his plastic ball came skirting across the hardwood floor in front of the television at a high rate of speed. The mostly white-furred guinea pig had spots of brown and black and dark eyes and a very cute little face. Julie had taken quite a liking to Winston.

Eventually Trevor came shuffling into the living room, still wearing his dirt-splattered practice uniform and looking a bit ragged.

"How about a shower before dinner," Julie said.

Trevor plopped down on the couch and tossed his school folder onto the coffee table. He had a tentative air that gave Julie pause. Had he failed a test? Possible, given the week they had just endured.

Julie set down her glass of wine as Trevor turned the channel from A&E to ESPN with speed that belied human capability. Trevor could have what he needed; he had done her a favor.

"How's Sam doing?" Trevor asked.

Julie gave her son an appreciative glance and pulled him in for a little hug. "Thank you for asking. He's not getting worse."

"But he's not getting any better, is he?"

Julie bit at her lip. "If by better you mean moving his arms or legs, then I'm afraid the answer is no."

A week of healing had mended the gash to Sam's chin, but his arms remained encased in casts with pins in the bones. His left leg, also in a cast, was suspended above the bed in a traction pulley system. His head CT read negative, and several neurosurgeons who had evaluated Sam had reached the same conclusion: the outcome could not be improved. Parts of his spine had been cut into pieces by shards of broken bone that acted as machetes.

There were more MRIs, more exams, and more tests, including electromyography, where multiple needles were inserted into Sam's body to assess electrical activity of his skeletal muscles and motor neurons. Every result disappointed.

"I'm sorry, Mom."

Winston came rolling by, his little legs churning

furiously. Trevor giggled, and the sound of her son's laughter brought a smile to Julie's face. Her first, it felt, in ages.

Julie redirected her attention to the folder and got her second smile of the week. Trevor had gotten As on both his history and science tests.

"Honey, this is wonderful," Julie said. "Well done."

"Yeah, it was easy."

"Or maybe you just applied yourself."

Trevor shrugged it off, but in his eyes Julie could see he agreed. Her son had so much potential. Getting him to do the required work continued to be the major obstacle.

Julie glanced at Trevor's agenda, which detailed the homework and projects due in the coming weeks. It should have been Trevor's responsibility to plan and complete all his assignments on schedule, but until he got back on track, Julie felt justified hovering in that helicopter-parent way.

"You're all set with *To Kill a Mockingbird*?" Julie asked.

Trevor's color drained. He rose quickly from the couch and nearly punted poor Winston like he was a soccer ball.

"Honey, what's wrong?"

Trevor did not answer. But she heard the sounds of him rummaging through his backpack. Trevor came storming back into the living room on the verge of tears.

"Everything all right?"

"That stupid book is at Dad's, and so is my English folder."

Julie checked the time. "That's no problem. We can get it out of the library. Or we'll take a drive to the store."

"My essay is at Dad's!" Trevor said. His shoulders slumped and his face crumpled.

"I'll just call your—" Julie stopped herself when she remembered that Paul had left town for the night.

"The essay is due tomorrow, and now I'm going to get an F and then you won't let me play soccer."

"Take it easy. Relax. We can tell your teacher. She'll understand, given everything that's going on. It's not going to be a problem."

The logic appeared lost on him. "You're gonna make me quit the soccer team. That's what you said if I got an F."

"No. No, I'm not."

"Any F and you're off the team. School is more important."

"This is an exception."

"It wouldn't have happened if I didn't have to keep track of my stuff. Between here and Dad's, I'm never just in one place." The tears that had been threatening began to leak out.

Julie understood that Trevor's frustration went far beyond this one English assignment. Behind it all—the fight in school, the falling grades, the incomplete homework—lay sorrow.

"Come, sit down," Julie said, patting the sofa.

Trevor remained standing, arms locked across his chest. Winston chose that moment to come scuttling by. He hit a wall, redirected, and was on his way once more. But the incident proved amusing enough to get a slip of a smile from Trevor.

"Honey, I get it," Julie said. "It's not easy having to jump around between here and Dad's."

"And now it's just going to be worse."

"Worse how?"

"Sam."

"Oh."

"You're not going to still marry him, are you?"

"Trevor!" Julie understood that kids could be direct to the point of being crass, but Trevor's comment had crossed a line.

"I'm sorry. I just mean—I like Sam. I think he's a really nice guy, and he's been great to me. You know? But think about what it would be like for me if you two were married and he was like, living here. He can't move his arms or his legs. He can't do anything for himself."

"For right now. He can get better."

The look Trevor gave his mother said he did not believe it. Deep down, going to that place she hated to go, Julie had to admit she felt the same.

"Him being here, with us . . . it would change everything."

Julie took a moment to collect her thoughts. Her throat had gone dry, which made it hard to speak. "I understand your feelings, here. Honestly, I do. Here's my promise to you. We're going to take this one day at a time. I don't want you to worry. You have enough on your plate."

"I just don't see why you can't fix it with Dad," he said.

"Fix it how?"

"I saw how you were with him at the hospital. You were close."

"And?"

"Why can't Dad just come live here again?"

And there it was. The real issue flushed out into the open where it belonged.

After the divorce, it had not taken Julie long to scrub the apartment of any traces of Paul. His artwork had been stripped from the walls, and his trinkets and favorite dishes took up shelf space in his new home now. This was her home and Trevor's home. No matter what happened with Sam, she would never live with Paul again. In her son's eyes, though, it remained a distant possibility.

"Come sit."

Trevor finally obliged and Julie pulled him in close.

"Your dad and I tried very hard," she said. "But we just couldn't make it work. I do like your father. He means well, and we're friends. Sometimes I want to slug some sense into him, sure, but I know how much he loves you. He'd do anything for you. But no matter what, your father and I aren't getting back together."

"Well, it sucks for me."

"Language, please."

"It stinks," Trevor said with some bite. "I can't keep track of my stuff. I don't even know when I'm supposed to be at Dad's and when I'm supposed to be here."

"This week has been hard on us all. It'll get easier. I promise."

"Yeah, but by then I'll have failed my other courses."

"Don't be dramatic. We'll deal with this English paper. Just take it easy on me right now. I'm going through an awful lot, and I need your support. Can I count on you?"

Trevor shrugged and said, "I guess."

Winston came back into view, ball spinning. Trevor picked him up. "I should put him back."

"When things get settled, we'll look at the schedule with your dad. Maybe we can simplify it. I don't know. And I'll e-mail your teacher after dinner about the essay. Okay? Now go wash up."

"Sounds good, Mom."

Trevor and Winston headed off.

"Trevor?"

He turned back around.

"I love you," she said.

"Love you too, Mom."

No pause at all from Trevor, no need to collect his thoughts. It was how he felt about his mother. Julie's heart swelled. She had made a vow after Sam's accident to say those three simple words to her son every chance she got.

CHAPTER 16

"Kill me, Julie. Please help me die."

Sam's anguished plea tore at Julie's heart. Fresh flowers filled the stark ICU cubicle with bright colors that failed to offset Sam's dark mood. He slept most of the day away, with Julie at his bedside every moment she got.

"You don't mean it. It's hard now, but it will get better." Julie entwined her delicate fingers around Sam's and gave his hand a slight squeeze.

Sam could not squeeze back. Nor could he touch Julie's face, or stand, or run, or feed himself, or do any of the countless things he used to do before the accident.

The gentle rise and fall of Sam's chest, the passing of his tongue across dried lips, the blinking of his eyes were the only indications he could move his body at all. The face that had been so full of life was sunken, his skin pulled close to the bone, dark circles marking the pain in his eyes. September became October, and in the weeks since the accident, Sam seemed to have aged a decade. With his beard shaved, Julie could better see how his face had lost its luster.

This was the new normal. Today was just another day in Sam's ongoing care in the ICU. It had been sixteen days since Sam fully regained consciousness and there were no major crises, no life-or-death medical procedures. All he had done on this day and the day before was to lie in his hospital bed, hooked to wires and tubes like a human marionette.

"Please, Julie. I can't live like this."

How many times had he asked to die? Julie had lost count, but it had started the moment Sam could speak again. Nothing Julie said could shake his despair. She understood it, felt it in her core.

"I'm sorry, baby," she said. "I'm so sorry for what you're going through. I've called someone who can help."

"Nobody can help me, but you. You've fought for death with dignity for years, now fight for me." Sam's voice was a hiss of air, a faint echo of his former self.

Julie shut her eyes to battle back another wave of distress. "It will get better. You have to believe it will."

"You're a hypocrite."

His words stung, but Julie understood his need to make it hurt.

"No, it's different for you. There's a lot of evidence that quality of life for—for people with your type of injury is about support and reintegration into the community."

"My injury," Sam said, the contempt almost palpable. "I'm quadriplegic and that's what I am going to be for the rest of my life. I don't want this. I don't. I'm going to live out my days helpless in a hospital of some sort, and you know it. You know it and you have to help me." Sam's body might have been broken, but his mind was crisp and working strategically.

Julie had made a career out of keeping people alive who were on the edge of death. The torment and pain she'd observed over many years had altered her beliefs about administering care to the supremely sick. She always did her job to the best of her ability, but welcomed the day when caring for patients would mean having the option to end their suffering in a dignified way.

Sam wanted to die. Should he have that right? Was Julie being a hypocrite? It was true her beliefs were easier to maintain when she had no deeply personal connection to the patient wishing to die.

"I believe you can make a life," Julie said, her voice not so convincing. "We can make a life together, and I want to be the one to help us do that. I know it can be a good life, too."

"You believe that as much as you believe Nancy Cruzan should have been kept alive."

"No. Nancy had no life whatsoever. It's different."

In one of her prepared talks about death with dignity, Julie had referred to the case of Nancy Beth Cruzan, who had been involved in an automobile accident that left her in a persistent vegetative state. Citing the due process clause of the fourteenth amendment, Nancy's parents went to court to get their daughter's feeding tube removed. In a five-to-four decision, the Missouri Supreme Court had ruled that individuals had the right to refuse medical treatment as long as they were competent to exercise that right. Without any clear and convincing evidence that Nancy Cruzan desired her treatment to be withdrawn, the tube remained in place. Nancy's parents eventually proved to the court's satisfaction that their daughter would not wish to be on life support. Nancy's feeding tube was eventually removed, and soon after she died. The case gave rise to the broad adoption of advance life directives.

Was it so different for Sam? As much as Julie wanted to believe the two cases were unalike, at the core both were about quality of life. Sam had no mobility. He was completely dependent on others for everything, and would remain that way, most likely, for the remainder of his life. To him, this was no life at all. He might as well be in a vegetative state.

Should Sam have the same right as Nancy Cruzan?

He was certainly of sound mind, and there was no mistaking his desire. But his vitals were improving, and with time his mental state might change as well. If Julie had learned anything from her years in the ICU, it was that people were deeply resilient and could adapt to almost any situation.

Julie glanced at the waves running across the screen in the six divided sections of the telemetry monitor above Sam's bed. The green EKG lead recorded a nice steady sinus rhythm, an indication of a healthy heart trapped inside a broken body. Sam could be fed, hydrated, and kept alive day after day, year after year. What he could not do was kill himself.

The pulse oximeter reading, a blue sinusoidal wave that mirrored the heart rate, showed Sam's oxygen saturation at 99 percent. His lungs, just like his heart, were functioning fine and allowed for breathing, but with help, probably forever, because his spinal injury

was complete—no motor or sensory function in the
lowest sacral segment.

Help came in the form of a curved tube affixed to
Sam's neck by a plate called a flange. The tube inserted
into Sam's tracheostomy stoma—a hole made in his
neck and windpipe—was permanent, but far better than
the alternative of long-term ventilation. The procedure
provided Sam with an open and clear airway, but made
speech more difficult because air no longer passed
through the vocal folds that produce sound. To facilitate
speech, Julie had to intermittently block the tube with
the palm of her hand to seal air inside the throat until
enough air accumulated to allow Sam to talk again.

Eating was easier than speaking. Despite the tube,
Sam could enjoy solid foods now, as much as he could
enjoy anything. He'd had a steak dinner not long ago,
specially marinated by the kitchen staff, but the meal
brought him no joy.

The arterial section of the telemetry monitor, colored
red, measured heartbeat to blood pressure. Sam was
stable here as well, a solid ninety-five over fifty-eight.
His meds would change over time, but he would always
need a lot of them to be kept alive.

"You know how to kill me so you won't get caught."

"I don't, Sam. Honest. They test for everything. And
even if I could, I would never. I couldn't."

Sam tried to speak, but no sound came out. Julie
capped the tube with her palm and waited a few moments while Sam labored to breathe through his nose
and mouth.

"The best care should be made available to every patient," Sam said in a raspy voice, "but a patient deserves

the right to hasten death to avoid inhumane suffering or escape from a life turned unbearable."

"Don't throw my own words back at me," Julie said.

"Then . . . you . . . are . . . a liar . . ." Sam was having trouble with his speech again.

Julie once more had to cap the tube, but was afraid he'd utter more hurtful words.

"Things may change in a few months," Julie said. "There have been cases."

"Don't . . . don't give me false hope. You understand the films better than I do, and I got a perfectly clear picture of the rest of my life."

Julie had a picture, too. It was indeed bleak. Sam would eventually be discharged to the rehab floor at White Memorial, where he could easily spend the better part of a year. And what would that year look like? In the mornings Julie would visit with him, feed him breakfast before the start of her shift. He would then have a sponge bath, and if he did not move his bowels in a diaper, he would most likely endure a second cleaning later on. Then it would be off to physical therapy where some young, able-bodied person would move Sam's limbs so that the muscles did not atrophy completely. If her schedule allowed, Julie could feed Sam lunch before the occupational therapists would try to teach him to do with his mouth what he had done with his hands.

His days would be an endless grind.

"I know it seems hopeless right now," Julie said as she caressed Sam's face. "But you have to believe me, because there is hope for better tomorrows."

"I resent your optimism."

Julie did not respond. She glanced down at her

watch. The visitor she had invited would be arriving here any minute.

"I understand," Julie said. "And I'm about to give you another reason to resent me."

At that moment, the door to Sam's cubicle opened. A thin woman entered, not tall, barely five foot four, with a pretty face, thick dark hair down to her shoulders, and large brown eyes full of kindness. She wore a beige cardigan sweater and black slacks, and some sort of ID hung from a lanyard around her neck. She acted unhurried, and by that alone Sam could have guessed she was not a doctor here. Her lithe body and graceful movements suggested past training as a ballet dancer.

"Hello, Sam, my name is Michelle Stevenson. Julie asked me to come see you. Is now a good time? I can come back later if you'd prefer." She spoke clearly, somehow striking the right balance between a professional tone and something more intimate.

Sam directed his frosty gaze up at the ceiling. Julie gently lifted Sam's head and readjusted the thin, firm pillows to give him a better look at this stranger.

"Why are you here?" Sam asked.

"I'm with an organization called Very Much Alive. And I'm here to convince you that there is a good quality of life for quadriplegics. Now, I know you disagree," Michelle said, preempting Sam's rebuttal, "but all I ask is your willingness to listen, and it will cost only your time. If I'm successful, and I believe I will be, I'll give something back to you that's very precious indeed."

"And that is?"

"Your desire to live."

CHAPTER 17

Julie had known about Very Much Alive before she contacted the organization. In fact, she was probably on their list of least favorite doctors. In disability rights circles, Very Much Alive was considered one of the most formidable. The group organized demonstrations, was active on the lecture circuit, wrote peer-reviewed papers for many respected journals, and engaged in constant battle online, in the media, and in the halls of Congress with organizations such as Humane Choices, which advocated for death with dignity.

VMA had some of the best counselors in the business, who were expert at convincing others to change their views, including several patients who had wanted to die and now were spokespeople for Very Much Alive. Their stories were displayed prominently on the organization's website with pull quotes, videos, and essays explaining how they came to their change of heart. Hopeful that VMA could reach Sam, Julie had made the call.

Sam's eyes narrowed into slits, his teeth clenched, and the veins on his neck bulged just as they had the day Julie stuck a needle in his chest.

"You should . . . have told me . . . she was coming." Sam labored to get out the words.

Julie capped his tube with her palm to fill his throat up with air again.

"In fairness to Julie, I'm the one who suggested we keep my visit here a secret. From what she told me about your situation, I was fairly certain you would have refused to see me. At least now I can plead my case, and all it's going to cost is a few minutes of your time."

"Please, darling. Five minutes. Hear her out."

Sam turned his head away from Julie. He would have gotten out of bed and left the room, if only he could.

"Julie told me about the accident," Michelle said, "and I want you to know how truly sorry I am for what's happened to you."

"Not as sorry as I am," Sam said.

Michelle cast her glance to the floor and nodded in agreement.

"What is it you want from me?" Sam asked.

"I'll get right to it. My organization opposes physician assisted suicide. We view it as a lethal form of discrimination against disabled people."

"What you call lethal discrimination, I call mercy," Sam said.

"With time, your thoughts and feelings may change. We've seen it with other people in circumstances similar to yours."

Sam nodded to Julie in a way that told her to cap his tube.

"There are drugs you can take that can induce temporary paralysis," he said. "Why don't you try living like me for a while and see how you like it."

Julie glanced at Michelle and had no trouble reading the woman's thoughts. This was going to be an uphill battle all the way.

"There's no question you're suffering," Michelle said. "But is it unbearable? Who is the judge?"

"On that point, I think I am," Sam said flatly.

"No. Your physician would actually become the ultimate judge, because he or she would have to take the steps to bring about your death. Right now, you might not be in the best place to guide that thinking."

This was one area where Julie had gone head-on with groups like Very Much Alive. Suffering was considered to be part of the human condition, as groups opposed to mercy killing often argued. Medicine, Julie said in her speech, was nothing more than a manufactured way to alleviate a natural process. Her argument went that mercy killing, as a means to end suffering, should therefore be treated as viable medicine. In her seminars, Julie asked, was it fair to force people to exist, often in agony, just for the sake of existing?

Sam eyed Michelle skeptically. "Are you suggesting I'm not rational, or that my judgment is somehow impaired? Want to quiz me on American history? I'll get a hundred. Guaranteed. Or better yet, I'll quiz you."

Michelle was well practiced at dealing with adversaries. "I'm sure you know our country's history better than I do," she said, a trace of a smile curving her full lips. "But that has no bearing on the fact that assisted suicide is not the answer."

Michelle had an ethereal quality, something inherently light, almost fairylike. She had high cheekbones and a slightly angular face. From their conversations, Julie had learned that Michelle had been married twice, and was close to fifty, but she looked easily a decade younger. She radiated warmth, and Julie cast aside any doubts she'd had about this meeting. If anyone could open Sam's mind to new possibilities, it was Michelle.

"Pardon me if I sound rude here, Michelle," Sam said, "but I think that I know best if my life is worth living."

Uh-oh, Julie thought. *Here we go.*

"I'm not saying you don't," Michelle answered. "We live in a society that values physical ability. It's completely understandable how your injury not only robbed you of your mobility, but of your dignity as well."

"Thanks for getting it."

Sam had never been sarcastic with Julie before, but the injury had changed much about him.

"At first blush, assisted suicide might seem like a good thing to have available," Michelle went on. "But dig deeper and you'll see the problems."

Julie shrank a little from the look Michelle gave her. She obviously knew all about Julie's papers and lectures advocating passage of death with dignity laws nationwide.

"It's fear of living a disabled life that makes you want to die," Michelle said. "It's fear of the indignity, of not being able to get out of bed, or use the toilet on your own. But this is new for you. Over time, you'll learn that needing help is not undignified, and that death is a far worse choice than assistance. Depression can be treated, Sam, but there's no known cure for a lethal prescription."

"Is this what you do for a living?" Sam asked. "Try and keep quads alive?"

His breathing had turned ragged. Julie gave him a drink of water, then capped his tube so that he'd be able to continue antagonizing Michelle.

"Not exactly," Michelle said. "What we believe is that legalization of assisted suicide and euthanasia will lead to policies that discriminate against the disabled, poor, and underinsured. We want to protect people from doctors who tell patients they have six months to live when the prognosis of a shortened life expec tancy is often wrong. And once society authorizes assisted suicide for the terminally ill, it's inevitable the scope will increase to include those who cannot self-administer lethal drugs."

"Well, that would be me," Sam said. "And you have yet to convince me that lethal drugs shouldn't be allowed."

"Right," Michelle said. "At first glance, your argument makes sense. Who better to make this decision than the person suffering from the condition? There's no question your perception of quality of life is going to have to change. But your brain is still sharp as ever, and technology has come a long way.

"You can still read, write, and share your ideas with others. You can still watch a baseball game, smell the fresh-cut spring grass, or taste a delicious meal. I'm not saying it's going to be easy, but it is possible to find enjoyment in new things, or a new appreciation for what you already know. There's a danger we all face if we allow the lives of disabled people to be viewed as not worth living."

Sam scoffed. "So now I have to be the poster boy for everybody else?"

"Not at all," Michelle said. "But I am asking you to give it more time. See if your perspective about quality of life changes. If you won't do it for yourself, then do it for Julie."

Julie set her hand on Sam's shoulder. She had not thought she had a single tear left inside her, but that familiar lump came back to her throat as her eyes watered.

"Give it time," Julie said. "Please, Sam, for us. Let's give it more time. Let's put our energy on living, not dying."

Sam motioned for Julie to cap his tube. Once he could speak more easily, he stayed silent long enough for the mood in the room to turn even more uncomfortable.

"What's your deal with this, Michelle?" Sam eventually asked. "Why do you care so much?" His voice had turned soft, and his eyes were heavy.

It was obvious to Julie that this conversation had taken an enormous physical and emotional toll on him. It had on her, as well.

"You ask a fair question of me," Michelle said. "And it's a story I think you may be able to relate to. Do you want to hear it?"

"Last I checked, I'm not going anywhere."

Michelle strained to smile. "We have to go back in time a bit, to my first husband. I was thirty-nine. I'm fifty now. Happily remarried to a doctor who works at this hospital, in fact. But back then I was happily married to a man I met in college—a man I thought I'd be with forever."

"I thought I'd be getting married to Julie and buying a new condo in Cambridge. Now I can't wipe my own ass. Funny how life throws us curveballs like that."

Michelle shrugged off Sam's aggression. Her eyes misted with memories. "Our curveball was a brain tumor. A grade IV astrocytoma, to be specific. He tried all the treatments—chemo, radiation, even surgery. Nothing helped alleviate his symptoms or his suffering. He was dying in the most horrible way. Seizures, nausea, blinding headaches, memory loss like an Alzheimer's patient. I didn't know what it was likc to watch someone I love suffer so much, but I can relate to Julie's pain because the experience was utterly excruciating."

"Then you should be able to understand why I want to die."

"I did and I do," Michelle said. "I understood so well, in fact, that I moved my husband and teenage son across the country to Oregon, where he could legally get the prescription you're wanting. And he got it, and he died. This was completely against my upbringing, my religion, but he needed my help and support."

Sam returned a grim smile, but Julie was glad to see any smile from him.

"You're making my case just fine," he said.

"But it wasn't fine, Sam. We're all going to die, no debating that. What I learned from my experience is that death can bring more problems if you do something to speed it up. My husband didn't die of a brain tumor. He died from the pills he ingested, the pills I helped him obtain. I thought the burden was mine and mine alone, but it turned out my son, Andrew, felt like he had a hand in killing his father. He didn't share his feeling with me until after his dad was gone, but later he expressed his guilt for not doing more to stop it from happening.

"Andrew wasn't sleeping. Started drinking, smoking, his grades went from As to Ds. He sank into a depression. I tried everything. Pills. Doctors. We eventually moved out of Oregon and settled in Massachusetts to get as far from the place where his father died as possible. It didn't help. He carried the guilt with him all the way across the country, and it followed him like a shadow."

Michelle's sadness was pronounced. "I knew when I got home and the house was quiet that something horrible had happened. I knew when I called Andrew's name and he didn't answer. I just knew."

Michelle closed her reddened eyes and put a hand to her mouth, head lowered. She stayed that way until her composure returned.

"I found him hanging in his closet. He was gone. He took his own life. He took his life because I took his father's. And that's when I knew that it wasn't just about my husband and his freedom of choice. It was about all the lives connected to him, including my son's. So I changed my tune about death with dignity and I turned my focus, my full passion, to preserving life at all costs. Death is coming for us all, Sam. And if you push Julie hard enough, she may just crack. She may move you to Oregon, or Vermont, or some state where you can legally order your own death. And you'll be gone, and Julie will live with that decision for the rest of her days."

Sam eventually broke the lengthy silence that followed. "I'm sorry for your loss, Michelle. You have my deepest sympathy. You've given me a lot to think about."

Michelle smiled. "Then I've done my job," she said.

In the protracted silence that followed, Julie sensed that anything she chose to say would be wrong. Except for the words, "I'm sorry," which Julie spoke in a soft voice, directed at Michelle.

Julie bent down and gave Sam a light peck on his forehead. As she lowered her head, Julie could see a few red dots marking the lower portion of Sam's neck. She stood, kissed Sam's lips, and said she loved him. Then she hugged him and hugged Michelle. For a moment the mood lightened.

Then, being the doctor she was, Julie shined her penlight on those skin abrasions. "Well, in addition to that prescription for Prozac, I'm going to get you another for an antihistamine," she said.

Sam returned a puzzled look. "Why is that?"

"From the looks of it, you're about to break out in hives."

"Hives? Oh, crap. Well, I guess when it rains it pours," he said.

Julie laughed because she could not stand to cry anymore.

CHAPTER 18

ONE WEEK LATER . . .

Julie finished a busy morning in the ICU, plus extra time on the phone with an obstinate agent from an insurance company. *Goodness, weren't they all?* This one refused to pay for Xolair because the patient had "asthma-like symptoms," not pure asthma. It did not seem to matter to her one bit that Julie's patient had failed standard therapy with prednisone. What mattered was that prednisone cost three dollars a month, and Xolair could run anywhere from five hundred to two grand, depending on the dose prescribed. It irked Julie to no end that someone in a cubicle without an M.D. was reviewing check boxes to see if all the criteria had been met.

"Has the patient been on a moderate dose of inhaled corticosteroids plus long-acting beta-agonists for three months?"

Come on now, Julie wanted to scream into the phone. *The patient is here, right now, and he's having a hell of a time taking in a good breath, not to mention he's had four emergency room visits in the last month.* Julie knew that Xolair would make a difference. The patient had an immunoglobulin E level through the roof, the exact area Xolair worked on.

"Is the patient's diurnal variation in peak expiratory flow greater than thirty percent?"

Do you even understand what that means? Julie wanted to say. She controlled herself. This was a game, and she was adept at playing. Her goal was to get the best treatment possible for her patients, while the insurance companies she battled wanted the least expensive/best treatment possible.

Therein lay the conflict: two little words with such an enormous impact. *Least expensive.* Julie knew she would win the Xolair battle eventually. After all, she had the MD. The game being played was one of attrition. If the insurance companies set up enough roadblocks, enough doctors would give up and settle for second best. It was a profitable strategy for the companies, but Julie was not about to be one who gave up the fight. She was compulsive about getting everything in order before even picking up the phone. The price Julie paid for her effort was a lot of extra time during nights and weekends, gathering her swords and shields for battle.

By one o'clock she was ready to head to the rehab floor, where she would have lunch with Sam. For today's feast, she had prepared a special meal at home with Trevor's help: buttermilk fried chicken and homemade coleslaw. The past couple of weeks had been difficult ones for Sam, compounded by a terrible outbreak of hives. But Sam was out of the ICU, and had sort of made good on his promise. He only asked Julie to help him die every other day.

Over the course of many conversations, Sam repeatedly expressed dismay at Julie's continued commitment to him and to building a life together. For a man used to giving of himself, he now felt like a burden to everyone. Often, Sam asked to be left alone. He confessed that Julie reminded him of all he had lost and would never get back.

Michelle insisted that "let me die" was a phase in the process. Indeed, Julie saw glimmers that proved her right. Sam had begun to sit in a wheelchair for a couple hours at a stretch before exhaustion forced him back into bed. Every day physical and occupational therapists stretched Sam's body to the absolute limit, and he seemed able to withstand the ordeal. The work kept Sam's muscles from atrophying completely, but did little to lift his spirits.

Sometimes during her lunch break, or after a shift, when Trevor was with Paul, Julie would climb into bed with Sam. Together they watched documentaries on YouTube detailing different stories of spinal injury and survival. For the most part, Julie found them life-affirming and deeply inspirational. Sam took it all in, and even asked a nurse to gather some information on assistive technologies. He was particularly interested in a computer that would allow him to type with his eyes. That was a positive sign, Julie decided. The speed at which cutting-edge communications technology was being blended with therapeutic and rehabilitative care was nothing short of astounding.

Close to the elevators, Julie picked up the pace and caught one going down. She was eager to play a song for Sam. Along with the cooler of lunch food, Julie had brought the iPod nano loaded with new music. She'd bought Sam the iPod a few weeks ago and downloaded a variety of music files from iTunes. Sam was not yet interested in listening to audiobooks; it took too much focus, he said.

Sometimes Julie would bring the iPod home and refresh it with more songs, organizing them into playlists for easier listening. Well, Trevor did the refreshing and playlist creation. It was his way of doing something nice for Sam. He was also much more adept with technology and was part of a computer programming club at school, The Bytes. Trevor had visions of MIT that did not yet jibe with his study habits, but his innate ability would take him places, Julie believed.

The iPod Trevor managed for Julie had a preponderance of jazz and blues, two of Sam's favorite genres, and lots of classic rock. Today she had added a song from the band Weezer, a tune that held special significance for both of them.

It had been a gray fall afternoon, much like this one. Sam had lured Julie to his classroom with some excuse about car trouble. When she arrived, the classroom was empty, until one by one a procession of Sam's students, silent as monks, filtered into the room and took up every available seat. Julie stood at the front of the class with a wary expression, unsure what to make of it all, and not getting any responses from the kids. The lengthy silence broke only when a student in the front row took out a pair of portable speakers and started to play "No One Else" by Weezer, a band Julie had discovered and adored while in medical school. One by one, in synchronized fashion, the kids held up cardboard signs with a letter neatly printed on each.

It took a minute for Julie to realize that the letters spelled out: "Julie I love you. Will you marry me?"

Sam had entered the classroom in a fine suit, holding a beautiful bouquet of white roses. His students had gone crazy, cheering and clapping as Sam went down on one knee to present Julie with a velvet jewel box.

Julie exited the elevator, wondering what impact the song might have on Sam's mood. Would he snap at her, as he had on several recent occasions? Or would the memory warm him, as it did her?

On the way to Sam's room, a voice broke out over the loudspeaker that stopped Julie midstride.

"Code blue, room 2206!"

That was Sam's room. Julie raced down the hallway and turned the corner just in time to see two nurses rush into the room. When Julie got there, one nurse had already started CPR and two others were busy setting up the bedside monitor. The adjustable lamp over Sam's bed illuminated his face, now disturbingly gray.

The nurses glanced up to see a look of alarm on Julie's face.

"Quick, tell me what happened!"

"I was just coming in to sit him up and get ready for you to feed him lunch," one nurse said. "He complained of feeling warm and light-headed. Then his eyes rolled back into his head and he became unresponsive. I couldn't feel his pulse, so I called the code."

The rapid response team, pushing various machines and a crash cart, burst into Sam's room and took up their respective positions. Dr. Hayes, a tall, gangly New

Yorker who was a board-certified physical medicine and rehabilitation specialist, rushed to Sam's bedside.

Julie responded with startling vehemence. "I've got this!"

Dr. Hayes retreated a few steps, making room for Julie to take over.

"I'm sorry, Henry. I'm sorry," Julie said to Dr. Hayes, finding a measure of calm she desperately needed. She directed her attention to a male resident. "Please take over compressions," she said.

Intubation could wait. There was no lingering animosity. Dr. Hayes understood no one was more qualified to lead the charge to bring Sam back from the precipice of death than an ICU doctor. Julie, however, understood that Sam would want her to do nothing.

She glanced at the IV bags and at the urinary catheter snaking from beneath the sheets. Somewhere within, she wanted to give him the everlasting peace he had begged for. At the same time, she felt an intense need to force life back into the waxy stillness of Sam's face.

"Okay, okay." Julie snapped back into herself, feeling the tempest subside as her mind clicked into task mode. "What do we see on the monitor?"

"Ventricular tachycardia at two hundred, no pulse."

"Charge to two hundred joules," Julie said.

There was an agonizing silence as a nurse turned the dial on the automated external defibrillator to 200. Another nurse attached two defibrillation pads to the chest to insure that the electricity got delivered to the right place on the heart.

"Draw up forty units of vasopressin," Julie ordered as she motioned a resident away from the bed. She pressed the charge button and immediately the hum of the machine grew louder, like a mosquito flying closer and closer to an eardrum.

"Step back from the bed," Julie called out. "Everyone, all clear!"

"All clear," almost everyone repeated, indicating a go-ahead to shock.

"Ready?" Julie said. "Shock!"

Julie pushed the red button on the top of the defibrillator. A metallic thump sounded as two hundred joules of electricity shot through Sam's chest and into the rest of his body. His paralyzed muscles did not respond to the jolt in the same manner as those of an able-bodied person. His body came off the bed just a little, but without the rigid arch that usually accompanied that much electricity.

"Any pulse?" Julie asked.

"No pulse," a nurse said. "Monitor looks like v-fib."

Julie glanced at the monitor and confirmed the read was indeed ventricular fibrillation. The ventricles of Sam's heart fibrillated, contracting in a rapid, unsynchronized way. The heart pumped little to no blood.

"Is the vasopressin ready? Give it now. Ready, charge to three hundred." Julie's voice was firm, but unagitated.

"Charging to three hundred joules," a nurse announced.

The hum of the machine again increased in volume as the nurse recharged the defibrillator.

"Charging to three hundred, ready."

"Clear!" Julie called out.

"All clear," many repeated.

"Okay, shock!"

Julie depressed the red button, repeating the previous

jolt. Sam's body barely moved as a metallic *thunk* sounded like a distant thunderclap.

"Any pulse?" Julie asked. A feeling of dread hit so hard it was as if someone had put the paddles on her own chest.

"No pulse, Dr. Devereux," a nurse announced. "He's still in v-fib on the monitor."

With alarm, Julie observed the jagged peaks and valleys of Sam's telemetry readout. Ventricular rate two hundred beats a minute, atrial contractions not discernable, P waves notably absent. Grim as it appeared, Julie knew Sam still had a shockable rhythm. There was still a chance he could come back to her.

Julie began to order medications to be given through Sam's intravenous lines. Epinephrine to help increase cardiac output, amiodarone to keep the heart beating normally, bicarbonate to counteract the lactic acid build-up, and even glucose, in case for some reason Sam's blood sugar had dropped too low. This was followed closely by a 360-joule countershock.

"Yes! We got something," a nurse announced with jubilation. "Monitor shows wide rhythm at forty-five. I can feel the femoral pulse, though it is weak and thready."

Julie held in a breath and watched the monitor, half expecting the readout to return to v-fib status at any moment. For the time being, it appeared to hold steady.

"Great job!" Julie said, feeling her own pulse decelerate. But how much of his oxygen-deprived brain would reawaken? "Okay, let's get IVF bolus five hundred milliliters of normal saline. And hang dopamine. Henry, please tube him now."

Julie appraised the assembled team, working side by side, each person focused on a specific task. She had been through this scenario hundreds of times before, but never with so much at stake.

"Dr. Devereux, we lost his pulse!"

Julie gave the nurse a horrified look. "What do we have now on the monitor?" Her composure was slipping.

"Slow and wide rhythm in the twenties. PEA."

Julie's heart sank. Pulseless electrical activity—no pulse whatsoever. Every inch they had gained in this fight they had just lost.

"Start CPR!" Julie snapped. "Give him more epi, one milligram."

Everything was done as Julie ordered, and with haste.

"Any pulse?"

"Sorry, Dr. Devereux, no."

The cardiogram still showed that slow and wide rhythm. Julie's body became damp with sweat.

"Let's use an escalating dose of epi," Julie said with force. "Three-milligram IV push. NOW!"

Chaos and pandemonium erupted.

"Hang an epi drip!" one nurse shouted. "Someone mix it, stat!"

The resident doing compressions had tired. Dr. Hayes took his place.

"Call cardiology," Dr. Hayes said. "Tell them to come fast. Get echo here! We need echo!"

"Epinephrine, three milligrams in now, Dr. Devereux," said a nurse. "We still don't have a pulse."

Julie tried to ignore the cold tickle of fear running down the back of her neck.

"Continue CPR," she said. "Give two amps of bicarbonate. Continue CPR. Come on!"

Cardiology arrived. The crowded room heated up as

more bodies crammed into the tight space, like canned sardines. The new contingent included Dr. Carrie Bryant from neurosurgery, a recent addition to the White Memorial staff.

"Keep up the compressions," Julie said. "We can still get a pulse. He just needs more drugs. More epi— please, do it now!"

From the corner of her eye, Julie caught an exchange of nervous glances. The sense of urgency was receding.

Dr. Bryant approached Sam and lifted his lids to shine her penlight into his eyes. She stroked his cornea with a piece of cotton, then applied slight pressure to Sam's forehead and nose. Her expression without optimism, Carrie stepped away from Sam's bed and groped Julie's arm.

"His pupils are fixed and dilated," Carrie said, looking Julie right in the eyes. "I'm so sorry, but he's gone."

Dr. Hayes came forward. "Julie, let me call it," he said.

The only response Julie could muster was a nod. Carrie gave Julie an embrace.

"That's it," Dr. Hayes said, glancing at his watch. "Thank you, everybody, for your efforts. Time of death is one thirty-five."

Defeated, Julie bowed her head and let her arms fall to her sides. The equipment was put away, the tube removed from Sam's throat, and the room quickly cleared. Julie resisted the urge to pump on Sam's chest herself.

Carrie said from the doorway, "You did everything you could, and you did everything right." With that, she was gone.

Julie stayed behind, too numb to cry, too emotionally drained to do anything but gaze at Sam's lifeless body. In one intense wave of emotion, the impact of what had just happened hit her full force. Her love was really gone.

He looked at peace. This brought Julie a measure of comfort. In the stillness of the moment, a thought struck Julie with force.

Sam's heart and lungs had been functioning fine. What caused him to suffer a sudden cardiac arrest?

CHAPTER 19

Autopsy means "see for yourself," and that was precisely what Lucy Abruzzo intended to do with Sam Talbot's body. She would see for herself what had killed him. Gowned, gloved, and masked, Lucy looked like any surgeon about to perform a procedure, except her patient required no anesthesia and she had no support staff on hand to assist. Lucy preferred it this way. She thrived in solitude, which was why she was equally comfortable running long distances or tackling virtual opponents in a spirited game of online chess.

The endeavor at hand was a chess match of a different sort: Lucy vs. death. But death was a wily opponent, and safeguarded its secrets the way a grand master could obscure a strategy until checkmate became inevitable.

The cavernous autopsy suite had an industrial look, with its gray-tiled flooring, fourteen-foot-high ceilings, and exposed ductwork. Lucy liked the utility of it all. Nothing here was wasted or decorative. Everything had a proper place and purpose. The room had three brand-new autopsy tables, plenty of good light, top-of-the-line instruments, and lab equipment organized neatly on stainless steel tables, or in glass-fronted cabinets securely mounted to the walls. Most everything here was new or in pristine condition, thanks in large part to Roman Janowski's skill at keeping the hospital coffers flush with cash. It was a fine place to work, and Lucy was ready for the task at hand.

As was her tradition prior to beginning, Lucy's eyes went to a sign in Latin that hung on a nearby wall. It read: *Ilic locus est ubi mors gaudet succurrere vitae.* Translated, it meant: *This is the place where death rejoices to help those who live.* The words mattered a great deal, reminding Lucy of her purpose here. Indeed, it was the very essence of her profession.

Ultimately—in a clinical sense, at least—everyone died of the same thing. The heart stopped beating, and blood stopped circulating through the body, two processes necessary for sustaining life. But many factors could come into play as life ended, and therein lay the value of an autopsy.

Autopsies had helped reveal misdiagnoses, uncover new diseases, and educate doctors—and humble them, and befuddle them—about the vast intricacies of the human body. Doctors, by their nature, did not easily embrace the possibility of being wrong. Over the years, Lucy had dug up plenty of medical evidence to wrinkle more than a few white lab coats. She had gone into pathology for the same reason she'd devoured mystery novels as a child. Lucy simply loved to figure out the real answers.

Because Sam Talbot was so severely injured, his death had not been a complete surprise. Cost and resources meant autopsies were rarely done without a compelling reason, such as death under suspicious circumstances, pending litigation, or a health threat to the general public. This procedure was a favor to a friend who'd requested it. Julie needed closure—deserved it, given all she had endured—so the stakes were high. Lucy was the boss, and did not have to ask anyone's permission to grant Julie's request.

Jordan, the diener, had already prepared the body, so when Lucy entered the autopsy suite she was able to get right to work. From her quick assessment, it was obvious Jordan deserved another raise. The X-rays were all visible on the viewing screen, and Lucy's tools, including the fine saws and scalpels she favored, had been laid out in perfect order.

Never had Lucy met a diener so committed to excellence. The word "diener" was German and meant "helper," which described Jordan to a T.

Pressing on the foot pedal, Lucy activated the overhead microphone and recorded the date, time, and location of the procedure: White Memorial Hospital.

"This is Dr. Lucy Abruzzo performing an autopsy on Mr. Samuel Talbot, who was deceased on Friday, the fourteenth of October, at one thirty-five P.M."

Lucy studied the X-ray images and rattled off her assessment as if she was reading from a book.

"Review of the X-rays demonstrates healing of the C4 burst fracture, type-two fractures to the ilium and pubis, left radial and ulnar fractures, right radial and ulnar fractures, and left olecranon fracture. Left femur fracture with rod in place, healing. All appear consistent with prior injuries, and no new findings identified. New hairline fracture noted in the sternum and fracturing anteriorly of bilateral ribs T5 through T8. Likely occurring during the resuscitation attempt."

CPR was a violent procedure that often cracked ribs and fractured the sternum. Pathology drilled home one undeniable fact: death was painless; living was not.

Lucy examined the body with her keen observational skills.

"First visual inspection shows a well-developed, well-nourished male in his forties. He is six feet tall, weighs one hundred ninety-five pounds, hair color light brown. Mild bruising appears on anterior chest, also likely a resuscitation injury. Significant bruising noted on the abdomen, most likely the result of injections and treatment for his spinal injury. Slight atrophy noted in the lower extremities, also consistent with his prior injuries and clinical history."

Julie had asked to observe this procedure, but ultimately agreed with Lucy that she'd be better served by reading the report. She did not need to see her fiancé cut open with a scalpel from the shoulder to the lower end of the sternum, and then cut again in a straight line over the abdomen to the pubis. What was seen could not be unseen, Lucy had warned.

Except for a bit of blood drawn out by gravity, Lucy's expert incisions produced almost no bleeding. A dead body has no blood pressure. Lucy was grateful that this was a limited autopsy, one that did not have to include the brain. It seemed invasive, especially on someone she knew, to open up the "black box" and poke around inside Sam's skull.

"After standard Y incision is made, there appears to be perimortem fracturing of the sternum and ribs anteriorly, as described on the X-ray."

Sam's cause of death would not be found in the bones. It was time for Lucy to cut the cartilage joining the ribs to the breastbone so she could enter the chest cavity and get to the organs. The bone saw whirred to life and made the necessary cuts almost effortless.

It was proving difficult, Lucy found, to remain her typically detached self. After all, she had lunched with Sam and Julie, had greeted him warmly when he came to the hospital for a visit, and had planned to attend their wedding. Now she was using rib spreaders and cranking the handle so she could open up his sternum and bones to get a good view of the inside of his chest.

She closed off her personal feelings, shut them down the way she could tune out pain on a long run, and began her inspection of the internal organs.

"Pericardial sac intact. Lungs appear normal. Minimal pleural fluid noted and sent for analysis." She made a new incision in the pericardium to conduct her examination of the heart. "Minimal fluid noted," she said. "The heart appears normal in size."

Then she moved over to the main vein, the inferior vena cava that carried blood from the lower body to the heart, and made another cut. "IVC appears normal in caliber and intact. After incision, no clot noted. Blood sent for routine toxicology and chemical analysis."

Gathering samples for the labs was something Lucy would deal with after the fact, but she was required to record her observations in keeping with proper procedure.

Now Lucy turned her attention to the pulmonary arteries, an area of interest to her. Evidence had pointed to an acute myocardial infarction—a heart attack—on the basis of Sam's EKG when he coded. But he had no indication of underlying, preexisting coronary disease, and the hole in Sam's heart from the pericardiocentesis had been repaired. Lucy suspected a fatal pulmonary embolism as cause of death, a clot traveling from veins in the legs to the lungs, completely stopping blood flow.

With this in mind, Lucy felt the pulmonary arteries, but detected no palpable clot. She made her incision.

"The left and right pulmonary arteries are clear."

Interesting.

She inspected the arteries lower down, in case the clot had been dispersed.

"Incision and inspection to the third-order branches are clear of clot," Lucy observed.

Whatever had caused his heart to stop beating was not going to be found in the lungs. Lucy removed both lungs, one at a time, and weighed them before turning her attention to the heart.

"Visual inspection of the heart shows normal size," she said.

She removed the organ and placed it on the scale. The heart weighed 385 grams, 35 grams more than the normal range. She placed the heart on the stainless steel table. Lucy felt uneasy, unusual for her, but then again she did hold the heart of her friend's fiancé in her hand. The moment for sentimentality was short; she had a job to complete.

"The circumference and appearance of the valves are normal," Lucy said. "The ventricular wall appears normal in texture and width." She searched hard for clues. A subtle scar could be a nidus for an arrhythmia, or an irregular heartbeat that would have caused his ultimate death.

She looked again and noticed something unusual

this time. The left ventricle appeared to be dilated. She inspected the bulge more closely.

"There is some bulging noted of the septum into the left atrium," Lucy said into the recording. The recording would pick up the excitement in her voice. "The right ventricular wall is normal in configuration, size, and thickness. The coronary arteries are patent with minimal atherosclerotic changes. Biopsy will be sent for chemical analysis, viral cx, and staining."

Lucy turned the heart over in her hands and studied the ballooned ventricle with intense interest. The anatomy here was incredibly unusual, even for a doctor who had held plenty of hearts in her hand.

"No significant coronary artery stenosis," Lucy said. "Nor is there significant fibrosis in the ventricular transverse sections near the apical or basal segment."

This was in line with Sam's medical history. If he had an underlying heart condition, Lucy would have expected to see abnormal narrowing in the arteries. Everything looked normal except for the apical ballooning of the lower part of the left vertical.

The bulging ventricle resembled a takotsubo, a pot with a bulbous base used by Japanese fishermen to trap octopuses. It was from this that the condition derived its name: takotsubo cardiomyopathy. It was a highly unusual coronary condition, one Lucy had never before seen in an autopsy. She might not have been able to identify its pathology were it not for her near-photographic memory. What made the discovery even more unusual was that takotsubo cardiomyopathy was almost always associated with older women, as much as 90 percent of the time.

Patients with takotsubo experienced a weakening of

the left ventricle, the heart's main pumping chamber, usually as the result of severe emotional or physical stress—or intense fear. More tests would have to be done for Lucy to make a conclusive diagnosis. But she believed Sam's lab results would reveal that he had been literally scared to death.

CHAPTER 20

Julie arrived at Michelle Stevenson's home in Shrewsbury at a quarter to seven. She came by car because her motorcycle was stored in a garage, where it would remain until it could be sold. Her riding days were done.

Motorcycle riding was not the only part of Julie's life that had gone into hiatus. She had contacted the head of the Mass Coalition for Choices and Dignity to tender her resignation from the board of advisors. She could no longer in good faith advocate for death with dignity laws in Massachusetts—or anywhere else, for that matter. Not after she went from opposing the views of Very Much Alive to partnering with them.

Did it mean she no longer believed in death with dignity laws? Or did it mean she believed in them as long as she was not personally affected? Either way, Julie could no longer serve on any of the committees, and she had canceled all her speaking engagements, with no reschedule date offered.

Today marked two weeks since Sam's death. Aside from funeral business, it was the first time Julie had been somewhere other than her home or the hospital. In that time, she had cried some, here and there, but mostly she walked through the days still with an impenetrable malaise, still numb to those who asked how she was doing. She had taken a week off, but welcomed the distraction she got from work. It was in the quiet moments that the guilt settled in and the gravity of the loss hit hard enough to take away her breath.

If only we had taken a different route. If only . . .

Trevor and Paul had shown true concern for Julie's well-being. Paul was readily and consistently available. He helped with shopping, with school, with carpooling. He showed a level of maturity to which Julie was not accustomed.

Julie always said that Trevor followed Paul's lead. In the wake of Sam's death, the flame that had fed her son's need for rebellion was extinguished, at least for the moment. His focus was on school, soccer, and not adding to his mother's distress. Julie was grateful for that, and for the many e-mails and sympathy cards she received—including one with a return address in Dorchester from a Mr. Max Hartsock, who had made full recovery from his MRSA infection. In his thoughtful note, Max included VIP passes to an upcoming Eagles game, which Julie gave to Paul to share with Trevor.

Julie rang the doorbell. She tucked the bottle of wine she'd brought, a cabernet sauvignon from Chile, under her arm and waited.

The door opened. Michelle greeted Julie with a warm embrace, drawing her into the foyer of the ranch-style home. The aromas from the kitchen were intoxicating. For the first time since Sam's death, Julie had an appetite.

Michelle took Julie's coat and the bottle of wine. She smiled when she read the label. "This will go perfectly with our meal," she said. "Speaking of which, we're having beef and ginger stir-fry. Hope that's all right with you."

"That's great. I'm glad you encouraged me to come. Whatever it is, your husband's cooking smells amazing."

"It'll taste amazing, too," a friendly voice called from the kitchen. "I'll meet you in the living room with appetizers in just a moment."

Michelle said, "Lucky for me, Keith loves to cook. Otherwise we'd probably starve. How are you holding up?"

Julie's expression was a bit strained. "It's been hard," she said. "But I'm hanging in there."

"Well, I'm glad you made the trek out west," Michelle said as she hung Julie's coat in the front hall closet.

"It's good for me to get out."

Michelle took the bottle of wine to the kitchen while Julie went to the living room. The furniture, mostly black leather and wood pieces, was tasteful, but not extravagant. Light from the fireplace warmed the room and cast a flickering glow across the beige walls.

It was harder to be in a couple's home than Julie had anticipated. She and Sam had talked long into the night about decorating the place they would buy together. For inspiration, Julie had gotten into Pinterest, and had pinned plenty of images to boards to keep track of her ideas. It was what couples did. That, and cook, and help with homework, and binge-watch shows on Netflix.

Julie's home was decorated with all the flair of a Pottery Barn catalogue. She was good at medicine, but lacked imagination when it came to interior design. That had been Paul's bailiwick when they were married, and true to form, his current place was a hip, industrial loft space with a neo-bohemian vibe. Julie had figured she and Sam would take advantage of his considerable skill with the table saw, and have lots of wood through-out their home—wherever that was going to be.

Now Julie would stay with her tried-and-true ap-proach: practical, affordable, and good enough. She had wanted to make home design decisions with Sam, and felt guilty for envying what Michelle and her hus-band shared.

Julie studied the art on the walls, which went well with the rest of the room's décor. Her attention was drawn to a black-and-white photograph of a handsome young man with a friendly smile.

"That's Andrew," Michelle said, returning with two glasses of wine. "That's my son who died."

"I'm sorry. He looks like you," Julie said.

Michelle's husband Keith emerged from the kitchen carrying a plate of baked Brie with almonds and one of shrimp cocktail.

"There's more where this came from," Keith said.

Julie knew Keith from work, and he had come with Michelle to Sam's funeral. The quick embrace they shared felt natural. Keith was a tall, handsome man, with neatly trimmed brown hair and eyes that sparkled when he flashed his brilliant smile.

An internist by training, Keith was part of a rela-tively new trend in health care. Hospitalists, which was Keith's actual job title, specialized in the care of hospi-talized patients. They could work on almost any floor and deal with every aspect of the patient's needs during their hospital stay. Like many hospitalists Julie knew, Keith moonlighted at other hospitals, which was a bit of a hush-hush practice, something not to be flaunted in the face of White's powerful CEO, Roman Janowski.

Julie's eyes went to something rather unusual hanging on the wall—two colorful beetles mounted with pins inside a wooden box frame.

Keith came over when he noticed Julie observing the specimens. "Lovely, aren't they," he said.

Julie grimaced slightly. "If anything with an orange body and green head landed on me, my first thought would be squish it, not frame it."

"Actually it's an orange abdomen and green thorax, but I get your point."

Michelle came over. "Keith's first field of study, his first love really, was medical entomology," she said.

"Diseases caused by insects have killed more people than bombs or bullets combined." Keith said this with a sardonic grin.

"I was a research scientist," he added, "traveled to exotic locales, collected specimens, tried to understand how these creatures potentially could harm or transmit diseases to humans."

"What changed your career trajectory?"

"Money," Keith said blandly. "Research just doesn't pay like traditional medicine. I had a son and one on the way. I dropped out of research, went to medical school, and became a doc. These lovelies, *Calodema regale blairi,* the male being the smaller of the pair, are somewhat rare and a nice little reminder of that time in my life."

"They actually are quite beautiful," Julie said, studying them closely.

"I've always been drawn to uncommon beauty, until I met Michelle."

Keith gave his wife a gentle kiss on the forehead, and though the moment was sweet, Julie found it painful. Reminders of all she had lost would be everywhere now. With time, she hoped, they would be easier to accept, though she doubted they could ever be ignored.

"He's still drawn to uncommon beauty," Michelle said, a hint of disapproval in her voice. "Now he has rats. A cage of them he keeps downstairs. What are there, six?"

Keith looked a little annoyed.

"About," he said. "They're actually wonderful pets, and much easier to take care of than dogs."

"But less cuddly than cats," Michelle felt inclined to add.

Keith rolled his eyes. "I think rats are marvelously intelligent and trainable," he said. "I breed them, it's a hobby. Happy to show you."

Winston had made Julie a little uneasy at first. She could not imagine how she would respond to a cage of rats, but she was not about to find out.

"I think I'll pass," Julie said.

Keith's expression took a serious turn. "I know you and Michelle have talked since the funeral," he said. "But I wanted you to know that the service was very moving. Your eulogy brought tears to my eyes."

"And he doesn't cry easily," Michelle said in a way that suggested some exasperation with her husband's stoicism.

"Thank you," said Julie.

The service had been well attended and utterly heartbreaking. Sam's parents flew back from Michigan, and other relatives and friends traveled even greater distances to pay their respects. Julie's father had died five years ago, but her seventy-nine-year-old mother was there, supportive as always.

Julie had managed to get through her speech. In it, she talked about Sam: his heart, his compassion, his love for his students, many of whom had come. Many of them were in tears.

"Ever since the funeral, I've been letting people turn in front of me," Keith said. "Your eulogy really made me think."

It had made a lot of people think, from what Julie heard afterwards.

"Sam loved to ride. It brought him tremendous joy," Julie had said at the service. "One thing I noticed on our long rides together was that Sam would always slow down and let another driver make a turn, or go in front of him. It wasn't simply a kind gesture on his part. He was saying something else. He was saying to the other driver, 'Where you are going is just as important as where I am going.' This was a theme of his life—your journey is just as important as my journey. He genuinely cared about the lives of other people, and wanted to know everything he could about their journey. And it was this that drew people to Sam's side."

"I had the same reaction as Keith," Michelle said. "It's like I have a whole new awareness."

"I'm glad to know that. I just spoke the truth. That was who Sam was."

"You must still be reeling," Michelle said.

"Well, to be honest," Julie said, "I've been a bit obsessed."

"Obsessed? How so?" Michelle asked.

Keith excused himself to fetch another bottle of wine from the cellar. "Don't get lost down there," Michelle said. Then to Julie, "I swear, that basement is like his own beetle burrow. He'll vanish for hours, fiddling away on different projects. Anyway, you were saying."

"Right, my obsession. The lab results from pathology came back and supported my friend Lucy's conclusion. Sam died of takotsubo cardiomyopathy."

Michelle gave a slight shrug. "Is that unusual?"

"Highly," Julie said. "It's atypical in men. Usually it's women over fifty who get it, but it's rare for them as well. It's sometimes referred to as 'broken heart syndrome.' It's a stress phenomenon that may be caused by a sudden surge of stress-related hormones, so it could also be triggered by fear."

"Is it always fatal?" Michelle asked.

"No," Julie said. "Often the condition reverses itself within a week. It feels like a heart attack, but it's extremely rare for it to be a fatal one."

"So it's different than a heart attack," Michelle said.

"It is a heart attack, but an unusual one. The EKG read is very distinct. It's typically not trigged by heart disease, because it's stress-based, and the autopsy confirmed Sam's arteries weren't blocked. Other than that ballooning, Sam's heart was perfectly healthy. I've never seen a case of it, and neither have any of the cardiologists at White I spoke with. It's very rare—two percent of heart attacks, maybe less."

"And you said it's mostly found in women."

"Menopausal women, to be precise, and yes, ninety percent of the time."

"So that makes Sam's case even more unusual," Michelle said, taking a sip of her wine.

"I'm looking for an expert on takotsubo," Julie said. "Someone who could review the slides."

"There's nobody at White?"

"Not the foremost expert that I'm looking for," Julie said. "You'd think with my contacts, I'd be able to find the right person, but it's not that easy."

"Not that easy for what?" Keith asked, returning to the room with a dusty bottle of red wine.

"Julie is looking for a medical expert who knows about cardio—something," Michelle said.

"Takotsubo cardiomyopathy," Julie said.

Keith thought hard a moment. "Ah yeah, I've heard of it. Ballooned ventricle. Very unusual."

He opened the wine, but left it on the table to breathe.

"It's how Sam died," Michelle said.

"We think," Julie clarified. "It's not definitive. But the up in a healthy markers are there. I'm trying to figure out why it showed up in a healthy male heart when there wasn't any associated stress event."

"Nobody at White could help?" Keith asked.

Julie shook her head, looking defeated. Never before had she spent more time in White Memorial's sizable research library than she had over these past few days. Her obsessive nature had gotten Julie through medical school, and it kicked in again to fuel her research into this rare heart ailment. Over the course of several days she had nearly drained a bottle of saline drops to keep moisture in eyes dried from hours spent gazing at the computer screen.

"Lots of dead ends and not a lot of leads. I got some names, but so far not a lot of callbacks. Look up 'busy' in the dictionary, and you'll find a picture of a cardiologist."

Julie was being kind. She had knocked on the doors of almost every cardiologist at White. Badgered them with questions until they stole glances at the clock or their pager. Most were polite, most respected her motivation, but all could give her only a smidge more than what she'd gleaned from her own research. The disease was too unusual for any of them to have more than a cursory understanding of it.

Every ailment had its guru to whom other docs turned for counsel, to whom their patients were referred. Julie needed to find that person for takotsubo cardiomyopathy, but he or she was as elusive as the reason Sam had suddenly presented with the condition.

"We deal with that callback challenge all the time," Michelle said. "Very Much Alive is always on the hunt for doctors who support our mission."

Julie's expression brightened. "You know, I should have asked you sooner," she said.

"Asked me what?"

"Very Much Alive—you guys are a global organization, right?"

"That's right. A lot of our focus is on US law, but there are international implications to what we do, sure."

"And you network with doctors all the time," Julie said.

Keith chuckled as if to say that was an understatement. "Michelle's more networked than an HMO," he said.

"So you must know how to find these doctors. Not only from various hospitals, but online too."

"We do monitor the Internet to look for trends," Michelle said. "It's one way we identify thought leaders in various fields."

"Then maybe you can help me find my takotsubo expert. I could post my questions to the more popular Web sites and message boards, at least. See if I get any hits."

Michelle nodded with enthusiasm. "Absolutely," she said. "I'd be thrilled to help. Especially if it can bring you some closure."

"But after we eat," Keith added. "Our food is getting cold."

Keith escorted everyone to a beautifully set table, served generous portions of his beef stir-fry, and poured wine into new glasses. Julie smiled and thanked him, but she was too anxious to eat. Michelle had given Julie something that had been as elusive as the expert she sought. She gave Julie hope she could find out exactly how Sam died.

CHAPTER 21

Lincoln Cole had been sitting for hours in the white cargo van parked across the street from Julie's apartment. Tell someone you work as a private investigator, and they'd probably conjure up an image of a wisecracking gumshoe with a thirst for adventure. The reality was much less glamorous, but Lincoln had had no delusions about the work when he left law enforcement for self-employment. He'd expected the hours of waiting for something to happen, and that was what he got: lots of waiting, lots of spying on cheating spouses, lots of surveillance work, lots of background checks, and lots of boredom.

Lincoln had skills, though. He was an ex-cop, after all—albeit one with an anger management issue, according to the brass who shit-canned him ten years back. The closest thing to a criminal is a cop, so yeah, Lincoln had all sorts of skills that he applied to his new trade.

As a general practice, private investigators did not

operate above the law, but Lincoln was adept at circumventing it. The straight-up corporate gigs paid well enough, but the ones that required him to cross some legal lines always paid the best. The question Lincoln had been asking himself of late was where to draw that line. He was fifty, and this was really a younger man's game. His savings were respectable, but Lincoln had no desire to live a respectable life. He wanted to be down in St. John's, sipping piña coladas and getting caught in the rain. He had no commitments here in Boston, no wife, no kids, and he still had his looks, thank God for that, but it would help to have the cash to attract the kind of women who appealed to his sensibilities: long on legs and short on needs.

To offset damage to his body from hours sitting in his van, Lincoln worked out religiously. For a man half a century old, he kept in fantastic shape. He weighed 180 on the nose and stood five feet eight inches tall, perfectly average all around, which was good for a business that often required him to blend into his environment. Despite having a slender frame, Lincoln could still bench 225 with ease, knock out 120 sit-ups in two minutes, and he moved athletically for a guy who never went beyond high school sports. He suffered from male pattern baldness, but thanks to a nicely round head could rock a buzz cut like Bruce Willis. He kept his face clean-shaven so he could apply various facial hair disguises, which went with the large collection of wigs he owned. Lincoln put on personas the way others did pants. It was a part of the job he loved.

The job tonight was Julie Devereux. She had been his sole source of income for the better part of a week. He had no idea why she was on his employer's radar. It was not his business to ask. He was paid to get information, which in this case required him to keep tabs on everything Dr. Devereux did and said, and to track everywhere she went.

Lincoln had been with the van the whole time, feeding the meter frequently because Dr. Julie had been out of his sight for hours. Even without visual contact, Lincoln knew exactly where she had gone. She had driven to Shrewsbury and back, which matched the plan Lincoln had heard Julie make on a phone call to a woman named Michelle.

Lincoln liked the new software from TrueSpy. It gave him total control over Julie's Android phone. Without her knowing, he could, among other things, listen in on her calls, read her messages, and track her location via the phone's built-in GPS. None of this was legal, of course. None of these tactics were sanctioned by the USAPI, the governing body of private investigators. But that organization could care less about Lincoln's modest savings account, or his plan to sip cocktails on some faraway beach with leggy blondes. So screw them.

From the shadows of the van, Lincoln watched Julie turn her car into the garage adjacent to her Cambridge apartment building. Evidently the good doctor could afford a deeded parking space in the lower levels.

Lincoln retreated to the back of the van, where he turned on all six fifteen-inch video monitors. The monitors were secured to a custom-made metal rig and stacked in two rows of three. Soon enough Julie would be back in Lincoln's sight.

In one of the center consoles, Lincoln watched Julie enter her condominium and hang her coat in the front hall closet. The camera recording her every moment was hidden inside a hollow plant holder that held a nice assortment of fake flowers. A few days back, while Julie was at work, Lincoln had entered her home and cut a small hole into that plant holder. He'd pushed the lens completely flush against the hole so there was no noticeable gap, and affixed the unit with duct tape to secure it.

Getting inside was easy. He could have picked the locks, but instead put on a janitor disguise and gained access to Julie's office at work. He snatched her keys and phone from her purse during a long hospital shift. He installed the TrueSpy software on her phone and had copies of the keys made at a place he knew did not bother to check ID. Lincoln returned the items, and Julie never knew they had gone missing.

The feeds from inside the condo were being broadcast wirelessly, through an encrypted channel. Lincoln could access them from his home computer if he wanted. But he'd told his employer he would be outside when she got home, and he'd keep watch until she fell asleep. It was their dime, after all. Lincoln had no idea where this job was headed, but his gut told him it would involve a lot more than illegal spying.

Again Lincoln thought about his imaginary line dividing legal activities from the other kind. How far was he willing to step across? He guessed the answer depended on how much his employer was willing to pay.

On a different monitor, Lincoln watched Julie wash her hands in the kitchen sink, then rummage through her fridge, ultimately electing to eat nothing. He had hidden this camera inside a wall socket near the toaster oven, which gave him a good view of the cooking area and the kitchen island where Julie and Trevor ate most of their meals. He had used wall sockets for a few other hidden cameras, including the ones in Julie's bedroom and the bathroom.

Lincoln thought this was a fine-looking home, much nicer than his apartment in East Boston. The kitchen was large and spacious, with stainless steel appliances, granite counters, cherry cabinets, and hardwood floors throughout. The other rooms were just as nice. Not that Lincoln lived in a hovel, but nothing about his apartment was upscale or inviting. He never entertained, and when he did sleep with women, it was always at their places, not his. Except for a few drinking buddies from his policing days, Lincoln kept few close ties. Most people pissed him off eventually.

Julie left the kitchen. The next time she showed up it was on the monitor in the bottom row, far left. She had entered the boy's bedroom. Lincoln knew her son was with Paul, but Winston, the guinea pig, had stayed behind. Julie checked the pet's water and food, then left that room as well.

In a different monitor, Lincoln watched Julie pee. It did not turn him on or anything—he was not sick like that—but when she changed into a nightshirt and underwear, he got a good look at her body and felt a little stir down there. For a woman in her forties, Julie Devereux was quite the looker. She was not the kind of taut twenty-five-year-old he fantasized about having his way with on the beach, but she had a respectable physique. He would have no qualms inviting her into the sack.

Anything he did to Julie, though, would require a cash payment from his employer. He could not think of one reason they would want him to do the horizontal bop, but he could conceive of other things they might ask.

How far over that imaginary line are you willing to go, Lincoln Cole?

He thought about those white-sand beaches and doing a whole lot of nothing all day long. Depending on the payday, he could cross that line as far as this job took him.

CHAPTER 22

Allyson led Romey into Suburban West's expansive boardroom. The members—four men and two women, business and community leaders from the western suburbs of Boston—sat along one side of the long cherrywood table. Allyson took a seat next to the vice chairman of the board, an owl-faced man in his sixties named Thomas Winn. Romey wore his best suit to the meeting—a solid blue Paul Fredrick number that hung just right across his shoulders and had a slimming effect when buttoned.

Tremendous effort had gone into preparing for this meeting, and Romey felt confident the outcome would be in his favor. He also came with more than just assurances of better days ahead. He could not simply offer up a carrot and expect these seasoned business leaders to follow him, salivating. He was no snake oil salesman. Romey had to guarantee the reward and thereby assume most of the risk, eliminating at least one major obstacle the board might present. The biggest wild card remained Allyson. Would she play Romey's game, or a game of her own?

Instead of sitting, Romey placed his briefcase on a chair and pushed it away, making room for him to stand. Standing made his short stature a benefit, as it allowed him to look down to make eye contact with each member of the board seated across from him.

He began immediately, with no introduction. He was on the agenda, and he had seen the e-mail that went around with his bio attached. No reason for redundancy. Administrators like Romey did not need an M.D. degree to be respected. They needed only to produce results, which Romey's resume supplied in spades. He had climbed from assistant comptroller at White Memorial to comptroller, with no other candidates interviewed for the position. Romey, who was a wizard at hospital finance, had saved the CFO from his own idiocy on many occasions. The CEO back then took notice, to the point of replacing the CFO with Romey. In this new position Romey pulled out all the stops and the hospital began not only to improve its financial position, but to flourish. When the CEO retired, the board wanted to continue the hospital's moneymaking ways and promoted Romey to the head position. He had never given the board cause to doubt their decision, something the White Memorial balance sheets made quite clear to the board at Suburban West.

"Health care is a changing industry and I am afraid, my friends, that your small suburban hospital is a dinosaur." *That's it, Romey—start 'em off with a bang.* He paused for effect.

"Even a repeal of the Affordable Care Act won't change what is afoot," he continued. "The changes being driven by Medicare are being picked up by private insurance plans and health systems. To profit in this new ecosystem, providers must become better, smarter—in a word, healthier. The job of the health system is to provide the right care, in the right place, at the right time." Romey could quote the Center for Medicare and Medicaid Studies the way Shakespearian scholars could recite a sonnet.

"CMS wants all Medicare patients to be served by a broad-based accountable care organization," Romey said. "And as we all know, Medicare is the bread upon which we spread our butter."

A board member seated across from Romey spoke up. "What is an accountable care organization? I've heard the term tossed around plenty of times but never quite grasped the concept, I'm afraid."

Romey returned a smile. The woman who spoke was Lydia Dutton, short-haired with a pointed gaze. She was the CEO of Dutton Capital, a financial services firm headquartered in Worcester. Romey had come to this meeting armed with a deep knowledge of each board member. Not the sort of sordid details he had dug up on Allyson Brock, though he would gladly go on another hunting expedition if any board member got in his way.

"It's a fine question, Mrs. Dutton," Romey said. "An ACO is a network of physicians, outpatient services, inpatient care, and other services like rehab and home health care. The goal of every ACO is to share risk with Medicare and private insurers. Some patients are sicker, some are healthier, but in the end the profits are larger because the network has cost efficiencies and is better at absorbing the cost of care differences.

"But the most striking difference in the ACO model

is how we get paid," he continued. "Because the money comes in up front, we are in fact more incentivized to keep people healthy.

"I'll give you an example. Let's say Medicare gives you a hundred dollars for the care of your uncle Paul and that's all the money they'll give. We want Uncle Paul to get well and not come back to the hospital. The more he comes back, the more he eats into our profits. But there's a problem. It's going to cost you a hundred twenty dollars to put Paul back together again, but it costs me only twenty because I have the right staff and equipment at my facility, plus my costs are lower because my buying power is higher. We're partners because we're in an ACO together, so you send Uncle Paulie to me, and I give you thirty for the referral and make fifty in profits. You made money, I made money, and Uncle Paul is back to playing his weekly tennis match. That's the ACO way, and it's why White Memorial has become the most profitable health-care system in Massachusetts—in fact, in all of New England."

"Thank you for clarifying," Lydia said.

"What's your pitch, Mr. Janowski?" Bernard Levy was the CEO of a large surgical and medical instrument manufacturer. His hobby was auto racing, and it came as no surprise that he wanted Romey to speed up the proceedings.

"What White Memorial is offering you is the opportunity to become a part of our accountable care organization," Romey said. "Join us, and in addition to the services you have here, you will be able to take advantage of the services we have in the city and share in the profit. Your patients will see no difference—only you'll now be able to offer them the backup of an expansive urban network."

Levy looked intrigued as he rested his chin on his hands. "So we get paid to send you patients. Is that it?"

"We share resources, and by resources, yes: patients are included. As a network, we all play for the same team—and not to sound boastful, but you want White on your team. We have three hundred sixty-seven physicians and mid-level providers, including our nurse practitioners and physician assistants. We also have a team of hospitalists and intensivists who manage all the inpatient care for our physicians. We are the premier trauma hospital in the greater Boston area and the first choice for ambulances transporting victims of gunshots and car accidents. And since we have inpatient rehab, patients can be transferred there earlier than at other hospitals, making their recovery swift."

"And the profits higher." Lydia Dutton smiled and Romey thought, *That's it, two in the bag.*

Vince Hanke, chairman of the board and owner of dry cleaning establishments across the western suburbs, piped up. "This sounds great for you big boys, but we are a relatively small hospital with only a hundred and thirty beds. And we know our patients like us as a neighborhood hospital."

"Well, Mr. Hanke," Romey said, "I'm afraid those days are coming to an end. Look at your last five years. Every year your volumes have dropped, and so have your margins. Allyson has tried to keep up through cost-saving measures, but it's like swimming against the tide."

Romey glanced over at Allyson, who kept up her

stoic expression, making it hard to gauge if she was going to go off script or not.

"If you don't jump on the ACO bandwagon now," Romey continued, "while the terms are favorable, a larger provider is going to come here and gobble you up and take all the profits with them. There is a premium I'm willing to pay for early entry. Further down the road another player, I'm afraid to say—even White—might not be so generous. And that day is coming sooner rather than later. Your own balance sheet is red flag enough."

A moment of silence allowed reality to sink in.

"How would you envision this moving forward, Mr. Janowski?"

Romey sensed that Vince Hanke would still take more cajoling. Change did not come easily to anybody, but at the end of the day, money was the motivator for everyone at this table.

"I want to start tomorrow by entering into a management agreement with you," Romey said. "White Memorial will send over a temporary CEO who will begin the process of converting your hospital to the ACO model. And I will begin the transfer arrangements for your patients who would be better served at our larger facility. Your rehab patients make a good place to start."

"What about our medical staff?" Dave Craig sounded angry, with good reason. A gastroenterologist and chief of the medical staff, he would bear the brunt of the upheaval.

"During the transition, your staff would practice just as always. As we move things along, we will train your physicians in the White ACO way of doing business. They'll learn how to integrate their treatment plans with the network available to them. We'll teach them how to move patients through our continuum of care, and by doing so minimize the cost of that care while maximizing the quality. I am certain that when your doctors realize the payback from risk-sharing with the feds and other insurers is robust, they will be happy to participate in this new system. Higher profits for you should trickle down to your physicians. This is a win for everyone involved."

"What if our patients don't want to go to the city for care? White Memorial hasn't always had the best reputation." The dissenting voice came from Rabbi Sarah Gertz, who represented the interests of the labor unions and members of the community at large.

"Ah, bad reputations live longer than they should, and new ones take a long time to get started," Romey said. "There is the old White Memorial under the old regime, and the new White Memorial under my direction. I think you'll find quite a difference between the two. Certainly we cannot force a patient to use White, but we count on word of mouth from the patients who do use the facility, and we offer a wide range of amenities to convince them to come back to us if they must. Once a person has been to White, will they spread the word? I'm betting a lot of capital on this arrangement that the answer will be yes."

"And our employees? What about Allyson?" Vince Hanke glanced over at Allyson, who looked increasingly uncomfortable in her seat.

Yes, what about her? Romey thought.

"Allyson and I have discussed this arrangement in great detail," Romey said. "All of the numbers are in the packet we provided for your review. She has gone over them carefully, as has your CFO. Allyson will of course assist with the transition effort as co-CEO, and we'll jointly manage PR to make sure the right messages are sent to the community, hospital staff, and to your patients. Naturally, we'll reevaluate Allyson's role and position with Suburban West once the transition effort is complete."

Vince fixed Allyson with a peculiar stare. "Allyson, is this true?"

Allyson straightened her suit and cleared her throat. Maybe it was only Romey who could see the strain in her eyes, who noticed her wan complexion. This was the moment of truth, and Romey felt a kick to his heart. If Allyson defied him, he would destroy her.

"Financially, this deal favors the board and the patients of Suburban West," Allyson began. "As a board member, and hospital CEO, I have a fiduciary responsibility to recommend what is in the best interest of Suburban West and its stakeholders." Allyson turned her head to look Roman Janowski squarely in the eyes. "Therefore, I recommend Mr. Jankowski's proposal without reservation."

Romey let go the breath he had been holding and finally took a drink of water. All that talking had left him feeling parched.

CHAPTER 23

It was a crisp autumn afternoon in early November, three weeks after Sam's death. Most of the leaves had escaped from their branches and the slate-gray sky held the stark promise of winter. Parents and friends on the sidelines watched the soccer game, draped in heavy coats and scarves. Some were cocooned beneath blankets pulled over their lawn chairs.

Julie knew most of her fellow spectators by name, but the soccer field was where their orbits collided. She stood next to Paul, who sipped hot coffee from a thermos. The game was almost over. The score remained a one-to-one tie.

Julie felt good to be doing something other than working or continuing her search for an expert's opinion on Sam's death. She held out hope that an expert would emerge from the shadows soon enough. With Michelle's help, they had posted Julie's inquiry on the most trafficked blogs and medical message boards. That seed-scattering approach should eventually bear fruit.

Right now, though, it was all about the game.

The left wing's pass to Trevor came as a perfect feed between two defenders. Trevor, patient and aware, waited until the first defender committed to the ball before he made his cut. Julie squeezed her hands together as the excitement built in her chest. The rest of the crowd, some twenty-odd spectators, must have felt it as well, because their collective voices rose to a fever pitch.

Matt Davis, the father of one of the midfielders, shouted, "Shoot!" so loud that Julie jumped a little. But Trevor did not fire off a rocket like he could have. A defender had quickly closed in and any shot Trevor took would most likely have been deflected.

Instead, Trevor pulled the ball back with his foot, then a scissor move, before cutting hard to his left. To Julie's adoring eyes, Trevor looked like The Flash dressed in his red uniform. Showcasing deft footwork, Trevor maneuvered the ball to his left foot as two defenders in white uniforms encroached on the ball with speed. Trevor's window of opportunity was closing fast.

Riverton Academy, a private school in Cambridge with 350 students in grades six through eight, prided itself on academics and athletics. The boys' and girls' soccer teams were the crown jewels of its sporting programs. Trevor had plenty of natural ability, but he'd lacked the drive to be more than a role player for the Riverton Hawks middle school team.

Since Sam's death, however, Trevor seemed to have found his wheels. The last game had been his first as a starter. He still had zero goals on the season, but that could change if he took the shot.

"Shoot, Trevor!" Paul yelled.

Julie sucked in a breath as her body tensed. How was it that a kids' soccer game got her nerves jangling like a code blue?

Trevor feigned a cut to his right, swung back his left leg, and brought it forward with speed. The ball shot off the ground with velocity and immediately gained height. It passed between two defenders without deflection and was on a trajectory to hit the upper right corner of the goal. Julie's hands went to her mouth.

The goalie, a tall boy with the body build of a marsh reed, leapt to his right with his arms outstretched. The ball curved as it spun. Julie held her breath as she watched the ball skim the goalie's fingertips and smash into the back of the netting.

Trevor dropped to his knees and thrust a triumphant fist into the air. He was soon swallowed by a sea of red jerseys that toppled on him in a gigantic pig pile of bodies. The referee blew the whistle that ended the game, with the Hawks taking the win on Trevor's magnificent goal.

Paul and Julie hugged, and Julie hugged some other parents who were just as excited as she was. They'd probably post pictures online before they returned to their cars.

After the game, the kids organized into two lines—one of white jerseys, the other of red—and did the walk where they slapped hands and said "Good job," or "Good game" in monotone voices. Afterward, the Hawks gathered on the sideline with their coach, arms draped around each other in a tight huddle, looking like they would be friends forever.

The whole scene got Julie choked up, especially the look of pure joy on her son's face. They'd had so little to celebrate of late that the small things in life took on a whole new significance. She was more keenly aware of the moments—how precious they were, how quickly it all slipped away.

"What a game," Paul said. "I told Trevor I'd take him for an ice cream. You want to join?"

"Maybe," Julie said, when her phone rang.

The caller ID came up unknown, which made Julie think telemarketer. She answered anyway, because she was curious.

"Hello," she said, using a hand gesture to excuse herself from Paul and the rest of the crowd.

"Hello," said a female computerized voice.

I knew it.

"This is a collect call from—"

"Brandon Stahl," said a real man's voice.

"—an inmate at MCI Cedar Junction," the female voice continued. "Will you accept the charges?"

Julie was too stunned to speak. Of course she knew the name Brandon Stahl—not only from the news, but also from White Memorial, where he'd worked as a nurse. After his murder conviction, Julie wrote an op-ed for *The Boston Globe* that did not condone his actions, but made a point of saying the tragedy should start a conversation about patient rights, and the right to death with dignity.

A day or so later, the comments section in the on-line version of the *Globe* article was disturbingly vile. What some people felt compelled to post online went beyond unsettling and bordered on threatening. Julie eventually had to stop reading. She had tried to make it clear in her op-ed piece that she was not an advocate

for murder, but rather for patient rights. Judging by the
slew of letters sent to White, it was a distinction lost
on many.

But that was several years ago. Why on earth would
Brandon Stahl be calling her now? And how on earth
did he have Julie's cell phone number? Her head became dizzy with questions, but she was with it enough
to accept the charges. She had to know what he wanted.

LINCOLN COLE had parked his van in the lot across
from the soccer field, where he could watch Julie without using his powerful binoculars. This had been
another slow day of doing lots of nothing at all. Lincoln
was beginning to wonder where this job was headed.
Not all of Lincoln's clients paid in cash, or paid this
well, so Lincoln was happy to stay patient. The talking
heads on sports radio jabbered on about Sunday's Pats
game. It amazed him how much mileage they could get
from one little running back controversy. So what if a
guy missed practice and got sent home? He deserved it.
And besides, the game had evolved to make the running
back the real walking dead.

Lincoln thought of changing stations when the
TrueSpy app on his computer began to chirp. Evidently,
Dr. Julie had received a phone call. Sure enough, out
the window Lincoln could see she had moved away
from the crowd with her phone pressed to her ear.

For just this reason, Lincoln kept his laptop charged
and running on the seat beside him at all times, like
a terminal from back in his patrol car days. TrueSpy
automatically broadcast Julie's phone calls through
his computer speakers, but Lincoln made sure the

entire conversation got captured as a digital transcript as well.

The start of the call left Lincoln puzzled.

"Hello, this is a collect call from—"

"Brandon Stahl."

"—an inmate at MCI Cedar Junction. Will you accept the charges?"

"Yes," Julie said.

Brandon Stahl?

Lincoln knew the name. The case had garnered big press around these parts. But why would a notorious prisoner want to call Dr. J? He thought they had worked for the same hospital, so maybe that was the connection.

"I don't have long, so I have to speak quickly," Brandon Stahl said. Stahl spoke in a subdued manner, not much edge. *Not the kind of guy who thrives behind bars,* Lincoln thought.

"Go ahead," Julie said.

"We worked for the same hospital, White Memorial."

"I know."

"I've been in prison for three years."

"I know that as well."

"They think I killed Donald Colchester."

"They don't think. You were convicted. What's this about?"

"I can't tell you over the phone. Not enough time. But can you make arrangements to come visit me in prison? Tuesdays are typically good."

"And why would I want to do that?"

"Because you're asking lots of questions about takotsubo cardiomyopathy, and someone thinks that condition is the reason I'm going to die in prison."

When the call ended, Lincoln made sure the TrueSpy app had properly captured a transcript of the conversation. His employers would want to know about this development right away.

CHAPTER 24

Imposing.

That was the first word that popped into Julie's head as she stood at the base of a twenty-foot-high wall topped by razor wire. The sun appeared as a pale disc behind a thin cover of clouds. It was Election Day in the Commonwealth, but the inmates would not be voting. Julie did up the top button of her camel hair coat to protect herself from a chilly November wind. The gray prison walls matched a bleak landscape that held all the warmth of a morgue.

Aerial photos of MCI Cedar Junction that Julie had sourced online showed something that resembled a college campus with concrete and brick buildings nestled close together, grassy areas for inmate recreation, black-top basketball courts, and even a regulation-size baseball field. From the ground Julie found it stark and profoundly intimidating. The massive walls kept out all noise, even birdsong, and the eerie quiet heightened her anxiety.

Julie parked in the visitor lot adjacent to the institution rotary and locked her car as required by prison rules. She followed signs to the visitor-processing trap and wondered again why it had such an ominous-sounding name. She half expected to find protesters camped out in front of the prison entrance, but without news cameras they had no audience and no reason to be there.

She pulled open the glass and metal doors to the front entrance and stepped into an austere lobby, sterile as any hospital ward. Julie swallowed hard as she approached the reception area, barricaded behind Plexiglas. She knew to leave her valuables in the car, including the engagement ring Sam had given her.

Underneath her coat, Julie had on black slacks and a white blouse because she had no idea what one should wear to a prison visit. She wanted something benign, not too dressy, but not too casual either, and hoped she had struck the right note. Turned out she was the best dressed here. Some of the other visitors (all of them women, who came in a variety of shapes, sizes, and colors) wore uniforms for retail jobs, or had on casual clothing such as baggy sweats and oversized shirts. These were hardened women who appeared to have led hard lives and were connected somehow to the hard men locked inside. Julie interacted with people from all walks of life at her job, so this part of the experience was not especially unnerving.

A heavyset woman wearing the red shirt/khaki pants uniform of a Target employee tried to pull open the entrance door. It was locked from the inside and Julie then understood the meaning of the visitor trap. This was a prison. You could get in, but you could not get out.

Following prison policy, Julie had scheduled her visit

forty-eight hours earlier, and slept poorly for two nights. Her thoughts swirled with possibilities as she tried to make a connection between a high-profile inmate in the state's maximum-security prison and her deceased fiancé. She got in line behind four other women and waited her turn at the processing window. Nobody spoke. This place did not lend itself to friendly chitchat.

A stern-faced woman dressed in a blue uniform took Julie's ID and ran it through a series of checks. Julie spent several minutes filling out the necessary forms. Once approved, Julie slipped her coat inside a locker and then passed through a metal detector on her way to the secured steel door just beyond. A trap guard, bigger than BC quarterback Max Hartsock, opened the heavy door as soon as everyone in the group had cleared the metal detector.

Julie followed the phalanx down a long, brightly lit corridor. There were no shadows here, probably by design. The door slammed shut behind her and Julie's heart jumped a little.

They marched in silence with the guard leading the way. Julie listened to the lonely slap of her footsteps against the linoleum flooring. The life energy here was utterly alien. She could not imagine a worse place a person could be.

Taking her assigned seat on a tall-backed metal stool, Julie turned it to face a scuffed Plexiglas divider marked by handprints and coated with a film of prison grime. Her side of the room was a big open space. A meager splash of sunlight filtered in through a row of hopper windows ten feet off the ground and covered in mesh wire. Other visitors took up the remaining stools and waited. They appeared practiced at this and far more at ease than Julie, who clutched her hands in nervous anticipation.

On the other side of the glass partition was a room big enough to walk single file. Julie could see a single metal door off to the left. At precisely 12:30 P.M. a loud buzzer sounded and a guard opened the door. In shuffled a row of severe-looking men, who, like the visitors, came in a variety of shapes, sizes, and colors.

Each man took a seat at his assigned window and the room instantly filled with chatter, indiscriminate as at any party. A man carrying a large manila envelope seated himself in front of Julie. She recognized him from various media reports, but he looked like a phantom of the image splashed across the evening news.

Julie's first thought was that Brandon Stahl was too frail to survive in here, among such men. He had a thin build, delicate face, and a smallish head topped by a wavy mop of brown hair that descended past his forehead to tickle his eyes. A full goatee, peppered with gray hairs, could not offset the liability of Brandon's high cheekbones, and did not give him the prison look of the other inmates. He had on a beige uniform reminiscent of the nurse's scrubs he'd once worn. The short sleeves revealed no tattoos, not that they would have made him any more threatening. His sunken eyes, dark like the rings surrounding them, conveyed profound sadness. Years behind bars had not hardened Brandon, but appeared to have drained him of life force.

After he settled, Brandon pushed a few strands of hair away from his face, picked up the phone on his side of the divider, and indicated Julie should do the same.

"Thank you for coming to see me," Brandon said into the phone.

He had the compassionate, gentle voice of a nurse—a tone she knew so well. Compared to the other voices Julie heard rattling about the visitation room, abrasive and angry as blaring horns, Brandon spoke with the sweet timbre of a flute.

Someone thinks that condition is the reason I'm going to die in prison. Brandon's words came back to her. Was it possible Julie was speaking with an innocent man?

"Needless to say, I was surprised by your call," Julie said. "I'm eager to know how you think your case is connected to Sam Talbot. And how you even know anything about him, or me, for that matter."

"You've been putting out a lot of queries online. That's how I know about you."

Julie believed him. She and Michelle had spent several hours posting to various Web-based resources looking for a takotsubo expert. This man serving a life sentence had been her only bite.

"I didn't know you had access to the Internet in prison."

"It's limited," Brandon said. "But that's not how I found out about you."

"I thought you said—"

"That's how my secret admirer found out about you."

"Secret admirer?"

"I have someone who believes in my innocence. He or she, I don't know, discovered your posts and brought them to my attention. My admirer also included your cell phone number."

The revelation unnerved Julie more than a little. Someone knew enough about her to pass along private information to a convicted murderer.

"Do you have any idea who this secret admirer of yours could be?"

"None," Brandon said. "But I'll tell you this. It's someone who really knows medicine."

"A doctor?"

"That's what I'm thinking."

"What can I do for you, Brandon? Why is it you wanted to meet with me?"

Brandon thought a moment.

"How much do you know about my story?"

"Only what I've heard on the news."

This was a bit of a lie. Julie had done extensive research on the Colchester murder case before her visit. She wanted to be prepared, but did not want Brandon to think she came here with any prejudgment. For this meeting to be of value, Brandon had to believe Julie could be an ally in his fight.

"I didn't kill Donald Colchester. Donald wanted to die, but I didn't help him."

This part of Brandon Stahl's case had been well documented during the sensational trial that took place several years ago. Donald Colchester suffered from end-stage ALS. The ravages of his disease had taken a significant toll, and prior to his death, Donald had become totally paralyzed. Though he was never a patient in Julie's ICU, Donald lived at White Memorial as a permanent resident in the long-term acute-care floor where Brandon once worked as a nurse.

Julie had reviewed Donald Colchester's medical records before this visit. She saw no reports of recurrent infections, pneumonia, sepsis, or kidney inflammation, all of which were common when an ALS patient neared death. He had maintained his body weight, and had no unexplained or refractory fevers, no changes in his level of consciousness. His labs showed no decrease in oxygen saturation, or an increase in tumor markers. Eventually he would present with all of those symptoms and more. But at the time of his death, Donald Colchester, same as Sam Talbot, was paralyzed and wanting to die, but incapable of committing suicide.

"You say you didn't kill Donald Colchester, but then how do you explain the recording?" Julie asked.

"I just told him that I'd help him die because he was so miserable. That's all he ever wanted. I said it thinking he would forget it or get over it. I just wanted to give him a little bit of comfort because he was in so much pain. I told him I'd use morphine, so he'd know it wouldn't hurt. Sometimes words heal more than medicine, you know? All I did was give him a little hope that his suffering would end soon, but I never would kill him—and I didn't."

The recording was the smoking-gun piece of evidence presented at Brandon Stahl's trial. And it had come into existence in a rather scandalous way. Donald's father, William Colchester, a Massachusetts state legislator representing the Fourteenth Suffolk District, became convinced the insurance company and hospital were denying Donald medical services that would improve his quality of life.

The senior Colchester received support from Very Much Alive and other players in the world of healthcare checks and balances. According to Michelle, with whom Julie had spoken about Colchester's case in generalities, denying care was a common practice these days, and something her organization would have fought staunchly to address.

The lawsuit filed by William Colchester attracted massive media attention because it was the representative's son at the center. The suit was ultimately dismissed due to a lack of evidence. However, William Colchester remained unconvinced. He took matters into his own hands and rigged his son's hospital room with a microphone to record conversations. He wanted to hear a doctor or nurse denying some treatment because of cost. What he heard instead was Brandon Stahl agreeing to help his son die.

"Donald Colchester begged me to kill him every single day. That's on the recording, too, if you give it a listen."

Julie felt a stab of pain as she recalled Sam begging the same of her.

Kill me, Julie . . . Please help me die.

"How long after Donald's death did that recording surface?"

"Weeks," Brandon said. "The media would have you think it was William Colchester banging the drum to get better care for his kid, but that's a load of crap. It was the mother, Pamela Colchester, behind it all. She was always on our case about giving her son the very best care. The dad was always pretty detached. I bet you anything bugging the room was her doing and not the father's.

"It was the mother who gave the recording a listen, no surprise there. The surprise came when she heard my promise, and I got arrested for murder. By then, Donald was already in the ground."

"What happened next?"

"My lawyers fought to get the evidence tossed. The Massachusetts wiretapping statute basically says it's illegal to record someone without a person's knowledge. They won. The evidence was thrown out, and the Colchesters were fined and given probation for the illegal wiretap. The case should have been dismissed."

"Except there was a witness," Julie said.

"Except there was a witness," Brandon repeated. "I knew the nurse who testified that she heard me make that promise to kill Donald."

"Sherri Platt," Julie said.

Sherri Platt had been big news during the trial years ago, and big news once again because of Brandon's failed appeal. Brandon's lawyers had argued during appeal that Sherri's testimony was improperly introduced during trial. The appeals judge did not agree.

"Why do you think Sherri waited to come forward during the trial?"

"She said she felt compelled to tell the truth when news broke that the wiretap evidence was ruled inadmissible."

"And you don't deny saying it?"

"I said it, all right. But I didn't mean it. Like I told you, I was trying to ease this guy's suffering. Placate him, you know? It's like a kid begging you to go somewhere. Sometimes you just make a promise without meaning it just to get them to stop asking. It was a stupid thing to say. Obviously, I regret it."

"As I recall, that wasn't the only bit of evidence against you," Julie said.

Brandon gave a nod. "Yeah, police found morphine in my apartment."

"Morphine stolen from White. Can you explain that?"

"No," Brandon said. "But I didn't take any drugs."

"No autopsy," Julie said.

"For a guy with end-stage ALS? Why bother?"

"And the court wouldn't exhume the body?" Julie said. "Cause of death could still be determined, I would think."

"My lawyer filed a request and the prosecution didn't object. Things were moving forward when BAM! The prosecution files a motion to deny the request. Suddenly Daddy Colchester is all upset about the idea of digging up his boy. The judge sides with Colchester, something about not revealing significant exculpatory evidence."

"Who was the judge?" Julie asked.

"The Honorable Robert Josephson, who, by the way, became a superior court judge a year after my trial. And guess which legislator was on the committee that appoints the judges to state court?"

"Um, William Colchester?"

Brandon broke into a lopsided smile. "That's right. You ask me, I'd say Judge Josephson got some favorable treatment for putting the kibosh on our motion to exhume the body."

"Why?"

Brandon shrugged. "No idea. I don't know how the morphine got in my apartment, either. Maybe William Colchester got cold feet about seeing his boy dug up. Or maybe someone made it worth Colchester's while to flex some political muscle."

"What does your secret admirer say about all this?"

Brandon opened the manila envelope he'd carried in with him. "I received this in the mail during the initial trial."

He held a piece of paper up against the window so that Julie could read the typewritten note for herself.

Your defense team is focused on the wrong issue.
Forget about the wiretap evidence. Look closely
at the enclosed EKG of Donald Colchester. Note
the ST elevation and fairly short QT interval.
Other ST-T abnormalities and QT prolongation
with large negative T waves occurring in succession. This readout indicates a rare heart anomaly
called takotsubo cardiomyopathy. The enclosed
cardiac echo shows apical ballooning consistent
with takotsubo. This is a stress-based condition
and the likely cause of death. Morphine did not
kill him. This did.

Julie knew an echo was not routine in chest pain protocols, but Colchester's high profile ensured that when
in distress he got the full workup.

"If you can cast doubt on the morphine theory—"

"I'm probably a free man," Brandon said.

"Show me the EKG and echo, please," Julie said.

Her pulse ticked up as Brandon fished out the images
enclosed with the letter. Who was his secret admirer?
Julie wondered.

Julie could not believe an inmate had access to Colchester's private files. What she could believe was that
the data existed. White Memorial had a state-of-the-art
EMR—electronic medical records—system that up-
loaded patient data to the cloud. Years of data were
collected and kept on permanent record. What Brandon
showed her matched what Julie had seen in Colchester's electronic medical record. It was convincing, but
she would want a cardiologist to have a look.

"What did your defense team do with this evidence?"

"ST-T abnormalities? QT prolongation? What do you think they did? They ignored it," Brandon said.

"Ignored?"

"Look, my parents are dead, I'm a bachelor. I didn't have a lot of cash on hand to begin with. I spent my entire life savings on my defense, which wasn't much. Sure, my team brought it up. Even hired a medical expert, some internist who couldn't explain how to tie a shoe. The prosecution's pathologists and medical experts argued pretty convincingly that the EKG and echo didn't show anything significant enough to have caused Donald's death. Heck, I believed them."

Julie understood. Ninety-five percent of takotsubo cases resolved with a complete recovery. An old adage in medicine went: *Common things occur commonly.* Combine the low probability of a fatal takotsubo event with an eyewitness who heard Brandon offer to kill Donald Colchester and morphine in Brandon's apartment, and the result was a life sentence with no possibility for parole.

"What do you want me to do?" Julie said. "Why did you call?"

"Help me prove that Donald Colchester died of the same thing that killed your husband."

Julie stiffened. "He was my fiancé."

"I'm sorry, my mistake," Brandon said. "And I'm deeply sorry for your loss. But listen, Doc, I'm going to spend the rest of my life in prison for a crime I didn't commit. Somebody thinks you're the only person who can help prove my innocence. I don't know you very well, but I'm willing to believe whoever sent me this information knows what the hell they're talking about."

CHAPTER 25

The day after her meeting with Brandon Stahl, Julie made the short three-block walk from the ICU in the Tsing Pavilion to the Barstow Building, home to White Memorial's famed Center for Cardiac Angiography, Angioplasty, and Arrhythmias, known as the C2A3. It was also where the director of C2A3, Dr. Gerald Coffey, kept a private office.

Dr. Coffey had been with White Memorial since the Pleistocene era, some staffers joked, but back in his day he had been at the forefront of new technical advancements in the field. He was a pioneer of acute myocardial infarction angioplasty, and had helped to perfect the procedure a decade before it became routine. He had completed his clinical training in cardiology at Harvard Medical School, his residency at Mass General Hospital, and a fellowship in cardiac medicine at Johns Hopkins, all best of the best.

The other cardiologists Julie had spoken with about Sam's case suggested she direct her inquiry to Dr. Coffey, but he had been unavailable until now. It was good fortune that his schedule cleared at a time when she had new and perhaps startling information to share.

Julie's legs ached as she hurried to make her appointment on time. She had spent the past five hours on her feet and desperately wanted to decompress in the hospital cafeteria with a cup of mud-colored coffee and *The Boston Globe*. Rare was the morning Julie had time to read the paper, and today was no exception.

Her Wednesday workday had begun just after sunrise, when she met with her ICU nursing staff and respiratory therapists before morning rounds. She was now on an extended lunch break. So far it had been a typically atypical day, with a variety of administrative issues and unpredictable patient ailments.

Julie took the elevator up to the third floor and proceeded down a quiet, carpeted corridor, as dimly lit as any casino. She found Dr. Coffey's office, fourth on the left, and checked the time. One minute before the hour. Good start. She knocked twice, and a voice softened with age told her to enter.

Dr. Coffey's spacious office had a window and a view of the quad. Julie tried to contain her envy; her office was a refurbished maintenance closet, a quarter the size of this one, without any natural light. Dr. Coffey rose from his chair behind an expansive oak desk, giving Julie a look at his thin frame. He extended his hand. His grip was firm as Julie introduced herself. They had never met, but with so many physicians at White, that was no great surprise.

Everything in the office was impeccably neat, from Dr. Coffey's desk to the bookshelves, to the fine mane of silver hair that topped a strong, square-shaped face. He wore black plastic glasses with thick lenses that magnified brown eyes set close to a snub nose. Under-neath a white lab coat he wore a rose-colored shirt adorned by a solid red tie. The office walls were plastered with framed diplomas and certificates, as well as a large photograph of Dr. Coffey playing golf with the mayor of Boston. Another photo showed him inside the cockpit of a plane he piloted.

"Please have a seat," Dr. Coffey said. "Can I offer you something to drink? Lemon water, perhaps?"

He has lemon water in his office?

"No, thank you," Julie said.

Dr. Coffey went to a small refrigerator (he had a refrigerator, too), poured two glasses, and gave one to Julie.

"In case you change your mind," he said. "Now, what can I do for you?"

"I want you to have a look at this EKG, if you wouldn't mind."

Julie produced several printouts from her purse and handed them to Dr. Coffey.

"The patient died," she said. "These were recorded shortly before death."

"You pulled this from an electronic medical record, I assume."

"Yes," Julie said. "The cloud-based system stores everything now."

"Cloud-based." Dr. Coffey said it with contempt. "To me a cloud is something puffy in the sky that one flies through."

"It's just a way of storing data," Julie said, though she did not fully understand the cloud herself. Her son Trevor could explain it to them both.

"Have you ever flown a plane?"

"Can't say that I have."

He pointed to the picture on the wall of him in the cockpit of one. "No feeling like it," Dr. Coffey said. "The only thing that makes me consider retirement is more time in the sky. That's why I'm very protective of my schedule. Got to make the most of every minute."

In her mind, Julie rolled her eyes. This was his not so subtle way of telling her to make it quick.

"I hope this won't take up much of your time," Julie said.

Dr. Coffey adjusted his glasses and cleared his throat, then took a sip of his lemon water.

"Very well," he said. "Let me have a look." He held the eight by ten printouts to his face, but did not study any image for long.

"Yes, I see the AVR elevated here, along with the anterior leads V2, V3, V4. Was the patient male or female?"

"Male."

"Over forty?"

"That's correct," Julie said.

"So it's atherosclerosis disease, buildup of plaque in the arteries."

"But there's no evidence of heart disease in the medical record," Julie said.

"Please," Dr. Coffey said dismissively. "Ten percent of patients have plaque we can't see."

"Can't see? Really?"

"Think of a Twinkie," Dr. Coffey said.

Julie looked baffled. "A Twinkie?"

"Yes. I use this analogy with my Harvard students every year. It connects with them. Now, imagine a large tube that has this Twinkie inside it, such that when you bend the tube where the Twinkie is, it cracks open, causing the white filling that represents free cholesterol to pour into the tube. That stimulates the clotting cascade and an acute thrombus forms. The body naturally produces elements like tissue plasminogen activator, which causes the clot to dissolve, and others that break the residual Twinkie plaque down like Pac-Man-gobbling ghosts. When you come back to the tube at the time of doing an angiogram, you find it clear of the filling and the Twinkie. But that's only temporary. The Twinkie comes back, cracks open again, and gets gobbled up again.

"Now, and I'm just thinking out loud because the EKG is very nonspecific, this could be a coronary artery vasospasm."

"And that is?"

"Smooth muscle constriction of the coronary artery," Dr. Coffey explained. "You can have nonexertional chest pain with ST-segment elevation. Patients may perform normally on the stress test, but constricted blood flow could result in ventricular fibrillation."

"Very well, but have a look at this. It's the patient's echo."

Dr. Coffey reached across his desk and took the printout from Julie's hand.

"Do you notice the apical ballooning of the left ventricle? This echo was taken around the time the patient began complaining of chest pain."

"Who is this patient?"

"Donald Colchester."

Dr. Coffey thought a moment before a look of utter surprise came to his face.

"Colchester? The murder victim from—what? A few years back now. What do you have this for?"

"I'll explain in a moment."

"The nurse who killed him—"

"Brandon Stahl."

"Right, Brandon Stahl, injected his patient with morphine, if my memory serves."

"You're correct. That was in the evidence."

"I don't have to explain to you that an opiate overdose has a high probability of causing a heart attack, do I?" Dr. Coffey looked at the echo more closely. "In this case I'd say Mr. Colchester had a coronary occlusion of the left anterior descending artery, the one that feeds the left ventricle."

"So you wouldn't say this was takotsubo cardiomyopathy?"

Dr. Coffey blinked several times rapidly. "Takotsubo cardiomyopathy? Why would you even say that? Is Mr. Colchester a menopausal woman subjected to some sudden stress event? No, of course not. It is what I said it is."

"A coronary occlusion of the left anterior descending artery," Julie said, repeating what Dr. Coffey had just told her.

"That's right. And what are you doing digging up one of White's most notorious skeletons, anyway? Does this have anything to do with that failed appeal?"

"In a way," Julie said. "And I appreciate the word of caution."

"Not enough to proceed with any, it seems," Dr. Coffey said.

Julie allowed a slight smile. The Donald Colchester

murder was one of the darkest days at White, and Dr. Coffey was right to think her line of inquiry was ill-advised. But some questions demanded answers, just as some convicts deserved their freedom.

"I want to show you something else. It's the pathology report from my fiancé's autopsy."

"Oh dear. That's right. Your fiancé was in that horrible motorcycle crash. I read that on a news bulletin that went around. I'm terribly sorry for your loss."

"Thank you. I appreciate it. But have a look at these slides. You can see the same apical ballooning of the left ventricle. And here the ST elevation registers on his EKG."

Dr. Coffey spent a moment examining the second set of printouts, these belonging to Sam.

"This is just more atherosclerosis. Both these men had heart attacks."

"Both of them had healthy hearts."

"You say healthy. Ten percent have plaque we don't see, remember?"

"The Twinkie."

"Yes, the Twinkie. But in one of these cases the man was murdered, so there's no odd correlation here. Again, I'm sorry for your loss, but it is what it is. You hear hoofbeats you think of horses, not zebras, and you certainly don't think of a unicorn."

"You're saying takotsubo is a unicorn?"

"Absolutely! What condition were these men in?"

"One had end-stage ALS, and the accident left my fiancé quadriplegic."

"So they had long-term, chronic stress for sure." Dr. Coffey paused. "But a *sudden* stress event? I doubt it. Wait a minute. I need to refresh myself."

From a bookshelf, Dr. Coffey pulled a large medical tome and opened to a page he found using the index.

"Here we go," he said. "Yes, that's what I thought. Takotsubo is an abnormal contraction of the left ventricle that extends beyond just one blood vessel. And here's the important part: a stressful trigger will cause an abnormal surge in adrenaline, constricting coronary arteries, which results in poor blood flow downstream. As the stress decreases, the arteries open up again, and the angiogram looks normal."

"Meaning?"

"Meaning if either of them had an acute stress event, which I'm telling you they didn't, when it was over their arteries would have opened up. Which is why takotsubo is so rarely fatal. These patients were men, not subjected to any sudden stress, who suffered *fatal* heart attacks," Dr. Coffey said. "That's not takotsubo. It's an undiagnosed coronary disease in the case of your fiancé, and murder in the other."

"Could you maybe pass these around to get some other thoughts?"

Dr. Coffey's face became a little red. "I don't have time to go through this again, and honestly I don't need you badgering my cardiologists with your questions."

"I'm sorry, I was just trying to understand."

"Oh please," Dr. Coffey said. "A graduate from a state medical school would understand."

Julie tried not to look offended. "I happen to have graduated from a state medical school. UMass Medical School, to be exact."

Dr. Coffey pursed his lips together. "Then try to understand this. We're all under pressure to perform financially and do what's in the best interest of our patients. I suggest you focus on caring for yours, and let me focus on caring for mine. I gave you the answer, so there's nothing more to say. I have another appointment elsewhere, so I'm going to have to end our meeting now."

"I'm sorry to be a bother," she said.

"And I'm going to hold on to these," Dr. Coffey said, slipping the printouts into his desk. His expression bordered on apoplectic. "White Memorial doesn't need a PR nightmare from some rogue ICU doctor making unsubstantiated claims about things she knows nothing about. And I sure as hell don't need Roman Janowski breathing down my neck thinking my department in any way condones your misguided exploration."

Julie stood shakily and backed toward the door. Coffey's rancor had jarred her, leaving her a bit off-kilter. This qualified as a sudden stress event, for sure. Maybe her heart would have a sudden onset of apical ballooning.

"Now, I'm sorry for being so harsh," Dr. Coffey added in a much softer tone. "You've lost your fiancé and I understand your need for closure. But I have a department to run, and what you're doing with this Colchester business threatens to make my life and my job more difficult."

"I assure you that's not my intention."

"Then prove it by dropping this matter entirely. Colchester was murdered, and his killer is in prison where he belongs. Your fiancé died of undiagnosed heart disease. That's it. That's the story. Though I do find it interesting."

"What is that?"

"You have a bit of a reputation here at White as a crusader, so I know all about your stance on patient self-determination. Do you condone what Brandon Stahl did to poor Mr. Colchester?"

"I am in favor of examining the laws with regard to a patient's right to die. I don't condone murder."

"Very well. At the risk of being a bit coldhearted here, I would think part of you would be grateful your fiancé was no longer suffering."

Julie seethed on the inside, but managed to keep her anger in check. "To be candid, Dr. Coffey, I don't need you to tell me what to think or feel, thank you very much. And you can have those printouts if you want them. I'll print out more if I need."

Julie stormed toward the door, but stopped when Dr. Coffey called her name. She turned around, expecting him to apologize.

"Remember, Julie, unicorns don't exist."

Julie thanked him for his time, even if she chose not to believe him.

CHAPTER 26

Julie left Dr. Coffey's office feeling ambushed and shaken. His explanation had some logic to it. Digging up unpleasant memories could call into question the competency of the cardiology department. After all, the group had access to the echo and EKG before Brandon Stahl's trial. Why not bring it forward? Dr. Coffey had a sterling reputation to protect, which could explain his inaction and his discomfort with Julie's findings.

Or perhaps Sam did have undiagnosed heart disease. And if that were true, Brandon Stahl was a murderer. Regardless of Julie's personal beliefs on patient self-determination, the law clearly stated that Brandon had no business killing Donald Colchester. Go to jail; go directly to jail.

What Julie wanted now was a cup of tea and some company. What she got were two text messages in short succession, from different senders. They could not have come at a better time.

The first text came from Lucy: *Checking in. What's going on? How are you doing?*

The second text came from Michelle: *Off to meet Keith for lunch but want to know how it went with Dr. C. Any progress?*

Michelle's text was bit more specific. She knew Julie had a meeting with Dr. Coffey.

Julie texted back: *Didn't go as hoped. Will explain later.*

Michelle: *I'll see Keith at dinner. Let's meet for lunch in fifteen. Okay?*

Julie called and invited Lucy to join them in the cafeteria in the basement of the Tsing Pavilion. Ten minutes later, Julie found Lucy, and the two women embraced with genuine affection. Neither felt they saw each other enough.

Both wore white coats over professional-looking outfits. Not all the docs here were dressed the same. A recent trend sought to do away with lab coats and neckties, because some studies cited them as culprits in the spread of infectious diseases.

Julie thought that was rubbish. The real villain was lack of basic hygiene. If all physicians took the time to wash their hands properly, those coats and ties would be as clean as any article of clothing.

Nevertheless, a movement had sprung up among the younger set to shun traditional attire altogether. Two camps had formed, those with coats and those without, and each wore their allegiance like Sneetches vying to be the coolest on the beaches. Julie and Lucy were old school. Roman Janowski was old school as well; he should have been opposed to dressing down, but he was shrewd when it came to recruiting talent. He made White Memorial a hip place to work.

Doctors dealt with life-and-death issues, and clothing

choice had no relationship to patient outcome. But it represented a subtle shift in attitude that seemed to mirror a not-so-subtle shift in the business of medicine.

White Memorial was just another hospital in a long chain of health-care providers to migrate from a traditional HMO structure to become an accountable care organization. Julie did not expend much of her energy on the business side of medicine. She had enough to manage in the ICU, and the MBAs were best suited to make sure that more cash came in than went out. But Julie did not live with her head lodged under a rock, either. She had read up on ACOs in an attempt to ascertain if it was just HMO-style managed care disguised by another name. After some serious contemplation, Julie concluded that ACOs were an evolution to a better way of doing medicine.

There was reasonable concern that the ACO model would lead to an increase in hospital mergers, greater consolidation of market powers, and higher prices. So far Julie had not noticed much of a change since White Memorial adopted the model. ACO or HMO, Julie still had plenty of sick people who needed her care.

Michelle showed up later than expected, introductions were made, and it was not long before the three women were drinking their respective beverages and chatting like old friends.

Julie caught them up on her contentious conversation with Dr. Coffey.

"He said what?" Michelle asked.

"He said that I'm chasing unicorns," Julie repeated.

Lucy was incredulous. "After he insulted her med school training. What an ass. You showed him the echo and EKG, I assume."

"Of course I did. But he's not at all convinced they mean anything."

"Well, Sam had a clean heart," Lucy said. "That should mean something to him."

"It's a Twinkie thing," Julie said.

Lucy appeared perplexed. "A Twinkie thing?"

Julie spent some time going over what Dr. Coffey had explained to her about the vanishing sponge cake.

"So what, then? Abandon the search?"

Michelle's question hit Julie hard. It was a reasonable one to ask, although the idea of accepting Dr. Coffey's explanation did not sit well. If it had just been Sam's case, Julie might have dropped the matter entirely. There was, however, this business with Brandon Stahl and his secret admirer to consider. The trio discussed this in detail as well.

"Who do you think gave Brandon Colchester's file?"

Julie shrugged. "That's a good question, Lucy. Nobody knows. It was someone who not only had access to the medical records system, but had a lot of knowledge as well."

Lucy pondered that. "You know, I have a thought there."

"Yeah?"

"I think this secret admirer of Brandon's may have paid me a visit as well."

"How so?" Julie was quite curious.

"Something to do with a cobalt poisoning case. I got results from a mysterious lab test that just happened to lead us to a correct diagnosis. I think I have an idea who might have sent me those test results, too. I'll do some digging and let you know."

"That's wonderful. Thank you, Lucy."

"Do you believe Brandon?" Michelle asked.

"He was very convincing. I guess I want to believe him."

Michelle reflected on this. "If he's telling the truth, then he has the worst luck imaginable."

"How so?" Julie asked again.

"Well, he gets caught on tape offering to kill Colchester, which honestly I find deplorable, but that's beside the point. Then Colchester dies of heart failure, but has the whole vanishing Twinkie thing, and Brandon gets sent away for murder. If that's how it went down, it's a shocking injustice."

"You're forgetting they found morphine in Brandon's apartment," Lucy said. "That taints him more than just a little in my mind."

"Mine too, I guess," Julie said.

Lucy said, "Let's agree Brandon didn't inject Colchester with a fatal dose of morphine, like he says. Then we're still talking a very significant medical anomaly here. Two fatal cases in one hospital is more than just a unicorn, it's a damn Pegasus."

"Explain," Julie said.

"Sam had a clean heart, and Brandon's echo, from what you told me, was clear of any blockages. This Twinkie thing is ten percent of heart failure cases at most. Isn't that what you said?"

"Well, that's what Coffey told me."

"Ten percent chance of it happening twice in the same hospital is an anomaly in my book. I'd love to get a look at that echo."

Julie made a tsk sound and grimaced. "I can't believe I let Dr. Coffey take those printouts," she said. "He had me so rattled."

"No worries. We can get it later."

"Maybe getting you rattled was his intention." Michelle tossed this out in a very matter-of-fact way.

It struck a chord with Julie. She took a long drink of tea and gave it some thought. "You think Coffey's covering something up?"

"I'm just saying his behavior sounds odd to me. But I'm not a doctor."

"You're married to one," Julie said. "That counts."

Michelle gave a laugh. "I suppose there's an osmosis factor I can claim. So I stand by my statement. Not only was Coffey being a jerk, he was being an odd jerk."

"But why?"

"You said it yourself. He's protecting his reputation."

"And an innocent man goes to jail for it?" Julie looked dubious.

"The morphine," Lucy reminded them.

"Hmmm . . . hard to explain away, isn't it?" Michelle said. "So where do you go from here?"

Julie shook her head. "Honestly, I'm not sure. Dr. Coffey made another good point. What could have produced such a scare or sudden stress event that it caused two rare heart-stunning conditions?"

"Fatal stunning at that, which makes it even more unusual," Lucy said. "It wasn't like Donald and Sam got a lot of varied experiences in their days."

Before anyone could answer, Julie spotted someone in line at the cafeteria—someone she had never met before, but wished to speak with urgently.

"Excuse me for a moment," Julie said, getting up from the table. "I'll be right back."

Julie caught up with the willowy blonde as she was

refilling a cup of coffee. Her tray held an apple and a blueberry Greek yogurt. Big meals in the cafeteria were a rarity—nobody had much time to eat.

Julie would not even have known about this woman had it not been for Brandon Stahl. After the prison meeting, Julie did some Googling and even a stint on the corporate intranet. She wanted to know more about Sherri Platt, the young nurse who essentially put Brandon Stahl away for life. According to her bio, Sherri had left her career in long-term acute care to work as an oncology staff nurse at White. It was a fairly significant career change, but jumping jobs in nursing was a common practice.

Julie gave the woman a tap on the shoulder. Sherri turned and tried to place the face.

"Sherri Platt?"

Julie had planned to ask Sherri some probing questions, at some indefinite point in the future. But the moment had found her, and Julie saw no reason to delay.

As Julie introduced herself, Sherri's expression changed. It appeared that she recognized Julie, perhaps because of Sam's accident.

"Dr. Devereux. What can I do for you?"

"I'd like a few minutes of your time, if possible."

Sherri checked her phone, the watch of the new millennium. Julie guessed Sherri's age to be about thirty, which meant she'd been in her late twenties during the Brandon Stahl trial. No ring on her finger, though she had a gold cross pendant hanging from a thin gold chain around her neck.

"I have to be back on the floor in fifteen minutes."

"No worries," Julie said. "This won't take long."

They found seats at an empty table and Julie exchanged a glance with Lucy, one she hoped conveyed that an explanation would be forthcoming.

"So what's up?" Sherri sounded genuinely intrigued and her blue eyes flickered with curiosity. She was a pretty girl, Julie thought, and she acted receptive, though beneath the surface something about her was off-putting, a noticeable detachment. Sherri radiated cold, like a gray morning in fall.

"I want to talk to you about Brandon Stahl."

In a flicker, Sherri's body language shifted from open to closed. She stiffened as she slid her chair back, and then folded her arms tightly across her chest, her hands clenched in fists. She broke eye contact, tilted her head down, and fixed her gaze to the floor.

"What about?"

"I went to see him in prison."

"Why would you do that?" Sherri's voice was soft, but with an edge.

Julie couldn't tell whether it was bad memories or something else making her so uncomfortable.

"I'm trying to figure out if there's a connection between his case and my fiancé's death. He died here a few weeks back."

"Yeah, I know. I'm sorry for your loss." Sherri did not sound sorry. She sounded as if she wanted to be anyplace other than here.

"I'm wondering if you can tell me a bit more about what you heard Brandon say that day."

"I already told that to the court."

"Yes, I know. I was just wondering why you didn't come forward when he first got arrested."

Sherri stood. "I've got to go. I'm going to be late."

Julie stood as well. "I'll walk you."

Sherri looked as if nothing could please her less.

"Look, that was a really horrible time for me. I don't feel like reliving it right before my shift."

"Why? Were you close to Donald Colchester?"

"No."

Sherri was moving now, at a quick pace too, and Julie followed. Passing the table where Lucy and Michelle sat, Julie held up a hand to let her friends know she would be right back. She hurried her steps to catch up with Sherri.

"Can you tell me why you waited to come forward?"

Sherri stopped walking, turned, and fixed Julie with fierce eyes. She jerked her head back as if needing space. Maybe she needed more air, too, because her breathing turned heavy, while her body went perfectly still. Sherri took her hand away from her mouth to speak.

"Because he was going to get off and I had to do something," she said in a shallow voice. "I had to do something or else he'd go free. So I told the judge what I had heard. I was coming down the hall pushing a cart of medicine and I happened to overhear a conversation between Donald Colchester and Brandon Stahl. It sounded private, and I didn't want to rush in and intrude, so I waited outside the door. That's when I heard Donald say that he wanted Brandon to help kill him, and Brandon saying he understood Donald's pain and that he'd be willing to inject Donald with morphine. Brandon said, 'You won't feel a thing. You'll just go to sleep like you want.' I didn't know what to do. So I left and gave Donald his medicine later. That's the truth."

Sherri shuffled her feet during much of her monologue, after which she fixed Julie with an unblinking stare.

"Okay," Julie said. "I'm sorry to have upset you. For all those weeks the evidence against Brandon Stahl was in question, and here you were sitting on a powder keg. That must have been difficult for you."

"What's difficult for me is you bringing this up now." Sherri pointed at Julie in an accusatory way. "Ambushing me like this. I don't appreciate it at all. Now, if you'll excuse me, I'd like to walk alone."

Sherri spun on her heels and took off at a good clip. Julie watched her go. She was not a trained psychologist, had never studied body language. But Julie had raised a son almost into his teenage years. One thing experience had taught her was how to detect a lie when she heard one.

CHAPTER 27

Lincoln Cole heard every word. Every single thing Sherri and Julie had just discussed. Julie's phone calls were not the only thing he could eavesdrop on. The TrueSpy software installed on Julie's phone converted the microphone into a sound transmitter. Without her knowing, Julie's conversations were being transmitted to a wireless receiver disguised as a hearing aid in Lincoln's right ear. He had bought the receiver for three hundred bucks on an online shopping portal specializing in that sort of gear.

Based on what he had heard, Lincoln knew his employer would want a full report. He would prepare it from his van. In a few hours, Julie would be done for the day and would then head for home. TrueSpy also gave Lincoln access to Julie's calendar. One device used for multiple purposes made Lincoln's job that much easier.

Lincoln had been loitering in the hallway outside the cafeteria, in full view of the two women he was spying on. He wore street clothes and was not worried Julie might spot him. She had not noticed when he followed her to the Barstow Building for her meeting with Dr. Coffey. He knew Sherri Platt, though. He knew Sherri very well, but she was too flummoxed to make the connection.

Dr. Julie was not Lincoln's first job for this employer. A few years back, Lincoln Cole had accepted a decent sum to bribe Sherri into making false statements about Brandon Stahl. It did not take much of a bribe, either; not that this was a surprise. As a cop Lincoln had seen plenty of illicit payments offered for dirty deeds done dirt cheap, as the band AC/DC put it. The hard rockers from down under really were on to something there.

Lincoln knew a number of dimwits who thought they were talking to a paid killer, not undercover police. They wanted spouses gone, lovers gone, ex-wives or husbands gone, and offered paltry sums to get the job done. They proposed five thousand, ten, and on rare occasions twenty large. People paid more for decking than they did for murder.

Lincoln kept his employer a secret, but Sherri guessed that he worked for the Colchester family. Of course, Lincoln would neither confirm nor deny her suspicion. Sherri had no idea she was picked for a reason. She had strong religious beliefs, worked on the same floor as the ailing Donald Colchester, and had a shift at the same time Brandon was caught on that recording.

Lincoln had paid a visit to Sherri's small house in Melrose, where she lived alone, and played her a copy of the recording the judge had disallowed. His instincts had been right. Hearing Brandon's offer to kill Donald Colchester did inspire her cooperation.

"This isn't some frame job," Lincoln had explained.

"Brandon is a legitimate killer, and he's going to get away with murder unless you help us."

Lincoln described the problem as a technicality in the law. If Sherri wanted to see justice done, they would need her help. Sherri wanted to see justice done, all right. Fifteen thousand dollars helped her along. A cash payment was made promptly, and thanks to her testimony, Brandon Stahl was put away for life.

What Lincoln had just heard in that tense conversation between Sherri and Julie troubled him a great deal. Sherri's personality had another aspect that might play against them: Catholic guilt. Sherri Platt did what she did for reasons other than a moral and religious imperative, and this left her vulnerable to suggestion. Judging by body language alone, Lincoln did not think it would take much poking for Miss Platt to crack like thin ice.

Back in his van, Lincoln phoned his employer and told him of the conversation he had overheard.

"Can you do surveillance on Sherri Platt?"

"I could bug her apartment," Lincoln said. "But it'll detract from the surveillance work on Dr. Julie."

The silence that followed lasted several seconds.

"No. It's an issue only if she goes back to Devereux. Keep your eyes and ears open, though."

"Dr. Julie is not going to stop."

"How do you know?"

"Gut feeling, I guess. She's like a dog, that one. Latches on and won't let go. The conversation with Sherri didn't help matters any."

"Does Devereux know Sherri's lying?"

"Sherri isn't too good at the conceal game, if that's what you're asking."

"What do you suggest?"

"If you want to give me a bump in pay, I can give Dr. Julie a good hard shove. A friend of mine doesn't appreciate her efforts to free his son's killer, if you get my meaning."

Another beat of silence.

"A bump it is. I'll leave the rest to your discretion."

"And if Sherri Platt suddenly sprouts a conscience?"

"There's plenty of money to take care of Miss Platt if it comes to that."

Yeah, Lincoln thought as he pictured the sun-drenched beach and the oiled-up women lying next to him. *And it'll cost a lot more than fifteen grand, too.*

THE DAY after her odd meeting with Sherri Platt, Julie saw Trevor off to school and then drove her Prius down the Jacob's Ladder Scenic Byway all the way to the town of Russell.

She had the day off, and knew exactly what she was going to do with it seconds after the schedule got posted. When the Westfield River came into view, Julie parked her car in the same scenic pullout where she and Sam had stopped on the day of his accident. It was Thursday, November the tenth, and Julie carried with her a bouquet of flowers. She wanted something to toss into the river to honor Sam's birthday.

She had spoken by phone with Sam's parents earlier. It was a pleasant enough conversation, but Julie knew that with time, communication between them would happen less frequently, until it stopped altogether. Death had pulled her out of Sam's orbit, and the lives connected to him were no longer tethered to her.

On the drive west, Julie could not help noticing all

the drivers distracted by their damn cell phones. Some drivers were gabbing with one hand on the wheel and the other on the phone. A few she saw texting, and she swore one was watching a video and laughing. What could be so important? Her mind flashed back to the Civic veering erratically from one side of the road to the other. All it took was a fraction of a second to shatter so many lives.

Julie knew very little about the driver who took away Sam's mobility and perhaps hastened his death. He was a twentysomething who had escaped grievous injury, but whose bright future would forever be clouded by a shadow of guilt. At least, she hoped he felt guilt.

A harsh wind blew in from the east and sent strands of Julie's hair whipping against her face. Streaks of sunlight struggled to penetrate a thin layer of clouds stretched across a slate-gray sky. She had on one of Sam's leather jackets, a pair of jeans, and a warm sweater, but could still feel a chill against her skin. Julie brushed the hair off her face as she climbed over the guardrail separating the pullout from the drop down to the river. It was a bit harrowing descending the steep pitch, but Julie made it to the riverbank without tumbling.

Movement overhead drew Julie's gaze skyward. She looked just in time to see a flock of birds—sparrows, she thought—circling. The tiny black dots moved as one and they appeared to be engaged in a dance of sorts, swooping and twirling, the shape always changing, but never seeming disorganized. The changes in direction happened startlingly fast and Julie was amazed the birds could hold their formation at such speed. As quick as they appeared, those birds were gone. Julie felt relieved. They were magical to watch, but seemed strangely ominous to her, like a black cloud swirling above her head.

Silly to think of them as omens, Julie thought. Then again, she had been unsettled ever since her odd encounter with Sherri Platt. Julie purged that memory from her mind. Right now this was about Sam. She tossed the bouquet of flowers into the fast-moving water and watched the current carry the bright colors downstream.

Julie made a solemn vow to Sam to find out the truth. Was Dr. Coffey covering up two fatal cases of takotsubo? If so, why? And what about Sherri Platt? Why had she lied to Julie about Brandon Stahl? What could she be hiding? And if Brandon Stahl was innocent, how did that explain the morphine recovered from his apartment? Maybe it *was* a heart attack that had killed Sam and Brandon, or was something else in play? Julie imagined that swarm of sparrows had taken the shape of a Pegasus.

Julie heaved and puffed as she climbed up the hill back to the scenic pullout where she had parked her car. She chided herself for lack of fitness and made a second vow to devote more time to the gym. Maybe she'd follow Lucy's example and take up running again. Certainly she would need to find something to fill the void now that Sam was gone.

Julie arrived back at her car a bit breathless and out of sorts. She turned around to face the river when she heard footsteps come up behind her. She whirled in the direction of the noise and froze. A jolt of fear spread up her spine.

Standing there was a man wearing a navy peacoat and a black baseball hat. His sudden presence would have been terrifying enough, but what truly frightened Julie was the mask he wore. It was made of hard plastic and was flesh colored so from a distance it looked like a human face, but up close it was smooth as porcelain. Holes were cut out for eyes, but he wore dark glasses underneath so to Julie it looked like two black moons were staring back at her.

"Turn around and look at the water again." The man spoke in a raspy voice.

Another ripple of fear swept through her. She was alone out here in this weed-strewn pullout littered with bottles and bits of trash. She noticed a motorcycle parked directly behind her car, but the make, model, and plate were all hidden from her view. Julie did as she was instructed and turned around.

"What do you want?" Her voice trembled.

"I represent someone who doesn't appreciate your efforts."

Right away Julie suspected this was about Brandon Stahl. Her visit to the prison must have attracted someone's attention. Julie contemplated hurdling the guardrail to slide down the hill to the river, but decided against it. *What if he has a gun?* Her heart pounded hard enough to make her feel light-headed and dizzy.

Behind her, Julie heard the sound of cars zooming along the scenic byway. If anyone driving even noticed, they'd see only a couple watching the rolling river.

"I haven't done anything wrong."

"And you need to keep it that way," the man said, still speaking in a low rasp.

Julie turned her head around enough to see the expressionless plastic face. The man grabbed her wrist and gave it a twist that sent a sharp stab of pain rocketing up Julie's arm.

"Did I say turn around? Look at the river. Keep your hands where I can see them."

Julie snapped her head back and did her best to keep it together. The alternative could result in her body floating downstream. If he wanted, he could choke her to death inside her car or behind the little shed off to her left.

Don't run . . . don't panic . . . just listen to what he has to say . . . maybe he'll leave me alone.

The man placed a cold hand against the nape of Julie's neck. She recoiled from his touch, but he latched on. His hands were rough with calluses and fear caused her skin to prickle. Her legs buckled as she sucked down a shallow breath. Her heart beat wildly.

"Your efforts to free a killer are not appreciated."

Julie stammered. "How do you know about that?"

"I have my sources."

"Well, I've done nothing wrong or illegal."

"You're opening old wounds."

"Brandon deserves justice." The sudden strength in Julie's voice surprised her.

"And he got it. Keep out of this business. What's done is done. My employer doesn't take kindly to crusaders."

"Okay—okay. I'll do what you ask. Just leave me alone."

"Now we're getting somewhere. I do trust you'll keep your word and won't talk to Stahl anymore. But to inspire your cooperation, I slipped a little something into your coat pocket. You can look at it when I'm gone. And don't try to follow me. I want you to count to one hundred with your back to the road, looking at the river. One hundred. Don't test me. Start counting now."

Julie's body quaked, but she cleared her mind enough to begin the countdown. "One hundred . . . ninety-nine . . . ninety-eight . . ."

Julie felt the man's presence retreat, then heard a motorcycle engine rumble to life.

"You ever ride one of these things, Julie?" the man shouted over the engine's din. "You should give it a try sometime. You might like it."

The man laughed and revved the engine hard before he zoomed away. Julie did not dare turn around. She kept her eyes closed and continued the count, trying to ease the tight band of fear that had wrapped around her chest.

Eighty-five . . . eighty-four . . . eighty-three . . .

Julie stopped the count at fifty. She listened. She heard no sound at all. No cars. No birds. Nothing. In that stretch of quiet, Julie found the courage to turn around. There were no motorcycles in sight, and she felt confident the man was gone. No trick; he just wanted enough time to get away.

Still shaking, Julie climbed back in her car and sat while she tried to catch her breath. When she felt settled enough, Julie reached into her coat pocket for the keys. Her fingers brushed against an envelope that had not been there before. She remembered the man had put something there to "inspire her cooperation."

She almost tore the contents as she ripped the enve-

lope open. She could not quiet the tremor of her hands.
Julie's breath caught when she removed a photograph.
She recognized the image right away. It was a picture
of Julie and Trevor taken at Wingaersheek Beach in
Gloucester sometime last summer. Trevor had posted it
on his Facebook page. Hopefully the police would view
it the same way that Julie did: as a threat.

CHAPTER 28

Lucy Abruzzo's office was nothing special, just a concrete room with a couple of windows, a desk, and a small conference table set off to one corner. An oval-shaped area rug warmed the space somewhat, but it lacked a personal touch. Lucy's diplomas used to take up floor space, but a custodian broke the glass on one, and by way of an apology, hung them all on her office wall. Her bookcase was filled with medical texts, though she had a shelf devoted to her favorite nonfiction books as well, which she lent out like a library.

Lucy was seated at her desk when Jordan Cobb knocked on her office door. He was dressed in his workday uniform, blue scrubs and canvas sneakers.

"Hi, Dr. Abruzzo," Jordan said.

Lucy peered out from behind her computer monitor. "Ah, Jordan. Good. Come in."

Lucy pushed the file she had been reading to the edge of her desk and absentmindedly left it splayed open. She got up from her chair and came around her desk to greet Jordan. He looked a little apprehensive; it was not every day the big boss asked to see him.

"Have a seat," Lucy said, motioning to one of the chairs around the conference table.

Jordan did as he was told, his large frame barely fitting on the smallish seat. Lucy took a seat as well.

"Tell me something, Jordan. What is it you want to do with your life?"

Small talk was never Lucy's strong suit. Jordan knew this, but even he was taken aback by her abruptness. He shifted uncomfortably in his chair.

"Excuse me?"

"The question isn't all that vague, I think. What do you want to do with your life?"

"I'm doing it," Jordan said, sounding more appreciative than defensive.

"You want to move dead people around, that's the extent of your ambition?"

Jordan shrugged. "It's honest work. And given my criminal record, my options are a little bit limited."

"Oh, let's forget about your criminal record for a moment, shall we? I knew all about it when I hired you. My question is, what else *can* you do?"

"What else?"

"Yeah, your other skills."

"Um—I tutor in math."

Lucy showed her surprise. "Really? I didn't know you were mathematically inclined."

"I understand it all right. Enough to tutor, you know? Taught it in prison."

"I see. Well, the reason I'm asking all this is that we're looking for a new lab assistant."

Jordan's face lit up. "Really? Like I could work with samples?"

"Oh, yes. The job involves processing specimens, preparation of tissue, bacterial cultures, staining for various smears, and of course preparation of human specimens for postmortem examinations."

With the notable exception of Sam Talbot, to Lucy the dead were specimens and nothing more.

A big smile came to Jordan's face, showing off teeth that would have benefited from braces if only he could have afforded them. "That would be . . . that would be incredible."

Quick as that smile came, Jordan's bright expression dimmed.

"What's wrong?" Lucy said.

"All I have is a GED," Jordan said. "You have to go through an accredited program to be certified as a lab assistant."

Lucy gave a nod. "You've researched that, have you?"

"I just—I just know how things work, that's all."

"I see."

Before Jordan could say anything more, Lucy glanced at her watch and appeared suddenly flustered.

"Oh, shoot. Jordan, look, can you wait here a moment? I have to go speak to a doc about a lab result, but I want to continue our conversation. I'll be right back."

The question was rhetorical. Of course Jordan would wait, but he nodded his agreement anyway. Lucy got up and left the room.

Jordan sat a while, but his eyes soon went to the folder splayed open on Lucy's desk. Even from a distance he could tell it was a pathologist report. As Jordan moved closer, he could see it was from somebody suffering from chronic inflammatory bowel disease. IBD—a notoriously uncomfortable condition.

The report of the endoscopic biopsy specimen was written clearly and succinctly, to deliver information to a busy clinician. Even a diener could make sense of some of it. The second line of the pathologist report was almost always reserved for the presence or absence of dysplasia, a term used to refer to an abnormality or a growth anomaly. What patients wanted on that second line was "negative for dysplasia." Second best would be "indefinite for dysplasia." The third and final choice was "positive for dysplasia." The dysplasia would be graded, high or low, and the lower the better. The more marked the cell change, the easier it was to make a diagnosis.

Jordan took a glance at the report and saw that this patient was negative for dysplasia. Good. Below that, though, was an image taken from the H&E stain, which was shorthand for a tissue section stained with hematoxylin and eosin. Jordan had worked pathology long enough for the nomenclature to become a fluent second language.

Jordan studied the image a moment, and felt his pulse tick up when he heard footsteps headed toward the office. He retook his seat just before Lucy reappeared. She looked a little frazzled as she hurriedly collected the patient file from her desk.

"Silly me," Lucy said. "I went to give the doctor the pathology report, and what did I forget? The pathology report, of course. Can you wait another minute, Jordan? I just have to give the patient the good news."

Lucy headed to the door, but Jordan looked at her uneasily. Lucy paused.

"Well, can you wait?"

"Um—um—"

"Yes or no? Not a hard question."

"Um—"

"Jordan, is there something you want to say to me? The doctor is waiting. His patient will want to know that he's cancer free."

"Yeah—um—Dr. Abruzzo."

Lucy set the folder down on her desk and crossed her arms. She gave Jordan a disapproving stare.

"Jordan, I'm in a hurry here. What is it?"

"Yeah, um—well—I was walking around the office, you know, waiting for you to come back and all, and well, I saw the file open on your desk."

Lucy's frown seemed to deepen. "Jordan, did you read a patient's confidential file?" Her tone was serious.

"I didn't mean nothing by it. Just caught my eye, is all."

"Well, it's my fault for leaving it out in plain sight, I suppose."

Jordan shifted his weight from foot to foot, eyes to the floor. "Yeah, well, I just noticed that you wrote he was negative for dysplasia."

Lucy glowered. "That's none of your business. And do you even know what that means?"

Jordan shifted again. "Well, you know, you work here long enough, you pick up the lingo. But I was just wondering if maybe you were in a hurry or something and you wrote the wrong word."

"Now why would you say that?"

Jordan gave this some thought. "Forget it."

Lucy glared at him hard. "No. No, Jordan. I won't just forget it. Why would you question me on this?"

"I don't know."

"Okay. Well, that was an odd little exchange we just had there. Wait right here. Let me deliver the good news and I'll be right back."

Lucy gathered up the folder. She made it to the door when Jordan called out her name. Her face almost a scowl, Lucy turned and shot Jordan an impatient glance.

"That patient is high-grade positive for dysplasia," Jordan said in a breathless voice. "You tell him he's clean and he's gonna die."

Lucy returned a quizzical look. "What are you saying?"

"I'm saying the picture of the stain shows an awful lot of cancer."

"Are you suggesting that I've diagnosed this patient incorrectly?"

Lucy's tone bordered on wrathful, as she got right up into Jordan's face. It did not matter that Jordan towered over her and outweighed her by more than a hundred pounds; he still shrank back. His eyes blinked rapidly.

"The cells look messed up."

"Messed up? Can you be a little bit more specific? I mean, you seem to absorb the language just fine."

"No—it's just messed up."

"Tell me exactly how it's messed up."

Jordan stayed quiet.

"You saw something. You have a point to make. Now make it."

"There's variability in the size, shape, and staining of the cells."

"Variability? You noticed that?"

"Yeah—the cells, they look, um . . ."

"Look like what, Jordan? Tell me, or I might have to find your replacement."

"The nuclei in the luminal half of the cells are stratified and show pleomorphism. That means there's a lot of distortion in the cells."

Lucy exhaled a loud breath. "Well, now. That *is* quite a lot of our nomenclature you've absorbed."

"Pleomorphism." Jordan's voice was barely audible. "That's a characteristic of malignant neoplasms."

Lucy stood with her arms akimbo. "I know what pleomorphism means," she said through clenched teeth.

Jordan bowed his head. "I'm sorry, Dr. Abruzzo. I shouldn't have said anything. I just—I just messed up, that's all. I'll wait right here while you deliver that report. But you shouldn't do it. This guy has lots of cancer. That's all I'm gonna say."

"Funny, I thought I was the doctor and you were the diener."

Lucy opened the report and studied it carefully. Instead of leaving, she took the top page of the report, and with a roguish expression ripped it in half.

"Well, lucky for us this patient doesn't actually exist," Lucy said with a smile.

Jordan was dumbfounded. "What?"

"I've noticed things around here. Relevant Web sites open to cases we happen to be reviewing, journal articles of certain importance left in the break room. But when you happened to stumble upon a mysterious lab report—one that seemed to have fallen out of the sky—and correctly diagnosed cobalt poisoning, well, let's just say my suspicions were roused," Lucy said. "But I couldn't prove it. I looked, but whoever used our medical records system to run that lab was a shadow. Even the IT folks couldn't find you."

"I didn't—I—"

"Jordan, please. I'm smart enough to know this fictional patient I baited you with was riddled with cancer. I'm also smart enough to know that you're a hell of a lot more than a diener. What I don't know, and what you're going to tell me right now, is why you sent Brandon Stahl the EKG and echocardiogram of Donald Colchester."

CHAPTER 29

The state police barracks in the town of Russell was a two-story redbrick building located a few miles from where a stranger accosted Julie. After navigating the curved driveway, Julie brought her car to a stop in a mostly empty parking lot and got out in a hurry. The man and his motorcycle could not have gone very far. They still had a chance of tracking him down.

Caught up in the urgency of the situation, Julie was having trouble settling down. She had never experienced fear like this. It transcended the emotional and became something physical, leaving her utterly drained. Whoever this man was, his presence lingered. If she closed her eyes, Julie could see that featureless mask and haunting black eyes staring back at her.

My client doesn't appreciate your efforts to free a killer.

Who could that client be? Julie had a good idea, and she planned to share those feelings with the state police.

In no time, Julie was seated in a cramped waiting

area, facing a Plexiglas window through which she could see patrol officers and dispatchers at work. A police officer eventually emerged from behind a steel door and introduced himself as Trooper Sean O'Mara.

He greeted Julie with a firm handshake. O'Mara wore the uniform of the Massachusetts State Police—blue shirt, dark blue tie, and dark pants with yellow stripes running down the legs. He was short and stocky, and seemed well suited for this type of work.

O'Mara had a stern face that Julie found slightly unnerving. She had expected someone older—a seasoned detective to hunt down an experienced predator. This stranger had known when to approach her, how to conceal his identity, and most important of all, how to get away.

"We'll go to the interview room," O'Mara said.

A small smile and a sympathetic look lessened Julie's anxiety. She had come here voluntarily and under duress, and she needed a dose of empathy.

O'Mara carried a clipboard with a police report attached into a small, windowless interview room. He invited Julie to take a seat across from him at a metal table. There was nothing on the gray-painted concrete walls. She provided all the requisite information, including her driver's license. O'Mara filled in the form, while Julie sipped from a bottle of water he had supplied.

"So in your words, tell me exactly what happened."

He had a young-sounding voice to go with his young-looking face, but Julie imagined he could ratchet up the intimidation factor when called upon. She also got the sense, after she explained in detail what had happened at the river, that this interview was not going to go as she hoped.

"Did he make a direct threat to hurt you?"

O'Mara asked the question in a leading way, so Julie would know the best answer would be yes. She tried to recall all that was said, but her thoughts were a bit jumbled.

"Not exactly," she confessed. "The whole encounter was a threat. And he did give me this."

From her purse, Julie produced the picture the man had slipped into her jacket pocket. O'Mara studied the photograph intently.

"Is this your son?"

"Yes. That's Trevor."

O'Mara turned the picture over and glanced at the back.

"There's nothing written here. Did he give you a note to go along with the picture?"

"No. Just the picture. But it's obvious, isn't it? If I don't back off, something will happen to me or to Trevor or to us both."

O'Mara studied the photograph again, but his expression implied nothing here was obvious.

"What is it he wanted you to stop doing?"

Julie sighed. "That's a long story."

"Try me."

"No disrespect, Officer, but shouldn't you be out looking for this guy? He was riding a motorcycle and had on a navy peacoat and a black baseball hat."

Julie got a flash of O'Mara's harder look.

"Any chance this guy dumped the coat and put on a helmet?"

"I suppose."

"Make and model of the bike?"

"I told you, I couldn't see it."

O'Mara pulled his lips tight. "Being honest here, you're not giving me a lot to go on."

Julie tried not to let her exasperation show. Inside, a simmering anger replaced what had been a lingering fear. This stranger had snuck up on her, unquestionably threatened her, and would suffer no repercussions for his actions.

"What about security cameras?" Julie asked. "Maybe they got a photo of the motorcycle and a license plate."

O'Mara cocked his head and paused. "Well, I know this stretch of road pretty well," he said. "There are no cameras in the vicinity where the incident took place."

"Maybe further down the road? Look at all the motorcycles."

"That's a lot of manpower and time," O'Mara said. "You don't have a make or model of the bike, and no real description of the man."

"Maybe he knew all this beforehand," Julie said.

O'Mara cleared his throat and jotted something down on the police report.

"Look, say we find this guy, which I'm not saying we can even do. We could talk to him, but I'm not sure we could charge him with any crime."

Julie was aghast. "He threatened me."

"There are possible crimes here; I'm not saying there aren't any. Criminal stalking, for instance, but that requires a pattern, a series of events over time. It's the same with criminal harassment. Did you at any point feel that your life was in danger?"

Julie looked O'Mara in the eyes. She understood he was not going to help her.

"I felt in danger the whole time, but he didn't specifically say he would hurt me. I told you that already. His entire demeanor was threatening."

"An extortion attempt?"

Julie pursed her lips and shook her head slightly. "No."

"Nothing stolen. No weapon."

"No to both."

"Well, maybe we can get him for violating your constitutional rights."

Julie went a little slack-jawed. "That's a law?"

"Section 11H. Sure is."

O'Mara wrote something down on the police report, while Julie returned the photograph to her bag. She tried to think what to do next, because this was going to take her nowhere. She got up from the table.

O'Mara peered up from his report. "The restroom is down the hall," he said.

"I'm actually going to leave. I need to get home to my son and I've got the sense there's not much we can do here."

O'Mara spun the clipboard around, pushing it toward Julie. As he did, he handed her his pen. He did not appear to disagree.

"I need you to sign this before you go," he said. "And as far as what we can do regarding this situation, without a description of the individual, make and model of the motorcycle, surveillance footage, I'm afraid you're right. There's not much we can do."

Julie signed the document. "Thank you for your time," she said.

She agreed only in part. There was not much they

could do *together,* but there was something Julie could do by herself.

IT WAS late Thursday afternoon when Julie parked her car in the garage near the Massachusetts State House. The drive east had not been an easy one, and her stomach clenched every time she saw a motorcycle.

She had phoned Paul from the parking lot of the police station and made arrangements for him to take Trevor after school. Of course she gave him her list of things to do. Trevor had a dentist appointment, and after that Paul needed to swing by Sports Authority to pick up a gift card for a boy's birthday party, and then bring Trevor to the same boy's apartment for a sleepover. Friday was a professional development day for the teachers: no school. Julie did not tell Paul anything about her frightening ordeal at the river, nor did she explain why she needed him to look after their son. Paul would worry and try to get involved, take over. He had that annoying alpha male, let-me-fix-your-problem gene.

She thought again of the stranger and her maddening conversation with Trooper O'Mara. The anger returned, and it was a good thing, too. Julie wanted as much venom in her as possible for the upcoming encounter with William Colchester.

A stout administrative assistant escorted Julie into Colchester's expansive, carpeted office. Julie had little hope she could arrange a meeting with the state legislator on such short notice, but had boosted her odds by using some rather convincing language.

"I'm Dr. Julie Devereux from White Memorial

Hospital, and I need to speak with Representative Colchester about his son's real killer."

That got the lawmaker's schedule shuffled around right quick.

William Colchester's office featured a stellar vista overlooking Beacon Hill, one of the more posh neighborhoods in Boston. As if to underscore his illustrious career as a public servant, the walls were tastefully decorated with framed photos of Colchester hobnobbing with local political and Hollywood elite. Two of Boston's brightest stars, Matt Damon and Ben Affleck, were featured prominently on his wall of fame. A cast-iron stand held an American flag at one side of his cherrywood desk, and on the other side stood the flag of the Commonwealth of Massachusetts. No doubt about it, William Colchester was a proud man of the people.

Though he was in his late fifties, William Colchester's complexion and dark hair, cut well above the ears and swept back with a generous application of Brylcreem, shaved more than a few years off his appearance. He was tall, fit and trim, and had the look of an amateur boxer because of a crooked nose. *Bar fight, perhaps?*

He possessed a charming albeit thin-lipped smile, and a handshake practiced at not being too soft or too firm. He had a father-knows-best quality, dignified and respectable in a tailored blue suit, white dress shirt, and bold red tie. He was also a born and bred Bostonian; Julie got the sense that when his suit came off, the Bruins jersey came on.

She knew his bio well enough, having read up on him prior to her meeting with Brandon Stahl. Community organizer, coach on the Hyde Park Hoopsters, director at City Year, and the list went on. Appreciation for his efforts came in the form of election results that had allowed him to legislate in the Massachusetts House for more than twenty years, and as such had amassed a powerful constituency and friends in many places—including, as Julie believed, MCI Cedar Junction.

"Thank you, Denise," Colchester said to his assistant. "Hold my calls, will you, please?"

Denise gave a nod that bordered on being a bow, and backed her way out of the office. Colchester pulled out a chair and motioned for Julie to take a seat at the round conference table. Polite, chivalrous, and all an act, Julie believed.

"I must say your call took my breath away," Colchester began. "You say you have important information to share about my son's murderer?"

He said it "murder-ah." Here at the State House the Boston accent was a mark of authenticity, and those who had it owned it with pride.

Julie collected her thoughts. The feeling of a man lurking behind her was nothing but a trick of the mind. Reaching into her purse, Julie took out the picture the stranger had slipped into her coat pocket and laid it faceup on the conference table.

Colchester examined the photo closely. "That's you," he said. "Is that your son?"

"That's what somebody put in my coat pocket a few hours ago. Somebody who didn't appreciate that I was looking into the possible innocence of Brandon Stahl."

Colchester flinched. The glint in his brown eyes dimmed. "I don't understand. What's this about?"

"It's about a man who threatened me and my son because of a conversation I had with Brandon Stahl in prison, but I suspect you already know that."

Colchester interlaced his long fingers and rested his hands on his desk.

"I'm sorry, I'm still lost. I canceled an important budget meeting because you said you had information about my son's killer. That was the message to me."

"Well, my message to you is this. Did you send someone to harass me? I want the truth."

Julie was shaking again. The rage had returned with a vengeance.

Colchester leaned back in his chair and gave her a hard stare. "I'm not sure I like what you're insinuating, Dr. Devereux. Now, if you have new information about Donald's killer, I want to hear it. But the right man is in jail. He was tried and convicted."

"Then why did you agree to meet with me?"

"Because anything about my boy takes priority," Colchester said, his voice gaining volume. "Anything, even people who I suspect came here to throw their misguided views about mercy killing right in my face."

"Excuse me?"

It was Julie's turn to be baffled.

"You think I'd schedule an impromptu meeting with someone without getting a background first? I read up on you. I know what you stand for. I know you think my son's in a better place. But you're wrong. Brandon Stahl had no right to take my son's life. Now, I'm sure losing the appeal got you and your activist friends all rattled. But let me tell you something. For what he did to me and my family, infinity isn't enough time."

An uncomfortable silence settled over the room. Julie needed a moment to collect her thoughts.

She said, "I think you're worried I'm going to find out what really happened to your son, and you don't want to see Brandon walk a free man. Why else would you harass me?"

Colchester brought his hands to his lap. If he reached for his desk phone, the call, Julie knew, would get her escorted from the building.

"Harass you? I don't even know you."

"You knew about my meeting with Brandon. Somebody at Cedar Junction tipped you off. Which means you know I have medical evidence that could link your son's death to the same rare heart disorder that killed my fiancé. Brandon says he never gave your son morphine, and I'm starting to believe him. Maybe you put the morphine in his apartment. Somebody framed Brandon and we both know it. Same as we know Sherri Platt lied about hearing Brandon offer to kill your son. You paid her off, didn't you?"

Colchester's face went red with anger. "I don't know what you're talking about," he said.

"You're lying. You're afraid I'm going to blow this whole thing wide open and that'll put you and Sherri in a lot of hot water. Were the two of you having an affair?"

"I never!"

"Why didn't you want your son's body exhumed?"

"Excuse me?"

"One moment you're fine with it and the next you're filing motions to oppose. Why?"

"You have a son, Dr. Devereux. How would you like to see him dug up after you've buried him?"

Julie cleansed the gruesome image from her mind.

"I find it an interesting coincidence that Justice Josephson landed a plum state appointment not long after the trial. And weren't you chair on the Joint Committee on the Judiciary back then?"

"I don't appreciate the insinuation," Colchester said. "I conduct myself to the highest ethical standards and I find it highly disingenuous to use my son's name so you can berate me with your unsubstantiated and wildly outlandish accusations."

Julie said, "What I'm saying may be unsubstantiated, but that doesn't mean it isn't true. I don't know why you want to see an innocent man rot in jail, but let me be blunt about something. If you ever send someone to threaten me again, I'll go to the police and file a formal complaint against you for violating my constitutional rights. And let's see how much your constituents like seeing you as the lead story on the six o'clock news."

Colchester was incensed. "Are you threatening me?"

"Not according to the law," Julie said as she stood up from the table. "I hope I won't be hearing from you or your—associate, again."

She opened the office door and walked out of the room.

CHAPTER 30

Julie headed in the direction of the parking garage with her head lowered to shield her from the cold, biting wind. Early afternoon, and it was dark as midnight already. She missed the autumn even though the official start of winter was still several weeks away. The shorter days and longer nights made everything harder, including making phone calls outside. Julie needed to reach Sherri Platt, right away, but doubted she could get a cell signal down in the garage. The wind was making the outdoors incredibly unpleasant.

Julie took shelter in a store alcove and dialed White Memorial's main number from memory. An operator patched her through to oncology, where Sherri had transferred after Donald Colchester's death. The duty nurse checked the shift schedule: Sherri was off and would not be back until morning. Julie pulled the doctor card, said it was important, and got Sherri's cell phone number. Home numbers these days were anachronistic.

What Julie needed now was a place to make her

phone call. Eventually, she found a warm place inside Emmet's Irish Pub. The noise level made it hard to hear and the smell of Irish coffee proved more than a little tempting. Julie could use a drink, just one, to settle nerves frayed from three intense back-to-back encounters—the stranger, the trooper, and the legislator. She found a quieter nook at the back of the bar and made a call that went straight to voice mail.

"Sherri, it's Dr. Julie Devereux. I'm sure you remember me from the other day. Listen, I know what happened to you. At least I think I do. William Colchester forced you into testifying against Brandon, didn't he? You never overheard Brandon speaking to Donald Colchester. I'm not saying you took a payment or anything, but I suspect the representative used some sort of intimidation. He did so with me. I was nearly attacked at a roadside stop earlier this afternoon. We need to stand together on this, Sherri. I need your help setting right what I think is wrong. I believe now there's a real possibility Brandon is an innocent man, and Donald Colchester's death may be linked to the same thing that killed my fiancé. We need to talk. Please, Sherri. You have to do the right thing here."

Julie left her number. Had she said enough? Brandon's life might well depend on it. The next stop Julie made was to the bar, where she ordered an Irish coffee. She'd had three sips of a truly magnificent beverage when her phone rang. Julie's heart leapt. It had to be Sherri calling back.

She glanced at her phone's display and wondered what reason Lucy might have for calling.

"Hey there," Julie said, blocking her left ear with her hand so she could hear over the noise.

"I figured out the identity of Brandon's secret admirer. He's my diener, Jordan Cobb."

"Your diener?"

"Yeah, I don't have a full story just yet. He was being a little cagey about it, because he was definitely looking at medical records he had no business looking at."

"But—but—he's a diener. The guy who contacted Brandon had to be an M.D. I'm sure of it."

"I tested him," Lucy said. "And trust me, this kid knows his stuff."

"Well, let me talk to him."

"I would, but he's gone. Said he had to get home to sit for his siblings. I wasn't about to hold him hostage, but I wanted you to know that you got your man."

"Can you give me his address?" Julie said.

Lucy had it on file. Julie was certain she had never been to Jordan Cobb's neighborhood before.

"What are you thinking?" Lucy asked.

"I'm thinking I'm already in Boston and it's not that far a drive from here to Dorchester."

PARKING IN Dorchester was no better than parking in Cambridge. The only difference was that the cars here were generally older models and a lot more street-hardened. Julie found a space in front of a boarded-up Laundromat and a tailor. Even though this was a vibrant neighborhood, with plenty of vehicle and pedestrian traffic, Julie was a fish out of water. The men fixed hostile expressions on her.

It did not help matters that Julie appeared to be completely lost as she tried to figure out if 48 Norton was on the other side of the street. Many of the stores were closed and the front entrances secured by metal roll-down doors, tainted by graffiti. There were no chain stores here. No Starbucks, no Hannaford's. Instead Julie walked past stores like Check Cashing, JP Wireless, and Peguero's Market.

A police car, siren blaring and lights flashing, zoomed by. Julie jumped a little as it passed. By the light of the strobes, she noticed a kid on a fixed-gear bicycle riding toward her. The kid, who looked to be about Trevor's age, wore a stiff-brim baseball hat and puffy down jacket. He slowed as he approached and circled Julie as if she were carrion to his buzzard.

"Yo lady, yo lady, whazzup? Whatchu doin' here, lady? Who you looking for?"

Julie stopped walking. This seemed to surprise the boy. Maybe he was accustomed to strangers picking up the pace, never making eye contact.

"Forty-eight Norton Street," Julie said. "Jordan Cobb. Do you know him?"

The kid laughed. "Yeah, yeah, I know him. Whatchu looking for him for? He in any trouble?"

"No. He's not, but I'm cold and I would like to get inside."

The kid seemed to appreciate Julie's straightforward approach. His bravado retreated a little as he pointed to a building on the other side of the street.

"He lives over there," the kid said. "Night, lady. Careful out here." The kid rode away.

Julie crossed the street and buzzed apartment number three. She waited. On the drive over, she'd thought about calling first, but what Lucy had said about him being cagey changed her mind. Better to catch Jordan by surprise. She waited for the intercom, but instead heard a young girl's voice call down from the apartment above.

"Who is it? Intercom's broken."

Julie stepped back and looked up at the silhouette of a girl leaning too far out the open window for Julie's comfort.

"My name is Julie Devereux. I'm a doctor at the hospital where Jordan Cobb works. Is Jordan home?"

"He's home."

"May I come up and speak with him?"

The girl poked her head inside, but reappeared a moment later.

"Look out," the girl said.

Julie stepped back as something dropped from the girl's hand. It hit the pavement with a clank. Julie looked at the ground and saw the girl had tossed down a ring of keys.

"Buzzer's broken too," the girl said.

CHAPTER 31

Jordan Cobb greeted Julie at the apartment front door. There was no foyer, so when Julie entered she stepped into a living room that barely accommodated the sofa, two chairs, and a television. The walls were painter's white, but decorated with a scattering of family photos. Aromas coming from the kitchen told her someone was cooking dinner.

Seated on the couch were two young girls, close in age, one maybe eleven and the other a bit younger. It was the older girl with mocha-colored skin, pigtails, and a pretty blue dress who had tossed out the keys. Both girls had books spread out in front of them and were doing homework while the TV played the kind of cartoon Trevor had only recently stopped watching.

Jordan, still wearing his scrubs from work, greeted Julie with an apprehensive expression.

"I'm in big trouble, aren't I?" he said.

"No, Jordan, you're not. But before we get into that, I'd love to meet your sisters, if I could."

The older girl jumped off the couch and approached

Julie with an outstretched hand. She had a firm shake and made eye contact the way Julie taught Trevor to do.

"I'm Teagen," the girl said, in a confident voice. "And this here is my sister, Nina."

"How do you do," Julie said, returning the keys to Teagen. "It's very nice to meet you both."

"Nice to meet you," Nina said in a softer voice.

She was the shy one, Julie thought.

"I see you're doing homework, so I don't want to disturb you. But I would like a moment of time with your brother. Is there a place we can talk?" Julie asked Jordan. "In private?"

Jordan gave a nod. He escorted Julie into a small but serviceable kitchen, where a pot of water heated on the stove and an oven gave off warmth. Julie looked around, wondering if Jordan's mother might be at home, but got the feeling Jordan was in charge.

"The girls are my half-sisters," Jordan said, stirring the pasta in the boiling water. He checked the chicken in the oven using a meat thermometer and turned over the asparagus on the bottom rack. "My mom's at work. She works for Marriott and does the overnight shift sometimes. I look after the girls when she's gone."

"Need any help with dinner?"

Jordan gave a laugh. "I think I got it, but fine if you want to pitch in."

Julie hung her jacket on the back of a chair and got right to work. Cooking always relaxed her, and memories of the eventful day faded as she strained the pasta, flavored it with Parmesan cheese, and added some seasoning to the chicken. Afterwards, Julie set the table even though Jordan said that was the girls' job.

"Gives them more time for homework," Julie said with a smile.

When the table was set, Julie poured three glasses of milk, but Jordan would not be sitting just yet. He covered his plate with another plate to keep his food warm.

"Nina, Teagen, you girls eat without me," Jordan called out. "I have to speak with Dr. Devereux alone for a minute."

The girls came running the way puppies might. Soon they were seated and eating, happy as could be.

Julie followed Jordan down a narrow corridor into a small, dark room where she could make out the outline of a bed and not much else. Jordan turned on the light and Julie's eyes went wide with surprise. The bookcases, of which there were several, sagged from the weight of all the heavy tomes. Julie had owned many of these titles because Jordan's collection belonged in any medical student's library. All the classics were there—*Essentials of Medicine, Gray's Anatomy, Sidman's Neuroanatomy* were just a few of the titles to catch Julie's eye.

The rest of Jordan's room was free of clutter, and his bed made to military standards. There was a wooden desk with a Dell computer on it and a chair well worn from hours of sitting. The desk alone was neater than any square inch of Trevor's room.

"It isn't much, but it's all mine," Jordan said, pulling out the desk chair for Julie to sit. He plunked down on the twin bed, which groaned and creaked under his weight.

Julie stood and gazed slack-jawed at his expansive library. "Jordan, how did you get this collection of books?"

"Would you believe one book at a time?" Jordan

said. His grin was endearing. "I don't buy much else. What my mom doesn't need, I spend on books and research materials."

"You've read all these?"

"Cover to cover. Understand it all, too. I've taken a lot of practice MCAT tests just to make sure."

"I read your notes to Brandon Stahl. I have no doubt you did fine. I just can't believe you're self-taught."

Jordan gave a shrug. She had seen him make the gesture before.

"I'm pretty confident I know my stuff."

He smiled again, and Julie saw why Lucy always talked so fondly of him. He came across as warm and kindhearted, with a sweet, inquisitive nature.

"Do you want to be a doctor someday?"

"I did," Jordan said, in a voice tinged with regret. "I always had a passion for medicine, biology, that sort of thing. When I was in seventh grade I made a model of the human body out of clay for an extra-credit science project. We're talking a *spleen,* made to scale. You could take out any organ and put it back where it belonged. I still have the index cards explaining what every body part does."

"Incredible to have such a clear vision and drive at that young age. I have a twelve-year-old son, and some days I think his only passion is Minecraft."

Jordan chuckled. "Yeah, well he and Teagen would be fast friends. We only have this one computer and it's a battle to get her off it. Nina, she's more like me, more into books."

"So why didn't you pursue a medical degree?"

Jordan's lip curled. "Not a lot of medical schools want to admit convicted felons."

Julie leaned forward. Lucy had never shared any information about Jordan's past.

"Convicted of what, if you don't mind me asking?"

"Possession with intent to distribute. It was marijuana, and a lot of it. It's hard out here—these streets, they can pull you in if you're not careful. I made a bad choice and it landed me in prison. Did five years hard time at MCI Cedar Junction, so I know Brandon Stahl's new home real well. In prison I kept at my studies. Read what I could. Petitioned publishers for their old textbooks, and a lot of them came through."

"You probably already know this, but there are medical schools out there that will overlook your past."

"Even if I found a school willing to take a chance on me, no way could I afford it. I still have to go to college. Before my arrest, my plan was to join the military. Become an army medic to help pay for school. My mom thinks everything happens for a reason. I agree, but I don't think it's God's hand at work. I think we make choices and live with the consequences. That's reason enough."

"Maybe your mom is right. If you had walked any other path, you might never have seen Brandon Stahl's medical record. Maybe that *is* the reason."

"Never thought of it that way."

"You've been browsing medical records at White to help fill in your knowledge gaps. Is that it?"

Jordan made that signature shrug of his, and looked a little uncomfortable about sharing. "Yeah, it's a hobby, I don't know how else to explain it. Just fires me up to learn. I figured out how to get into the system without being caught. I took some online computer classes."

Julie glanced at the old laptop computer on Jordan's desk. "My goodness, you're a self-taught hacker, too."

"I come from the DIY generation—that's do it yourself."

"Yes, I'm familiar with the acronym. My son uses the same lingo. So, what made you look at the Donald Colchester file?" Julie asked.

"It was high profile. A nurse from our hospital kills a state rep's son. He's moving into my old home. How could I not look? Wasn't thinking anything strange at first. Just looking, you know? Results from the cardiac troponin were high, so I didn't even need to check the EKG to tell he had a heart attack. But I looked anyway. It was a pretty strange reading."

"How good are you at reading EKGs?" Julie could not contain her surprise.

"I'm no cardiologist," Jordan said, "but I get by."

"What made you think takotsubo cardiomyopathy? That's not an easy determination to make."

Jordan motioned toward his bookshelf. "It's all there. Just got to know how to look. For this one, I dug like an archeologist. The weird EKG made me look at the echo and, well, I'd never seen a heart valve look like that one before. Didn't look like a heart attack brought on by morphine to me. Looked like something else entirely."

"Takotsubo is a very rare stress phenomenon, so I'm not surprised you hadn't seen it before. Well, I am surprised, because you're a morgue technician with a physician's mind, but you get my point."

Jordan gave a laugh. "Thanks. If you ask me, I'd say it's obvious Brandon Stahl's defense team got it all wrong. But there's nothing I can do about it now. Appeal is over. He lost."

"What do you think about the morphine they found in Brandon's apartment?"

"I thought about that a lot before I wrote my letter. There were two possible explanations. I don't think he killed anybody, so either Brandon's a junkie and that's tough luck, or somebody heard that recording and wanted to make sure Brandon did the time for that crime."

"You think somebody planted evidence?"

"Wouldn't be the first time it happened to an innocent man."

"Let's play out your theory, because I have the same suspicion, but for reasons we won't get into. Donald Colchester suffers a fatal heart attack after Brandon Stahl is caught on tape offering to kill the legislator's son. The tape isn't heard until after the body has been buried. Someone thinks Brandon is going to get away with murder, so they make sure they pin it on him by bribing Sherri Platt to testify and planting evidence in Stahl's apartment. That sound about right to you?"

Jordan's eyes turned fierce. "More than right."

"I'm pretty sure I know who's behind it, too."

"The father," Jordan said.

"Yes. William Colchester. He's got motive to keep Brandon in jail. Maybe his wife pressured him into it. According to Brandon, she was the hawk monitoring Donald's quality of care."

"So how do we help Brandon? I think the guy is innocent."

"We'd have to prove there's a pattern of takotsubo cases at White Memorial. My fiancé died of the same thing. I'm not a stats geek, but the probability of an unlikely event being isolated to the two cases we just happened to stumble upon is pretty darn low. I'm going to dig through the medical records of everyone who died from a heart attack at White and see if I'm right. It's a long shot, but maybe it's enough to overturn Brandon Stahl's conviction. Maybe in the process I'll figure out what really killed my fiancé."

Jordan's expression was skeptical. "I don't know if I would do that if I were you."

"Why not?"

"When I accessed Donald Colchester's file, I noticed somebody had altered his medical records. I couldn't tell who, or what they did exactly, but I do know they deleted information from his file."

"Deleted?"

"That's what it shows in the logs. Somebody used the same superuser access I have to delete some data from Colchester's record. The date stamp showed it happened postmortem. Now, why does somebody want to alter a patient record after someone has died? I didn't think much of it, until you started talking about looking for information. Maybe someone was trying to keep a secret."

Julie's brow furrowed. "Can you check Sam's file for me without anybody knowing you're in the system?"

"Sure. I can do it from here using the superuser ID. It gives me admin access, plus I know how to mask my IP—that's my Internet address—so I can't be traced."

"Do it."

It took Jordan a few minutes to bring up White's electronic medical records system. He used a special key that generated a onetime password. The key, the size of a credit card and nearly as thin, generated a series of numbers that cryptographically authenticated the user. It was the same technology Julie used to access the records system from any remote location, typically her home.

"Where did you get hold of one of those?" Julie asked.

Jordan was typing furiously as screens of meaningless data scrolled by at a rapid rate.

"Um, some questions I think I'd rather not answer."

He went quiet for a bit, with the intense concentration and focus of a surgeon. Then his eyes opened wide. "Look here, you can see the date Sam's record was created."

Julie peered over Jordan's shoulder at a screen titled Transaction Log. The date was the day of the accident, and it brought back dark memories.

"The transaction logs show limited data. You can see the date a record was created, and there's a transaction type for records being added, modified, or deleted."

"It doesn't say what exactly was done to the record?"

"No. I've actually read up on that, because I had the same question. I don't know any EMR system that records every adjustment to the medical record itself. It would create too unwieldy a file. You'd have to invest a lot of money to get a system robust enough to handle something like that. Transaction logs are used for IT troubleshooting only. Your typical techs don't know a tibia from a femur, but they can understand transaction types just fine."

"Did someone delete something from Sam's record?"

"Look right here."

Julie focused where Jordan pointed and she saw a record deletion entry made on the same day Sam had died.

"Whoever deleted the record used a superuser ID to make changes. Just like with Colchester's EMR, I can't tell who altered it or what they deleted."

"Let me have a look. Maybe I can remember."

Julie took her time to examine Sam's extensive medical record carefully. It was all there: treatments, medications, operations, a complete compilation of an unfathomably expensive stay in the hospital. But for the life of her, Julie could not figure out what was missing from his file. Everything seemed to have been recorded properly.

Jordan came back from checking up on the girls. "What did you find?"

"I don't see anything," Julie admitted.

"Two cases of this rare fatal heart disease and two altered records tells me that someone isn't going to like you digging around a bunch of EMR files on a treasure hunt. Know what I'm saying?"

"Not exactly."

"Let me do the digging for you. I know how to get into the system and poke around without being spotted. You go in as you, and you're broadcasting yourself to anyone who wants to keep something hidden." '

Dr. Coffey and William Colchester were two names that popped into Julie's head as possible secret keepers. Sherri Platt was another.

"I don't want you involved with this, Jordan. Can you teach me how to do it?"

"Depends. How good are you with tech?"

Without embarrassment, Julie told Jordan she had needed Trevor's help to load a music player with digital files. Jordan's look told her plenty.

"Yeah, that isn't going to work too well. Again, let

me do it for you. I want to do it. Heck, I got this far, I should see this to the end."

Julie thought about the man at the river and her tense meeting with William Colchester. She did not want Jordan involved, but on the flip side she wanted answers. She hesitated before extending her hand. They shook.

Partners.

LINCOLN COLE sat in his parked van, waiting for Julie to come out of Jordan Cobb's apartment. What he needed now was some direction. He had given Julie a little shove down by the river, and then driven his motorcycle into the back of his van. He had parked right off the exit to hasten his vanishing act. He figured that after the scare, Julie would take some time off her crusade to think things over. Instead, she surprised him by paying Colchester a visit, calling Sherri Platt, and getting Jordan Cobb from White Memorial involved in her little quest.

Lincoln guessed the sizable man escorting Julie back to her car was the morgue tech. He knew Jordan Cobb by voice only. Soon he'd know everything there was to know about him. His employer needed to make some hard choices based on this new information. For now, Lincoln would do his job. He would follow the doctor. But these latest developments were very troubling. If Lincoln's gentle shove had not done the trick, something more punishing might be in order.

Those considerations were for another time. Julie had pulled away from the curb.

And Lincoln did the same.

CHAPTER 32

Julie arrived home a little after nine o'clock and parked her Prius in her designated space. She trudged to the apartment building entrance as if she was dragging a cinder block chained to her leg. The day had drained her completely. Jordan had invited Julie to stay for dinner, but she politely declined. Best that he and the girls managed the evening routine without her interruption.

The girls were delightful, and Julie was glad to get to know the Cobb family. She was also glad Trevor was out for the night. She needed her space, quiet, and time to collect her thoughts. Julie had white wine chilled in the fridge and a new *Downton Abbey* on the DVR to watch. Except for Winston, the guinea pig, the apartment was hers alone for the night.

Jordan had an incredibly time-consuming task ahead of him, but he was ready to get to work. He would have to sift through all the recent deaths at White, and look at echocardiograms and EKGs for any signs of takotsubo. A third case should be something Dr. Coffey could not so easily brush aside with his Twinkie theory.

As she neared the door, a shadow cut across Julie's vision. She stopped walking to look in that direction. An uneasy feeling took hold as a figure emerged from the darkness, a silhouette on approach. The pounding of Julie's heart was louder than her footsteps had been. Her throat closed up, but Julie's fear morphed into confusion when William Colchester stepped under a light. He wore a beige trench coat over his suit and Julie took special notice of his hands encased in leather gloves.

She did not like the gloves.

"What are you doing here?" Julie's voice carried a hard edge as she squeezed her hands into fists.

"We need to talk."

"We did that already. This is harassment. I told you as much. I'll call the police."

"I want to make a deal."

"A deal?"

"That's all. I came here with an offer."

"How the hell do you know where I live, anyway? And how long have you been waiting for me?"

Colchester gave a sideways smile. "Long enough. And let's just say I have a lot of loyal constituents."

"Yeah, I know all about them. They like to share my private conversations with you and shake me down at the river. What is it you want?"

"I want you to leave this Brandon Stahl business alone."

"And why should I do that?"

Colchester made two sidelong glances, as if worried somebody might be watching or listening. A conspiratorial look came to his face.

"There are some legislative bills coming before the House that, if passed, are very favorable to White Memorial—taxes, zoning, matters of that nature. What's good for White could be advantageous to you. I'd be happy to do a little lobbying if you stop trying to free my son's killer."

Julie's mouth dropped open.

"Are you bribing me like the others?"

"Ugly words. I'd prefer to think of it as a mutually beneficial arrangement."

Julie paused. Her heart continued to race from the scare, but anger also entered into the mix. "You have no business confronting me like this," she said.

Colchester took in a ragged breath. He stepped forward. Under the harsh light, Julie could better see the pain in his eyes. Much of the color had drained from a face marred by desperation.

Without provocation, Colchester reached out with a fast hand and seized Julie by her wrist. He squeezed hard, but not so hard that it hurt. Reflexively, Julie jerked back her arm, but Colchester would not let go. He held on like a drowning man clinging to a rope.

"Brandon Stahl is a nightmare my family is trying to put behind us. I called my wife after you left my office, and told her what you said, and she's been crying ever since. People are going to be hurt by your actions, and you'll accomplish nothing. Please, just stop. I'm begging you to leave this alone!"

His last words came out almost as a hiss. Julie twisted her arm and ripped free of his grasp. She rubbed where he had touched her. Her eyes blazed with fury.

"Touch me again and I'll have you arrested for assault. Show up here again and I'll file formal harassment charges. You have no business telling me what to do."

Colchester sank back into the shadows.

"People will be hurt by what you're doing," he said.

"What I'm doing is finding out the truth."

Colchester lowered his head and dropped his shoulders in a look of defeat.

"Remember what I told you," he said. "Just remember that." He stuffed his hands in his coat pocket and trudged up the garage ramp to the street level.

Julie watched him go. She continued to watch even after he was out of sight. Back in her apartment, Julie almost cracked a smile as she poured herself a glass of wine. Colchester was the cap to what had been an utterly insane day. From the riverbank of western Massachusetts, to the State House, to the streets of Dorchester, the day's events—some terrifying, some maddening, some truly baffling—played back in her mind like a disjointed dream.

After she fed Winston, Julie sank into the sofa and got three minutes into her show when her cell phone rang. She figured it might be Lucy wanting an update on her meeting with Jordan Cobb, but the caller ID came up as SHERRI PLATT.

Julie became animated. Her pulse quickened.

"Sherri, I'm so glad you called."

Sherri made heavy breathing noises, and it sounded to Julie like she was crying.

"I want to talk," Sherri said.

"Good. I want to know the truth."

Sherri's breathing remained uneven.

"I need some time . . . to make some arrangements first." The young nurse was clearly distraught.

"When do you want to speak?"

"Tomorrow," Sherri said.

"I get to work at eight," Julie said.

"Meet me after my shift in the cafeteria. I get off at three. I'll tell you what I know—what I did."

"You lied in court. Didn't you? Just tell me that?"

"Tomorrow. I'll tell you everything."

CHAPTER 33

Even with all that had happened in the last couple days—months, really, going back to Sam's accident—Julie brought 100 percent of herself to the job. She could compartmentalize with the best of them. It was how she dealt with death on an almost daily basis and still managed to cook dinner for her family with a smile on her face. Sam had found this ability of Julie's a little unsettling.

"Sociopaths can't turn it off like you do," Sam once remarked.

"Who said I'm not a sociopath?" Julie had answered with a wink.

She compartmentalized for Trevor and for herself, because what happened at White Memorial did not need to follow her home like some gloomy shadow.

Today, however, Julie was having a hell of a time placing her upcoming meeting with Sherri Platt into her mental lockbox where it belonged. Loads of sick and needy patients needed Julie's attention until three o'clock rolled around. Julie also had Jordan Cobb weighing on her heavily. He should be locked up inside another of her mental compartments, but she could not help but wonder what he might find. She also regretted his involvement with this whole affair. William Colchester's words came back to her, and hard.

People will be hurt by what you're doing.

What people? Julie wondered. Sleep had not come easy last night, and with so many unanswered questions tumbling about her head, three o'clock could not get here fast enough.

By quarter to three, Julie had not eaten, nor had she sat down. The day had been extremely busy with the usual array of ICU happenings: respiratory disorders, a stroke, heart failure, trauma, and a case of sepsis similar to what the BC quarterback, Max Hartsock, had experienced, only without the catheter siphon.

Julie's legs suffered the usual midday ache. Still, the ICU was stable, and another doc, Bill Goodman, came in to work, making it easier for Julie to slip away. Arriving five minutes early at the cafeteria where she and Sherri first met, Julie made a quick check of the place. Sherri was nowhere to be seen. Julie waited fifteen minutes before calling Dr. Goodman.

"Bill, it's Julie. I was wondering how things are going up there. I'm supposed to meet someone, but they're running late."

"Everyone is still sick," Dr. Goodman said. "But your presence is not immediately required, if that's what you're asking. You're supposed to be off in an hour anyway. Why don't you just call it a day? Things here are well under control."

Julie thanked him, ended the call, and then texted Sherri Platt, but got no response. Another ten minutes went by with no sign of the nurse. Sherri had sounded anxious to meet with her. Maybe she got caught up with some work crisis on the floor. It happened all the time in the ICU. Julie called oncology and was patched through to the duty nurse.

"I'm sorry, Sherri called in sick today," the nurse reported.

Julie cursed under her breath and used her doctor card to get Sherri's home address.

IF JULIE had left an hour earlier, it would have taken her half the time to get to Melrose. Now she was caught in bumper-to-bumper traffic on I-93, stuck behind an eighteen-wheeler that spit exhaust like dragon's breath. Sherri had not answered her phone or responded to any of Julie's texts, so this whole journey might prove to be time wasted. She should be home with Trevor, who wound up having to go with Paul at the last minute. The guilt trip he had saddled her with was justified. Her kid had begged for some consistency, and here she was giving him the exact opposite.

Julie had a guess that Sherri's sickness had something to do with a sudden change of heart. If Colchester could offer tax breaks for White Memorial, he could certainly come up with something compelling to purchase Sherri's continued cooperation.

According to the GPS, Julie was five miles from Sherri's Melrose home when Jordan Cobb called.

Julie spoke the command, "Answer phone," and her hands-free Bluetooth system connected the call. Thinking of a certain white Honda Civic, Julie permitted herself to talk and drive only if her hands remained on the wheel at all times.

"Hey there," she said, changing lanes.

"I've got one."

Julie tightened her grip on the wheel. "And?"

"I started with people who had died recently, and whose death was classified in the system as a heart attack. I'm just getting rolling because there's a lot of data to sift through, and it's really slow going."

Julie gazed out the window at the standstill traffic.

"I can relate," she said.

"Wish I could write queries against the database, but I can't. If I could, I might be able to pull up records for myocardial infarctions that also have a record delete transaction type in the transaction logs. That's the pattern we're looking for."

"I thought you were a superuser," Julie said.

"The superuser access is for viewing, adding, and editing records. The database stuff is with IT."

"But you said you got one. How?"

"I was looking at names and remembered a guy I wheeled to the morgue, Tommy Grasso. He used White Memorial like a Comfort Inn. So I checked it out."

"And?"

"And he didn't have an echo on file, but his EKG looked a lot like our two other cases. ST-T abnormalities, QT prolongation with large negative T waves occurring in succession. So I checked the transaction log and there it was—a record of a deletion logged postmortem."

"Any history of heart disease?"

"No. It's the lungs that were killing him, not the heart."

"The EKG is telling, but not telling enough. We need an echo to definitively show takotsubo type ballooning."

"That's gonna be tough to find."

Julie did not disagree. Protocols for chest pain always involved an EKG. The twelve-lead setup, six on chest and four on the arms and legs, could be done in a few minutes, and computer algorithms gave interpretations immediately. Echocardiograms, by contrast, were not routine. White did not offer a twenty-four-hour echo service like some hospitals with cardiology fellowship programs staffed night and day.

"I'll keep looking," Jordan said. "There's something to this, Dr. Devereux. Especially with those deleted records. It's a pattern."

"No, it's a start. Look up Colchester's file for me. Let's compare his EKG with Tommy's."

"Hang on a second."

Jordan's second was more like a couple of minutes, in which time Julie inched her car forward maybe forty feet. She drummed her fingers restlessly on the steering wheel while waiting.

"Hey Doc, check this. That record is gone."

Julie's vision went white and cleared in time for her to hit the brakes before finding the bumper of the car in front.

"What do you mean gone?"

"As in, the record doesn't exist in the EMR system anymore."

One name came to Julie's mind.

Dr. Coffey.

Coffey had made it clear Julie's investigation was unwelcome, and now he was making sure it was impossible. Maybe Dr. Coffey had discovered something on his own to make him and the department look bad, or perhaps something that would make it hard to keep

Colchester's killer behind bars. A cold chill spread across the nape of Julie's neck. Just how far was William Colchester's reach?

Jordan checked the database and found Sam's record was still in the system. But with Colchester's EMR gone, Julie no longer had definitive evidence of two cases of takotsubo at White. What she had was smoke, but no fire.

"What are you thinking?" Jordan asked.

"I'm thinking I can't get to Sherri Platt's place soon enough."

CHAPTER 34

Roman Janowski walked alongside Allyson Brock as they headed from the main entrance of Suburban West to the rehabilitation unit. Her strides equaled two of his, and he had a feeling Allyson hurried to make it as uncomfortable for him as possible.

White Memorial had gobbled up Suburban West like a great white shark snatching a meal in a single bite. The biggest obstacle to the takeover had always been the board of directors, but the numbers Romey put forward were so favorable his negotiation skill could have been second-rate and would have still closed the deal. Romey's lawyers had the papers drafted and the details ironed out well in advance of that meeting. Based on projections, West's chairman of the board, Vince Hanke, was doing everything in his power to speed up the process.

Brilliant.

The full transition would take time, but there already were some tangible benefits in bringing Suburban West into White's accountable care organization. The benefits could be even greater, but Romey had heard from the other CEO that Allyson kept her foot too heavy on the brake. Romey had come here to force that foot over to the gas.

ACOs were the media darlings of the moment, with almost daily news reports of savings to Medicare projected in the billions. With ACOs, the average spending per patient was expected to plunge forty to fifty dollars per month in the coming years. Multiply that by millions of patients, and the trend was worth some attention.

The media could write whatever stories they saw fit, but Romey's accountability was to his board, which mandated he deliver profits and patients. Before Romey took over White Memorial, those were thought to be mutually exclusive objectives. Allyson would learn the hard way they were not.

The looming takeover left Romey little time for exercise, or for screwing around with either of his two mistresses. It had been all work and no play, and indeed that made Romey a dull boy. His suit pants did not fit as well, and his notoriously slow metabolism probably had something to do with how snug his blazer felt across his chest.

The stress of the merger did not seem to bother Allyson any. Her weight had not fluctuated one iota. She still looked fine in her business suit, her rear end filling out her black slacks to perfection. *Who said walking golf courses wasn't exercise?* Romey lamented not getting a chance to bed her. It could have happened, too, but Romey always put business before pleasure.

"How are things with Knox Singer going?" Romey asked.

Allyson's counterpart had come from Boston Community Health, better known as BCH. Knox had already given Romey an earful on how things were going.

"I think we're making progress," Allyson said in a voice too sweet, too saccharine.

"Any trouble spots?" Romey was much better at lying.

"Nothing we can't handle," Allyson said.

"Good," Romey said. "I read the report from Dr. Lucy Abruzzo. It seems you two had a good meeting."

"We did. She's a very directed person, not much small talk with her. It was an extremely productive working session, and I'm sure there are efficiencies we can gain by leveraging the resources of her pathology department."

"Dr. Abruzzo may have a certain way about her, but she's supremely competent. I'm sure whatever ideas she's come up with will benefit our respective hospitals and our patients."

When they reached the rehab unit Romey walked the floor, checking in on the rooms.

"No available beds," he noted.

"We've been busy," Allyson said. "It's good for the hospital and the patients. They have to go somewhere."

"Shouldn't some of them have gone to White? You've seen the numbers, or have you forgotten?"

Romey led Allyson beyond the nurses station, out of earshot of the staff. A few patients were out on guided walks around the floor. Most got around with the aid of a walker.

"I hadn't forgotten, Romey," Allyson said. "But it's a lot easier to move these patients on paper than it is in real life. They have families nearby and don't see the benefit of going to White."

"Because you haven't made them see the benefit."

"I thought my job was to run this hospital," Allyson said with some bite.

Romey returned a half smile.

"The staff is a reflection of their leadership, is all I'm saying. If the staff believes it's better for their care, the patients will believe it, too."

Romey put his hands behind his back and walked with an exaggerated tilt from side to side, like he was out on a leisurely stroll. He popped into a unit where a frail, thin man could barely be seen beneath all the tubing connected to his body. Romey went to the patient's bedside after Allyson introduced him to the nurse.

"Hello, I'm Roman Janowski, CEO of White Memorial and the newest member of the board here at Suburban West. And who do I have the pleasure of meeting?"

A nose cannula supplied oxygen to this patient, but Roman knew for a fact he had been on mechanical ventilation not too long ago. He also knew this patient had chronic COPD and no hope of ever living anywhere but at Suburban West or some other long-term-care facility.

The man spoke in a whispered voice, weak with disease, and introduced himself as Albert Cunningham. Albert was a Vietnam War veteran, and onetime public address announcer for the Boston Red Sox.

Romey was patient with Albert, who got winded easily as he recounted his bio. The young nurse seemed taken by Romey's attentiveness and evident compassion. Suits rarely mingled with the guests. Romey might not have been blessed with six-pack abs, but he made up for it in other ways. At the end of their brief conversation, Romey took hold of Albert's hand to shake goodbye and commented on the substantial scarring there.

"Is that from the war?" Romey asked.

Albert explained it was a leftover from a bad case of hives.

"Seems like something's trying to get me at every turn," Albert said. "My lungs might be crap, but at least the ticker's still going strong."

Romey wished him well. Then he and Allyson were back in the corridor.

"Nice fellow," Romey said. "What the hell is he doing here?"

Allyson returned a blank stare. She had no idea how to respond. "Um, he's sick and needs to get better. I'm sorry, but I thought that's what a hospital was for."

"He's not going to get better, and he's eating your profit. He doesn't belong at White—or here, for that matter. He belongs at a long-term-care facility or a nursing home."

"He refuses to go there. He thinks that's where you go to die."

"So you send him home, and then he comes back here again."

"What would you like me to do, Roman? Put him on an ice floe with old and sick Eskimos?"

"I guess what I'd like is to go to your office so we can talk in private."

ALLYSON SAT behind her expansive desk in a spacious top-floor office. Romey stood and gazed out the window at the parking lot below. Not a great view, not great furniture or carpeting, but what could be expected from a suburban hospital bleeding red ink?

Allyson did not want her pro golf career to eclipse her accomplishments as a businessperson with a passion for health care. She had an open-door policy, and was happy to meet any doctor or nurse who had ideas on how to improve Suburban West's operation. She was loved here. Knox Singer was Romey's guy, and a perceived threat. Something had to give.

"Allyson, you've done a great job here at West."

"You're firing me, aren't you?"

Romey turned to face her, with arms behind his back, and his eyes momentarily to the floor. He paused before finally meeting her harsh gaze.

"The board agrees that this pond isn't big enough for two fish to swim."

"Oh, are you setting me free? Is that it?"

"I like the visual."

"It's better than the truth."

"And what's that?"

"I've been gutted, flayed, and served for dinner."

"We all have our perspectives."

Romey took a folder from his Tumi carrying case and set it on Allyson's desk.

"You'll find the terms are quite favorable. And of course I'll be an unqualified reference."

"That fills me with such warmth, I can't tell you."

"Just be grateful I've given you a graceful exit. I could have buried you, Allyson, and taken Suburban West over in the same day."

Allyson sent an icy smile. "Forever in your debt, Roman." She opened the folder and perused the three-page document within. "I'll have my lawyer look this over and get back to you."

"Have it signed by tomorrow," Roman said. "Or I'll make it ugly for you."

With that parting salvo, Romey strolled out of Allyson's former office.

CHAPTER 35

Sherri Platt's suburban street reminded Julie of Sam's neighborhood. Julie did not have to look for reminders of Sam; they were everywhere, and she never felt prepared for them. The episodes always left her sad, depleted, yet she wanted those remembrances to continue. They made her feel close again to Sam.

She had parked on the street. The sloping driveway accommodated tandem parking, and Julie did not want to block in the blue Toyota Corolla already parked there. The Toyota probably belonged to Sherri Platt. Julie did not know Sherri very well, had no idea of her personal life. Several reporters covering the Brandon Stahl trial had referred to Sherri as unmarried, a description that stuck in Julie's mind because it seemed superfluous, as if marriage somehow defined a woman.

That was years ago. Now Sherri could be married, or living here by herself, or with her parents. Julie had no way of knowing.

Sherri lived in a brick, two-story, single-family home with a small, hilly front yard. It was 4:30 in the afternoon and the sun had already set. And to think winter was still weeks away. No lights were on inside the home, and the garage door was closed. Someone had left an outside light on, so Julie could see the lawn was free of fallen leaves. A few pruned shrubs planted in a bed of light brown mulch provided a nice backbone to the thoughtful landscaping. The only thing differentiating Sherri's house from the others on the quiet street was an eerie feeling Julie could not shake.

She rang the doorbell, then cinched her overcoat tighter. No answer, so she rang it again. Two chimes sounded, hollow to her ears.

Julie looked around. Nothing suspicious here, quiet suburbia as far as the eyes could see. Standing on the front steps, Julie phoned Sherri, and then texted. Nothing. She turned the doorknob. Her desire to get Sherri's confession trumped better judgment.

To Julie's surprise, the knob turned. She opened the door a crack and called out into a darkened room.

"Sherri? Are you home?"

Julie opened the door a bit wider and jumped when an orange cat streaked from the darkness, slipped out the door, and brushed against her legs. She snatched the cat off the front step before it could venture any further. The cat made a weak protest—a soft meow. Julie set the pet down inside and it scampered off into the darkness, somewhere in the stillness of the silent home.

A moment passed before Julie became aware of something sticky on her hands, and felt certain the cat had just peed on her. In the dark it was hard to tell, so Julie used her phone's built-in flashlight for a better look.

She gasped as she saw a partial paw print, colored red, stamped on the palm of her right hand. Julie put her hand to her nose and breathed the familiar scent. Coppery. Metallic. Blood. She wiped the blood off on her pant leg and went inside the home. She called Sherri's name. No response. Her heart beat erratically. Perspiration dappled the back of her neck.

Feeling the wall for a light switch, Julie found one to the right of the door. No foyer here. The light illuminated a well-appointed living room with hardwood floors. The furniture was a bit old, a bit tired, and Julie wondered if Sherri lived here with her parents. It was immaculate, though, with no turned-over chairs, or broken mirrors. No signs of struggle. Where had the blood come from?

Julie set her gaze on a set of bloody paw prints forming a trail that vanished through a square entranceway. She put her hand to her mouth to stifle a cry.

Julie called Sherri's name again. No response again, so she ventured further into the home. She took a gulp of air and froze when the floor creaked from her weight. She took more steps forward, following the bloody paw trail through the entranceway. She knew it was irrational to head upstairs. She should call 911 and get the hell out of there. But she was a doctor and Sherri could be inside somewhere, injured, in need of help.

Julie peered up a dark stairwell and found a light switch on the wall. She flicked it on and now had a view into a kitchen and a hallway space adjacent to the stairs. A coatrack stood by a door to what Julie thought was the garage. No men's coats hung there, and the boot tray held only women's shoes. The home was remarkably uncluttered and the décor suggested a lone female resident. If Julie had to take a guess, she would say Sherri Platt lived alone.

Julie searched for anything out of the ordinary, a sign of an intruder, something that might necessitate a hasty retreat. All appeared normal, except for the bloody paw prints that were harder to see on the carpeted stairwell. Julie followed them up.

"Sherri?" Julie's voice sounded anxious. "Sherri, it's me, it's Julie from White Memorial. Are you all right? Please answer me."

Julie's voice sank into the upstairs gloom. She took each step slowly, pausing to listen. A faint meow emanated from a darkened doorway above. Julie picked up a sickly-sweet odor, a musty kind of smell. She gripped the handrail tight and felt a knowing in her gut. Something was horribly wrong here.

At the top of the stairwell Julie heard the cat's meow coming from a darkened doorway. She reached into the doorway, feeling around blindly until her fingers found the light switch. A bright glow spilled out into the hallway and a blur shot from the door at Julie's feet. She jumped, but relaxed when she saw it was just the orange cat with bloody paws.

Julie swallowed a breath and walked into the light. Sherri Platt lay facedown and spread-eagled on the floor. Her pink terrycloth bathrobe was splattered in crimson. The blood came from a hole blown through the back of Sherri's skull. There was no weapon on the ground, but Julie did not think this was a self-inflicted injury. Sherri's hair was matted and stuck together at the site of the wound.

Julie made a low moaning sound as she rushed to

Sherri's side. She did her best to avoid the blood, but it covered too much surface area around the body. Bloody paw prints marked the pristine tile like gruesome ink stamps. Sherri's head was tilted to one side, her expression a blank. Areas on Sherri's face were mottled with purplish markings, the result of lividity. Parts of her legs, visible where her bathrobe had splayed open, had the same ghastly shade.

Julie knelt at Sherri's side and felt for a pulse. She found none. None was expected. The skin was cool to the touch, and Julie felt the stiffness of rigor mortis. The blue of Sherri's eyes had faded to the hue of a cataract and a dark stripe cut horizontally across the sclera. Tache noire, the black spot of death.

Julie stood shakily and turned to face the bathroom mirror. She drew in a ragged breath, eyes wide with horror reflected back at her. Written on the mirror in crude lettering with red lipstick were three unmistakable words.

FOR BRANDON STAHL

CHAPTER 36

Java du Jour, a new coffee shop that had opened near White Memorial, sold copies of *The Boston Globe*. Michelle bought one and brought it over to the table where Lucy and Julie sat sipping their morning coffee. The day after Sherri Platt's murder, *The Globe* ran a feature front-page story. It had also made national news because of the macabre connection to Brandon Stahl. Three days later, the story was relegated to the Metro section of the Boston papers. Without leads, there was little to hold the interest of a media-saturated public with a short attention span. The national outlets left coverage to the local press. With no suspects, police had opened a tip line seeking the public's help in finding the killer.

The going theory was that Sherri Platt was the victim of some zealot, one of Brandon Stahl's supporters, a misguided defender of patient self-determination, who had developed a personal vendetta against Sherri because of her testimony. When Brandon lost his appeal this deranged individual snapped, and took revenge.

Many of the initial news reports included a photograph of Julie taken off the Internet without her knowledge or permission. Trevor was horrified and begged to stay home from school on Monday, anxious about all the attention he would receive. Julie relented, but had to go the police station for more interviews, so Trevor went to his father's.

He spent the weekend with Julie, though. It was relatively quiet. Calls from reporters eventually died down. Julie told them what she had told the police, with a few omissions. The media hounds did not need to know of her ongoing takotsubo investigation. Even if she had conclusive evidence of some rare heart condition plaguing patients at White, Julie would never go to the press without good reason. She also kept secret her belief that Sherri Platt had lied on the witness stand during the Brandon Stahl trial.

Those details, and others, Julie shared with the police during hours of interviews. The detectives did not know what to make of the takotsubo connection among Sam Talbot, Donald Colchester, and Tommy Grasso. Nor did Julie get the sense they viewed William Colchester as a suspect. The timing of Sherri's murder and Julie's meeting with her was most likely coincidental, one detective had said.

Julie did not believe it for a second.

"The funeral is on Sunday," Michelle noted as she skimmed the article. "Are you going?"

Julie's face showed the strain of a string of difficult days. "Yes, of course," she said. "I'm taking Jordan Cobb with me. He knew her—not well, but I think her murder really shook him up. I can't get the image of that poor girl out of my mind. It's just been awful."

Lucy set down her coffee. "You still think William Colchester was behind it?"

"I do. To silence Sherri Platt," Julie said. "She was going to open up to me; I'm sure of it. And I think that's what got her killed. I think Colchester bribed her to lie on the witness stand. Heck, he tried to bribe me, said he would do something on his budget committee to benefit White Memorial, and then he told me people would get hurt if I didn't back off."

"When did he say that?" Lucy asked.

"He came to my home after I met with Jordan," Julie said.

"And the police weren't a little concerned about that?" Michelle's sarcasm had bite.

"According to the detectives, Colchester had an alibi. He also said there's been no communication or texts between Colchester and Sherri. They think there would have been something if he had offered Sherri a bribe. But I say, if Sherri was going to come clean about taking a bribe, it certainly gave Colchester a motive."

Lucy made a look of disgust. "So a crooked state representative will get away with murder?"

"It's possible," Julie said. "The police have to do their jobs and I'll do mine. There's still a chance we can overturn Brandon's murder conviction if we can somehow show there's a pattern of rare heart attacks in seemingly healthy hearts."

"Won't explain the morphine, or Sherri's testimony," Michelle said.

"I don't think anything can explain Sherri's testimony now," Julie answered.

Lucy said, "I looked at the medical record Jordan sent me to review."

Julie shot Lucy a glance, her eyes showing concern. "You mean our helper. I don't want his name getting out."

"All secrets are safe with me," Michelle said. "I feel a connection to this, too. I want to be of help."

Julie gave Michelle's arm a slight squeeze. Getting to know Michelle, the friendship that had formed, was one of the few bright spots to emerge in the aftermath of Sam's accident.

"What's your take on Tommy's file?" Julie asked.

"My take is I'm not a cardiologist," Lucy said. "How the heck did our *helper* learn so much?"

Julie nodded her agreement. "It's pretty remarkable."

"Well, the EKG does look unusual for a typical heart attack. I wish he'd had an echo done. Even without one, I wouldn't dismiss a takotsubo incident, but I wouldn't diagnose it, either."

"Someone deleted something in that record postmortem," Julie reminded her.

"Are you suggesting a cover-up?" Michelle asked.

"My best guess is Dr. Coffey locked me out of Colchester's file for a reason. But I know there were deletions in Sam and Tommy's records, as well as Donald Colchester's. And all three had the same unusual EKG, and we know for sure about left ventricle apical ballooning in two of the cases. Something isn't right here. Not right at all."

"Forget the EKGs for a second," Lucy said. "Explain to me how someone with chronic COPD like Tommy, a quadriplegic like Sam, and guy with advanced ALS all suffer a stress-induced heart attack. What kind of stress event could they have had? It's honestly never made sense to me."

Julie sighed aloud and recalled how Dr. Coffey had said something very similar. Nothing was adding up. It never had. Takotsubo was an instant reaction to an extreme stimulus. These men were all debilitated in some capacity. What kind of stimulation could they have possibly experienced?

Julie's stomach rumbled. She had not eaten breakfast, and the line at the counter was not long anymore.

"I'm going to grab a muffin," Julie said. "I'll be right back."

She asked the counterperson for a banana walnut muffin and realized she had been rude not to get something for her friends. She decided to surprise them with a breakfast treat and ordered two more of the same muffin. She brought the treats back to the table on a plate.

"I got one for each of us," Julie said.

Lucy picked up her muffin, examined it closely, and set it back down.

"Do you know if this muffin has walnuts in it?" she asked.

"Yeah," Julie. "It's banana walnut, to be precise. I've had them before. They're delicious."

Lucy pushed the muffin away. "Oh, good. You promise to give me CPR?" She said this with a twisted grin.

Julie slapped her forehead. "Oh my gosh. I'm so sorry. I completely spaced."

Michelle got it. "Nut allergy, I'm guessing."

"Horribly allergic," Lucy said. "Growing up I was the only girl in my school with an EpiPen in her backpack. Now they're as common as erasers, it seems."

Julie perked up and looked at Lucy in a curious way. She picked up the muffin and examined it closely, turning it over in her hand, studying it as though she'd never seen a muffin before.

"See if they'll exchange it for a blueberry," Lucy said.

"No, it's not that," Julie answered, her voice a little distant. "It's what you said earlier. What kind of stress event could Sam and the others have experienced? It doesn't make sense, right?"

"Right," Lucy responded.

"What are you getting at?" Michelle asked.

Julie set the muffin back down on the plate. "Let me ask you this, Lucy. Could that acute coronary pathology have manifested as an allergic phenomenon?"

Lucy's eyebrows lifted as she mulled this over.

"I never gave it any thought," she said, "but I suppose it's possible. It could have been an allergic reaction, yes."

"Which means it might not be takotsubo after all," Julie said with some excitement.

"Then what could it be?" Michelle asked.

"To be honest, I have no idea," Julie said.

"It's worth looking into," Lucy agreed. "But there's a problem with that theory."

"Which is?" Julie could not mask her disappointment.

"We did slides of Sam's heart muscle to look at the muscle fibers. If it was an allergic reaction, we should have seen mast cell activation and a differential increase of eosinophils."

"What are mast cells and eosinophils?" Michelle asked.

"They're both part of the immune system," Lucy said. "Eosinophils are white blood cells that, along with mast cells, control mechanisms associated with allergy and asthma. If it was some sort of allergy, I would expect those cells to be present in large quantity. But that's not what the slides showed."

"Is there any chance the slides were done incorrectly?"

Lucy shrugged. Years in the autopsy business taught her that anything was possible.

"Sure. If the tech was distracted or a wrong stain was used, it's possible."

"Would you mind checking for me?"

"You're my sister from another mister. Of course not."

"Sounds like we've made some progress here," Michelle said as she flipped a page in the newspaper.

"You know what I'm thinking." Lucy's expression showed concern.

"What?" Julie asked.

"I'm thinking, look at what happened to Sherri Platt. Julie, are you really sure you want to dig into this any deeper?"

CHAPTER 37

The automatic doors of the ICU swung open and in came Shirley Mitchell. Shirley was not Julie's first patient to come back to the unit on a hospital bed, nor would she be the last. This time, instead of pneumonia coupled with peripheral artery disease, Shirley had returned to the ICU with serious GI bleeding. The nurses watched her carefully throughout the morning, but her bleeding persisted and her blood pressure had begun to drop. Shirley received one unit of blood and two more were on the way.

Julie put on her protective equipment: a blue plastic gown, gloves, and mask with a splatter shield. She would be prepared for any brisk bleeding. During the initial examination, Shirley was agitated, swatting at the nurses, refusing to have leads placed for telemetry, and making a grab to pull out the IV. At one point she yelled, "The movie is over and I don't want any popcorn!"

Clearly, Shirley was not at all herself. Julie checked the readouts after the nurses finally attached her to the telemetry monitor, blood pressure cuff, and pulse oximeter.

Oxygen level was only about 87 percent on three liters nasal cannula. Her heart rhythm was irregular and fast, alternating between 115 to 120 with frequent bursts to the 140s. Blood pressure rang off as critical: seventy-eight over forty-four. They were behind. The bleeding was obviously profuse and Julie needed all hands on deck. She started with the litany of orders needed to save Shirley's life.

"Nancy—hang two liters of nasal saline, wide open."

"Vicky—call the blood bank and tell them to send two units of blood superstat. And to prep for four more units."

Marie, the secretary, poked her head around the corner. "Dr. Devereux, I seated the family in the waiting room. I told them it would be a while until she stabilizes. Anything else you need?"

"Thanks, Marie, I'm good."

Julie examined Shirley's battered arms. No nurse would be successful in finding another IV site anytime soon. Placing a central line seemed inevitable. But to start, Julie needed to develop a plan of attack to stop the bleeding.

Her first phone call was to the gastroenterologist, Dr. Morgan. After some negotiation (necessary when dealing with a specialist) it was decided to proceed with a CT scan of the abdomen, to be followed by a colonoscopy after the patient stabilized. Dr. Morgan was betting on diverticulosis as the cause, which in 90 percent of cases would stop bleeding on its own. But when Julie got a call from the lab, plans needed to change quickly.

"Shirley Mitchell's troponin is ten point four," the lab tech reported. "And her hematocrit is only twenty-two."

Julie, her face grave, announced the news to her team. The job of keeping the blood going into Shirley's body from coming out was easy to say, but harder to do. Those labs indicated the job was far from complete. The CT came back as expected: nonspecific findings. Julie gave Dr. Morgan another call.

"I would consider a colo," Dr. Morgan said, "but right now, with her lung disease and her heart in bad shape, it's just too risky. She'll arrest on my OR table."

"But, Jim, she needs a better blood count to stop the heart attack, which won't happen unless you get in there and stop the bleeding."

"Seriously, Julie, this lady is a train wreck. I don't need the quality safety committee after me when she dies from the colonoscopy. Call interventional radiology, I think Kim is on. She'll help you."

Julie picked up the phone and was connected to Dr. Kim Sung in interventional radiology. Arrangements were made and soon enough Shirley was carted off to radiology. After two hours, Julie took a call from Dr. Sung.

"Hey Julie, I tried my best. I coiled a couple of places, but she is oozing everywhere. She's like a pincushion. Nothing seemed to help. I think you've got to get surgery in on this. I have a page for you. Sorry I couldn't get it done."

Julie thanked Dr. Sung for her efforts, but had her doubts about the surgery. If GI would not consider a colonoscopy because of Shirley's cardiac and pulmonary risk factors, it was likely she would get even more pushback from surgical consults.

Only one option remained—Shirley would have to stay in the ICU, get drugged up, get more swollen, and deal with the pain and bleeding as it came and went like the tides. Julie could provide little in the way of meaningful therapy.

Shirley was brought back to the ICU and awake when Julie checked up on her again. Her eyes were open, but dull as if they were covered with film. Her short hair lay matted and without luster. Her lips were two bloodless threads on a starkly sallow face.

"Shirley, how are you holding up?" Julie asked.

"I want to die," Shirley managed to say in a weak, gravelly voice.

The words hit Julie hard, and of course she thought of Sam.

"Well, we don't want that to happen," Julie said.

"I do. The pain is horrible. I want to be with my Bobby. I want to go with him."

Bobby was Shirley's husband of fifty years. There were children and grandchildren in the picture, some now in the waiting room, but in this condition Shirley took no joy from them. Everything hurt, and hurt horribly.

Julie locked eyes with Amber, the young nurse who had cared for Shirley the last time. Shirley's predicament was indeed dire, and Julie believed the sick woman was justified in her wish to end her suffering. All Julie could do now was manage the pain with a little help from Dilaudid.

While conducting her exam, Julie noticed significant erythema on the back of Shirley's left hand ringing the 18-G IV. It had not been present at the last check. The red inflammation looked similar to Sam's outbreak of hives, but distinct enough for Julie to know it was not the same condition.

"How long has she had this redness?" Julie asked Amber, a tinge of concern in her voice.

Amber looked at Julie, a little flummoxed. "I just noticed it now," she said.

Julie called for a stat surgical consult and while waiting, began her procedures. She placed an internal jugular central venous access line and right radial arterial line. Shirley would need aggressive resuscitation for hemorrhagic shock using fluids and pressors. A full panel of lab work was repeated. Results came back fast, and one got Julie's attention right away. Shirley's blood gas reading showed her oxygen level was now below sixty millimeters of mercury, which meant respiratory failure. Shirley actually looked worse than her blood gas indicated. She was pale and sweaty, mottled on her arms and legs. Julie called out to the staff: "We need to intubate in here!"

Additional nursing staff charged into Shirley's room. Tammy, the respiratory therapist, began bagging Shirley with an ambu bag while Julie set up her endotracheal tube. One nurse was drawing up etomidate and another busied herself with the suction tubing.

The intubation went as smoothly as expected given the circumstances. Shirley was heading toward unconsciousness and very little sedation was needed. Her blood pressure, however, tanked, as usually happens after an intubation, and additional boluses were given.

The surgeon, a handsome man with a Harvard pedigree, finally arrived to do his assessment.

It's about time, Julie thought.

He was immediately distracted by Shirley's arm.

"Julie, good thing you called. Looks like she has a NSTI infection."

Necrotizing soft-tissue infections were increasingly more common at hospitals everywhere, for reasons Julie could not quite fathom. Poor woman. Not only did she have hemorrhagic shock, but septic shock as well. One hour later, Shirley was on her way to the OR for emergency debridement, a procedure she was deemed fit enough to survive despite her fragile condition. The timing of Shirley's departure coincided with the end of Julie's workday, but she was not headed for home. She had a stop to make first.

MCI Cedar Junction.

LUCY FOUND Dr. Becca Stinson with her eyes pressed against the lens of a microscope. She tapped the young resident on the shoulder, which caused a bit of a scare, but got her attention.

"Becca, do you have a minute?" Lucy asked.

The question was rhetorical. Everyone always had a minute for the boss.

"Yes, of course," Becca said.

Lucy brought a clipboard that held printouts with the lab order for Sam Talbot's stains. She handed the clipboard to Becca. "Do you recall doing these stains?"

As part of their training, residents learned the equipment and procedures by doing tests typically handled by the lab techs. For Becca and her peers, processing stains and reviewing path slides was as common a practice as checking e-mail. Equally common were long hours without sunlight. Lucy noticed Becca's peaked complexion and how her wide eyes had rings around them, a mark of too many hours gazing through a microscope. Lucy brought the paper trail of Sam's extensive lab tests, hoping a quick review would refresh Becca's overtaxed memory.

"This is Sam Talbot, Julie Devereux's husband, right?" Becca said, while leafing through the pages.

"Fiancé," Lucy corrected. "And yes, that's right. I was wondering if you remember anything about the stain."

Becca's expression went blank. "Like what?"

"Specifically if the eosinophils in the stain showed up pink."

Becca strained, trying to recall.

"I think that's right. It was a long time ago, though. I thought I had put something about allergic reaction in my lab report, but it's not what's indicated in the report you handed me, so I guess I'm mistaken."

"Take a look at this, then. It's the actual slide."

Lucy went to the digital slide scanner and in no time had the slide of Sam's heart on the display screen for Becca's review. It was the same image Lucy had studied in her office after the autopsy and again moments ago. A sea of purple dots covered darker patches to indicate denser tissue morphology. Each slide was like a little painting, and Lucy found the variations, the differing contrasts, and abstract shapes endlessly fascinating. Like paintings, each slide had a story to tell, but the interpretations were seldom subjective. White Memorial used an automated system to apply the H&E stains, the gold standard for this procedure, and the slide on the screen clearly showed elevated neutrophils. The purple coloring was a common occurrence in myocardial infarctions, but also supported Lucy's takotsubo theory. End of story. If Sam had experienced some sort of allergic reaction, as Julie speculated, the eosinophils in the slide would have stained pink during the chemical reaction, but such was not the case.

"Like I said, it was a while ago and I've done a lot of stains since then. So I guess my memory isn't so great after all."

Lucy thanked Becca, who did have a memory to rival Lucy's. But slides were slides, and memories were not always to be trusted.

IT WAS a repeat of the last time Julie was here. It was how prison life was designed to be—the same thing, day in and day out. Julie had made the call forty-eight hours earlier and gotten on the visitors' list. A different employee with the same stern look processed Julie's ID through a standard series of checks. Julie was cleared to go inside. While waiting for the trap guard to show, she phoned Dr. Goodman in the ICU.

"How's Shirley Mitchell?"

"She's out of surgery but not hemodynamically stable. Could take another twenty-four hours."

Or longer than that.

The dark thought passed quickly. There was every chance Shirley Mitchell would never be stable enough to be taken off mechanical ventilation. Julie's conversation with the sick woman came back to her. "Let me die," she had said, or something to that effect. Sam had asked the same of Julie, Julie had championed that very right, and Brandon Stahl might be imprisoned for fulfilling that very wish. Julie ended her call with Dr.

Goodman and was soon led down a familiar corridor, stuck in the middle of a grim processional.

The trap guard escorted Julie to an empty partitioned section. She took a seat on a metal stool bolted to the floor, and waited. A loud buzzer went off. Looking to her left, Julie saw Brandon Stahl enter the room behind the glass. This time, Brandon did not need to prompt Julie to pick up the wall-mounted phone. He still looked frail to her with his mop-top hairdo, twiggy arms, and a face incapable of hiding his humanity.

"How are you, Brandon?"

Brandon's expression was grave. "I should be asking you."

"You heard the news about Sherri, I take it."

"We may be locked up from the outside world, but we're not cut off completely. Tragic."

Julie returned a skeptical stare and said nothing for a time.

"You don't think I had anything to do with her death, do you?" Brandon asked.

"Did you?"

"No," Brandon said emphatically.

"I saw the bullet hole in Sherri's head, and it's not something that will leave me anytime soon."

Brandon's eyes flared. For the first time Julie saw in them a look befitting a hardened criminal.

"Have you come here to tell me you're not going to try to help anymore?"

"No."

"Good. Because I had nothing to do with that poor girl's murder. I don't care if she testified against me or not. What happened to her was a horrible crime. But

I didn't send any inflammatory messages to my so-called devotees, like some of the news reports implied. Contrary to popular belief, I do not want to be, nor should I be, the poster child for mercy killing. Don't thrust that mantle on me."

Brandon jabbed with his finger. "I never asked one person to stand outside the prison and protest on my behalf. They send me letters all the time with stories about their sick mothers and fathers, aunts, uncles, whatever, and ask for my advice on how to kill them. How do they get the drugs? How do they properly inject them with a needle? Like I'm Dr. Kevorkian's protégé or something. That's my legacy. I'm the how-to-do-it guy for murder." Brandon shook his head in disgust. "That's not me. That's not who I am." His eyes narrowed. "I'm just a nurse. That's all I ever wanted to be."

Tears almost came to Brandon's eyes. He could cry, and would not be alone. On both sides of the partition tears flowed freely, and the emotions spilling out were raw and unfiltered.

"I want you to try and remember something for me," Julie said.

"Okay."

"Did Donald Colchester have any allergic reaction that you can remember?"

"Allergic reaction?"

"Anything that stood out in your mind."

"That's a long time ago, and I've had a lot on my mind since then."

"Understood. But I'm looking for a link between Sam's case and Donald's."

"And you think it could be allergy related?"

"We're having a hard time coming up with an event

that could cause these disabled men to have been scared or stressed to death."

Brandon leaned back in his chair, lowered his gaze, and folded his arms. "Did you look at Sam's medical record?"

"I did," Julie said. "But nothing jumped out at me."

Brandon rubbed his chin, deep in thought.

Julie's mouth formed a grimace. She wanted an answer, a bit of light shined in the dark.

"Are you thinking an anaphylaxis-type allergic reaction?"

"Doesn't even have to be that severe."

"And there was *nothing* in Sam's file?"

"No. And I looked it over very closely."

"What about Colchester's file, then? Did you look at that?"

"It's gone."

"Gone?"

"As in, deleted from the EMR system, or some glitch. IT can't figure it out. Believe me, I've asked. Best I came away with is a help desk ticket, which is why I'm counting on your memory."

"Seems funny, you know. You looking into this and then Colchester's EMR file goes missing."

"Yeah, though 'suspicious' was the word that popped into my mind. The doctor who took my copy of the file suddenly isn't answering my calls and surprise, surprise, I can't seem to get a meeting with him, either."

"I don't know." Brandon held a breath. "I mean, we're talking a long time ago. Years."

"Just try." Julie leaned forward and put her hand against the glass. "Was there anything?"

Brandon groaned, closed his eyes tight, and grabbed

a clump of his hair as if it hurt to think that far in the past, to think about it at all. Then his eyes sprang open and he looked almost pleased.

"I got something," he said. "I just remembered. It was horrible, too, because he was paralyzed."

"What was horrible?"

"Urticaria," Brandon said. "Hives. A bad case of them, too. They just broke out one day. We gave him antihistamines of course, but I spent a lot of time putting cold compresses and wet cloths on the affected areas."

Julie's stomach dropped at the same time her mouth fell open. So much had happened since the accident. It was all a blur. She had cared for Sam, eaten lunch with him, cried with him, nurtured him, brought in Michelle so he would stop begging to die—all while working her job and looking after Trevor. Of course it could slip her mind. Hives. And Julie now knew exactly what entry someone had deleted from Sam's medical record.

CHAPTER 38

The overcast day seemed a perfect match for Trevor's somber mood. Poor kid, he wanted to be anywhere but in the car driving with his mom to Beverly Municipal Airport on Massachusetts's North Shore.

For the past few miles Trevor had kept his face in his phone.

"What time are we going to get back?" Trevor asked. "Jake wants me to come over."

Julie mulled it over a moment. "Well, to be honest, I thought we could spend the day together," she said. "After this jaunt we could maybe get a bite to eat, catch a movie or something. The IMAX isn't too far from here."

Julie came up with this plan only after her son tried to make a plan of his own. She wanted time with Trevor, as much of it as she could get, but had been so preoccupied with this upcoming rendezvous it had not occurred to her to make a day out of it.

Trevor contemplated the offer, and eventually he gave a gentle nod.

"Sounds like fun, Mom. I'll see what's playing." He returned to his smartphone.

"Nothing too violent, please."

Trevor gave a sidelong glance with a perfect "come on now" expression.

"Okay, how about nothing crazy violent," Julie said. "Superhero violence, fine, but no serial killers, or assassins or ninjas or any of that. Deal? I just don't think I can handle it."

Trevor reached up and touched Julie's shoulder. She could see in his eyes he was thinking about his mom and Sherri Platt.

"Maybe let's just go for lunch somewhere," Trevor suggested.

Julie gave Trevor's hand an appreciative squeeze. "Sounds good to me, honey," she said.

With everything that had happened, Julie was not about to leave Trevor home alone while she went on this jaunt. It did not take an M.D. to know Dr. Gerald Coffey had been intentionally avoiding her for days. She had called and e-mailed, all without reply. She even resorted to camping out in front of his office only to learn he was off for the week. A staycation, his assistant had called it. The same assistant also made a point of saying Dr. Coffey was available for patient consultation if needed. This meant he should have been available to answer Julie's numerous calls.

What Julie wanted were answers, and those answers could not wait for Dr. Coffey's return. Someone had intentionally deleted data from Sam's file, and from the file of Tommy Grasso, and quite probably from Donald Colchester's as well. Julie confirmed with Lynn Golden, Tommy Grasso's respiratory therapist, that not long before Tommy died, he'd developed a bad case of hives. Stunned by the revelation, Julie double-checked Tommy's EMR and found no entry of the reaction anywhere. Jordan double-checked and had confirmed a single deletion in the transaction log. They both saw reasonable cause to correlate the two. Someone had answers, and Julie hoped that someone was landing at Beverly Municipal Airport on time.

This rendezvous would not have taken place, at least not in this way, without Trevor's help. Julie knew Dr. Coffey owned a plane. He'd made a point of bragging to her about his flying during that awful meeting. On a whim, she'd asked Trevor if it was possible to track down a pilot by their flight plan. Not that she expected Trevor to know, but she thought he might be able to figure it out. Trevor jumped on the assignment in a way he rarely did with homework, and in a matter of minutes came up with the answer.

"I just searched Gerald Coffey's name in the FAA's online registry and found a record of his plane," he had said.

Julie had been in Trevor's bedroom, staring over his shoulder in astonishment as he typed with dazzling speed. It seemed a new Web page loaded with each blink of his eyes. In the background Winston could be heard scampering about his cage, seeming as excited as Julie. The FAA page Trevor found showed an entry for a Diamond DA40 owned by Dr. Gerald Coffey.

Julie had Trevor do some additional research. "Made in Canada and Australia, the four-seat aircraft is considered a first choice for discerning pilots." At $184,000, one would have to be very discerning. Trevor searched for flight plans on a Web site called FlightAware. There were none, though he soon discovered that flight plans were not required for private planes.

Julie's disappointment was short-lived.

"When there's cloud cover he would have to fly IFR, and that requires him by law to file a flight plan," Trevor said, reading a Web page on the topic.

"You're brilliant," Julie said, ruffling his hair.

The forecast for the weekend was overcast, so in the morning Julie asked Trevor to do the search again. Bingo. Dr. Coffey planned a flight from Beverly to Providence, Rhode Island, and back to Beverly again. He would be landing at 11:30 in the morning.

Julie had contemplated surprising Dr. Coffey at his Marblehead home, but what she wanted was neutral territory. She worried that he would see her questions as threatening. If Dr. Coffey were involved in some kind of cover-up, a conspiracy of some sort, he might act erratically, might claim self-defense when the police arrived to find Julie's lifeless body in the same gruesome state as Sherri Platt's.

How hives and rare heart attacks in healthy hearts could be tied to Dr. Coffey and William Colchester, to Brandon Stahl's murder conviction, and to the deaths of Tommy Grasso and Sam Talbot, Julie could not begin to fathom. Lucy's findings were inconclusive. Becca, whom Lucy claimed possessed a steel-trap memory, recalled Sam's pathology slide as showing an allergic reaction, but the actual slide showed nothing of the kind. Julie could not explain the discrepancy, just as Brandon Stahl could not explain how morphine ended up in his apartment.

Julie and Trevor arrived in plenty of time to find

parking and to get settled in the small airport's lounge. Through a bank of tall picture windows, Julie watched Dr. Coffey's D40 descend from the overcast sky, appearing almost to the minute of when he was scheduled to land. Trevor's expression was priceless. He had figured out where Dr. Coffey would be, and seeing his theory prove out made him beam with delight. Julie hugged her son to her body and kissed the top of his head.

"Good work, sweetheart," she said. "Now when he shows up, I want you to wait over by the Coke machine. This has to be a private conversation."

The lounge area was a spacious room with navigation maps on the wall, a few vending machines, some tables and chairs, and not much else. A few minutes after he landed, Dr. Coffey entered the lounge looking every bit the pilot. He had on a brown leather jacket and gold-rimmed aviator sunglasses, which he wore despite the cloud cover. Every one of his silver hairs looked perfectly placed. He walked with purposeful strides until he came to a hard stop the moment he realized the figure in the middle of the lounge was Julie. He exchanged his sunglasses for his other spectacles, the ones made of black plastic with thick lenses, the ones that magnified his surprised eyes.

"Dr. Devereux, what on earth are you doing here?"

"Dr. Coffey, what a funny surprise."

Judging by Dr. Coffey's glower, he found nothing funny about it.

"You know, I was thinking about you. Thinking there must be something wrong with my phone," Julie said. "I called you a number of times and e-mailed as well, but never got a response. Lucky for me I bumped into you, in the airport of all places. Was that you who just landed? Beautiful plane."

"It was. But again, what are you doing here?" Dr. Coffey's voice had the edge of an ax.

Julie pointed to Trevor. "My son is an aspiring pilot. He likes to come and watch the planes land."

"Really? I've never seen you here before," Dr. Coffey said.

"We go to different airports," Julie said without hesitating.

Dr. Coffey glanced at his expensive wristwatch.

"I'm afraid I'm in a rush, Julie," he said. "It's nice to see you. Best to your boy."

Dr. Coffey walked past her, but Julie reached out and gently took hold of his arm.

The doctor whirled on his heels, his cheeks reddening while his nostrils flared like those of an angry bull.

"Oh, no worries, I'm in a hurry, too," Julie said in a calm voice. "This won't take but a minute."

"Perhaps another time," Dr. Coffey said.

"I just want to know if you had anything to do with my no longer having access to Donald Colchester's medical record?"

Dr. Coffey's lips were closed, his expression serious. "Why on earth would you ask me something like that?"

"I gave you my copy of Colchester's file and the next thing I know, I don't have access to the electronic version. I'm just curious. Do you know anything about that?"

"That—that—has nothing to do with me, I assure you."

Julie took note of Dr. Coffey's brief stutter. But she studied his body language a moment, and decided he was a better liar than poor Sherri Platt.

"I would like to have the file back, if I may," Julie said.

Dr. Coffey shook his head. "I'm afraid that's impossible. I shredded those documents after you left. There was no reason for me to keep them."

"I guess you didn't realize I wouldn't be able to access them again."

"To be honest, none of this is really my concern."

Julie caught a nervous glance from Trevor. He could tell this conversation was tense, and conflict, especially in the wake of his parents' divorce, was something he worked hard to avoid.

"Let me ask you something medical, if I may."

Dr. Coffey sighed aloud. "If you must."

"What kind of allergic reaction could cause a heart attack?"

The sneer on Dr. Coffey's face was meant to intimidate.

"I would think you would know a life-threatening manifestation of allergic disease is usually the result of anaphylaxis." He eyed Julie a little darkly. "You're not back on the takotsubo bandwagon, are you?"

"Something like it," Julie said. "Of course, my first thought was of anaphylaxis, but what I was looking for was an allergic reaction similar to takotsubo."

"And I asked you to let that go."

"Allow me, if you will, to share a little something I found out. You see, I may have graduated from a state medical school, but even I know how to do a Google search. And do you know what you get when you search 'allergic reaction similar to takotsubo,' those exact words? You get a link to Kounis syndrome."

Dr. Coffey folded his arms as if to say he found Julie's revelation and investigation a personal affront.

"Kounis syndrome," Julie continued. "Allergic angina, allergic myocardial infarction—I'm not telling you anything you don't already know."

"No, you're not."

"So in your professional opinion, could Kounis syndrome be misdiagnosed as takotsubo?"

Dr. Coffey pondered the question in a thoughtful manner. "I guess it's possible."

"Type one Kounis syndrome is an acute allergic event found in patients without predisposing factors for coronary artery disease. That sort of coronary artery spasm could cause apical ballooning in the left ventricle, could it or could it not?"

"Am I on the witness stand, Dr. Devereux?" Dr. Coffey gave a tight-lipped smile.

"It's just a question," Julie said.

"Sure. Why not. You seem to have all the answers. What do you need me for, anyway?"

"What if the allergen didn't show on the pathology slide?"

Exasperation now from Dr. Coffey. "Then I'd say the lab tech screwed up the stain, or someone switched the slide."

The twinkle in Dr. Coffey's eyes made Julie uneasy. *Someone switched the slide.* Her thoughts went whirling. *Could it be possible?* If someone did that, could they also have planted morphine in Brandon's apartment? Bribed Sherri Platt into testifying to ensure a conviction? If so, what was being covered up, and what was Dr. Coffey's part? *Why would he even plant the suggestion that someone switched the slide?* Julie wondered. Overconfidence, she thought. Perhaps he considered her an unworthy adversary. He got a rush flying planes; maybe he was addicted to risks, like a criminal who left clues for the cops trying to catch him.

"If you don't mind, I'd really like to go home now," Dr. Coffey said. "I had a great flight, and I don't want anything to spoil what has been until this moment a terrific day."

Julie returned a wan smile. "I'm wondering if you know of any drug that could cause a Kounis syndrome reaction? Something that might have a connection to, I don't know—hives."

Julie held a breath. This was the moment. This was why she wanted to confront him in person. How would he react? What would he do or say?

A defense lawyer could not have coached a better facial expression. Dr. Coffey was stoic, utterly emotionless. He shook his head to show his disbelief.

"You can't let this go, can you?" he said in a harsh voice. "I've seen you all over the news. Everywhere you go, Julie, bad things seem to follow. Why don't you just leave this one alone?" Dr. Coffey looked over his shoulder at Julie's son, and held his gaze long enough for Trevor to shrink under the weight of his stare. "For everyone's sake, just leave this alone and move on with your life."

"I can't do that," Julie said.

Dr. Coffey shrugged. "Fine. Have it your way. But if you confront me like this again, I will report you to the Mass Medical Board for erratic behavior and have your license pulled faster than I landed that plane. That's a promise. You have a nice day."

Dr. Coffey exchanged his regular glasses for his aviator sunglasses and marched away without looking back.

LINCOLN COLE watched as Julie and Trevor walked from the airport lounge to her Prius, parked in the public lot not far from his sedan. He called his employer and relayed the conversation as he remembered it. Some of the medical jargon was a bit much, but Lincoln had a good enough grasp to convey the key points. His level of knowledge might have been on a need-to-know basis, but Lincoln was right in thinking what he overheard meant big trouble for his employer.

"This has to be handled."

"Sherri Platt handled?" Lincoln asked.

"Yes. But we need discretion."

"Not another national media story?"

"That would be preferable."

"I happen to know Julie is taking Jordan Cobb to Sherri Platt's funeral and bringing him home."

"And that matters why?"

"Mr. Cobb doesn't live in the best neighborhood."

"Well then, it seems we're all set here."

The call went silent. The beach, Lincoln Cole's early retirement, was very close, so close he could almost feel the sand against the soles of his feet.

CHAPTER 39

Sherri Platt's funeral was tragic in every way. It was the second funeral in as many months Julie had attended for a person who left this world well before their time. Sherri's family and friends spoke eloquently of a woman with a kind heart who loved helping others and loved being a nurse. The pews of the small Congregational church in Melrose were full of mourners, and the tears flowed freely. Many of Sherri's colleagues had come to pay their respects, but Julie was most impressed to see Roman Janowski, White's CEO, there as well. He spoke with Julie before the service.

"How are you holding up? It must have been such a shock to make that horrible discovery," Roman said.

"It was, and I'm doing all right. Thank you for asking."

"If you need time off, we'll make it happen. Don't you worry there."

"Thank you, Roman. But I'm glad to be at work. Honestly, I need the distraction."

"Please, call me Romey. All my friends do."

"Romey it is."

Julie thought about sharing her concerns over possible Kounis syndrome in patients at White, but knew better than to go to Roman without absolute proof. Dr. Coffey would certainly call foul, accuse Julie of harassment, and while she wanted answers, Julie also wanted to keep her job.

"You're a wonderful doctor, Julie," Romey said. "Just know that we're here for you in any way you need. You've been through an awful lot these past few months."

Roman gave Julie a quick embrace and she realized they were about the same height. He always seemed taller to her, perhaps because of how he carried himself.

During the service, Jordan Cobb sat in solemn silence beside Julie. He looked handsome in his dark suit, but from the way he shifted in his seat, Julie could tell Jordan was more comfortable in a pair of scrubs. The service had deeply moved him and after the final eulogy Jordan wiped tears from his eyes. Julie was touched by his emotion, but she was crying as well. The service brought back disturbing memories of a cat with bloody paws, of Sherri's collapsed skull and inert body on a blood-soaked bathroom floor, of those chilling words (For Brandon Stahl) crudely scrawled on the mirror in red lipstick.

Therapy had helped Julie deal with her divorce, but she questioned if anything could get her over the gruesome discovery and the guilt that had followed. Julie kept telling herself, if only she had not pushed for answers, Sherri Platt might be alive. The guilt reminded her of a phrase she uttered constantly in her head after Sam's accident.

If only . . .

The afternoon service ended after five and Julie made the drive to Dorchester in the dark. Even if Jordan owned a car, Julie would still have offered to drive him to the service. They were both connected to Sherri Platt through Brandon Stahl and it felt fitting to be together on this solemn day. The world outside her car windows seemed to have slowed. Thanksgiving was on Thursday, and the coming holiday might have tamed the city's typical kinetic energy. Paul would be joining Julie, Trevor, Julie's mom, and a few other friends and relatives for a Thanksgiving meal at her Cambridge home. Julie was grateful her divorce was amicable so she and Paul could share holidays together, but it was still a solo effort and there was much to prepare. Julie was way behind schedule.

Julie and Jordan's talk of the funeral turned to talk of their fledgling investigation.

Jordan said, "You still think Colchester had Sherri killed to keep her quiet about lying on the witness stand?"

"That's my best guess," Julie said. "I think he made it look like it was one of Brandon's supporters to cover his tracks."

"What's the motive?"

"Bribery is not good for a political career, and I'm sure he wanted to keep Brandon in jail, as well. It's why he planted the morphine. He believes for certain Brandon killed his son and had to make the case airtight. Couldn't happen without the drugs and Sherri's testimony."

"Makes sense," Jordan said. "But you told me Colchester played the grieving dad only to the media."

"He did. And you make a good point. I think his

wife had something to do with it. Colchester said something about her being emotionally fragile. What if she was so convinced Brandon killed her son that William Colchester made it a reality for her well-being?"

"I'd say that's a pretty twisted marriage."

Julie said, "Though, I wonder why Colchester didn't initially fight the request to exhume the body? That came after. Strange."

Jordan gave it some thought.

"Maybe a doctor he consulted with told him exhuming the body could cast doubt in the minds of the jury." Jordan tossed out the idea with a shrug. "Like it would muddy up the waters," he continued, "make it harder to prove morphine did him in. I'd say that's enough of a motive for Colchester to grease the judge's palm."

"Maybe the doctor he consulted was named Coffey."

Jordan exhaled loudly. "Coffey? Why him?"

"Heart attacks in healthy hearts at White? It's the equivalent of a politician caught making a bribe. Not a good advertisement for the hospital, and it's a fast track to professional ruin. Coffey's protecting his ego and reputation while jeopardizing patients' lives, that's what I think. Suppose he was following Brandon Stahl's case closely because he knew it was really Kounis syndrome that killed him. If that were true, I'd say he knew about the motion to exhume the body, and then approached Colchester with some free advice about it, if you know what I mean."

Jordan mulled it over. "Makes sense," he said. "But if it's Kounis syndrome killing the patients, how do you explain Sam's slides? There was no indication of allergy there."

A car that had been tailgating Julie gave an angry honk, changed lanes without signaling, and passed quickly on her left. Ah, the joys of driving in the city never ceased.

"It's simple," Julie said. "Dr. Coffey knew Sam would be autopsied, so he somehow switched the slides. With know-how and access, it's easily done."

"So let me get this straight," Jordan said. "After the wiretap evidence gets tossed, Colchester bribes Sherri and plants evidence to get Brandon convicted."

"Yes."

"And we think he did this to help his emotionally unstable wife move on."

"Theory, yes, but I like it."

"Meanwhile, something is causing allergic reactions in healthy hearts at White. Coffey knows about it; he's afraid of it for some reason. He plays to Colchester's fears about Brandon going free. It's fear enough for Colchester to bribe the judge into denying the request to exhume his son's body, and Coffey's dirty secret about Kounis syndrome stays buried in the ground. That about sum it up?"

"That's my take."

Jordan shook his head in disbelief. "Dr. Abruzzo has a saying anytime she comes up with an unusual cause of death," he said. "It doesn't have to be probable, it just has to be possible."

Julie made a slight chuckle. "We'll have to keep searching those medical records for cases of undiagnosed Kounis syndrome."

"No more takotsubo, right?"

"No, this is allergic, not stress related."

"Maybe interview staff to see if they remember patients breaking out in hives," Jordan suggested, "and then see if there are matching records in the system."

"I like that plan."

Something still tugged at Jordan.

"How did Colchester know Sherri was going to come clean to you?" he asked.

Julie thought this over, but could not come up with an answer.

AS THEY drove into Dorchester, Julie stifled a yawn. She was bone tired, and the thought of getting the Thanksgiving preparations under way, under-caffeinated, was less appealing than driving through these confusing Dorchester streets.

"Do you know anyplace I could grab a good cup of coffee for the ride home?"

Jordan made a "pfft" sound, as if to say, but of course.

"Rico's is one of the best coffee shops around and it's right down the street from my apartment. The owner is a Puerto Rican guy named Juan, and if you think Colombian coffee is good, wait until you try his brew."

Lucky for Julie, she found parking close to the quaint coffee shop. It was a nippy November evening and the streets were relatively quiet. The less walking she had to do in this unfamiliar neighborhood, the better.

Jordan escorted Julie into Rico's. She had volunteered to drop him at home first, but he refused her offer.

"Better if I hang out with you while you're in my hood," he said.

Julie did not disagree.

The aromatic coffee shop had plenty of character but

not a lot of space, and the few tables for seating were all occupied. One good whiff and Julie understood why. She went right to the counter, and was ordering her coffee, when a deep baritone voice spoke to her from behind.

"Dr. Devereux?"

Julie whirled and broke into a bright smile. The tall man with broad shoulders standing behind Julie was the quarterback for the Boston College Eagles whose life she'd once saved.

"Max Hartsock!" Julie exclaimed.

Max opened his arms and gave Julie a warm embrace.

"What are you doing here?" Max said with an accompanying head scratch. "Rico's might be the last place I thought I'd run into you."

Julie gave a little laugh.

"You're not the first person I've surprised like that lately," she said. "I'm bringing Jordan Cobb home. Do you two know each other?"

"Know him? Jordan's my homey," Max said, as he and Jordan went through a mesmerizing series of choreographed handshakes and slaps. "Wouldn't have made it through algebra without him."

"We were just at a funeral for a colleague of ours, Sherri Platt," Julie said. "You may have read about her in the papers or seen her on the local news."

"Local and CNN," Max said. "Heard all about her and *you*. That's a horrible discovery to make. I hope you're doing all right."

"I'm hanging in there. Thank you."

Max invited Julie and Jordan to join them at his table. Once seated, Max again offered his condolences about Sam. Julie thanked him for his thoughtful note and for the football tickets.

"Paul took Trevor to the game. Speaking of which, what are you doing here? I would have thought Thanksgiving was all football all the time."

"Yeah, well, we played yesterday. Game on Saturday against Louisville. Revenge, I should say." Max followed a devilish grin with a wink. "Anyway, Coach gave us the day off so I came home to help my grandma get ready for the holiday. It's kind of a tradition. You have not lived until you've had my grandma's sweet potato pie."

Julie laughed. She was glad to hear Max doing so well, and even better, looking and feeling so well. He was back on the field after his near-death experience and, according to Trevor, putting up some impressive stats. Forget playing football: the fact that Max Hartsock was even alive, talking to Julie, sharing stories, praising his grandmother's cooking, was something awe-inspiring and beyond gratifying.

These were the moments when Julie loved being a doctor, and they balanced out the difficulties of caring for the ultra-sick. Max represented the best outcome possible—a return to health with a high quality of life. For Sam, this was not to be, nor was it likely for Shirley Mitchell, who remained on a ventilator, or for any number of patients Julie could name off the top of her head.

After a few more minutes catching up with Max, Julie got her coffee in a to-go cup and said her goodbyes. Paul would be dropping Trevor off in a couple hours, and the thought of all she had to do was overwhelming.

Jordan walked Julie to her car. "Take care, Doc," he

said. "We'll figure this thing out. Just know I'm on your team all the way."

"I know it. Want a ride?"

Jordan pointed. "I'm just down the block. It's cool. I'll walk."

There was a hug, and then Jordan waited curbside until Julie got settled in her car before he headed down the street for home. She pushed the Start button on her Prius and the engine came to life, not that Julie could easily tell. The thing was silent as a panther on the hunt. Even though she had owned the car for a few years, it took a bit to get used to the quiet engine. She had grown accustomed to the roar of her motorcycle and to the vibrations it gave off. Julie set her coffee in the cup holder and took a moment to fiddle with her GPS. These streets would be impossible to navigate without some kind of assistance.

She'd just placed her hands on the steering wheel when a man stepped directly in front of her car. He was tall, with long braided dark hair covered by a black knit cap. He wore a puffy dark jacket and dark baggy jeans. His arms dangled at his sides, but one hand appeared unnaturally elongated. It took a moment for Julie to realize he was holding a gun. Before her terror had a chance to take root, her driver-side door flew open and another man was there, looming over Julie as he leaned into her car. He held a gun to her face and glared at her with angry eyes. He was close enough to bathe her in his hot breath. Julie gripped the wheel hard, her head dizzy with fear.

"Give me the keys, bitch, and move over. I'm taking this here car for a ride."

Julie had several thoughts, but they came to her too fast to register as anything conscious.

I'm being carjacked!

That was one.

Give him the keys.

That was another.

And then came a third thought, which materialized with the speed of reflex.

He doesn't know the car is already running.

Julie's mind was gummed with terror, but a notion had been planted. The man at the door continued to shove his way inside, pushing against her, while the other man stationed in the front of her vehicle continued to block her way. Now she got it. Neither man knew the car was running. The engine was silent.

Julie screamed for help as she slammed her foot on the accelerator. The Prius responded instantly and shot forward at a high rate of speed. The man forcing his way into the driver's seat was caught by surprise and dropped his gun in exchange for a grip on the wheel, which kept him from being sucked under the moving car. The man standing in front lifted his hands in a pointless attempt at self-defense.

A second later, the front of the Prius made a loud thud as it slammed without slowing into the man's midsection. With a sound of folding metal, the man toppled over like a rag doll. His skull slammed against the hood of the moving vehicle hard enough to leave a dent. Then he vanished from view underneath the chassis, as if the Prius had swallowed him whole.

The other man reached down, and with one hand managed to rip Julie's foot off the gas pedal. The car rolled ahead, but slowed considerably. With his other arm, he uncorked a vicious strike that connected his elbow solidly with Julie's temple. The blow left Julie dazed, and the man had no trouble ripping her from her seat. She and the man toppled to the road in a heap. The driverless Prius rolled ahead, and the man Julie had run over became visible on the ground nearby. He moaned, but did not move much.

Stunned from the blow to the head, Julie was not moving much either. Her attacker took advantage and climbed on top of her. He pinned her arms above her head with one hand, and with the other produced a knife from his boot big enough to carve a Thanksgiving turkey.

"I'm going to make this sting."

He cocked back his arm and Julie braced herself for the pain. She had treated plenty of stab wound victims over the years, and the anticipation was its own form of torture.

A blur of motion rose up behind Julie's attacker like a great dark wave.

Max Hartsock barreled from the darkness, airborne, arms held wide as if he were making an open field tackle. He slammed into Julie's assailant and knocked him to the ground. He then went tumbling, still entwined in Max's massive arms, into the middle of the road. Cars in both directions came to a screeching halt.

A small crowd had gathered, but no one came forward to assist. Plenty of people, however, were filming the fracas on their smartphones. Max and the other man tussled a moment, but the contest was very much one-sided. Max was the quicker and stronger of the pair, and soon had Julie's attacker facedown with one arm wrenched behind his back at an unnatural angle. The man yowled in pain.

"Max, come on, man, it's me, bro. It's Dominick."

The man Julie had run over recovered some of his

sensibilities and took aim with his gun. Julie, aware of the danger, rolled to get out of his line of sight. He leveled his weapon, but blood loss made it impossible for him to keep a steady hand.

The delay gave Jordan time to push his way through the crowd. He dove on top of the armed man, pried the gun from his hand, and with little effort had him pinned, and then had the gun to his face.

Dominick continued his protest. "Come on, Max. Let me go. It was just a game, man. Some dude paid us to scare the lady. Nothing more. We got a grand to freak her out, that's all. We wasn't gonna do nothing to hurt her. Truth. Come on. Let it go."

Max answered by tightening his hold. Off in the distance Julie heard the wail of police sirens on approach. Her body shook from all the adrenaline. She locked eyes with Jordan. She and Jordan had the same thought: someone had paid these two—not to scare her, but to kill her.

CHAPTER 40

Lincoln Cole drove away before the police arrived, before they could start to question witnesses, before those two gangbangers he had paid could identify him. He drove past a convenience store on his way out of town and thought about buying a pack of smokes, even though he had quit the habit years ago. The stress was starting to get to him. He was not accustomed to so many setbacks. He was not accustomed to killing, either. He had not thought it would have bothered him so, being a cop who had seen lots of horrible things, but at night Sherri Platt's voice came to him like whispers from the grave. He heard her pleas, could see her trembling lips, the shake of her body in the grasp of an unimaginable terror.

After Sherri called in sick to work, Lincoln put the gun to her head. He'd felt sick to his stomach when her eyes bugged out and her mouth opened in a silent scream. He told her to turn around. He could not look at her face and do the job he was paid to do. He told her not to scream. He told her she would be fine. He lied.

The only thing Lincoln loved about taking Sherri's life was the money. He would have taken Julie's life for the same reason, but came up with what he thought was a better plan. It seemed like a stroke of genius to make Julie's murder look like a carjacking. In hindsight, it was foolish to let those numbskulls orchestrate the attack. Lincoln passed a second convenience store and slowed. He imagined the taste of smoke dribbling into his lungs. The urge was almost impossible to resist, but to cave now would be a sign of weakness, an indication that events had spiraled beyond his control. Lincoln would show restraint and light up a fat stogie on the beach once this was all behind him.

He pulled into the store's parking lot anyway, but remained inside his van to make the call. He explained to his employer what had happened.

"What now?" Lincoln asked.

"You'll have to leave that one to me." The call went dead.

Lincoln spat out a curse. He got out of his van and gave a stretch. His gaze turned toward the store's warm interior. *One pack of Camels won't hurt anything,* he thought.

THANKSGIVING WAS off, or at least that was Paul's assertion. He had brought Trevor home and gone up to the apartment to see if Julie was really doing fine, as she'd professed on the phone. After hugs, Trevor retreated to his bedroom, supposedly doing his homework, with his headphones on as usual, which meant he could not hear his parents' tense conversation.

"I said I'm fine, Paul. I don't need go to the hospital

and I don't need a knight in a jean jacket and ponytail to protect me."

Gingerly, Julie touched the red welt on her temple that continued to throb. She needed more ice, but would wait for Paul to leave just to make the point she really was okay.

"Well, maybe you need this ponytailed knight to talk a little sense into you."

Julie picked up her cup of tea and glared at Paul from over the rim, but said nothing.

"Since you've started on this path, you've been harassed, found a woman dead—shot in her home —and nearly got carjacked. All for what?"

"The truth," Julie said.

Paul fixed Julie with an angry stare and spoke through clenched teeth in an effort to cage his temper.

"The truth is William Colchester flexed his muscle to keep you from unnecessarily opening old wounds. The truth is a crazy zealot killed Sherri Platt because the courts wisely refused to let Brandon out of prison. The truth is you tried to pop some doc's inflated ego and he got a bit snippy with you. And the truth is you put yourself in a very dangerous part of town where getting carjacked isn't, I'm afraid to say, so damn uncommon," Paul folded his arms as if he'd said all that needed to be said.

Julie looked at him, incredulous.

"You can't possibly believe what you're saying. Look at everything that's happened, and you think there's nothing to it? That it's all in my head, is that it?"

"Now you're putting words in my mouth."

"I don't need to do that, Paul. You're belittling me perfectly fine all on your own."

"Well, that's just great," Paul said with disgust. "You keep making headlines and I'll keep making sense."

Julie crossed her arms and glowered at Paul. Their argument seemed a reversal from the ones they'd had while married, with Paul accusing Julie of acting irresponsibly.

"Listen to me, Paul. Thanksgiving isn't canceled," Julie said. "And I'm not going to take a leave of absence from my job, as you so strongly advise. And no way in hell am I going to stop pushing until I get some real answers here." Julie smacked her hand against the kitchen table, the slap like a gunshot, her face red, hot with anger.

Paul stood from the table, his face also in a rage.

Before he could respond, Julie's phone rang. It was Michelle calling. Julie ignored Paul's glowering look and answered the call.

"Oh my God," Michelle said. "Julie, are you all right?"

"I'm fine, I'm fine."

"It's all over the news. Keith and I are so worried about you. What do you need? What can I do?"

"Nothing, Michelle, nothing. Thank you though for checking in, but really I'm fine. It was just scary, that's all, and thankfully it had a good outcome."

"Well, I'm here if you need to talk."

"Thanks. But right now I'm actually talking with Paul. Can I call you later?"

"Yes, of course, call anytime," Michelle said. "Sending hugs."

Julie ended the call and met Paul's furious gaze.

"Just remember, Trevor's my son, too," he said, pointing to the bedroom. "So let's say that you're right. Not that I believe it, but let's just say it, okay? Are you willing to put him in danger to find out if your fiancé died of some—some allergy?" Paul held up his hands as though they were the scales, options for Julie to weigh. "Think about it, Julie, while I go give my son a hug good-bye. I really hope you'll give what I said some serious consideration. If you're right, or I'm right, either way don't you think it's best to leave this matter alone?"

JORDAN SHOWED up for work at 8:30 on Tuesday, a day and a half after the attack, feeling sluggish, sore, and uncharacteristically unmotivated to cart around the dead. He'd had a horrible night's sleep, plagued by disjointed and disturbing dreams. In one, Jordan rushed to Julie's aid and took a bullet to the side from a mysterious gunman. In another, it was a knife to the gut. He felt out of breath when he awoke both times, body drenched in sweat, eyes darting about the darkness in search of hidden dangers.

Jordan knew the two assailants; not personally, but by reputation. Dominick and the other one, who went by the name Lil' P, were gangbangers, members of the notorious Wilcox Street Boyz. Tough as they come, with a rap sheet longer than any Jay-Z lyrics. The cops carted Dominick away in the back of a cruiser, but Lil' P left in an ambulance. He had suffered major trauma—a broken pelvis and femur shaft fracture, Jordan suspected, and judging by the shallow and rapid breaths, a possible pneumothorax. But nobody asked the diener's opinion.

The police did have questions for Jordan, but those had nothing to do with medicine. He gave them his statement, but felt more perp than good Samaritan. The detective who jotted things down in a black notebook seemed strangely focused on what Jordan was doing with Julie Devereux in the first place, how he knew the woman who was nearly carjacked. It was certainly different for Max Hartsock, because he was a known commodity, a local hero.

The press, vultures with police scanners, sped to the scene and had a field day with the story: "BC Quarterback Saves Local Doc Who Saved Him." Julie being in the news so recently, with her discovery of Sherri Platt's body, gave the press even more fodder.

Jordan's nightmares were certainly stress induced, but maybe they had hidden meaning. He would take bullets for Julie in every way because he believed in her, he trusted her, which was not something he could say about many people, including the police.

Jordan had plans for the day. He would do his job, but sneak away during breaks to go on a hunting expedition. Somewhere in the vast medical archives was a connection between healthy hearts and hives that Jordan was determined to find. He made it down to pathology with only a few stops to recount last night's terrifying ordeal for curious colleagues.

When he finally arrived at the lab he saw Lucy standing outside her office, speaking with a woman he did not know. The other woman looked far more suit than doc in her blue blazer and knee-high skirt. When Lucy saw Jordan, her expression did not brighten as it usually did. She appeared crestfallen, not a look he was accustomed to seeing from the typically phlegmatic doctor.

"Mornin', doc," Jordan said with a smile.

Lucy pursed her lips, clearly agonized by something.

"Jordan, could you please come into my office for a moment," she said.

Jordan obliged, of course, and took a seat at the conference table at Lucy's direction. Lucy sat as well, as did the woman she was with.

"Jordan, this is Val Mesnik from our human resources department."

Jordan's pulse ticked up. Something wormed in his gut, a feeling of impending doom.

"I'm going to let Val explain what's going on here."

From a leather workbag, Val took out a thin manila folder, which she splayed open on the table. She reached into the bag again, this time for her reading glasses. She scanned the first page.

"Jordan, here at White Memorial we put a premium on patient privacy. The requirements outlined by the HIPAA act are quite specific when it comes to policies around individual medical records."

Lucy's forlorn look only deepened, as if she knew the outcome of this conversation, and it would not be to anyone's benefit. Jordan felt uncomfortable in his chair and the room seemed to get sauna hot.

"I know about HIPAA," Jordan said.

Val pulled her glasses to the bridge of her nose and eyed Jordan sternly.

"Do you now?" she said in a soft voice. "Well then, you'll understand why the IT department was concerned about all the superuser access to the EMR system from locations that they couldn't trace. Someone, it seems, was accessing patient records and intentionally trying to hide their IP address. You wouldn't know anything about that, would you?"

"Oh, cut the Nancy Drew crap, Val," Lucy said with

an eye roll. "Jordan, IT looked over the dates and time stamps in the logs of some of these sessions and matched it to security camera footage that shows you on the terminals at the time. There were other sessions they couldn't match up, but they think those happened at a home using IP-masking technology and our one-time passkey."

Jordan's body tensed. "You think I did it?"

"I told Val, and her fellow hounds from HR, that it's not conclusive proof of anything. And besides, I gave you permission to look at records as part of your employment here. In my mind, this is a nonissue."

"But you didn't give permission for Jordan to mail Donald Colchester's medical records to an inmate at Cedar Junction, did you?"

"No, Val," Lucy said, "because I told you, I did that myself."

Val glanced at her notes. "I see. Which you know is also a serious violation."

Lucy locked eyes with Jordan. "Here's what happened. During a routine search of Brandon Stahl's cell, they apparently found Donald Colchester's medical records tucked inside a book." Lucy put the word "routine" in air quotes. "Val here thinks you had something to do with it because of these superuser sessions. I, of course, told her that's ridiculous. But evidently that wasn't good enough for Val here, who wanted to fire you on suspicion alone, which I think is BS. So I told her the truth: I sent the files to Brandon to help with his defense because I thought he was innocent. You shouldn't get in any trouble for what I've done."

Val cleared her throat. "Yes, well, that's why I've

asked for this meeting," she said. "The computer access suggests the possibility of a different scenario, and I want to give Jordan a chance to state his innocence as a matter of record."

Jordan looked at Lucy, who nodded her head slightly, making it clear what answer she wanted him to give.

"What's going to happen to Dr. Abruzzo?" Jordan asked.

"What's going to happen is I'll take care of myself," Lucy said.

"It's a matter for the hospital to look into," Val said. "But the hospital's position on this sort of thing is very clear."

"Could she lose her job? Her medical license, even?" Jordan's nervousness showed.

"What happens to me is not your concern," Lucy said.

Val did not bother to answer Jordan's questions, which told him all he wanted to know. For several long seconds Jordan gazed at his lap, deep in thought. When he looked up, he made eye contact with Lucy.

"Dr. Abruzzo, after all you've done for me, I can't let anything happen to you. Not one thing. I'm sorry."

From the pocket of his scrubs Jordan fished out the thin, credit-card-sized passcode generator and put it on the conference table in front of Val.

"I used this to access the records," Jordan said. "And I'm the one who mailed Brandon those files, not Dr. Abruzzo. It was me and me alone."

Val smirked as she picked up the thin device.

"Jordan, I'm afraid this is a very serious situation," Val said.

"He's my employee," Lucy said. "I'll discipline him."

"If by discipline you mean fire, by all means, Dr. Abruzzo."

"I'm not firing Jordan."

"No. I suspected you wouldn't. But that's okay. Because I am. Jordan, I'll need you to come with me."

Jordan got up from the table. Lucy did the same.

"Jordan, this isn't over," Lucy said, a shake to her voice.

Jordan came over and gave Lucy a long embrace.

"I agree," Jordan said to Lucy. "It's not over by a long shot."

CHAPTER 41

Julie had just finished her morning cup of coffee when she bumped into Michelle, who was on her way into the ICU. The two women embraced with a bit more intensity than a typical hug between friends.

"Oh my God, Julie," Michelle said, looking her friend over head to toe. "Are you doing okay? Should you even be here?"

"I'm sorry, I should have called you back. I'm fine, really I am," Julie said, sounding assured. "It was scary, but it's over now."

"Yeah, like all over the news."

Julie made a half smile. "It's a little weird, I have to admit, to have my name out there so much. I even got an e-mail from Roman Janowski."

"The CEO?"

Julie returned a nod. "He was very sweet, very concerned, and didn't seem at all bothered with my being so prominent these days. But still, you don't like getting e-mails from the big boss."

"I'm sure. Say, can you meet for a late lunch? One thirty? I want to catch up."

"I think so," Julie said. "What brings you here today?"

Michelle gave a little laugh. "Unfortunately, this is where a lot of my customers hang out."

It was Julie's turn to chuckle, though the rest of this conversation would have to wait until lunch. Amber emerged from Shirley Mitchell's room with a concerned look on her face.

"Dr. Devereux, there's a problem with Shirley's central line. Could you take a look, please?"

"Yes, of course. I'll be right there."

Julie said a quick good-bye to Michelle and reconfirmed their plan to meet. Perhaps Lucy would be available and could join them. As if on cue, Julie's phone rang. It was Lucy calling. Julie declined the call and sent it to voice mail. Then Jordan called, and Julie felt a little pang of concern. Why would both of them call in such short intervals? The answer would have to wait. Shirley needed immediate attention.

As Julie predicted, Shirley had not stabilized enough to be weaned off mechanical ventilation. It had been several days since Shirley's return to the ICU, and her relatives could no longer maintain lengthy bedside vigils. Shirley was alone most of the time, breathing with help, and unaware in her blissful propofol slumber.

"She must have thrashed about and pulled out the line," Amber said, concern in her voice. In time, the young nurse would realize these things happened. A patient pulling out their central line was not as rare as Kounis syndrome by any stretch, but it was not a common occurrence either, which was what had Amber on edge.

A trickle of blood oozed from a thin gap in the central line where it had detached from the skin. The catheter affixed to Shirley's jugular vein had been sutured in place, so Shirley's thrashing must have been considerable in order to dislodge it. It was standard procedure for Julie to put in a new central line. She did so without issue. The line had to be flushed, though, to make sure it was clear.

"Amber, please hand me a saline flush, will you?"

The saline flushes were commonly used items and kept in each ICU room for quick and convenient retrieval. Amber handed Julie a ten-milliliter syringe, though three milliliters of saline would be more than sufficient. Julie undid the wrapping and inspected the site for any redness, swelling, or signs of infection. She scrubbed the catheter hub with an alcohol swab for fifteen seconds, then removed the sterile cap. She inserted the open end of the syringe into a hub on the catheter, followed by a twist to lock it. Next, Julie opened the valve mechanism and slowly injected the proper amount of clear saline into the catheter.

"All set, Amber," Julie said as she handed the syringe to the nurse for disposal. Julie left Amber to tend to other matters.

Five minutes later, Amber, sounding more anxious than before, called Julie back into the room.

"Dr. Devereux, Shirley Mitchell's blood pressure just dropped."

Julie rushed to Shirley's bedside and immediately noticed a nosebleed so brisk it soaked though several applications of gauze. Alarm bells rattled in Julie's head when she observed how all of Shirley's IV sites were oozing. Red rivers snaked down Shirley's bloated arms and marked her mottled neck. Closing the drape, Julie lifted Shirley's hospital gown to examine the belly. Signs of bruising appeared as if by magic before her eyes, while pools of blood started to well up from between her thighs. Worry squeezed like a vise around Julie's chest.

Oh, goodness, no . . .

"Amber, quick! Call for four more units of blood," Julie said in a crisp and direct manner. "Draw a set of labs now. I think she is going into DIC."

The proteins controlling Shirley's blood clotting had become overactive. It was not unheard of for a patient with a necrotizing skin infection to suffer disseminated intravascular coagulation (DIC) and possibly die because of sepsis, but it was a highly unusual complication. Another nurse came running into the room with a liter of saline to hang as a bolus. Julie stayed calm. She had no intention of announcing Shirley's time of death.

While Amber prepared to draw her labs, Shirley's heart rate began to drop precipitously.

"Dr. Devereux, she's bradying down."

"Bradying" down was medical speak for a slowing heart rate. Shirley's had plummeted into the twenties.

"Quick, an amp of epi and call a code blue," Julie said with force.

Alarms sounded and much commotion followed. A swarm of people burst into the room and took their respective roles in an effort to pull Shirley out of her nosedive. But Shirley's EKG went flatline, triggering more alarms, more noise, more commotion. Amber and a second nurse took turns performing CPR at a grueling rate of one hundred compressions per minute, while Tammy got the respiratory bag going.

A nurse called out, "Three minutes, another epi, Dr. Devereux?"

"Yes, please."

Labs were quickly drawn, including a complete blood count, liver enzymes, chemistries, and a full coagulation panel. Two units of packed red blood cells arrived and the nurses hung the bags of medicine and hooked them to the infusion pump.

Come on now . . . come on . . .

Shirley continued to be asystole with no cardiac electric activity, no output or blood flow. Julie knew she was running out of time. A nurse delivered that third dose of epi.

"Any pulse?" Julie asked.

Compressions came to an abrupt stop as many hands felt Shirley for a pulse.

Nothing.

"Resume compressions," Julie said.

No change. Still flatline.

"Is the family here?" Julie asked.

"No, nobody has arrived yet," a nurse said.

"Okay. Okay, everyone. I'm calling it."

The mood turned somber. Julie glanced at the clock on the wall.

"Time of death, ten fifteen A.M.," she announced in a solemn voice.

Grim faces all around. Death was a regular visitor to the ICU, but never a welcome one. Julie left for the break room. She needed to clear her head, decompress, but she could not stop reviewing the case in her head.

Where did things go so horribly wrong?

CHAPTER 42

"I got fired," Jordan said.

The wind was blowing hard, distorting Jordan's phone call and making it difficult to hear. Julie thought she'd heard him right, but it still did not make any sense.

"You got what?"

"Fired," Jordan repeated. "I'm out of White. Gone as of this morning."

"Oh my goodness. I'm so sorry. Tell me everything."

It's my fault was playing in the back of Julie's mind.

She was seated at her desk, hours after Shirley died, and only now understood why a different diener, a man she had never met before, had come to collect the body. Julie would have to cancel her lunch plans with Michelle. She and Jordan needed to speak in person. Jordan told her the saga in brief.

"Routine search, my foot," Julie said after Jordan finished his explanation. "William Colchester must have put someone up to it. He has connections at the prison. I'm sure of it."

"Yeah, well, Dr. Abruzzo was going to take the fall

for me. I couldn't let that happen, so I had to confess to what I did."

"I'll get you your job back," Julie said. "Don't worry."

Jordan breathed a loud sigh that rose above the howl of the wind and told Julie his worry was going to stick around for some time.

A nurse poked her head into Julie's cramped office, a broom closet compared to where Dr. Coffey worked.

"I've got the lab on the phone. They'd like to speak with you. Said it's urgent."

"Jordan, I'll call you in a minute. Hang tight, okay?"

Julie took the lab's call at the nurses station.

"Hi, Dr. Devereux, this is Dr. Becca Stinson down in pathology. The criticals for Shirley Mitchell are back. Sorry they took some time, but the tests needed to be repeated. They still don't make much sense."

Julie motioned for a nurse to hand her a pen and piece of paper.

"Give them to me over the phone. I'll write them down."

Julie jotted down each result as it was dictated to her. She blinked, because to say these did not make sense was more than an understatement.

Wbc: 13.6
Hct: 21.0
Platelet count: 274
Pt and inr: 14.0 and inr 1.0
Ptt >100
Fibrinogen 400
d-dimer: 3
Heparin anti xa level: >3.0 (nl between 0.3–0.7)

Julie's mouth fell open and her body went numb.

"Read that last one again."

"Heparin anti xa level greater than three point oh," Becca said.

"Three point zero? Well, that's a mistake," Julie said. "Shirley Mitchell had a GI bleed. The last thing we would give her is an anticoagulant and blood thinner. Let me talk to Lucy."

"I'm afraid Dr. Abruzzo—um—isn't available," Becca said.

Something cagey about Dr. Stinson's answer unsettled Julie.

"Tell Lucy to call me as soon as she can."

"Yes, Dr. Devereux."

The results made no sense whatsoever for several reasons. Concern over Jordan's unceremonious firing took a sudden backseat to this new and deeply troubling development.

A nurse rushed over to Julie while she was lost in thought.

"Dr. Devereux, we need you in room six. The patient's oh two sat level is dropping."

Julie tried to clear her thoughts so she could focus on this new crisis. She headed off to room six, but found it impossible to shake away her gnawing concern. Those lab tests were not just strange; they were downright sinister.

JULIE TRIAGED the patient in room six for the better part of an hour. The end of the busy workday came, and not much had changed except for Julie's lunch plans. Jordan was still an ex-employee of White, Shirley Mitchell was still dead, Lucy still MIA, and Julie still baffled by the test results. Julie was in her office, doing paperwork, preparing for the next round of battles with the insurance companies, when her desk phone rang.

"Dr. Devereux here," Julie said.

"Dr. Devereux, this is Marilyn Bates, Mr. Janowski's personal assistant. I've been asked to see if you could please come up to Mr. Janowski's office right away. The matter is urgent."

A pit opened in Julie's stomach. "What is this about?"

"I'm afraid I don't know. I only know that it's extremely important."

JULIE HAD never been to Roman Janowski's office before, but eventually she found it on the fifth floor of the Wilcox Building. A dour woman with curled gray hair sat at a desk near a set of shuttered double doors made of burnished wood. The nameplate on the woman's desk read MARILYN BATES. She managed a look Julie felt was one part contempt, one part glee, and one part empathy.

"Roman is waiting for you inside."

Perhaps Ms. Bates's monotone was meant to be intimidating. Julie's heart thundered as her stomach went through a series of somersaults. She had no clue what this meeting was about, but gut instinct told her it was not going to be anything good. The feeling was confirmed when Julie opened the door and saw Roman Janowski, Lucy Abruzzo, and Amber, the nurse who had cared for Shirley Mitchell, all seated at the large conference table in his spacious office, with grave looks on their faces. Three people dressed in business attire like Roman, two men and a woman, were also present.

"Please take a seat, Julie," Roman said in a joyless voice.

Roman sat at the head of the table and pointed to an empty chair directly across from him. There was no handshake hello, no trace of the warmth he had shown at Sherri's funeral. The CEO's dead-eye stare chilled Julie's blood.

"This meeting is being recorded," Roman said. "I should advise you that you have the right to refuse to be on record, but just know we will consider your lack of cooperation justification to have you escorted from these premises and your employment suspended as a result."

"Roman, what on earth is this about?"

There was a tremor in Julie's voice, unusual given how many orders she had uttered in life-and-death situations that day.

"It's about what happened to Shirley Mitchell," Roman replied.

Julie's eyes went wide and she directed her gaze toward Lucy, who was seated closest to her on the left side of the table. "Lucy, what is happening here?"

"Because you may not know everyone, I'm going to repeat introductions for the record," Roman said. "Seated at the table are Dr. Lucy Abruzzo, White's chief of pathological services; Amber Ellis, ICU nurse; Dr. Julie Devereux, pulmonary and critical care physician; Max Gilbride, director of patient safety; Val Mesnik, from human resources; and Bob Anderson, legal counsel for White."

"Roman, please, I demand an explanation," Julie said.

"I would like to lead this discussion, if you don't mind, Dr. Devereux," Janowski replied, his eyes boring into her. "Amber, would you please repeat what you told us right before Dr. Devereux arrived."

Amber, who sat next to Lucy, shifted uncomfortably in her chair and refused to make eye contact with Julie.

"After Shirley came back from radiology, I heard her say 'I want to die.'"

Bob Anderson said, "And at the time did you think Dr. Devereux heard these comments?"

Julie's face flushed with anger. "I demand to know what this is all about," she repeated.

Lucy shot Julie a stern look that said *keep calm, stay quiet, and be controlled,* all with a glance. Lucy had never admonished Julie before, and the experience was as unpleasant as it was unfamiliar.

"Yes, I'm sure Dr. Devereux heard those comments," Amber said. "We looked at each other like, okay, that just happened. Let's move on."

"Move on, all right," Roman grumbled as he slid a manila folder down the table. The folder scraped across the smooth surface and needed a push from Val to reach Julie, the intended target.

"What's this?" Julie asked as she picked up the folder.

"Please have a look," Roman said. "I would like you to confirm the contents. It's articles, op-ed pieces and such, written by you that espouse your stance on death with dignity—patient self-determination, as you call it. Your views on mercy killing."

"We've had these on file for some time." Bob Anderson felt this was legally relevant to share, for reasons Julie could not fathom.

She glanced through the folder and claimed authorship for every document within.

"Okay, so I wrote these," Julie said, waving the folder in front of her face like a fan. "But I wrote these before my fiancé's accident, and to be honest, my views on the subject have changed since then. In fact, I believe my views are still evolving. I'm sorting it out. But what does this have to do with anything? These are policy opinions about medicine, not related to any of my patients or patient care. Certainly not related to Shirley Mitchell."

Julie set her gaze on Max Gilbride, the beady-eyed director of patient safety, who sported jowls like an orangutan's.

Lucy cleared her throat. Her expression was deeply pained. "I was very concerned with Shirley Mitchell's labs," she said. "In a typical DIC, the platelets would be low, the PT and PTT high, and the fibrinogen would be low. The labs on Shirley came back showing the opposite."

A knot formed in Julie's stomach. She understood now what was happening here.

"Those levels made me look beyond DIC as a cause of the bleed, which is why I asked Dr. Stinson, one of our residents in pathology, to look for heparin levels. For the benefit of those who do not practice medicine, the heparin xa level should be less than point one in anyone not on heparin. Shirley Mitchell was three-point-zero. The only possible way she could have a level that high is if someone injected her with heparin."

The hairs on the back of Julie's neck began to rise as she fixed Lucy with a wide-eyed stare.

"What are you saying, Lucy?" Julie's mind was reeling.

"And why was Dr. Devereux in the patient's room?" The question from Gilbride was directed at Amber.

"Someone pulled out the patient's central line and it needed to be reconnected."

"Wait, wait, wait," Julie said, glaring now at Amber. "*Someone* pulled out the line? That someone was Shirley Mitchell."

Gilbride cleared his throat. "She was on what dose of propofol?" he asked. Max Gilbride, an internist turned bureaucrat, was the internal affairs equivalent for doctors and put the A in a-hole.

"Thirty mic per kig," Amber said.

Julie translated the dose in her head. Propofol is a weight-based drug and thirty was a high dose per minute.

"In other words, Shirley was pretty out of it," Gilbride said.

"Yes," Amber answered in a quiet voice.

"What are we thinking here?" Julie asked the question and sent nervous glances around the table.

"I'll tell you what we're thinking, Julie," Roman answered. "I'm not here to waste your time, or ours. Shirley's bleeding began minutes after you flushed the central line."

"Yes, with saline I got from Amber."

"That couldn't have been just saline," Roman said. "Somehow Shirley was given heparin, a blood thinner, and that caused her to bleed out."

"Well, how would that have happened?"

"We don't know," Romey said. "We're hoping you or Amber could enlighten us."

Julie said, "Honestly, Roman, I have no idea."

"We tested the rest of the flushes taken from that

ICU room," Lucy said. "They all came back as normal saline."

"Well, there you have it," Julie said.

"But that doesn't mean someone didn't use a little sleight of hand and swap a package containing a syringe of saline for one containing a syringe of heparin."

Gilbride's smug look made Julie want to explode. She felt her body heat up beneath her white lab coat.

"That's perhaps the most preposterous thing I have ever heard in my life. You're implying Amber or I had something to do with this. Lucy, please, you can't possibly accept this rubbish as fact."

Lucy was expressionless.

"How did she get the heparin, Julie?" Lucy asked.

Bob Anderson glanced at his notes and said, "According to Amber's statement, the patient's blood pressure dropped minutes after you flushed the line."

"We believe that was the moment of injection," Gilbride added.

"Given the levels of heparin in Shirley's blood and the timing of her pressure drop, I would have to concur," Lucy said.

Julie glanced around the table, looking for a sympathetic face, and found none. "I can't believe what I'm hearing. You've got to be kidding me. Are you suggesting I killed Shirley Mitchell on purpose?"

Gilbride reached for the folder of Julie's papers. "I'm suggesting you have motive, Julie. You've been feeding it to the public for years now."

"I—I—I just don't know what to say."

"You and Amber were the last to treat Shirley," Roman said.

"That's true," Julie answered.

"Then until we get more facts, both you and Amber are being suspended from White with pay until a thorough investigation can be conducted. You will not have access to these facilities or any hospital systems during this suspension period. Val is here to work through your exit paperwork."

Amber burst into a sob, shaking her head in disbelief. "I didn't do anything wrong. I swear it."

Janowski eyed her with disgust. "If our findings show malice, being fired will be the least of your concerns. I fully intend to report this matter to the authorities, and you should expect an investigation and possible charges."

"Charges?" Julie asked. "What sort of charges are we talking about?"

Bob Anderson got up from his seat and buttoned his suit. "The biggest charge would be murder."

CHAPTER 43

Julie refused to sign any of the paperwork required by HR; not without her lawyer present, she said. She advised Amber to do the same, but the poor girl was utterly shell-shocked, too young and inexperienced to defy authority.

Amber sorrowfully followed Val to her office down the hall, while Julie was stripped of her badge and unceremoniously escorted out of the building by security. Nobody gawked because nobody knew what had gone down, but soon word would spread via social media and Julie's troubles would become White's version of a viral video. Julie felt weightless and strange in her own skin, as if this experience was happening to someone else and she somehow had become a detached observer.

From her car, Julie phoned Lucy.

"Please come to the parking garage. I'm on level B2 near the elevator. Let's talk," Julie said.

Ten minutes later, Lucy, cocooned inside her warm jacket, opened the passenger-side door of Julie's Prius with the bent front fender and dent in the hood. As she climbed in, Lucy looked straight ahead in an effort to avoid Julie's penetrating stare.

"Hey, hey, Lucy, it's me, it's Julie, your friend, and I need you now more than ever." Tears came to Julie's eyes and blurred her vision. Lucy gave in to the tugging on her arm and turned to meet Julie's gaze.

"Did you do it?" Lucy asked in a harsh whisper.

Julie could not contain her look of disgust. "How could you even ask me such a thing?"

"Because I know what you believe," Lucy said. "The articles in that folder weren't exactly a surprise to me."

Julie's mouth fell agape. "I can't believe you just said that to me."

"If you did it, you have to own it," Lucy said.

Julie knew Lucy could be distant, but her icy treatment caught her off guard and hurt deeply.

"If I did it," Julie said, "I'd have been a hell of a lot smarter than to use heparin. I could have used bupivacaine, for goodness' sake. I'm not stupid, Lucy, and I'm certainly not a killer."

Lucy's eyes narrowed. She knew about the anesthetic drug. "Bupivacaine wouldn't have been too smart, either," she said. "I would have noticed the QT prolongation on the EKG and run a tox test for it. I'd still have caught you."

A slip of a smile came to Lucy's face and Julie broke into a laugh that sounded like she had stifled a sob. Even under duress, Lucy's brain worked in overdrive. She simply could not help being the brilliant pathologist she was. It was a moment between them, one that gave Julie hope Lucy was not completely lost to her, hope she could still be an ally in this fight.

They fell into a heavy silence, broken when Lucy asked, "What do you want me to do, Julie?"

The desperation in Lucy's voice implied they had arrived at some sort of impasse.

"Just be open-minded right now," Julie said. "I just need you to hear me."

"I'm listening."

"While I was waiting for you, I had time to think a little more clearly about things. Isn't it a bit coincidental that Jordan and I got fired on the same day?"

Lucy's face turned taut. "Are you suggesting someone killed Shirley Mitchell to get you out of White?"

"I'm saying we can't stop looking for Sam's true killer. Whatever it is that caused his heart to stop, it's killing others at White, maybe elsewhere, and somebody doesn't want us to find out what's really going on."

"Julie, stop. Just stop it."

"No. I can't and I won't."

"I don't know what's happened to you, hell, even me, for getting so involved in this whole affair, but it's gone too far. I should have turned Jordan in when I found out what he was doing with the patient records. I should never have brought the two of you together."

"I didn't kill Shirley."

"Honestly, I don't know if that's true. You're asking me to swallow an awful lot here. What's not debatable is that someone injected Shirley with heparin, and by all accounts it appears to have been intentional. You had the means, motive, and opportunity. You don't have to be a mystery novel enthusiast to know those are three criteria for proving a murder. I might be able to buy some weird drug allergy causing fatal heart attacks. Maybe something we didn't know about, something we potentially could have uncovered in this investigation of ours. It's possible, I grant you that. But now you're saying someone was murdered to throw us off the trail? Think about it for a moment and try to see it through my eyes. Shirley Mitchell was a very sick woman, the kind of woman whose right to die you would have fully supported."

"Supported only if it was the law."

"What do you want from me, Julie?"

"I need you to find samples and run some tests. Jordan and I no longer have access to the computer systems, and I don't believe that's an unintentional consequence. Someone didn't want us to find other victims."

"Do you even hear yourself?"

"Yes, other victims," Julie repeated with more emphasis. "I hear myself perfectly well, thank you. We need you monitoring the EMR system for patients with hives who later die of a heart attack. The hives will be deleted from the patient's record postmortem. I promise you this is true. Test the tissue from the corpse for various allergy-causing antigens and foreign substances. Whatever is killing these patients, we'll find it in that test."

"Who, Julie? Who is doing this and why?"

Julie shook her head in frustration. "I don't know. But somehow William Colchester and Gerald Coffey are involved, I'm sure of it."

"Yeah? Well, I'm sure of this: if I do anything to help you, I'll lose my job, and I sincerely doubt I'll get another."

"Please, Lucy. You're my only hope."

"My opinion? You need to focus on yourself and

your family. Romey is coming after you for Shirley's death and that's a fact, not an opinion. Somebody has to take the fall for the heparin and it's going to be you, not Amber. So please, don't ask me for any favors right now."

"Why, Lucy?" Julie's voice cracked. "Why won't you help us?"

"Because this job is all I have," Lucy said. "I don't have a partner, kids, a pet, anything. I run. I read. I play chess. But what I really love, my life's purpose, my passion, is pathology. You're asking me to risk everything for something I don't fully believe. To put myself on the line to support you when I have doubts about your innocence here. Put yourself in my shoes and see if you would do the same."

Lucy opened the car door and got out. She had nothing more to say.

CHAPTER 44

It was Wednesday morning, the day before Thanksgiving. The kitchen should have been the most active room in the home, but the stove burners were off and the refrigerator mostly empty. Paul sat at the kitchen table drinking coffee Julie had brewed for him. Trevor was in his bedroom, packing his bags and preparing for a lengthy stay with his father. With all that had happened, Julie could not deal with meal preparation, hosting, or even being with others. The turkey would stay put in the freezer until she got around to thawing and cooking it.

Everyone who had been invited to Julie's home for the Thanksgiving meal made other arrangements, including Julie's mother, who made no secret of her worry and concern.

"I'm fine, honest, Mom," Julie said to her mother, one of the few people who still called the landline. "Everything will get cleared up. Just give it time. Okay?"

Julie must have had this conversation with her mother half a dozen times since her ouster from White only a day ago. She might have sounded convincing, but it was not exactly how she felt. Worry lingered about how the investigation into Shirley Mitchell's death would ripple through all facets of Julie's life and how it would impact her son.

As if her thoughts had summoned him, Trevor lumbered out of the bedroom with his overnight bag slung across one shoulder. "I'm all set," he announced.

Julie did not believe in keeping secrets, and had told Trevor what had happened to her at White and how the incident was under investigation.

Trevor took the news in stride. "I've seen you at work, Mom," he'd said. "I know you wouldn't do anything to harm that woman on purpose."

I didn't harm her at all, Julie thought.

No point being defensive. Julie thanked Trevor for his support. What she needed now was a way to prove him right. She did not question that heparin had entered Shirley Mitchell's blood, but how did the drug get there?

Julie was not the only one suffering. Jordan felt despondent over his predicament and Julie's. They had spoken by phone, but had not met in person. During their conversation, they agreed—without Lucy's support, their investigation was at a complete standstill.

Trevor had forgotten something in his room, and went back to retrieve it.

"You sure you don't want to join us tomorrow night?" Paul asked.

"I feel terrible saying it, but I'd rather be alone. Just not feeling up to any company."

The apartment buzzer sounded and Julie's heart jumped. She went to the intercom.

"Who is it?"

A gruff voice responded, "Detective Richard Spence and Detective Howard Capshaw of the Boston PD. We'd like to have a word with you, if we may."

Paul rushed over. "Not without a lawyer," he whispered in Julie's ear.

Julie returned an annoyed look to tell him she could handle this. "Yes, please come up."

Paul glared at Julie. "Are you crazy?" he said.

"No, I'm innocent. I've done nothing wrong and I have nothing to hide. I don't need a lawyer when I have the truth."

"For a brilliant doctor, you're acting pretty naïve. These guys don't care about the truth. They care about closing cases, and they'll do whatever they can to trap you."

"Thank you for your concern, Paul," Julie said. "I promise to be careful."

A moment later came a knock on the door. Julie checked the peephole and saw both men flash official-looking badges. Introductions took place after Julie opened the door for them. Spence was thin with graying hair and a hard-bitten face. Capshaw had a bit more heft, less gray in his thinning hair, but like Spence had a hard-bitten face with a ruddier complexion. Both wore suits and neither had smiles.

"Thanks for meeting with us," Spence said.

"Thanks for the surprise visit," Paul said with sarcasm.

"Paul, why don't you help Trevor get his things together? I'll see the detectives to the living room, and then I'll see you both out. Detectives, if you'll come with me."

Paul huffed his displeasure, while Julie escorted the

two detectives into the living room. She offered them coffee or water, which they declined. She left them there and went to say her good-byes to Trevor.

"Be good to your dad," she said. "I'll take care of Winston, and I'll see you soon."

Trevor was anxious. "What are the cops doing here, Mom?" he said in a low voice.

"It's nothing, honey," Julie assured him. "They just have to ask some questions, that's all." She ruffled Trevor's long hair, and crouched to look him in the eyes. "I love you, sweetheart. Everything is going to be just fine. Trust me."

A tickle of doubt made Julie wonder if she had just told him a lie. Trevor had a hard time looking his mother in the eyes, probably because she would see how anxious he was feeling. Trevor left with an extra-long hug that brought a lump to Julie's throat.

Julie returned to the living room to find Detective Spence there, milling about, checking things over, looking in places she had not invited him to look. Detective Capshaw was not in the room, but entered from the hall. It was likely he'd been examining the rest of the apartment. Julie mulled this over and regretted not taking Paul's concerns more seriously.

Capshaw and Spence took seats on the sofa while Julie pulled up a chair. Spence took out a notebook.

"It's not often the same person is connected to two different murder investigations," he began.

No friendly smile there, no glint in the eye: this detective had elevated the stone-faced look to an art form.

"Regarding Sherri, I don't really know what to say other than what I told the detectives I spoke with. I be-

lieved, and still do, that William Colchester had something to do with Sherri's murder."

Capshaw said, "Yeah? I read that in the report. So
did Colchester inject Shirley Mitchell with whatever it
was that killed her?"

Unlike Spence, Capshaw sported a crooked smile.
Julie thought of a cat toying with a cornered mouse. In
that moment, Julie hated everything about these detectives. Their air of superiority and smugness, evocative
of Dr. Coffey, made it clear that these two were hardly
on her side. Julie launched into an explanation of events
the way she understood them. The detectives took careful notes.

"Let's go through this one more time," Spence said,
a friendlier look on his face, as though trying to clear
hostility from the air. "You injected the deceased, Shirley Mitchell, with a syringe filled with—" Spence
glanced at his notebook. "—herapin, and that's what
caused her to bleed to death."

"It's called heparin, and no," Julie answered emphatically. "I cleared Shirley's central line using a saline
flush, and somehow a high quantity of heparin got in
her bloodstream."

"So you had nothing to do with that," Capshaw said.

"I did not."

Spence leaned forward and looked Julie in the eyes.
"She was going to die, wasn't she?"

Julie shrugged. "We're all going to die," she said.

Spence nodded in agreement. "You know what I
mean," he said, kind of on the sly. "This lady was spitting the last bit of air from her lungs, wasn't she? So
you just pushed her along."

"We've read some of your, well, call them provoca- tive essays on the subject, so we know how you think about these things," Capshaw said.

"And we don't disagree with you," Spence added. "Hell, it's how I'd want to go."

Julie pursed her lips and tried to get her pulse to set- tle. "Detectives, I know what you're trying to do here and I'm not going to bite, because nothing you said is true. I didn't intentionally inject Shirley Mitchell with heparin, and it's a horrible way to die. As someone who has written extensively about death with dignity, I can tell you that suffering a massive bleed through pretty much every orifice, including the rectum, is hardly a dignified way to go."

Capshaw cleared his throat and shifted in his seat uncomfortably. "Well, what's your theory on how she got the drug in her system?"

"I don't have one, Detective Capshaw," Julie said. "If I did, I would certainly share it with you."

Spence gave his partner a nod, and Capshaw took it as his cue to stand. He handed Julie his card.

"Please be kind to Amber," Julie said. "She's as in- nocent as I am."

"Thanks for the opinion. If you can think of any- thing, give us a call," Capshaw said.

"Am I still a suspect?" Julie asked.

"I'll answer your question this way," Spence said. "If you're planning on going out of town in the next cou- ple of days, let us know."

FROM THE front seat of his white cargo van, Lincoln Cole waited for the call like a fisherman anticipating a tug on a slack line. He had chartered boats in the Caribbean before, glided across pristine blue waters in search of bonefish, wahoo, tuna, but this was a different sort of exhilaration. His employer was undeniably crafty. Lincoln had a good sense of people from his years on the force and it was obvious he was working for a highly intelligent individual, someone who understood human behavior as well as, if not better than, most detectives.

Lincoln had never worked with Spence or Capshaw during his years on the force, but they seemed fairly competent. They had asked Julie the right questions, had pushed her just hard enough. If Lincoln had been in the room he might have told Julie how Amber had flipped, just to gauge the doc's reaction, but the criticism was a quibble. Those two had nothing and they knew it. At most, Julie would be fired from White, but Lincoln doubted she would be arrested for murder.

Julie still had to be dealt with in a permanent fashion, which Lincoln knew was his employer's plan all along. Get her out of the hospital first, and then get her dead. But killing her and the diener had to be—Lincoln racked his brain for the right word—organic.

He checked his watch. No way to know when the call would come in, but it would come. He trusted his employer implicitly. The waning sun in a cloudless sky offered only the illusion of warmth. Lincoln used a portable battery-powered heater to keep from shivering while he waited in his van parked at a meter down the street from Julie's home. On the seat beside him was the uniform for Lincoln's new job— armed security guard at Suburban West hospital. In the wake of so many mass shootings, armed guards at suburban hospitals were an increasingly common sight, and Lincoln's background in law enforcement added authenticity to his hire.

It was no surprise to Lincoln that his employer had enough pull to get him the gig, but he was still impressed with how quickly it had come together. If all went according to plan, Julie and Jordan would soon be sneaking into Suburban West.

What would Lincoln do should he stumble upon a pair of armed intruders on his first day on the job? Why, he would have to defend himself. Lincoln would of course be justified in shooting to kill. One victim was a convicted felon and the other a suspected murderer, which would only bolster Lincoln's self-defense claim.

The sound of ringing jangled in Lincoln's headphones. His TrueSpy application was picking up a phone call to Julie. Lincoln smiled, imagining this was the first big tug on his fishing line. Would the caller be the person he was expecting? Lincoln listened intently.

"Hello, this is Dr. Devereux."

Doctor. The word choice was interesting. *Was a queen without a court still a queen?* Lincoln asked himself.

"We don't know each other," a female voice said, "but we may be able to help each other."

"Who is this?" Julie asked.

Lincoln could not suppress a smile. This was indeed the bite he had been waiting for. Lincoln pantomimed the motion of pulling back on his imaginary rod to set the hook.

"My name is Allyson Brock. I'm the former CEO of Suburban West."

A pause.

"What can I do for you, Allyson?"

"I received an anonymous note in my mailbox. It came in a blank envelope with my name on the front. No stamp and no return address, and no signature, either. I would like to read it to you, if I may."

"Yes, of course."

" 'Dear Ms. Brock. I'm sending you this message because I believe you can help my friend, Julie Devereux, and help yourself at the same time. You lost your job at Suburban West and I want to give you the chance to take revenge on the person responsible for your ouster as CEO— Roman Janowski. I have been asked by my friend to look for a very specific tissue sample. I am being watched too closely to help her. You are not. Call her. She can explain what she's looking for. You'll know what to do when you hear what she needs. Believe me when I tell you if she's successful, it will crush White and do major damage to Roman Janowski. The samples have to be prepared properly, so tell Julie to bring a secret admirer. She'll know what it means.' The note had your phone number at the bottom," Allyson said.

Lincoln gave another hard tug on that imaginary line of his.

"Who sent it to you?" Julie asked.

"I have no idea," Lincoln heard Allyson say "It was signed, 'A Friend.' "

"Lucy," Julie said in a soft voice.

"Excuse me?"

"Nothing. I'll tell you what I'm looking for. Are you ready?"

"Yes."

"I think there's something very wrong at White. Some combination of drugs, something, I don't know what, causing an allergic reaction, triggering fatal attacks in patients with relatively healthy hearts. I need tissue samples so we can test for allergy-causing antigens. But the samples can't just come from anybody. They have to be from people who had healthy hearts, who died suddenly, and who had previously broken out in hives."

The call went silent. Lincoln mimed the motions of reeling in his catch.

"Let me get this straight: you want access to one of our cadavers?"

"That's right," Julie said. "But you've been fired from Suburban West. I knew about that even before you read me the note, so I'm not sure how you can help."

"I've been fired, yes, but I still have access to my office—I'm allowed to use it while I'm searching for my next position. That was the deal the lawyers worked out."

"So you have a badge?"

"A badge that can access all of the facilities, yes. I could get you inside. But tell me, do you really think this would hurt Roman?"

"If you can help me find the right sample, I think White will have to clean house, and Roman Janowski would be the first to go."

Lincoln's audio feed distorted when Allyson chortled.

"I'd like that very much," Allyson said. "The sample needs to come from a patient who had hives, is that right? And death from cardiac arrest with no history of heart disease?"

"That's right on both accounts."

"I have a friend who can check for me. In fact, I have a lot of friends there. Nobody likes what White Memorial, Roman specifically, has done. Let me get back to you."

Lincoln tensed with excitement as a lengthy wait put him on edge. In time, the phone rang again.

"Julie, I think there's a body you can take a sample from. He died on Monday. The body is still in our morgue because the family can't agree where he's going to be buried; actually met him a week ago, while I was giving Roman a hospital tour. Albert and Roman talked about a number of things, including scars Albert said he got from hives."

"Sounds like post-inflammatory hyperpigmentation," Julie said.

"I'm looking at his medical record right now and that's what it says. No mention anywhere of heart disease. Does that help?"

Lincoln laughed out loud. It was too easy, too perfect.

"I think it helps tremendously. What was the patient's name?" Julie's voice was ripe with excitement.

"Albert Cunningham," Allyson said. "He was the public address announcer for the Boston Red Sox."

"Tomorrow is Thanksgiving," Julie said. "The hospital will be quiet."

"That's right. Why?"

"Do you really want to help me?"

"I really want to hurt Roman Janowski."

"This might. I think this just might."

"Then I want to help."

"Give me your address. I'll come over tonight if that's all right with you. I'll get the badge and we can work out the logistics. Tomorrow, I'll go get the sample."

"Works for me," Allyson said, and she gave Julie her address.

It worked for Lincoln Cole, too. His first shift at Suburban West happened to be scheduled for the next afternoon.

CHAPTER 45

At five thirty on the afternoon of Thanksgiving, Julie drove her Prius into a sparsely filled parking lot at Suburban West and picked a space away from the building and far from any floodlights. She was composed, but her insides were quaking. Never in her life had she brazenly broken a law, but now she felt out of options. This was no longer about figuring out what killed Sam. Julie truly believed others would die if she did nothing. The killer, it seemed, had found a new feeding ground at West.

Jordan shared Julie's sentiments, but was quiet on the drive. He was too occupied reviewing the process and techniques of producing human tissue blocks for testing purposes. He could apply various media to embed the samples in molten, melted, or paraffin wax. Being an ICU doc gave Julie confidence that she could do the biopsy well enough, but she knew nothing about the machines required to produce routine tissue embedding. Thankfully, her partner—her secret admirer—was more than capable around a lab.

Julie put the car in park and cut the engine. She turned her head and saw the basement entrance to the pathology lab, just as Allyson Brock had described. As Allyson promised, no security cameras were mounted to the outside walls. It gave Julie confidence that everything Allyson said about the lab, the layout, and the location of the body would be accurate as well.

"Did you ever get in touch with Lucy?" Jordan asked.

He was referring, of course, to the note Lucy had written and stashed in Allyson's mailbox.

"No. She doesn't feel safe, it's obvious from what she wrote to Allyson. But she's done plenty for us. If we can get her the sample, she'll find a way to test it where she's not being watched."

"Who is watching her?" Jordan asked.

"It's got to be Coffey and Colchester."

"Yeah, gotta be. But I still don't fully get the motive."

Now it was Julie's turn to fall silent, head bowed in thought.

"It's a cover-up, I'm guessing," she said. "Let's say a powerful drug comes on the market for treating something unrelated to the cardiovascular system, but it can also cause a fatal allergy. A symptom of the allergy is hives. It could be very expensive for the manufacturer, so Coffey gets hush money to keep a lid on the potential allergic reaction. A similar thing happened with GM not too long ago. They knew the ignition switches were faulty, but it was cheaper to stay quiet about it than deal with the problem, and it cost lives. And later a whole lot of GM's cash."

"So how does Colchester fit in?" Jordan asked.

"I still think Colchester was working overtime to get Brandon convicted," Julie said. "Like I said, maybe he was doing it for his wife, I'm not really sure. But he was damn well determined to see what he thought was justice get done. I think he bribed Sherri and planted the drugs. During the trial, Coffey approached Colchester with his thoughts about exhuming Donald's body. The people who paid Coffey enough hush money to buy him that plane couldn't let that happen. Colchester wants his conviction and he's willing to reward the judge to get it. Maybe he takes a little extra cash from Coffey's employers for his campaign war chest as a bonus. Who knows?"

A twitch in Jordan's eye became a little more pronounced. "Never did have much love for politicians," he said.

JORDAN'S FIRST thought when he turned on the lights: there was no comparing Suburban West's pathology lab to the one at White Memorial. This space was about half the size, the ceiling low enough for Jordan to be aware of its proximity to his head. No cobwebs or corrosion on any of the equipment, but it was antiquated and some of the microscopes might have been borrowed from a high school chemistry classroom. A powerful stench of formaldehyde was at least one thing the two facilities had in common.

Jordan stepped into the hallway. Julie was right, Thanksgiving was a perfect time to steal some tissue samples. The place was as quiet as the dead they had come to visit. Both he and Julie wore white lab coats that Jordan brought from home. It would provide an air of authenticity should someone happen upon them. Perhaps with a little luck, and a lot of conviction, they could be convincing enough to be left alone.

A blue sign hanging from the ceiling pointed the way to the hospital morgue. Jordan made his way down the quiet corridor with Julie close behind. He was first into the morgue's anteroom. He paused by the cold stainless steel table where bodies could be properly weighed, measured, and photographed by a wide-angled camera mounted to the ceiling.

"You good?"

"Good," Julie answered.

He picked up the nervousness in her voice and wondered if she would have gone through with this alone.

Jordan led the way into the autopsy suite, an open space with a rust-colored floor ideal for camouflaging bloodstains. The walls were lined with stainless steel racks filled with surgical supplies, and plenty of empty rolling carts for moving bodies around. In the middle of the room stood several freestanding sinks with attached exam tables and scales hanging above the basins for weighing organs.

They passed the specimen preparation and storage area before entering a chilly room behind a sealed door where the bodies were kept. Allyson had described the area well: a row of metal lockers, three bodies per stack, each cooled to 51.2 degrees Fahrenheit. With a tug on the handle, Jordan opened the top locker of the middle row, number eight. The body inside was sealed in black plastic. Jordan slid the tray out and undid the zipper. A toe tag confirmed it was Albert Cunningham. Refrigeration had kept Albert in decent shape, with little decomposition and only a slight rotten smell. Tufts of gray hair poked up from Albert's oval-shaped head, and he had no expression on his waxy face. Jordan raised the height on the cadaver lift and slid Albert out of the storage unit. The lift lowered with a foot release.

"All right, Doc," Jordan said. "You get the tissue sample, then I'll take over."

"Right."

Biopsy time.

Jordan wheeled Albert into the autopsy suite, over to one of the freestanding sinks. Albert was thin and light, and Jordan had no trouble transferring him to a rolling stainless steel cart, but did not bother moving him to an exam table. He'd be going back to his storage unit soon enough.

Julie scoured the supplies for the needed equipment. She gathered her materials expeditiously and carefully laid the instruments on the steel exam table next to the sink. Jordan inventoried the items: forceps, scalpel, tissue hook, needle holder (a long scissors-like implement good for suturing, with a locking mechanism at the base to hold a needle and thread), specimen bottle, gauze, and a suture. No risk of infection and no pain meant no need for lidocaine or any sterilization. However, they both wore surgical gloves, and had them on from the start so they would leave no fingerprints behind.

Holding the scalpel like a pencil, Julie made an incision in the abdomen using a number ten blade, with Jordan pulling on the skin to provide counter traction. Julie's incision went completely through the dermis and sank deep enough to see subcutaneous fat. Her technique and steady hand impressed Jordan. In two cuts she had exposed subcutaneous tissue and had done so using care worthy of the living. The cut went deep enough for Jordan to see Albert's liver. He knew this was a good choice for the sample. If a toxin were involved, it would still be present in the liver. The tissue could also be tested for the presence of an allergen.

Julie took a large sample of liver tissue using the forceps and scissors and then carefully placed the sample inside the specimen jar. Then she sutured the wound closed.

"It should be enough," she said. "But I think I'll take some more tissue from the airway just to be sure."

"I know Albert won't mind, but let me check the hallway, make sure we're still in the clear," Jordan said.

At that moment, the door to the autopsy area swung open with force and a burly security guard, gun already drawn, burst into the room. He aimed his weapon at Jordan and in a commanding voice yelled, "Get down on the floor!"

Jordan held his ground even though the guard pointed his weapon at Jordan's head. Julie came out from behind the autopsy table, her hands up to show she was not a threat, and approached with caution. The guard swiveled and trained his weapon away from Jordan and onto Julie.

"It's fine, it's fine. I'm a doctor here," Julie said, holding up Allyson's badge as proof. The picture on the badge of course would not match the woman holding it, but Jordan thought the quick flash was convincing enough. Julie spoke with the authority of a physician and the security guard should have backed down. The gun, to his surprise, did not lower even an inch. Why? It was inconceivable the guard knew all the doctors working here. He should have been embarrassed, should have acted contrite, and then he should have gone away.

"I'm here with my assistant finishing up some important work," Julie said. Her voice carried a little uneasiness.

The guard's arm stayed rigid like steel, and the gun did not waver in his steady hand. He seemed to ponder his next move. Jordan's heart began to hammer away. Prison was not someplace he wished to return anytime soon. The guard cleared his throat.

"Yeah, I don't think so," he said.

"Excuse me?" Julie looked confused.

"I'll clarify," the guard said, with a twisted smile. "I don't think you work here, Dr. Devereux."

Julie stammered, "How . . . how do you know my name?"

The guard closed in on Julie with startling quickness. He aimed the gun at her but did not pull the trigger. Something about him seemed hesitant.

"This isn't easy," he said.

What isn't easy? Jordan stood frozen.

"I know so much about you," the guard said.

The statement was directed at Julie, and Jordan did not know what he meant.

"And about your son, Trevor, and your ex, Paul, and your poor dead fiancé. I know you sing in the shower and I like you best in your black bra and matching underwear. It's a good look for you."

"You," Julie said, her voice quavering as realization came to her. "It was you at the river, wasn't it?"

Jordan remembered that story.

The guard returned a nonchalant shrug. "Yeah, and it was me in Sherri's home before you got there," he said. "And it's me here now. Actually, I would have been here sooner, but my new boss is quite the chatterbox.

Damn. I thought it might be easier a second time, but I think I was wrong."

"What do you want?"

The guard took in a breath and aimed his gun a bit higher.

"Look, I'm really sorry," he said.

Julie was shaking. Jordan snapped out of his daze enough to notice two guns stashed in the back pocket of the guard's uniform. Two guns. Quickly, Jordan understood. This man was here to kill them. He would shoot them both and then plant guns to justify the killing as self-defense. They were intruders, after all. Somehow the guard had known they would be down in the autopsy room at this hour. Had Allyson betrayed them? Was it a setup from the get-go?

With a slight turn of his head, Jordan saw a metal bowl on the exam table within his reach. Jordan lunged for it, and with one hand, slid the bowl off the table as he fell to the floor. Then, with a flick of the wrist, he flung the bowl Frisbee-like at the guard's head.

The guard must have caught a blur of motion in his peripheral vision. He ducked an instant before the steel would have connected with his temple. The bowl sailed past him and clattered noisily onto the floor. The guard spun from the waist and aimed his gun at Jordan. He got off a shot that splintered the concrete near Jordan's leg.

Jordan rolled twice, and two more shots fired.

CHAPTER 46

The moment the guard burst into the autopsy area, the carjacking incident came into sharp focus. Julie's immediate instinct was to grab something for self-defense. The closest thing to her was the scalpel, which she stashed in the pocket of her lab coat. While Julie's heart shook with fear, her mind stayed sharp as she gave the guard what sounded like a plausible explanation.

"I'm a doctor . . . I work here . . . this is my assistant . . ."

A flash of the official Suburban West badge should have been enough to send him away. But this was no ordinary security guard. He was here on a mission. When he pointed the gun at her, Julie thought she saw murder in his eyes. Julie's mind reeled with unanswered questions. How did he know those details about her life? How did he know they would be in the autopsy suite?

The answers would have to wait. The bowl Jordan tossed might not have found a target, but it created enough of a distraction for Julie to get the scalpel into her hand. As the guard fired his gun at Jordan, Julie raised her arm and brought it down in a sweeping arc. The scalpel's steel blade penetrated the guard's muscled shoulder to the handle and pushed deep enough into flesh to stick upright even after she let go. The guard howled in rage.

A look of pure terror stretched across Julie's face. She whirled in the direction of the morgue and took off running.

BITCH, STABBED ME.

Lincoln Cole was seething. The reservations he had about committing two more murders were gone now. It had not occurred to him that Julie might have armed herself. The oversight was almost unforgivable. This whole episode was supposed to be a simple two-shot deal, followed by a frantic phone call to his supervisor to report the incident. *Helluva first day you had, son.* Lincoln had met the head of security, Bert Stone, an hour before the start of his first shift. He did not know the old-timer at all, but imagined it was something his new boss might say.

Helluva first day.

Lincoln suppressed the urge to shoot Julie as she ran. Forensics would have no trouble telling the difference between entry and exit wounds, and it would be hard to argue self-defense if the doc had potholes in her back. Lincoln took off after Julie, thinking he would catch her in three strides, four at the most.

He left the blade in his shoulder, prioritizing Julie over its removal. He reached with his free hand and seized the back of Julie's lab coat as it billowed behind her like a flapping cape. He tightened his grasp and gave a hard yank.

Julie's feet continued forward while the rest of her traveled in reverse. She went airborne a moment before gravity plunged her to the unforgiving concrete floor with a thud. Her skull made a notable sound when it made contact. Dazed from the blow to the head, Julie lay on the floor, gasping for breath, the air knocked out of her lungs.

Lincoln eyed Julie and tried to imagine how a shot to the head would look to investigators. It would look unusual, he decided, so he aimed for her heart instead.

JORDAN MIGHT not have joined a gang in prison, but he had learned how to fight from people who were in gangs. Exploding from the hips, Jordan launched himself into the air at the exact moment the guard considered his shot. As the guard's gun came level with Julie's chest, Jordan wrapped his arms around the guard's waist and got his shoulder firmly rooted against the brawny man's body. With the full force of his momentum, Jordan drove the guard hard to the ground. The angle of impact pressed the upright scalpel deeper into flesh. Judging by the sound of the guard's scream, the pain must have been electric. The blade might have scraped bone.

The impact dislodged the gun from the guard's hand. Jordan had little trouble flipping the guard, weak and disoriented, from his side onto his back. This was tactical for two reasons: it gave Jordan a physical advantage, and it barricaded the other guns beneath the guard's body. In no way did it mean Jordan could relax. He knew not to underestimate fists as a weapon.

Jordan straddled the guard's waist, but he failed to get the man's arms pinned to his sides. With the guard's arms free to attack, Jordan expected one of two countermoves. The guard might decide to clinch him, but it would leave his head exposed to punches. He might try to shield his head, but if he did, Jordan could shimmy up the body and put him in an even stronger hold. Jordan had seen plenty of prison fights where one guy had his arms pressed against his ears and the guy on top went for the throat. Never ended well for the guy on the bottom.

For the moment, at least, Jordan had the upper hand. But he could feel his opponent's legs pumping furiously in an effort to break free, and he wondered how much longer he could maintain his hold.

RAGE OWNED Lincoln Cole, but not enough to make him do something stupid like shield his head. What he wanted to do was put a bullet through the morgue tech's eye. But his guns were inaccessible, and Lincoln had to give it to the kid. He'd been strong and skilled enough to get Lincoln to the ground, and had him pinned in a mounted hold.

But the kid was also clueless about what to do next, and Lincoln had a plan. Flexing his ankles, Lincoln made a base with his feet, rooting them firmly to the floor. With a thrust, Lincoln bucked his hips hard enough to toss Jordan forward like he was being thrown from a bronco. He did this repeatedly. With each toss, Jordan's hold weakened considerably.

Lincoln bucked again and this time as he did, he rolled to one side, brought his knees through Jordan's legs, and rolled onto his back once more. In this position, Lincoln was able to wrap his legs around Jordan's waist while getting his arm secured around Jordan's neck.

Now, Lincoln began to squeeze. With any luck, he'd crush the windpipe in the next few seconds.

JORDAN FELT strangely light-headed. In that moment he believed he was going to die, and die horribly. The guard secured a python-like chokehold around Jordan's neck. Jordan could feel the man's bulging bicep press against his windpipe hard enough to cut off the air supply. Bit by bit Jordan's vision went dark, though he could still make out Julie lying on her back not far from him. Her head lolled groggily from side to side as she fought to come to her senses. Jordan struggled to break free, fighting for each breath, flailing his body in a panic.

Then, in a strange reversal, Jordan began to relax. It took a moment for him to realize he had hit oxygen debt. Unconsciousness was probably seconds away, death soon to follow. Terror and pain gave way to a feeling of peacefulness. An eerie blackness came at him like a fast-moving eclipse. Jordan resisted the shadow at first, but gave in to a feeling of euphoria as he let himself fall into the abyss.

JULIE SOMEHOW managed to get to her knees. She had no memory of doing so, and was dazed. The idea of seeing stars was no longer a figure of speech. Her head throbbed, but her vision had cleared enough to see Jordan on top of the guard. It appeared he had the upper hand, until Julie realized the guard's arm was wrapped tightly around Jordan's neck. The guard also had his legs knotted around Jordan's waist to keep him from pulling free of the hold.

Julie tried to stand. Her knees buckled, so she

crawled toward them, unsure what she would do once she got there.

Weakened from her fall, and down on the floor with no real leverage, Julie tugged on the guard's arm. All that did was get his attention. He snapped his head in Julie's direction and his eyes blazed with venom. *You're next,* his look said.

Instinct, nothing more, made Julie open her mouth and lunge at him with her head. She sank her teeth into the exposed flesh of the guard's forearm and bit down hard enough to coax out a warm gush of blood. Blood filled her mouth. The taste went beyond repulsive, but the attack proved highly effective. The guard let go of Jordan's throat, so he could direct the force of his attack on Julie.

LINCOLN TRIED to ignore the pain rocketing up his arm. He wanted to keep his hold a little longer. The morgue tech was almost dead. If Lincoln could give it a few more seconds, he would surely finish the job. But Julie had latched on to his arm with force, and would not let go. Her teeth tore into his flesh, and the pain went from bothersome to excruciating in a blink.

He had to get her off him, so he snapped his arm as if cracking a whip. He managed to dislodge her, and in the process struck her face with his knuckles in more than a glancing blow. Julie tumbled back to the floor. Lincoln forgot all about the morgue tech as he reached for Julie. Hurt whatever had just hurt him was all he was thinking. It was blind fury taking over, not really his best option.

With air in his lungs again, Jordan recovered his wits along with his mobility. Jordan's next move took Lin-

coln by surprise. Somehow he got his arm wrapped
around Lincoln's neck, and he drove his shoulder while
pushing with his legs. Jordan's hips came forward as
he rolled onto his side. From there, Jordan was able to
squirm free of Lincoln's flimsy grasp and scramble to
his feet.

Lincoln did the same. Instead of bull-rushing Jordan,
though, Lincoln tried to draw a gun from his back
pocket. The weapon got caught on the fabric of Lincoln's pants, and he fumbled to get it free. Once he
did, he aimed the gun not at Jordan, but at Julie.

THE GUN getting stuck was good fortune, Jordan thought,
but not entirely surprising. Back pockets were not designed to be gun holsters. The effort afforded Jordan a
few precious seconds he did not think he had. It was
enough time to attack.

Julie was on the ground, trying to get her bearings,
trying to get to her feet, but she was too disoriented
even to stand. Jordan lowered his shoulder and charged
the guard at a sprinter's pace. He slammed into the
guard's exposed side, and momentum carried them
both into the cart holding Albert's body.

The cart toppled over with a loud clatter, spilling Albert to the floor. Somehow both men managed to stay
upright. The pair bounced off the cart and stumbled
into the exam table where Julie had laid out her instruments for the biopsy.

With his left hand, Jordan grabbed hold of the
guard's right wrist, effectively pinning the hand holding the gun. The guard pushed back, his arm shaking
as he struggled to position his gun in front of Jordan's
face. Jordan's back was pressed up against the exam

table. He latched his right hand to the lip of the table, which improved his leverage considerably. Even so, the guard was still overpowering him. The gun continued to inch closer to Jordan's face.

Jordan turned his head to get maximum distance from the gun barrel, when he caught a glint of something silver in his peripheral vision.

In a leap of faith, Jordan let go his grip on the table so he could reach for the silver object. In doing so, Jordan's grip on the guard's arm weakened. The barrel came swinging toward his face. Jordan clutched the curved seven-inch needle holder in his hand like a talon. He brought the surgical implement toward the guard's left eye with force.

A bullet exploded from the gun barrel and a searing pain erupted near Jordan's temple. Even so, Jordan's strike was on target. There was some resistance at first when the tip of the needle holder hit the eyeball. The resistance did not last long. Jordan felt something give and then heard a pop as he drove the instrument through the guard's eyeball and deep into the skull.

In an instant, the guard's knees buckled. The gun tumbled from his hand. Then the guard crumpled to the ground, where his body went into spasm. The guard flailed for a moment before he came to a full stop alongside Albert's perfectly still body.

CHAPTER 47

Jordan slumped to the floor, exhausted and breathing hard. Sweat mixed with blood where the bullet had grazed his temple. The bleeding came briskly, and Jordan's dazed expression suggested he was in shock.

Julie was not faring much better. Her face and head throbbed where she had taken blows, and the taste of the killer's blood continued to foul her mouth. With great effort, Julie stood, wobbly on her feet, and staggered over to Jordan. She did a quick visual exam and used the flashlight feature on her phone to check his pupils. They reacted briskly to light and constricted consensually. Good sign.

Her senses and balance returning, Julie found a box of gauze, which she applied in generous quantities to stanch the bleeding from Jordan's head wound.

"Keep pressure on it," she said, while wrapping a bandage around Jordan's head to hold the gauze in place. "We need to get you to a hospital."

Jordan actually laughed. "Aren't we in one?" he said.

Despite it all, Julie could not suppress a little smile.

It dimmed, though, when her gaze traveled to the security guard with the needle holder sticking up grotesquely from his eye socket.

"I don't mean this one," Julie said. "We have to get out of here. Now."

"I can't hear very well from my left ear," Jordan said.

"The ringing should go away with time, but we have to go."

Adrenaline coursed through Julie's veins like a river. She could not quiet the shaking of her body.

"No," Jordan answered.

Julie looked at him, bewildered. "What do you mean?"

"Give me the badge."

"Why?"

"Because if we both go down for what happened here, nobody is going to get the sample tested."

"What story could you possibly give?"

"The truth. I got the badge from Allyson Brock, who I know through Lucy. I came here to do some research in the lab. I was here with her permission and the security guard attacked me."

"The police aren't going to believe you," Julie said. "You have a record."

"I'll take my chances."

Jordan clutched his bandaged head and winced in pain. Talking hurt. So did standing, which Jordan could do only with Julie's help. Jordan retrieved the specimen jar and handed both the jar and the cooler to Julie.

"Whatever is in Albert's tissue is worth killing us over," Jordan said. "If we don't do this now, whoever is behind it will go underground. They'll hide the evidence the way they did hives in the victims' medical records. Get the sample to Dr. Abruzzo and get it tested. Call Allyson Brock and make sure she knows what's coming her way."

As much as Julie hated to agree, Jordan made good points.

"Who do you think he really is?" Julie asked, pointing to the guard. "He's been spying on me, following me."

"I don't know," Jordan said. "But I got a feeling that Dominick, the punk who tried to carjack you, he knows. He kept saying someone paid him to scare you. What I think is someone paid him to try and kill you, and when that didn't work, whoever is behind this got us both kicked out of White and set the trap here."

"You think Allyson is involved?"

"I don't, but that's just my gut. Same as I don't think Lucy set us up. She wouldn't. But how did he know we were going to be here?"

Julie thought it over and pointed at the dead security guard. "He's been watching me. Maybe he's been listening to my calls as well."

She held up her phone and showed Jordan the call she received from Allyson.

Jordan agreed. "These days, with all the spying and whatnot, it's not that hard to do. I'm not going to be able to check into it, but maybe Trevor can. Tell him to look for root type programs. If he doesn't know what that means, tell him to Google it. He's smart like you. He'll figure it out."

"Jordan, I can't just leave you."

"I'm putting Albert's body back where it belongs, and then I'm pulling the fire alarm. Go. I'll be all right. I'm going to be arrested and I'm not going to get bail. I know that. But I have faith in you. I trust you and I want you to trust me. We have one chance at this. Let's not blow the opportunity."

Julie bit at her bottom lip and held Jordan's gaze a moment. Then she hugged him and gently touched his cheek. Her vision was watery from the gathering tears.

"I'll come through for you," Julie said. "That's a promise."

THE ONLY person Julie knew who might be at home and alone on Thanksgiving was Dr. Lucy Abruzzo. Lucy made her dislike for the holiday known every year when it came around. She would say it was gluttonous and complain it memorialized the genocide of an indigenous people. Julie would jokingly call Lucy a "Debbie Downer." She would also invite Lucy for Thanksgiving dinner, an invitation invariably declined, but always with a show of thanks.

Julie was not about to call Lucy to announce her pending arrival. Phones were not to be trusted. Her attacker had spied on her, perhaps using her phone as a window into her life.

Julie's nerves crackled for the entire drive into Boston, while her thoughts swirled. What was happening to Jordan? What were the police saying? Would they come looking for her? Every police car Julie came upon sent an icy chill down her spine. Who set them up? Everything, she believed, hinged on the test results—meaning everything hinged on Lucy.

Julie found street parking and rang the buzzer to 6C. Lucy lived in an apartment building on Commonwealth Avenue within walking distance of Kenmore Square.

The apartment, which Julie had visited on several occasions, featured a lighted glass staircase, a clear-sided Jacuzzi tub resembling an aquarium, and a marble steam room with an intricate inlaid mosaic design, all of which enthralled everyone except for the apartment's lone occupant.

"The architect had bad taste, but the place has a great view," Lucy said in reference to her home's ultramodern design.

Julie rang the buzzer and waited. A moment later a voice came through the intercom.

"Who is it?"

"It's Julie, I need to see you right away."

There was no hesitation. The buzzer sounded to let Julie inside.

LUCY HAD been in the middle of a game of chess with an opponent from Seoul, who was not very good at keeping control of the board's center, when her intercom sounded. One look at Julie's pale and drawn complexion implied trouble. Her friend's battered face suggested trouble on a large scale. Julie's breathing was so erratic she practically had to spit out the words.

"Someone tried to kill us, Jordan and me, but we killed him, I mean Jordan did. Jordan's in jail or he's headed there, I don't honestly know, and I need your help testing a tissue sample I took from a cadaver at Suburban West."

Lucy blinked several times and kept quiet as she took it all in. Then she said in a calm voice, "Well now, that's quite the conversation starter. Tell me again, who did you kill?"

"A security guard at Suburban West. He attacked us. But I don't think he was real security, or if he was, he was there to kill us both."

"What on earth were you doing at West?"

This puzzled Julie. "Allyson Brock."

"Who?"

"The former CEO at West. She called me because of your note," Julie said.

Lucy tilted her head to the side. "My note?"

"Did you send Allyson a note telling her to call us, that she could be of help with the tissue sample?"

Now it was Lucy who looked puzzled. "I did no such thing."

Julie stared at Lucy with mouth agape.

"We need to talk," Julie said.

Lucy led Julie over to a plush sofa in the center of a sparsely furnished and rather undecorated living room. She left only to pour them each a glass of Jameson. A few sips proved enough to calm Julie somewhat. Then it was Lucy who did the listening and Julie who did the talking.

Afterwards, Julie asked, "Do you believe me?" She sounded nervous.

"Why wouldn't I?" Lucy said.

Julie looked bewildered. "Well, because of Shirley Mitchell, of course."

Lucy waved her hand as though brushing the incident aside.

"I go by logic and facts," Lucy said. "With Shirley Mitchell there was evidence to counter the narrative you supplied. In this case, I have nothing to go on but your word. And I do trust you. Why would you lie?"

"To convince you to test the tissue sample I took."

Lucy patted Julie's leg. "If that were the case, I'd help you out of respect for your creativity."

Julie hefted the cooler she'd carried in. "I need to know what's inside this sample. There is an allergy-causing antigen at work here and we need to find it. Whoever sent Allyson that note knows it, too. They just didn't think we'd get out of there alive to test it."

Lucy considered all possibilities. Logic dictated that if she believed Julie about the attack at Suburban West, about it being a trap, she also had to believe Julie's claims about Shirley Mitchell. Which meant someone must have replaced saline with heparin. In Lucy's mind, she was left with only one option.

"You may have been fired from White, but I wasn't." Lucy kept a deadpan expression.

"So?"

"So, to learn what's in that tissue, you and I have to go to the lab."

CHAPTER 48

Julie was in rough shape, so Lucy drove them to the hospital. On the way there, Julie tuned the radio to WBZ. A broadcaster reported breaking news of a homicide at Suburban West hospital. No names had been released, but the broadcaster said a suspect was currently in police custody.

Lucy took it all in. "I'm sorry," she said to Julie.

"For what?"

"For ever doubting you."

In transit, Julie used Lucy's phone to call Allyson Brock. The conversation was tense, as expected. The snippets Lucy heard made it sound as if Allyson was more concerned for Allyson than anything else.

Julie ended the call with a look of disgust. "Well, I don't think she set us up," Julie said, "but I don't think she cares what happens to us, either. Her biggest worry was that she was going to get arrested. I told her to wait for the police to show up, which they will, and tell them she gave Jordan her badge as a favor. It will back up Jordan's story."

"What's the worst they can do to Allyson?" Lucy asked. "She's already been fired from West."

"That's what I said. The most they can do is revoke her access privileges. Anyway, she's going to try and figure out who the security guard was, when he was hired, who hired him, that sort of thing. Allyson still has the loyalty of the employees at West. She'll get info. The guard told us it was his first day on the job, but I don't know if that's true or not."

"If it is true," Lucy said, "you realize that whoever pushed through his hire, or called in a favor, is probably the person who wanted you dead."

They arrived at White a little after nine. It was dark, chilly enough for Lucy to lend Julie a warm jacket, which she wore in place of the bloodstained lab coat. And it was quiet. Everyone was with family, except for the sick and their caretakers.

Lucy parked in a rear lot reserved for staff and she and Julie made it to the lab without incident. A police officer, evidently unaware that Julie had been fired from White, waved as the two docs walked by. Jordan must have kept Julie's name out of his conversations with the police. That would buy them some time.

The lab was empty, as expected for a holiday evening, and Lucy took her time getting the equipment set up. She enjoyed this part of the job so much that for a moment Lucy forgot where the sample had come from, and how it had come to her.

"The test is called an immunohistochemistry," Lucy explained. "It's a process we use to detect antigens, things like proteins, in tissue cells. We use this type of staining widely in the diagnosis of abnormal cells. Here we'll be looking for a concentration of mast cells. I'll be using immunophenotyping to understand the various proteins expressed in the cells."

"Lucy, no offense, but I don't think I care how you do it," Julie said. "I just want to know what's in that tissue."

"No offense taken," Lucy said with a shrug.

Others might have been put off by Julie's candor, but Lucy appreciated it. No reason to explain something to someone not interested.

Julie used a website accessed from one of the lab's computers to listen to news reports about Suburban West, while Lucy went about her work. She was not an expert in allergies by any stretch, though she knew sneezing and runny noses were symptoms. The reaction itself took place in the genes, and got expressed through the immune system. The process Lucy was using would allow her to identify the antibody in the tissue sample so she could reverse-engineer it into the corresponding allergy-causing antigen.

Gowned and gloved, Lucy prepared a sample by fixing the tissue in formaldehyde, and then embedded it in paraffin to maintain the natural shape. She used a machine called a microtome to section the tissue to five millimeters, a thickness required for the test. The slides she coated with a gelatin adhesive. The sections were dried in the oven.

"Staining and immunodetection is up next," Lucy said after the initial tasks were done. Her voice was almost joyful; she so loved this work.

Julie was on the computer, no longer glancing at news sites about the murder, but instead researching causes of hives.

"What else did these patients have in common besides hives?" Julie asked.

"I'm not sure," Lucy said, snapping off one set of gloves in exchange for another.

"Sam, Donald Colchester, Tommy Grasso, Albert Cunningham. There's a thread we're missing."

"They're all men," Lucy said.

"More than that, I would think."

"They were all in the hospital," Lucy said. "Some were sicker than others."

"Were they?" Julie sounded a bit animated. "Was Donald Colchester with his advanced-stage ALS really worse off than Sam? Or what about Tommy Grasso and his chronic COPD, and Albert Cunningham, suffering from the same? Each was living a marginal existence, including Sam."

"I see your point."

Julie fell silent, but some thoughts had begun to percolate.

Lucy returned to her work. Detecting the target antigen with antibodies was a complex, multistep process. When the samples were ready, Lucy applied an alcian blue dye and began to examine the mast cells under a microscope, looking for antibody-antigen interaction. Anything stained purple meant the presence of an epitope—an antigen recognized by the immune system.

Lucy saw something, all right, and it surprised her greatly.

"Julie," she said. "Do me a favor and run a search for meat allergy."

"Excuse me?"

"A meat allergy," Lucy repeated, her eyes glued to the microscope lens. The slide showed evidence of an antibody binding to a sugar carbohydrate found in beef, lamb, and pork called alpha-gal.

Julie clicked a few Web sites. "There's an article here about alpha-gal."

"That's it," Lucy said. "Summarize for me, please."

"It talks about a tick bite causing an unusual reaction to meat," Julie said.

"Go on."

Lucy had not looked up because her microscope was revealing a fascinating world, one of profound vastness constrained to a tiny slice of human tissue.

"The allergy produces a hivelike rash," Julie noted with some excitement. "In some people it can cause an anaphylactic reaction. Why do you want to know this? Did Albert Cunningham have an alpha-gal allergy?"

"Read on," Lucy said.

"It says the allergy is only found in people bitten by the lone star tick, which is mostly in the southeast, though it's been appearing farther and farther north, especially Long Island."

Lucy was listening intently while looking at her slide.

"People bitten by the ticks develop antibodies against the alpha-gal sugar," Julie said. "But it's a delayed reaction, sometimes up to eight hours after ingesting meat, so they aren't always aware of the connection between a case of hives and the meat they ate."

This inspired Lucy to abandon her microscope and come over to Julie, who did not look away from the computer screen.

"The symptoms of the allergy range from the minor, like itching, to the more major, like hives and even anaphylaxis with weakness, swelling of the throat and tongue, and difficulty breathing."

"No fatal heart attacks like Kounis syndrome?" Lucy asked.

Julie entered a keyword search into a medical database using the terms "Kounis syndrome" and "alpha-gal." There was plenty of information about allergic reactions resulting in myocardial infarction, but nothing specifically linking Kounis syndrome to alpha-gal. And yet according to the antibodies in the stain, Albert Cunningham had suffered an alpha-gal allergic reaction. But an alpha-gal allergy alone did not trigger a heart attack, so Lucy wondered if another agent played a role in the event, a combination of alpha-gal and something else.

Julie read on. "This is interesting," she said.

Lucy leaned in closer.

"The cancer drug cetuximab produced a similar reaction in people who were later found to be alpha-gal allergic. Some people being treated with cetuximab showed severe hypersensitivity reactions. Doctors found these drug reactions were localized mostly to the southeastern United States. Researchers were able to link allergies to cetuximab to patients who were bitten by the lone star tick."

"So for those patients, receiving a dose of cetuximab was like ingesting red meat."

"Exactly," Julie said. "Was Albert Cunningham ever given cetuximab?"

"I can test the tissue to see."

"I wonder what would happen to someone who was made alpha-gal allergic by a tick bite and then given a large dose of cetuximab?"

Lucy looked thoughtful. "It would be like ingesting pounds and pounds of meat," she said, "but in a concentrated form. The body would become overwhelmed trying to fight off the allergy."

"Overwhelmed to the point the heart suffers a massive allergic coronary?"

A heavy pall settled over the lab.

"Let me test for the drug."

Julie was smart to have taken the sample from the liver. It was the best tissue for use in postmortem toxicology, because it was where the body metabolized most drugs and toxicants. The process of testing was complex and required every bit of Lucy's expertise. But a specific toxicology screen could detect cetuximab. The drug was so unusual it would never have been picked up on a typical tox screen.

It took a couple of hours. Julie spoke with Trevor and Paul on the lab phone, but told them nothing of her ordeal. When the results came back, Lucy was shocked, but not entirely surprised.

Albert Cunningham's tissue showed a huge quantity of the cancer drug, far greater a dose than would ever have been prescribed.

"Did Albert have head or neck cancer?" Julie asked, referring to the two most common cancers the drug treated.

Lucy had access to the Suburban West medical records system as a result of the merger. She made a quick scan of Albert's record.

"No. He did not have cancer."

Julie gasped. "Then Albert was murdered. He was somehow made alpha-gal allergic and dosed with a high quantity of cetuximab to induce a fatal allergy-triggered heart attack."

"You know what this means, don't you?"

"Yeah, it means Sam was murdered too."

CHAPTER 49

The Nashua Street Jail was a big brick building housing more than seven hundred pretrial detainees, Jordan among them. Jordan maintained a calm, measured demeanor as he spoke to Julie on the other side of the glass partition. He massaged his fingers repeatedly, while swiveling on his metal stool, but these were the only outward signs of his nervousness. The wound to his temple had been sutured, and the area protected by a bandage.

Julie's heart ached for him. Seeing him here, dressed in prison orange, fueled her resolve to get him out. As Jordan had predicted, the presiding judge denied bail at Jordan's arraignment. They had led Jordan out of the courtroom in handcuffs with his mother and sisters crying, and Julie looking on dolefully.

Julie had not yet been linked to the murdered security guard. She planned to keep it that way until the time was right for her to come forward.

Jordan had been confined to a cell for two days, but

reassured Julie he was doing just fine. The guards were treating him well. He was familiar with the routine and joked about how it was like riding a bicycle.

"Word I heard is the guy who tried to kill us was an ex-cop turned PI named Lincoln Cole," Jordan said.

"I heard the same on the news," Julie said.

"What you didn't hear is that Dominick ID'd Cole as the guy who paid him to scare you."

"Scare me? We both know that wasn't the plan."

"He still isn't owning up to what he was really going to do."

"You believe him about Cole?"

"Sure as heck, yes I do."

Julie concurred.

"Who hired Cole to be a guard?" Jordan asked.

"That's what we're trying to find out," Julie said. "I'm waiting for a call from Allyson. When I get it, I'm going to see Detectives Spence and Capshaw. Then I'm taking down whoever murdered Sam. That's a promise."

Jordan gave Julie a sideways glance. "You know who it is, don't you?"

"Let's just say I have my strong suspicions."

"How did they do it? The Kounis syndrome, how was it induced?"

Julie knew this conversation was being recorded. If her visits to Brandon Stahl had taught her anything, it was that the less she said the better.

"Let's just say you're not going to be in here for long," Julie answered.

A guard whistled. It was her time to go. On the way out, Julie stopped to retrieve her personal items from the locker. She saw a missed call followed by a text from Allyson. This was a new phone, but Julie had Trevor look it over to be safe.

Her son had lived up to Jordan's expectations. With help from Google, he had found a program called TrueSpy installed on her previous phone and learned about what it could do. Julie told Trevor it was a practical joke, and never to do such a thing to somebody else. It was unclear if he believed her.

She read Allyson's text.

Julie had thought she knew who got Cole that security job.

And she was right.

CHAPTER 50

Detectives Spence and Capshaw kept their brows furrowed throughout most of Julie's story, but she believed they would come around to her side eventually. They were crammed into an interview room with one-way glass and not enough heat. For this meeting, Julie had chosen a business suit from Lord & Taylor and the detectives both wore jackets and ties, making this a nicely dressed ensemble to discuss the dirty business of murder.

The conversation was being recorded, as the detectives made abundantly clear on several occasions. Also made clear was Julie's right to have an attorney present. However, she came alone, against Paul's wishes and those of Lucy, who had wanted to attend. A lawyer would get in the way, and Julie worried Lucy might confound the detectives with her science. She had one chance at this pitch, and it had to be a strike.

The detectives were cordial, much more so than when they came to chat about Shirley Mitchell. This time Julie had come to them, so perhaps they saw no need to apply pressure. They wanted answers as much as anyone. Julie had just finished giving them part of the story, including her involvement with Lincoln Cole's death.

Spence said, "We could charge you for that, you know? Probably a number of other felonies in addition to murder."

Capshaw agreed. "Like crimes against the dead."

"What I did was get a tissue sample proving a murder took place. I think the district attorney will go easy on me."

"Maybe," Spence said.

"It's a chance I'm willing to take, but I like my odds. And as for Lincoln Cole, Jordan killed a man who had come there to kill us, who attacked us first. Cole had two extra guns on him. Let me ask you, who did those guns belong to?"

Spence and Capshaw exchanged glances, then shrugged.

"We don't know. Someone filed off the serial numbers," Capshaw said. "Did a good job of it, too. Makes it real hard for forensics. We're still looking into ownership."

"Check your records. I don't own a gun, and I certainly don't know how to buy one with an expertly filed-off number, or file it off myself."

"Yeah, well, maybe your pal from Dorchester knows his way around town, if you know what I'm saying."

Julie flashed Spence a hard look. "You don't really believe that, do you? The only scenario that's going to add up and make all the pieces fit together is the one I'm telling you."

"You should have come forward when Jordan did." Capshaw's tone was only slightly admonishing.

"If I had, then I wouldn't have been able to get the sample tested."

Julie showed the detectives the lab results Lucy wrote up for their benefit.

"At first I thought it might have been an unknown drug reaction killing the patients, my fiancé included," Julie said. "Something a drug manufacturer would be willing to bribe, cheat, and kill to keep secret. But I was wrong."

Spence looked confused. "It's not a drug reaction?"

"No, it is," Julie said.

"Oh, I got it," Spence said. "Wait, I don't got it. Do you confuse your patients like this?"

"What I mean to say," Julie continued, "is that it's not an accidental drug reaction. Someone is making the targeted victims alpha-gal allergic."

"You told us about that. Alpha-gal is a—a—" Capshaw fumbled for the right words.

"It's a carbohydrate that's not found in humans or primates, but it is found in the meat of other mammals," Julie said. "People who are allergic to the alpha-gal sugar in mammal meat will experience delayed anaphylaxis. The shock can be anywhere from four to eight hours following ingestion of meat, including beef and pork."

"This isn't some condition PETA invented, right?"

"No, Detective Spence, I assure you it's quite real. Researchers think there's something in the saliva of the lone star tick that makes people allergic to the alpha-gal in mammal meat."

"So we're fine so long as we stick to cannibalism." Detective Capshaw smirked.

"In a way you're right. I think the killer tested

potential victims for alpha-gal sensitivity by feeding them meat. If they broke out in hives, they were essentially marked for death. Someone with access to the medical records system at White deleted the hives incident from the patient's EMR, which was a smart move."

Spence leaned forward in his chair. "Why smart?"

"We inventory the EMR system from time to time for health trends. Someone might have been curious about why White Memorial had a statistically significant outbreak of urticaria."

Capshaw turned to Spence. "That's doc jargon for hives," he said. Then to Julie, "I had 'em once. Awful. Just awful."

"How did these guys get tick bites?" Spence asked. "The vics were pretty limited, your fiancé included. I don't think they were doing much hiking."

Julie had been wondering the same thing for days.

"I don't know," she said. "I just know these victims were somehow made alpha-gal sensitive, and then they were killed."

"Killed by using—" Spence glanced at his notes. "Cetuximab."

"That's right," Julie said.

"But not heparin." Capshaw sounded dubious, though seemed pleased he had remembered the drug name.

"Shirley wasn't killed in the same way as the others. Her death was much more obvious, intentionally so, as a setup to get me out of White."

"Why?"

"Because I was too close to the truth."

Spence and Capshaw seemed willing to accept this just to move forward.

"So, speaking of obvious, with—cetuximab, wouldn't

that be picked up in an autopsy?" Capshaw was looking at his knuckles when he asked the question.

"No. As Detective Spence so aptly put it, most of the victims were very sick and would not have been autopsied. Even if they were, like Sam was, there'd be no trace of the drug unless we specifically looked for it in a forensic toxicology screen, which is far more comprehensive than what might be ordered for, say, an overdose in the ER. We wouldn't do a screen like that unless we had a good reason."

"Like a court order to exhume a body."

Julie had already given the detectives her theory on William Colchester's involvement.

"Precisely. There was a chance that a full forensic toxicology screen might have yielded traces of cetuximab in the tissue, especially given the quantity we found in Albert Cunningham's body. I think someone was worried what a full tox screen on Donald Colchester would reveal. Ask me, I'd say someone preyed on William Colchester's fears, told him exhuming the body would get Brandon's charges dropped. I'm sure he wasn't told why, but like you said, docs can be confusing. Wouldn't be hard to convince him of some falsehood."

"You're saying Colchester didn't know about the cetuximab?"

"In my opinion, no," Julie said. "William Colchester had one goal and one goal only: convict Brandon Stahl for the murder of his son. He bribed Sherri to get her testimony, and then offered another bribe to the judge so he'd deny the request to exhume his son's body. I'm figuring Colchester's the one who planted the morphine in Brandon's apartment. That's what I believe."

Spence said, "And you think William Colchester killed Sherri and blamed it on a Brandon Stahl supporter because she was going to confess to the bribe?"

"Yes."

"So this cetuximab stuff is really what killed his son, Donald, by causing that weird heart thing?" Capshaw looked proud of himself for following, and even better, contributing to the conversation.

Julie nodded. "Yes, what we thought was a condition called takotsubo cardiomyopathy was all along Kounis syndrome, an allergic cardiac event triggered by a massive overdose of cetuximab in a person who was alpha-gal allergic."

"Alpha-gal allergic because of a mysterious tick bite."

"Or not a tick bite," Julie clarified. "Like I said, I don't know how the victims got the allergy. But I do know anyone who had the sensitivity and was later infused with a high dose of cetuximab would suffer a massive and fatal coronary that would look exactly like takotsubo to any pathologist. Wouldn't matter if the person's heart was sick or healthy, it was going to develop a ballooned left ventricle before it stopped beating."

Capshaw said, "And so your big plan is to get this guy to confess."

"That's right."

"Why would he?" Spence sounded dubious.

"This individual tried to have me killed, Detectives. We know that's true, or you would have me in handcuffs right now. I'll show him the evidence from Albert Cunningham's tissue sample. Then I'll tell him I'll bury it, in exchange for him guaranteeing my safety and the safety of my son. Something happens to either of us and my lawyer brings the evidence to you. I think he'll believe me. I'm counting on it."

Capshaw said, "Why is your suspect even doing this? What's the motive?"

"Think about the victims. They were all very ill, severely incapacitated, or at the end of their lives," Julie said. "I think the killer was taking a patient's right to choose death and removing the patient from the equation."

"Angel of Mercy kind of thing, is that it?"

"Yes, he's picking the victims for that reason. That's my belief."

Actually, it was one possible theory—enough to convince the detectives to help, Julie hoped—but she had another theory, one she kept to herself. Lucy had coached her to think of this conversation like a chess match: "Always stay three moves ahead," she'd said. So far, Julie had played it well.

"Since you and he share some of the same beliefs on death with dignity, he might just believe your offer to keep tight-lipped about it," Capshaw said, thinking aloud.

"This all sounds very dramatic," Spence said, "but in real life people can get really hurt."

"And in real life people are being murdered at my hospital. I need to do something to stop it."

"You're sure of this guy?" Capshaw did not look convinced.

"Absolutely," Julie said.

Spence and Capshaw exchanged glances, and some sort of understanding passed between them. It made Julie think of Jordan and the night they became partners at his apartment.

"If we get a green light—not saying we will, but if we do—you'd have to wear a wire," Spence said.

Julie shook her head. "No. No. I can't do that. I know him. He'll suspect me going in. I'll be searched, and then we won't get anything."

"We'll be there. We'll have your back." Spence acted so sure of himself.

"I can't. I'm sorry."

"Then this conversation is over. You go home and we'll talk about charges when we come to arrest you," Spence said.

Julie hated being in this position, but she had put herself there. She knew going in they might demand she wear a wire, but what choice did she have? Jordan depended on her, Brandon too. And she faced jail or another attempt on her life if she did nothing. The only way to set things right, and bring the hammer down on those responsible, including William Colchester, was to get the police involved.

"Look, maybe you could try something else. Bug the office or something. There's this technology called TrueSpy, my son found it on my phone. I think Lincoln Cole put it there. It secretly records phone conversations. Your team could use that, couldn't they?"

The detectives' expressionless gaze said no.

"I've done this rodeo plenty of times now," Capshaw said. "Our tech guys have a way of doing things. We can't just throw in something new, something we haven't heard of or used before, and think it's going to work. We have a process, and that's the process we have to use. Now, I hear you, Julie. I get your concern, I really do, but these devices are so small nobody is going to notice them. I promise. You'll be fine."

Julie agonized. "May I make a phone call? I'd like to talk it over with my friend."

"Sure. Call away."

"In private," Julie said.

Capshaw shut off the recorder and he and Spence left the room without protest.

Julie phoned Lucy on her new cell phone. The two talked at length until a decision was made. Julie invited Spence and Capshaw back into the room.

"If you can make it happen," Julie said, "you've got yourselves a deal. But on one condition."

Capshaw sighed. "We're listening."

"My friend Lucy is allowed to be with you as an observer."

"Why?"

"Because I'm going to be scared out of my mind and, no offense, you two aren't exactly a comforting presence."

Again with the glances, and again the detectives reached a nonverbal agreement.

"Fine," Spence said. "She'll be in the equation. But we need the name of the guy we're taking down."

Julie said, "His name is Dr. Gerald Coffey."

CHAPTER 51

Thin clouds stretched across a slate-gray sky and snow was in the forecast for this first day of December. Lucy had dressed for the weather in her warmest sweater, though the back of the surveillance van was plenty warm thanks to all the body heat. The full-size white cargo van had a decal on the outside panels advertising a company called JP Pest, but inside the van was crammed with high-tech surveillance equipment unlike anything Lucy had ever seen. There were wireless transmitters, sound recorders, sound amplifiers, a mixing board, cameras, various wires, even a working periscope and controller. It was all highly sophisticated, and when Lucy saw it she understood why they could not use new technology that had not been properly vetted and field-tested.

Detective Spence was in the back of the van, along with Lucy and two technicians from the Boston PD who knew how to operate the equipment. To increase usable space, the van's seats had been removed and replaced with benches bolted to the floor. Detective Capshaw was seated up front, reading a copy of the *Boston*

Herald and looking a lot like a guy from JP Pest enjoying his lunch break. Scattered around the hospital campus were a number of other undercover police officers, but Lucy did not know where they were positioned or how they had been disguised.

Detective Spence had made it clear that Lucy's job was to keep Julie calm. Other than that, he expected her to stay out of the way. His prickly demeanor did not ruffle Lucy in the least. She respected it, in fact. This was his domain, his job, his operation to run, and his neck on the line if things went south. And things were going to head south. Lucy was sure of it.

Getting Julie inside White was not a problem, because she had Lucy's badge. "The badge switch worked before, it can work again," Julie had said during a late night planning meeting with the lead detectives. All the warrants, including those for the wiretap, were in place, and steps had been taken to ensure Dr. Coffey would be at his desk. In fact, he was scheduled to meet with Lucy—only it would be Julie who walked through his office door.

"Okay, let's do a mic check," a technician said.

Spence gave Lucy a nudge. "You're on," he said.

Lucy wore a headset with an attached microphone. She got comfortable in her seat and took a deep breath. She was not one to get easily rattled, but this was her friend venturing into treacherous waters, and Lucy played a vital role in the mission's success.

"Julie, it's Lucy. Can you hear me?"

A crackle in the headset and then, "Yes, loud and clear."

Julie's voice was also being broadcast into earpieces worn by all the police. "What's your—um, location?"

Lucy did not know the proper lingo. Spence had told her to just talk naturally. "Where are you?" Lucy asked.

"I'm inside the lobby of the Barstow Building," Julie said. "I'm using my phone's earpiece so it looks like I'm having a normal phone conversation, but I'm worried you can't hear me. The microphone is pretty far from my mouth."

"I hear you loud and clear," Lucy said.

Spence gave a thumbs-up as well.

The miniaturization of the wire Julie wore had stunned Lucy. Gone were the days of bulky contraptions and sweat streaming down faces of worried snitches fearing the dreaded pat-down. "Wire" in the age of wireless meant cameras and recorders so small they could be hidden practically anywhere. The recording device Julie wore was hidden on the button of her white lab coat. The device captured audio only, because Julie insisted on wearing the smallest possible device that would meet the need.

Now was the moment of truth, and Lucy's anxiety came on strong.

"Red Leader, this is Red One, I have Julie in our sights. Confirming her position in the lobby of the Barstow Building."

"Roger, Red One," Detective Capshaw responded.

"How's the disguise working?" Lucy asked.

"Nobody has come over to ask me to lunch," Julie said.

During the planning meeting, Julie had pushed for a simple disguise to wear to help conceal her identity. She was concerned that former colleagues might approach her and inadvertently tip off Dr. Coffey. A wig turned her from a brunette to a blonde, and the glasses she wore were intentionally oversized as well as tinted to hide her eyes and much of her face.

"Are you ready for this?" Lucy asked.

"I'm ready as I'll ever be," Julie said.

Lucy checked the time on the van's digital clock. "Okay, you're expected in Coffey's office in five minutes."

"Got it. Or Roger. Or whatever I'm supposed to say."

Julie went quiet.

"Red Leader, Red One, she is on the move. Repeat, Julie is on the move, she's past security and into the building. We have lost visual."

A sudden numbing apprehension overcame Lucy.

Spence took notice of her pale complexion. "Do you need water?"

Lucy nodded. "Yes, please."

Chatter in the van went silent. Everyone's attention was focused on the equipment, listening to Julie's footsteps, and then the ding of an elevator. She was on her way up. The crackle of a microphone in Lucy's headset made her heart jump.

"Red One, are all teams in position?"

"Roger, Red Leader. All exits are covered. We're prepared to take our target."

The plan was to use overwhelming force. Dr. Coffey could be armed, and the biggest concern was that this mission not turn into a hostage crisis. They had coached Julie when to back off, and to stay near to the door so she could make a fast exit, and to make sure she knew how to find the stairwell. With luck Julie could get out of there with no problem, and later the police would make the arrest with no risk to public safety.

Lucy lowered her head and fixed her gaze to the floor of the van.

Come on, my friend . . . be okay . . . just be okay . . .

Lucy glanced at the digital clock. It was a minute past the designated meeting time. The microphone made a jumble of noise and suddenly stopped picking up any sound. Lucy flashed Spence an edgy look.

"Where is she?"

Spence was looking anxious himself. "Hey, Red One, we have any visual?"

"Negative, Red Leader."

"All right. Hey, Dave, check the equipment."

Dave, one of the two technicians in the van, ran through a series of checks. "Um, Detective Spence, we have an issue here."

Spence went over to Dave. "And?"

"And I'm pinging her transmitter, but I'm not getting a response."

"What does that mean?"

"It means the device is offline, sir."

Spence went red in the face. "Oh, that's just great. Just great!"

The sarcasm was biting. Lucy came over to them, her concern much more pronounced.

"We lost her," Spence said.

"We lost her?" Lucy flashed anger. "Well, what does that mean?"

"It means her mic isn't transmitting."

From the front seat, Detective Capshaw slid open a partition so he could communicate with the team in the back of the van.

"I got nothing in my earpiece," Capshaw added.

"Nobody does," Spence said.

"What do we do?" Lucy asked.

"Give it a minute," Spence said.

"What if he has her as a hostage, or something," Capshaw said. "We've got no visual and no recording. That doesn't fly. We gotta get in there."

Spence did not disagree. "All right, Red One. This whole operation is a Charlie Foxtrot. We got to go in there. We got a warrant to search Dr. Coffey's office so we'll use that. Go! Go!"

Lucy bit her lip. This obviously was not how things were supposed to happen. She could hear the chatter in her headphones as the police swarmed into the Barstow Building.

"Red One, we are through the lobby," came a voice.

Lucy imagined the scene as best she could: Boston Police in body armor with guns drawn racing through a hospital lobby, flashing badges and shouting orders to gain entry. The sound of echoing footsteps marching up concrete stairs blasted in Lucy's ears. She heard grunts and the issuing of various commands, most of them unintelligible.

Spence leaned forward in his chair. Lucy glanced at him. His jaw was set tight and he was grinding his teeth. The tension on his face produced deep creases across his brow. Lucy leaned forward in her seat, her eyes closed, concentrating on every word, every sound she could pick up.

"Red Leader, there's a blond woman outside Dr. Coffey's office. She appears to be fine. Go! Go!"

Lucy heard a door slam open, then shouting—a lot of shouting.

"Down! Get down on the floor! Hands behind your head! Don't move! Do not move!"

"What's this about? What's going on here?"

It was Dr. Coffey's terrified voice, Lucy believed.

"I said down. Get facedown on the floor, hands behind your back!"

The commanding voice was so loud it distorted in Lucy's headphones. The commotion continued for some time.

"Red Leader, we have a situation here."

Spence uncoiled in his seat. "What situation?"

"Sir, it's the blond woman."

"What about her?"

"Well, she's got the wig, all right. But it isn't Julie Devereux. This girl here says her name is Becca Stinson and that she works for Dr. Lucy Abruzzo."

"Where the hell is Julie?" Spence shouted.

"Sir, we don't know."

CHAPTER 52

Julie strode past the desk of Marilyn Bates, where the gray-haired sentry kept watch, and burst unannounced into Roman Janowski's spacious office. Of course Marilyn followed, a frantic look on her craggy countenance, bracing for a stern rebuke over her failure to guard.

Romey was hardly amused by the intrusion, but he displayed no outward signs of anger. He simply rose from his chair.

"Marilyn, would you leave us, please?" he asked. "And close the door behind you."

Julie hovered near the door, her hands clenched into fists, electric currents racing through her body.

"What on earth are you doing here, Julie?" Romey's tone revealed both puzzlement and annoyance.

"Surprised to see me, Roman?"

"How did you get into the building?"

"I used Lucy's badge, same as I used Allyson's badge to get into West."

"Clever girl. We'll have to address that security lapse, won't we? What is it you want, Julie?"

"I want to cut a deal."

"A deal about what?"

"A deal that will keep me and my son alive and you out of prison. I think we have a lot to discuss."

Romey reclined in his high-back leather desk chair, folded his arms across his chest. Julie found his expression obnoxiously sanguine.

"I have no idea what you're talking about," Romey said. "But I do know I'm busy and you've been fired from White, which means I'm going to have you forcibly removed." Romey reached for his desk phone.

Julie approached with caution, ignoring the fear bubbling in her gut, the tremor in her heart. "I have proof," she said. "Cetuximab and alpha-gal. I know how it works."

Romey set the phone back on its cradle and returned his hands to his lap. He rolled his chair forward and leaned his elbows against his uncluttered desk.

Julie was intentionally vague, wondering how Romey would respond and what she would do if he attacked, if he pulled a gun on her. She inched forward and got to within a few feet of his desk, close enough so she could read the time on his brass clock. By now Spence and Capshaw would have a big surprise on their hands and the police would be grilling Lucy and Becca for information. With luck, it would all be sorted out soon enough.

Romey glared at Julie. "What do you want?"

"I told you, a deal."

Romey's face turned thoughtful. "How do I know you haven't already cut one?" he asked. With his fin-

ger, Romey pointed up and down Julie's body and then
touched his ear.

This is it, Julie thought. *This is the moment.* Her
excitement began to build, but her fear remained. "Always be three to four moves ahead of your opponent,"
Lucy had said.

"I see your point," Julie said. She directed her gaze
to a white lab coat hanging on a metal coat tree tucked
in a corner—something she had noticed on her last visit
to Janowski's office.

"What if I put on that lab coat," she said, "and wear
nothing underneath?"

A slip of a smile came to Romey's face, with a leer
Julie found disgusting.

"I'd say it would work for me if it works for you."

Romey rose from his chair, adjusted his suit, and
then retrieved the lab coat.

"I'll watch," Romey said.

"What? You don't trust me, Roman?"

"No. I don't."

Julie locked eyes with Romey and did not avert her
gaze while she removed her car keys and phone from
the pocket of her trench coat. She set those items on the
corner of Romey's desk and dropped the jacket to the
floor by Romey's feet. Underneath, she wore a blue
blouse and black slacks. She had given Becca the wig
and glasses in a bathroom exchange made in the lobby
of the Barstow Building, but not the lab coat with the
wire in the button. Julie had walked out of the building not wearing any disguise, while Becca stayed behind. On her way to Romey's office, Julie kept up the
ruse by conversing with Lucy in the surveillance van.
When it was time, Julie ditched the bugged lab coat in

a trash can after crushing the device under the heel of her shoe. Now she was here, about to get undressed, and everything was going according to plan.

Romey took in Julie's figure, clearly imagining what was to be revealed to him, reveling in it. The anticipation excited him, Julie could tell. She undid the buttons of her blouse and lowered the zipper of her black slacks. Romey kept his eyes on her the entire time, and it was obvious he found the experience arousing. He dangled the lab coat in front of Julie like some reward she had yet to earn. Julie struck a stolid expression as she stepped out of her pants and took off her blouse.

"Everything," Romey said, eyeing Julie's body with a wolfish grin.

Julie took off her bra and underwear, anger eclipsing any embarrassment. Once she stood naked before him, Romey handed Julie the lab coat, but pulled it away the second she reached for it.

"I may never have this view again," Romey said.

Julie snatched the coat from Romey's hands and did up the buttons as quickly as she could with her own hands shaking. Romey stashed Julie's clothes in a gym bag and walked the bag out of his office.

"Leave that where it is," Romey said to Ms. Bates. "And hold all my calls, cancel all my meetings for the day. I'll be leaving after this."

Julie crossed the room toward Romey and stopped halfway between the door and his desk. She circled so that her back was to the door and Romey's to his desk. It gave her a quick exit, but there was another reason she took up the position. Roman would learn what it was soon enough.

Julie felt naked even though the lab coat covered most of her body. The chill on her legs was an unpleasant reminder of her vulnerability.

"So, then," Romey said, motioning to the conference table. "Do we want to sit so you can tell me about this deal of yours?"

"I'm fine to stand," Julie said. "The deal is I want my life and I don't want anyone to come after me or Trevor. That's the nonnegotiable."

"Who said anyone would?"

"I could put you away for life with what I have on you."

"Then do it, Julie. Put me away."

"I don't know how many Lincoln Cole types you may have employed."

Romey set his hands on his hips. "I see."

"Why did you do it, Roman?"

"Who said I did anything?"

"It was the money, right? You and your bottom line."

"You're making grand accusations now. I'm owning up to nothing."

"Cetuximab doesn't come cheap, but it must have been worth it, or you wouldn't have done it. So tell me, Roman, how much was Sam going to cost you? How much did you save by killing him?"

"Killing him? You must be crazy."

"How much? Tell me, or I'll turn in the evidence and take my chances you can't get to us from prison."

"Money is not the point. Is it? You of all people should agree. The point, my dear, is that health care should be just that. Health. Care. At some point in time, we've turned it into sick care. We've gotten to a place where all we do is spend money to keep people alive. Our job as healers is to heal. Our job is not to simply perform more tests and provide more services on people who will very likely die anyway.

"You ask what does the death of a patient like Sam save me," he said. "I ask you, what did it save him? Years of being treated like an experiment, of enduring the next grand hope, the next big promise for the possibility that one day he might get a taste of what a normal life is like again. What would those years have been to him? Isn't it better to die quickly than to live in misery enduring test after test, treatment after treatment? Isn't that the right you fought so hard for?"

"I fought for the patient's right to choose," Julie said. "Not for you to make the decision for him."

"Maybe some patients need a push."

"Just like some politicians."

"We all have our motivators."

"How much did it take to motivate William Colchester?"

"Excuse me?"

"My guess is the devoted dad was more devoted to his bank account than to justice. So I want to know how much it cost you to keep Donald Colchester in the ground."

"I don't know what you're talking about."

"Of course you do. When the recording surfaced, you probably felt a little anxious wondering what it might reveal. Lucky for you it picked up a fall guy. When the recording evidence got tossed, you scrambled to make the case against him stick. You knew the mother wouldn't stop until she got some answers. She'd been fighting for her son from day one. The last thing you wanted was an investigation into Donald Colchester's death, so you got Sherri Platt to turn on Brandon, and you or your goon planted the drugs in his apartment. But you couldn't get to the judge who might have agreed to exhume the body. William Colchester had to do that for you. So tell me, what does it take to buy that kind of cooperation?"

The mention of Colchester's name disturbed Romey. "He's a small man."

"I want to know how small."

"Are you trying to figure out a sum for yourself?"

"I have no income, no hope of getting a job with Shirley Mitchell hanging over my head. So yes. What did you pay him? Because I think I'm worth more. With what I have on you, I'm confident you'll agree."

Roman gave this serious consideration. It was actually something Jordan had said that allowed Julie to piece it all together. "How did Cole know Sherri was going to come clean to you?" Somebody knew because they were eavesdropping on Julie's conversations. And that somebody was Lincoln Cole, not William Colchester.

"Two hundred thousand," Romey said.

"Two hundred grand to get William Colchester to bribe the judge?"

"Yes, that's what I paid him and that's what I'm willing to offer you."

Julie broke into a smile. "Good," she said.

The door to Romey's office burst open and seven armed agents from the FBI stormed in with guns drawn. They ordered Romey to the ground and he cooperated without resistance. He was immediately handcuffed, brought to his feet, and read his rights.

"What are the charges?" Romey asked.

Julie took delight in the fear on his face.

"U.S. Code 201," an agent from the FBI said. "Bribing a public official."

"What is this? I never—" Romey said. "And don't trust her. She's been fired from White. She has reason to hurt me."

Julie retrieved her cell phone from Roman's desk and held it to his face.

"It might look like my phone's turned off, but it's not," Julie said. "It's running an app called TrueSpy and recording everything we just discussed. The Boston police weren't so keen on my using it, so I went to the FBI. They told me they couldn't get a warrant for murder because it wasn't a federal crime, but turns out bribing a public official is a different story. Trust me, Romey, you'll still go down for murder, you son of a bitch."

Julie used the bathroom in Romey's office to change back into her street clothes while her phone was bagged and tagged as evidence, and Romey got carted away in handcuffs.

The Boston police had given Julie the ultimatum to wear the wire or face arrest, so she played it the only way she could. She'd said yes to their deal, while secretly cutting a separate deal with the FBI to get Colchester. Roman was Julie's real target, but she needed someone for the bait and switch. Dr. Gerald Coffey had served that need well.

Neither organization knew what the other was doing, so now the FBI had another job to do—make nice with Spence and Capshaw and get Lucy and Becca out of hot water. Julie had another job to do as well. Somehow Sam and the others were made alpha-gal allergic. But how? She knew someone who might have an answer—someone who knew a lot about bugs.

CHAPTER 53

Michelle Stevenson poured a little more wine into Julie's glass. They were back in Michelle's nicely appointed living room where a framed beetle hung on the wall near a picture of Michelle's son, Andrew. Julie had gone to the home of Keith and Michelle to talk arachnids—specifically, the lone star tick. Julie's theory was that somehow the tick saliva had been synthesized and then injected into the patients to turn them alpha-gal allergic.

Julie looked at the picture of Andrew with a renewed feeling of gratitude for her own life, for her many blessings, for Trevor, and a sense of peace she felt now that Lincoln Cole and Roman Janowski were no longer threats.

"Will they charge Roman with murder?" Michelle asked.

"The police are working on it," Julie said. "That's why I need your help. Roman certainly had access to the patients, and giving an injection of cetuximab isn't so hard to do. What I can't figure out is how he made them positive for the alpha-gal allergy."

Keith, dressed comfortably in jeans and a navy polo, made a sound suggesting that he was at a loss as well.

"For such a small critter, the tick's salivary glands are incredibly complex," Keith said. "I mean, it's really quite remarkable. It's certainly a key to their evolutionary success. The bioactive component exhibits a range of pharmacological properties. I'm not sure how it would be synthesized, but I suppose it's possible, or elements of it at least."

Michelle said, "What was Romey's motive in all this?"

"Well, he didn't come right out and say it, but profit, I'm sure," Julie said.

"How so?" Keith asked.

"Moving from fee-for-service to the accountable care model changed the profitability equation. The extra money an ACO can earn from Medicare kicks in only if the patient's cost for care is lower than expected. What better way to control costs than get rid of the expensive patients? Hospitals' revenues are up, but margins are down because of climbing expenses. A patient like Sam could cost up to a half million dollars, maybe more. Get rid of enough patients like him, put a stop to unnecessary tests and treatments, and it combines to make a big difference to the bottom line. We don't know how many people Roman murdered, but to make it worth his while it had to be a lot."

"Judging by the ones we know about, they had a lot of tests and treatments coming their way," Michelle said, sipping her wine. "Though Very Much Alive would argue those were hardly unnecessary."

"I agree," Julie said. "But it was a point Roman made before the FBI came barging in to arrest him."

"Oh, I would have loved to see the look on his face when that went down," Keith said.

"You should have seen the looks on the faces of the Boston detectives," Julie said. "They were none too pleased, and the FBI was gloating a bit, but they got Lucy and Becca out of trouble, thank goodness. I guess intra-agency competition is a normal thing. I'm just glad I was able to put Roman where he belongs."

"And poor Dr. Coffey," Michelle said. "What a scare. I'm surprised he didn't have a coronary."

"He's a pompous ass with a heart of stone, so I'm not surprised at all," Julie said. "He had nothing to do with this, but he earned his place in the operation."

Keith stood, shaking his head in disbelief. "Crazy. Just crazy. Let's break for dinner, and then afterward we'll dive into the nuances of tick saliva," he said. "I've got braised chicken with artichokes in the oven. I'd hate for a lengthy discussion about tiny bloodsucking arachnids to ruin our appetites."

"I'll help you get it ready," Michelle said, rising from her chair.

Julie stood as well. "May I use the bathroom?"

"Of course, you know where it is. Down the hall next to the study."

When Julie got out of the bathroom, she could hear Keith and Michelle having what sounded like a heated conversation. Marriage was hard, Julie knew, and she wandered into the study to give the couple some space to finish their disagreement. She scanned the bookshelves, noting many medical ethics texts, some novels, a few classics mixed with mysteries and thrillers. Keith had his own section for medical texts, but some remnants from his past life as a bug enthusiast lingered, including a large volume specifically on arachnids.

Julie took the book off the shelf and turned to the index, where she found an entry for the lone star tick. She opened to that page and a shiver tore through her body.

The page was marked up, highlighted, words scribbled in the margin. Several loose pages from a notebook were folded up inside. Julie flipped through other pages in the book, but only the entry for the lone star tick had any markings on it.

Taking care to be quiet, Julie unfolded the loose pages tucked inside. It took her a moment to understand what she was looking at. Gripped with a sudden terror, Julie put her hand to her mouth to silence her gasp.

The pages contained diagrams of what appeared to be a complex incubation system. There were instructions for light and food sources, specific details on moisture and temperature, along with diagrams of the life cycle of the lone star tick from egg to larva to nymph to adult. There was also an illustration of a very large cage and a crude rendering in pencil of rats in the cage.

Julie felt sick. She poked her head out of the study and could hear the tense conversation between Keith and Michelle continuing.

Keith . . . my God . . . it's Keith.

Julie's heart went to her throat, her thoughts racing.

They hadn't synthesized the saliva at all. He was using real live ticks to make the patients alpha-gal allergic. But how would he harvest them? From the rat cage he kept in the basement, that's how.

She recalled snippets of what Michelle had said. "He has rats . . . a cage he keeps downstairs." Didn't she say something about Keith spending hours down there?

Julie walked silently down the hall. She could hear the discussion between Keith and Michelle a bit more clearly. She closed the bathroom door and left the light on inside, hoping it would look like she was still occupied if anyone came looking for her.

"Spare me how in touch with my feelings you are, Keith. You don't get it and you don't get me, and let's stop pretending you do."

The fight sounded familiar to Julie. It could have been a squabble she once had with Paul. It distracted Keith, though, and allowed Julie to descend the front stairs down to the lower level.

Just like the time she made her way through Sherri's darkened home, Julie used her phone as a flashlight to go exploring. The basement was a multiroom design, with a bathroom to her right, and a room directly across from the bathroom that functioned as a wine cellar. One end of the hall had a door that probably opened to the garage. At the other end was a second closed door. It was this door Julie opened. She stepped into a utility room covered in drywall with linoleum for flooring.

The flashlight from Julie's phone cut through the darkness. She scanned one side of the room, bouncing her light over stainless steel tables and shelves with various pieces of lab equipment—all very modern looking, like something Lucy would have in her lab at White. Behind her, Julie heard a sound of scurrying feet.

She whirled and saw a cage on a wooden stand. The cage was far bigger than anything sold at a pet store. Custom-built, Julie speculated. Inside were eight rats, crawling over a floor made of moss and grasses. They were playful creatures, all in good health, it seemed. Julie's nervousness spiked as she opened the top of the cage.

The rats sensed her presence and the scurrying intensified. With her heart thundering, terror percolating in her throat, Julie reached a hand into the cage and felt around for one of the rats. She had experience in handling Winston, so this was doable.

The rats lunged at the intruder. One nipped at Julie's fingers, another brushed the skin of her hand with its taut tail. Julie pulled her hand away in a panic, but reached in again, this time seizing one of the rats by its plump midsection. The rodent's legs kicked furiously, scraping against Julie's hand with sharp-clawed feet.

Julie held the squirming animal with one hand and used the flashlight in her other to check its fur. At first she saw nothing, but a closer examination revealed various protrusions coming up off its body.

Julie held the light closer and saw a tick embedded in the animal's skin. But not just one tick, at least a dozen on this rat alone. Julie did not need a field guide to know these were lone star ticks.

Julie had just dropped the rat back into the cage when her world went dark. A pain exploded on the side of her head and her knees buckled as she toppled to the floor, sprawled on her back at an odd angle. The throbbing in her temple became an intense, searing pain. She felt a gush of warmth as blood poured from the wound to her scalp. A light came on. Her vision returned, but was blurred.

Julie moaned and tried to stand, but a figure loomed over her and pressed a foot against her sternum to hold her down. Now she could see him clearly. Keith wielded a frying pan in his right hand. He glared at Julie with a look of scorn.

"Quiet. I don't want our neighbors to hear you." He knelt on Julie's chest, and with his hands to her throat, he began to squeeze.

Julie's throat closed. An urgent need for air overcame her. It was like being underwater, swimming for the surface, while the surface moved farther and farther away. She writhed and wiggled to get free, but Keith had her pinned with his knees. He increased the pressure against her throat.

"I'm sorry, but it will take some time to end you."

"Michelle . . ." Julie managed. "Help . . ."

"I'm afraid Michelle can't help you now," Keith said.

Can't help me because he hurt her, Julie thought. *Can't help me because she's got a knife in her chest and she's dead on the kitchen floor.*

Julie tried to scream, but all that came out was a hiss of air followed by a pitiful wheeze. Julie's life began to race through her mind in flashes, not vignettes, but images coming to her thoughts and leaving in flickers. One thought dominated all others.

I want to live. Live! Live!

Julie thrashed and pawed at Keith. She whipped her head from side to side, trying to break free of his hold. Blackness was coming. It was moving toward her like storm clouds swallowing the landscape, like a coming tornado.

With time, Julie's struggles abated. She became still, no longer feeling the pressure on her throat. No longer feeling anything but lightness. Peace settled over her like a warming light. A light. The bright light replaced the darkness.

A sound came, a loud clanging that reverberated from somewhere not far away. A sudden rush of air filled Julie's lungs, as if powerful bellows had pushed it there. The sound came again. Julie lolled her head to one side, and through dim vision saw Michelle bring the frying pan Keith attacked her with down on top of his head.

Michelle lifted the weapon and brought it down again, and again, until Julie heard a crack, followed by another. Keith's skull had collapsed in on itself. His body went into violent spasm before it went completely still. Blood covered the linoleum floor in a wash of red.

Michelle crawled over to Julie, blood splatter dotting her face in a gruesome design.

"Oh my God, Julie, Julie, can you hear me? Are you all right?" Michelle caressed Julie's face, her hair.

Julie could see her friend's eyes swimming with worry and fear. She tried to speak, her voice coming out in a rasp.

"I'm alive."

"Yes, thank God," Michelle said. "You're alive."

"It was Keith," Julie said, still on her back, chest heaving, spitting out each word. "Keith—he was killing the patients. He killed Sam."

"No, Julie. No."

"Yes—it's true. I found proof. On the rats—the tick is on the rats."

"No, Julie. What I mean is, Keith didn't kill Sam. I did."

CHAPTER 54

Michelle left the room, but only for a moment. She came back with a first-aid kit and wrapped a towel around Julie's head wound. Julie was too woozy and disoriented to try and stand, let alone get away. Julie let Michelle get her into a seated position with her back pressed against a wall.

"Don't worry, Julie," Michelle said. "I'm not going to hurt you. I promise. I swear to you it's true."

Julie's eyes brimmed with fresh tears. "You killed Sam. Why?"

"I did it for him," Michelle said, her voice cracking with emotion. "Because it was what he wanted for himself."

Julie shook her head in disbelief. Nothing made sense.

"Your work, your mission with Very Much Alive, was to keep people alive and get them the care they deserved."

Michelle's gaze traveled to Keith's dead body and his concave skull.

"Come. Let's get you into the kitchen. I'll properly bandage your head and tell you everything."

Julie let Michelle help her get upstairs and get seated on a kitchen chair. Michelle applied a fresh field dressing to Julie's head wound. She was practiced at it, the way a nurse would be. Julie had a glass of water on the table, but could not take a drink. Her throat ached too much for anything, talking included. The shock of what had happened proved almost paralyzing, and yet Julie was not afraid. Not in the least. Michelle's wide eyes were gentle, filled with kindness and sympathy.

"My mission was to prevent the kind of suffering I endured," Michelle said.

"I don't understand." It was hard and it hurt for Julie to speak those few words.

"You see, I wanted my first husband to die," Michelle said. "He wanted to die, and it happened just the way I said. The way I told you and Sam."

"But Andrew?"

"Yes, Andrew took his life. That's also true. But I did tell you a lie. I never stopped believing that what I did for my husband was the right thing to do. Death was his best option. But look at what I lost in the process. I lost my son. I lost my reason for living.

"So I joined Very Much Alive thinking I could make amends. I tried to become a zealot for life at all costs, because what I had done had cost me so much. It had cost me Andrew, my only child. I joined Very Much Alive with the intent of carrying on their mission, but all it did was to put me face-to-face with people like my husband, people who wanted, who needed death with dignity.

"I didn't believe in the mission of Very Much Alive,

I never did. I was lying to myself, fooling myself thinking I could. I thought God took Andrew from me as punishment for what I did, and my penance was to fight for life at all costs. But faced with so much suffering, I couldn't suppress my true beliefs. In my heart of hearts I believe ending my husband's suffering was the right thing to do. So after a time, I helped others who wished to die."

"Helped them?"

"I killed them," Michelle said. "I did it so their loved ones wouldn't have to. So their loved ones wouldn't have to suffer the guilt and maybe even the loss I did. I picked the patients who I believed didn't want to live anymore, or who in secret confessed this desire to me, and I helped end their suffering."

"How many?"

Michele's gaze grew distant. "Ten or so," she said. "Maybe more."

"But—Keith—Romey?"

"Keith found out what I was doing. He found the potassium I used, other drugs too. He told me I would get caught eventually. Actually, I thought he was going to turn me in, but that wasn't his plan. He had been researching alpha-gal. It was a hobby really, but when he discovered what I was doing he thought it over and realized it could be about money, not mercy."

"Keith went to Romey."

"Yes, Keith went to Romey. And as a hospitalist, Keith had access to patients all over—different floors, different hospitals too, including West."

"Keith killed Albert Cunningham?"

"He did," Michelle said. "We needed to have a real

reason for you to go to Suburban West. I was against it, of course, but what could I do?"

"But you killed Sam?"

"Yes, I did. But I wasn't supposed to do it. Keith gave him the tick bite, but that was before Roman told us he didn't want anything to happen to Sam."

"Why?"

"Because Romey knew you would get Lucy to perform an autopsy. As long as nobody saw the pathology of the heart, nobody would ever know how these patients were dying.

"But once you started down the path, you wouldn't stop. Romey tried to throw you off the trail. He made sure Coffey felt some heat about his department— performance pressure, that sort of thing—so he would become an obstacle, not an ally." Michelle took a drink of water.

"What about Tommy Grasso and Donald Colchester?"

"I killed them both with cetuximab. But I did it because of mercy, not money. And as for Donald, I had no idea his mother had bugged the room."

"Weren't you heard on the recording?"

"No. Donald was asleep when it happened. Keith thought we caught a lucky break that Colchester's mother listened to the recording after her son was put in the ground. But he knew she would press hard to get Brandon convicted. We had to make a convincing case."

"Who bribed Sherri?"

"That was Romey. Actually it was Lincoln Cole, Romey's guy. Cole planted the drugs in Brandon's apartment, too."

"Did Lincoln Cole bribe Colchester?"

"No. That was Romey's doing. He's skilled at finding the right levers to pull. Same as with Keith, money was Colchester's motivator, not compassion. It was a win-win all around."

Julie could not believe her ears. Then she could not believe her memory, because now she recalled Michelle being on the ICU floor when Shirley Mitchell had trouble with her central line.

"It was you who pulled out Shirley's central line, wasn't it?"

"And replaced the saline in the room with heparin. So in a way I killed Shirley, too. I felt horrible about setting you up, but not about killing Shirley. By that point, you were too close to the truth."

"My God, Michelle. What have you done?"

"What I did was listen to Keith."

"What is that supposed to mean?"

"It means I was forced—coerced, I guess, into going along with the scheme he pitched Romey. Moments ago, right before he attacked you, we were fighting about what to do because I was ready to turn myself in. It was never about the money for me, Julie. I promise you that. It was always about mercy. Somewhere on my righteous path, I guess I lost my way. But I've found it again. I've found it by taking his life to save yours."

Julie was too numb to feel anger, but it was there, lurking below the surface, wanting to come out.

"What now?" Julie said.

Michelle turned her back to Julie, reached into a kitchen cabinet, and came out holding a pistol.

"Now I have to say good-bye."

Julie's eyes went wide with fear. "No, please. My son."

"We could have been great friends. Please know how sorry I am for everything."

Michelle raised the pistol. Julie covered her face with her hands, a silly reflex because it was not going to stop the bullet.

Instead of firing at Julie, Michelle put the gun into her own mouth.

And she pulled the trigger.

EPILOGUE

A group of them were waiting outside MCI Cedar Junction for Brandon Stahl to emerge from prison. Julie was there, of course, along with Paul and Trevor; Lucy; Becca Stinson; Jordan; his sisters, Teagen and Nina; as well as Jordan's mother. Brandon's family was small, but a scattering of his friends had come.

Not present, or at least not in any great numbers, were people who supported death with dignity and branded Brandon their ambassador. He had not done what many had believed; he'd played no part in Donald Colchester's death.

The most surprising of all the attendees on that March afternoon, gathered under gunmetal skies, was Pamela Renee Colchester, mother of Donald Colchester, wife of disgraced politician William Colchester.

Pamela, a slight woman with graying hair, dressed in a navy pantsuit, stood quietly, composed. Julie had not spoken with Pamela since her husband's indictment on bribery charges. The disgraced judge caught up in the scandal had resigned, but William Colchester remained in office. Defiant as he was, an announcement of his resignation was expected any day. A fickle public could overlook many things, but what William had done was not one of them. Pamela had not issued any official statements, but word was that she would stand by her man, and not move out of the Hyde Park home they had shared for thirty years.

Julie stiffened as Pamela approached. She did not know what to expect. Rage? Sadness? A mixture of both, perhaps? Pamela's expression revealed nothing.

"You're Dr. Julie Devereux, am I right?"

A breeze came and tousled Julie's hair. "Yes. That's right. How are you, Mrs. Colchester?"

"Pamela, please," she said. Her manner of speech was a bit clipped, her voice a little plummy. "Is this your son?"

"Yes, this is Trevor," Julie said.

Pamela's eyes welled up a little. "Nice to meet you," she said, shaking Trevor's hand. "May we speak in private?" she asked.

"Yes, of course."

Trevor went with Paul.

Pamela and Julie stepped away from the crowd.

"My husband is not a horrible man," Pamela said. "But what he did was wrong. In his defense, Roman Janowski misled him into believing our son's killer would go free if they exhumed Donald's body. He never thought Brandon was innocent, but obviously the money Roman offered clouded his better judgment."

Julie gave her a nod. "I'm sorry for what you've gone through," was all she could think to say.

"I've done my research. I believe you and your friend, Jordan Cobb, saved many lives, not to mention what you've done for Brandon."

"We just wanted the truth."

"Well, there's something I would like to share with Jordan. I was hoping you could introduce me."

Julie called Jordan over and made the introductions. Jordan wore a shirt and tie and looked handsome, though his expression was uneasy.

"Jordan, what you have done, the risks you took, the commitment you showed to serving truth and justice, deserve merit and reward."

Jordan gave a shrug. "Thank you, but I was just trying to help."

"You did more than that. What happens to my husband from here is not your concern. His motives were good, but his methods deserve reprobation. You, on the other hand, deserve our admiration—both you and Dr. Devereux."

"Thank you," Jordan said. "Kind of you to say."

"It's more than kindness. I have a letter from the mayor of Boston indicating in strong language that you should file for an official pardon request for your past crimes. I believe you'll be granted one without delay. In addition, I have commitments from several medical schools that would welcome you into their programs and provide substantial financial aid."

"You mean I could become a pathologist?"

"If it's your wish."

Jordan beamed. Lucy came over and heard the news and soon others had gathered around Jordan to share congratulations. His sisters—each wearing a dress, the older girl in blue, and the younger one in white—clung to him with proud looks on their faces.

All the adulation gave Pamela a moment to continue her conversation with Julie.

"I want you to know how sorry William is for what he's done. Donald's death was a relief to him. In some ways his death was a relief to me, if I'm being honest. To see my son suffer was—well, it was hard on us all. I'll just leave it at that. But I do believe William was sincerely concerned for my health. He knew it would be a devastating blow to me if I thought Donald's killer went free. I'm sticking by my husband's side. I'm not proud of what he did, but ultimately I believe he did it out of love."

"Michelle was driven by compassion, too," Julie said. "But that doesn't make it right."

"No, it doesn't," Pamela said. "I'm sure if he knew what Roman Janowski was really up to, he would never have bribed the judge."

"If he did it only for justice, he would have done so without requiring a cash payment first," Julie said.

"I suppose that's true," Pamela said. She removed an envelope from her purse. "William wrote you a letter and I promised him I would deliver it to you personally. Julie, I'm truly sorry for everything."

"You have nothing to apologize for," Julie said. "You've done nothing wrong. You're a mother who suffered a terrible loss."

"That's true, I am. But I don't need to be culpable to care. Compassion is what binds us. It's what makes living worthwhile."

Julie thought of her life's work and believed Pamela

was right. She also thought of Michelle, who had become what Brandon once was: a symbol for the mercy movement with regular visitors to her grave. In a way, Michelle had shown great compassion to her victims. But without the patient's choice in the matter, or the support of the law, Michelle's compassion had been nothing less than a crime. As for Julie, her stance on death with dignity remained clouded. Sam's case had made her more open to the opposing views of legalized assisted suicide.

The two women hugged briefly, then Pamela walked away. Lucy, Trevor, and Paul came over to Julie.

"What was that about?" Lucy asked.

"It's about love and grief," Julie said.

Paul pulled Julie into a side hug. He noticed Trevor looking.

"I'm very fond of your mom, son," Paul said with a wink, "but we're not getting back together." Then Paul turned to Julie. "But I'm damn proud of her, and I couldn't ask for a better mom for my son." Paul gave Julie a gentle kiss on the forehead.

At that moment a loud buzzer drew the crowd's attention to a gated entrance topped by razor wire. A door behind the enclosure opened and out stepped Brandon Stahl, dressed in street clothes, a big smile on his face, looking just like a man enjoying his first taste of freedom.

ACKNOWLEDGMENTS

My father sometimes quipped that he loved having written books more than writing them. The ideas didn't always come easy. Perhaps for that reason he kept a motivational note taped to his computer monitor that read: **This is hard**. The other note taped below it read: **Be fearless**. My dad brought the discipline and work ethic he learned as a doctor to the craft of writing. It was his nature to attend to each word as if it were an expertly applied suture.

The bottom line: The work was lonely for him. He thrived in the chaos of the ER. Book writing meant hours of solitude and day after day of mental gymnastics. It could be isolating. My father drew the inspiration to work hard and be fearless from his readers around the globe. It was the connection he made to you, and the one he had with his team at St. Martin's—the editors; artists; public relations, sales, and marketing personnel—that reminded him the book business wasn't quite as lonely as it seemed.

To that end, I wish to thank those who contributed

their time and expertise to this novel. Dr. David Grass, whose knowledge and expertise continue to astound me, was present in mind and spirit for every word on every page. In reading *Mercy,* you might wonder if I had snuck off between books to earn my M.D. from an esteemed medical college. I assure you, I did not. However, Dr. Marya Koza-Saade shared her expertise as a critical care physician and in doing so allowed me to bring Dr. Julie Devereux's story to life. If you look at all the doctors who contributed to this novel, I think I have most of the medical specialties covered. I wouldn't have known anything about Xolair, among other tidbits, without the guidance of Dr. William Goodman. Dr. Peter Wertheimer is a wellspring of ideas and medical knowledge that he has kindly shared with me at the bus stop on many occasions. Dr. Ethan Prince, an interventional radiologist and my dear cousin, walked me through some very tricky procedures. Dr. J. James Rohack, an esteemed cardiologist, was my expert on all things related to the human heart. Without the help of Dr. Steve Adelman from Physician Health Services, a Massachusetts Medical Society corporation (where my father worked as a director), I would not have found Jim or Marya, and would thus have been extremely handicapped in completing this novel.

I enjoy making this a family affair. My aunt, Susan Palmer Terry, sister to my father, spent her career consulting on the business side of medicine; she enlightened me about accountable care organizations and helped shape Romey's story line. Other shaping came from the careful reads of Judy Palmer and Clair Lamb. A special nod of appreciation goes to my wife, Jessica, and my children, Benjamin and Sophie, for their continued love and support. My brothers, Matthew and Luke, both talented writers—Matthew with several published thrillers of his own—offered encouragement and creative inspiration on multiple occasions. And thanks always to Meg Ruley and the gang at the Jane Rotrosen Agency, who believed all along I could do this job. To that end, my deepest gratitude goes to Jennifer Enderlin, my father's beloved editor for many years, who entrusted me with his brand.

A great deal of gratitude also goes to you, the reader. It's challenging but incredibly rewarding to continue my father's groundbreaking work in the genre of medical thrillers. My hope is to keep that legacy alive in a way that is satisfying and entertaining to readers of the genre and most important to my father's many fans. I'm not an imitation of my father, nor do I think it's possible to replicate another's distinctive voice. But my personal pledge is to deliver novels that adhere to my father's sensibilities, to his innate understanding of drama, and to his knowledge of what makes characters compelling and stories hard to put down. My stated goal is simply to do him proud.

In that regard, I hope I have succeeded.

Daniel Palmer
Hollis, New Hampshire

Read on for an excerpt from the next book
by Michael Palmer and Daniel Palmer

THE FIRST
FAMILY

Coming soon in hardcover from St. Martin's Press

CHAPTER 1

The terror never went away. It should have by now. After all this time, she should not have been so afraid. Her long legs shook beneath the silky fabric of an elegant red gown. She inhaled deeply to calm herself, but perspiration coated her fingers anyway. *That could be a problem.* Her ears picked up each twitch, rustle, and breath in the cavernous room. They were watching her every move. Her delicate face stared back at them with a blank expression that hid her mounting anxiety.

The concert hall was sold out. Thunderous applause for her had just died down, and this was the brief interlude before the music began. Her heart beat so loudly she feared the microphone would pick up the sound. She stood alone in the center of a large stage, a spotlight targeting her as if this were a prison break. In her right hand she clutched a violin with a bright amber finish and stunning marbled flame, expertly antiqued.

Scanning the hall, she searched for the rangy man with square shoulders and the slender woman who was an older version of herself. There they were in their usual location, third row: Doug and Allison Banks, her parents. Her name was Susie Banks, and she was their only daughter, their pride and joy. Without their support Susie would not be standing on the stage of the Kennedy Center, chosen from hundreds of hopefuls to open the National Symphony Orchestra's evening performance with a solo piece.

This moment had seemed inevitable from Susie's earliest days. She was two years old when she played her first song on the piano—a ringtone from her mother's cell phone she had replicated by ear. Soon she began plinking out melodies she heard on the radio. By the age of five, Susie could play Bach's Minuet in G Major, never having taken a lesson. Words like "prodigy" and "special" got bandied about, but Susie did not understand what it all meant, nor did she care. She had found this amazing thing called music and the music made her happy.

The day her mother put a violin in her hand, Susie's whole world came into even sharper focus. She felt a kinship with the instrument, understood it in a profound way. One year into her study she flawlessly performed Mozart's Violin Concerto No. 5 during a student recital. For Susie, the notes were more than dots on the sheet music. As she played, she could see them dance before her eyes, swirling and twirling like a flock of starlings in flight. She would practice daily, hours passing like minutes, her joy unfettered and boundless. She did not have many close friends growing up, always needing to practice, or rehearse, or perform. Yet she never felt lonely, or alone. Music was her constant companion, her first true love.

Now nineteen, Susie was poised for a professional career. She had taken a gap year between high school and college to work on her craft. With hundreds of concerts on her resume, she had hoped her stage fright would be a thing of the past. But it was present as always and would remain with her until she played the first note.

This was a hugely important showcase. The conductor of the Chicago Symphony Orchestra was in the audience specifically to hear her play. If all went well, it was possible she would be moving to Chicago.

Susie set her chin on the smooth ebony chin rest and pushed the conductor from her thoughts. All sound evaporated from the room. She had no sheet music to follow. She had long ago committed the Chaconne from Bach's Partita #2 for Solo Violin to memory.

She took one last readying breath, drew the bow across the strings, and conquered the powerful opening double stop like a pro. The audience, the hall itself, seemed to vanish as she drifted into the other place where the music came from. Her body swayed to the rhythm and flow as Bach's notes poured from her instrument.

The bow and her fingers became a blur of movement. Susie kept her eyes open as she played, but she saw nothing while she felt *everything*. A brilliant shrill wafted from the violin, a melody sparkling and pure in triple time, followed by an austere passage of darker, more muted tones. Years of dedication, all the things she had sacrificed, were worth it for this feeling alone, such indescribable freedom.

She had reached measure 89, near the halfway point. Drawing the bow toward her, Susie geared up for the next variation, where the bass became melodic and the diatonic form resumed. Up to that point her playing had been perfect, but suddenly and inexplicably came a terrible screech. Susie's arms jerked violently out in front of her, the bow dragging erratically across the strings. Her chin slid free of the chin rest as her violin shot outward.

A collective gasp rose from the audience. Shocked, unable to process what had happened to her, Susie repositioned the violin. Her professionalism took over. Her reset was more a reflex than anything. She drew the bow across the strings once more, but only a warbling sound came out. The next instant, her arms flailed spastically in front of her again in yet another violent paroxysm, as if her limbs had separated from her body and developed a mind of their own. She tried to regain control of her arms, willing it to happen, but it was no use. The wild movements occurred without her thought, like those body starts she'd been having before she fell asleep: first the sensation of falling, followed by a jarring startle back into consciousness. Only this time she was wide awake. No matter how hard Susie strained, she could not stop her arms from convulsing. It was the most terrifying, out of control sensation she had ever experienced.

When the next spasm struck, Susie's fingers opened. The violin slipped from her grasp and hit the stage floor with a sickening crack. Another gasp rose from the audience, this one louder than the first. Susie was helpless to do anything, but stand facing everyone with her arms twitching like two live wires. As suddenly as those seizures came on, her limbs went still, as if a switch had been turned off. She raised her arms slowly, studying them with bewilderment. Then, she directed her gaze to the violin at her feet. For a moment she could not breathe. Murmurs from the audience reverberated in her ears.

Bending down, she gingerly retrieved the broken instrument, fearing another attack was imminent. She stood up tall. The violin dangled at her side with a gap in the wood like a missing tooth. She searched the audience for her parents, but could not see them through the haze of lights and the blur of tears.

Frozen in the spotlight, her cheeks red and burning, blinking rapidly, Susie gave one sob as she backed away. A voice in her head howled: *"What happened to me?"* She stumbled into the back curtain, fumbling for an escape, pawing at the fabric, desperate to get away. Realizing her mistake, she reoriented to the right and dashed off stage.

The quiet concert hall carried only the echo of Susie's heels, tapping out a fast, unsteady beat.

ROW EIGHT, center seat.

His name was Mark Mueller, but those who knew him well called him Mauser—a reference to his favorite weapon, the German-made Mauser C96 semiautomatic pistol, last manufactured in 1937. Mauser kept his thick blond hair combed back to expose a wide and flat forehead. The green shirt he had picked out for this concert covered his tattoos and fit snugly against a body that bulged with muscles from years of pumping iron in the yard.

Calmly, Mauser watched Susie come unglued. His gray eyes sparked and his top lip curled, putting an arch in his bushy blond mustache. When people in the audience got up from their seats, Mauser did the same. He strode into the foyer with his cell phone out.

"It happened," Mauser said. He described what he'd seen.

It was all the information Rainmaker needed to mark Susie Banks for death.

CHAPTER 2

Distilled to a few words, Karen Ray's job description was: *protect the President's family with your life*. The family consisted of Ellen Hilliard, aka FLOTUS, the First Lady of the United States, and Cameron Hilliard, the first family's sixteen-year-old son and only child. She had done this particular job for six and half years now. When she started, Karen had towered over Cam, but these days, standing only five-foot-four in heels, she was considerably shorter than everyone she protected.

Ellen thought Karen looked like Sandra Bullock with shoulder-length, auburn hair. Karen could not see the resemblance herself, but as a woman approaching fifty, she took the comparison as a compliment.

Karen was a special agent, not a "suit guard," a term popular with members of the Uniformed Division. The differences in the divisions of the Secret Service were not subtle. Uniformed guards interacted with the public, wore mostly white shirts and black slacks, and intentionally did not blend. Karen wore tailored Ralph Lauren suits to work, and her domain consisted of anywhere members of the first family happened to be.

At the moment, Cam Hilliard was still in his bedroom on the second floor of the White House. If he stayed there much longer, he would be late for school. Again. The First Lady had instructed Karen to make sure that did not happen.

Ellen was busy with a television interview, and her order had sent Karen off in a hurry. She took the same elevator President Geoffrey Hilliard used when his bum hip made it difficult to take the stairs. The elevator could make eight stops, from the sub-basement up to the third floor. Karen exited on the second floor.

She marched down the Center Hall, an airy seventeen-foot-wide corridor adorned with landscape paintings and comfortable sitting areas arranged by the First Lady. Compared with the ornate décor of the previous administration, Ellen Hilliard's style was more understated, in keeping with her middle-class upbringing.

The President embraced Ellen's choices wholeheartedly. He had a measured approach to just about everything and cared more about public perception than aesthetics. Anything that did not create controversy (think: expensive remodeling) he supported fully. There was good reason that Ellen Hilliard's favorability rating seldom dipped under eighty percent.

The two floors the President and his family occupied comprised thirty-six rooms and fifteen bathrooms, but these days Cam confined himself mostly to his bedroom. It seemed just yesterday he'd been bouncing around the third-floor game room, or building with

Legos in the spectacular solarium that the Clintons had constructed. But Cam had been a nine-year-old boy back then, sweet-faced and innocent, unsure of his family's newfound prestige and privilege. Now Cam was entering a new phase, carried forth on a raging river of teenage hormones. Perhaps when his father's second term in office ended, Cam would emerge from this period of seclusion like a bear waking from hibernation.

Bigger kids, bigger problems. That was how Ellen summarized her recent challenges with Cam—a saying that applied to most parents, regardless of stature. Karen could relate. Her twenty-five-year-old son, Josh, knew perfectly well how to use a phone but rarely bothered to call.

From a distance, Karen could hear the steady beat of electronic music coming from Cam's bedroom, directly across from the Yellow Oval Room where Ellen frequently entertained. Aside from pulsating music, the floor was library quiet. Secret Service agents seldom patrolled the upper levels, and the White House staff was busy elsewhere. Karen and Cam were alone.

She knocked on his door—softly at first, then again with a bit more force—but Cam did not answer. Karen thought she knew why.

Chess.

She peeked inside and saw Cam, his back to her, intently staring at a digital chessboard on his computer. She figured Cam was winning, because he always won.

Cam was serious about chess, supremely talented, and committed to playing tournaments, each functioning as a rigorous exam, so he could become one of a handful of young players to earn the title Grandmaster, the highest level of chess mastery. Karen did not know how close Cam was to obtaining his lofty goal, but if she had money to bet, hers would go on Cam.

She spoke from the doorway.

"Cam, it's Karen."

She did not have to identify herself. Karen was Cam's shadow; he knew her voice perfectly well.

"Your mom sent me to get you."

Cam held up a finger—a give-me-a-minute gesture.

Karen checked her watch. A minute was all they had.

"You're going to be late for school if we don't leave now."

At first glance, it would be hard to tell a teenager lived in this tidy room. The only giveaway was a mini-mountain of PlayStation games scattered on the carpeted floor in front of the television Cam had fought so hard to have in his bedroom. When it came to winning arguments, Cam's persistence and tenacity could rival some of the President's toughest adversaries. But that was the Cam from before—the kid with spunk and spirit, not the boy who had become withdrawn. For a kid accustomed to the limelight, always quick with a smile, lately Cam had trouble making eye contact.

"Knight C3," Cam mumbled to himself. "Why didn't I see that?"

To Karen's ears, Cam sounded distraught. He was out of his pajamas and dressed in his school uniform—a good sign she could still get him there on time.

"Cam, let's go. You're going to be late."

"Please, Karen, can you give me another second?" Cam said. "It's super important."

His pleading tone won out.

"My queen's got the high ground," Cam said under his breath. "Try to castle, Taylor, go ahead and try it."

Taylor.

Now Karen understood Cam's intensity. Taylor Gleason, a high school classmate of Cam's, was the son of the chief White House physician, Dr. Frederick Gleason, and the second-best junior chess player in D.C. To Karen's knowledge, Cam had never lost a match to Taylor, and he did not intend to start losing now.

Cam adjusted the volume on his computer speakers and a mechanized voice rose above the din of electronic music.

"Rook takes E5."

Cam smacked his hand hard on his desk, and Karen could not help but think *gunshot*. Her whole body tensed.

The computer voice spoke rapidly as the next sequence of moves occurred in quick succession.

"Queen takes E5. Queen takes D7. Rook A8 to D8. Queen takes B7. Queen E3, check."

"Got you now, Taylor."

Karen was pleased. Cam sounded animated when lately talk of chess seemed to bring him down.

The match went on a bit, until the computer announced Taylor's last move: "Bishop B6, checkmate."

Cam clutched the sides of his head as if experiencing an intense migraine. He lowered his hands and took a drink of water from a glass on his desk. After a swallow, he swiveled in his chair, cocked back his arm, and hurled the glass with force at the wall near his bed. The glass shattered on impact.

Karen rushed to him.

"Cam! What's going on? Are you all right?"

Cam rose from his chair and began to pace. He was a tall boy, slim like his mother, with short, sandy-colored hair. Beneath his wire-rim glasses, Cam's eyes were cornflower blue, also like his mom's, and a jaw line was starting to emerge as the cute boy transformed into a handsome man.

"Cam, talk to me. What's wrong?"

Instead of answering, Cam muttered incoherently while he continued to pace.

"I'm going to call Dr. Gleason," Karen said.

"No!"

Cam barked the word with force. Karen had not expected such a protest, but then again it did mean seeing the father of his rival so soon after a painful defeat.

"Not him. Don't call him."

Cam's shoulders were slumped as he got into bed. He pulled the covers over his head. Karen sat on the edge of his bed. She was his protector, and over the years a bond had formed that went well beyond anything written on an employment contract.

"Talk to me, Cam. Tell me what's going on."

Cam poked his head out from beneath the covers, his eyes reddened as he fought back tears.

"I don't know what's wrong," he said. "I don't get it. He beat me. He never beats me, and I'm losing to him now."

Karen was glad to hear him acknowledge that *something* was wrong.

"Is it the pressure, Cam?" she asked. "It's got to get pretty intense at times. There's no stigma in needing help for—well, your mental health."

Cam bristled.

"You sound like Dr. Gleason. He thinks it's all in my head. He's run all sorts of tests and whatnot, but he doesn't get it and now he has my parents convinced I need a shrink."

Karen and Ellen were close, confidants even, but for whatever reason Ellen had kept these developments a secret.

"They're wrong. There's nothing wrong with my head. I'm just—off."

"Have you tried talking to your parents about it?"

"Yeah. A bunch of times, but you know how much influence Dr. Gleason has over my dad."

The answer there was "plenty." Dr. Gleason, a Navy doc, had come to the President's attention through the True Potential Institute, a unique educational center dedicated to helping D.C.'s most gifted children develop mastery in a variety of disciplines. It was where Cam and Taylor both studied chess. A friendship blossomed between Dr. Gleason and the President when they discovered a shared a passion for sports, golf and tennis especially, though Gleason was by far the more competitive of the two. Their camaraderie led to Gleason getting the plum appointment to head up the White House Medical Office. Cam's point was well-taken. The President had complete confidence in Dr. Gleason.

"They won't listen to me," Cam said. "They only listen to *him*. Maybe if those stupid tests showed something, they might change their minds."

Karen mulled this over. She believed Cam. The way he had been acting could support Gleason's theory, but perhaps something else was amiss, something undetected. The President might not be open to outside consults when it came to his family's health, but the First Lady was a different story.

Karen said, "Let's get you to school and I'll work on this from my end. It's possible I can convince your parents to consider the opinion of somebody other than Dr. Gleason. Do you trust me?"

Cam might have caught the mischievous glint in Karen's eyes. He returned a small smile as he climbed out of bed, the blue sport coat of his school uniform now a bit wrinkled.

"With my life," he said with a wink.

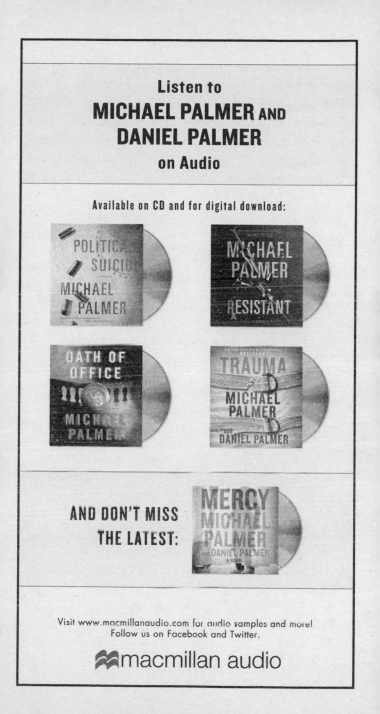